TALES OF ALE AND CHAINMAIL

VOLUME 1

ASHLEY BRAVINGTON   ALAN KENT

JONATHAN MALONEY   DAVE DEICKMAN

KATE LONGSTONE   LUCINA NYX   CRYSTAL ROLES

THOMAS D MOORE

SKYNATION PUBLISHING

Tales of Ale and Chainmail
(Vol 1)

This is a work of fiction. Names, characters, places, and incidents
either are the product of the author's imagination or are used
fictitiously. Any resemblance to actual persons, living or dead,
events, or locales is entirely coincidental.

Copyright © 2023 SkyNation Publishing

All authors assert his/her right to be known as the author of this
work.

All rights reserved. No part of this book may be reproduced or used
in any manner without written permission of the copyright owner
except for the use of quotations in a book review. For more
information: contact@skynation.info

ISBN 978-0-6455708-1-6 (paperback)
ISBN 978-0-6455708-0-9 (hardcover)
ISBN 978-0-6455708-2-3 (digital online)

www.skynation.info

CONTENTS

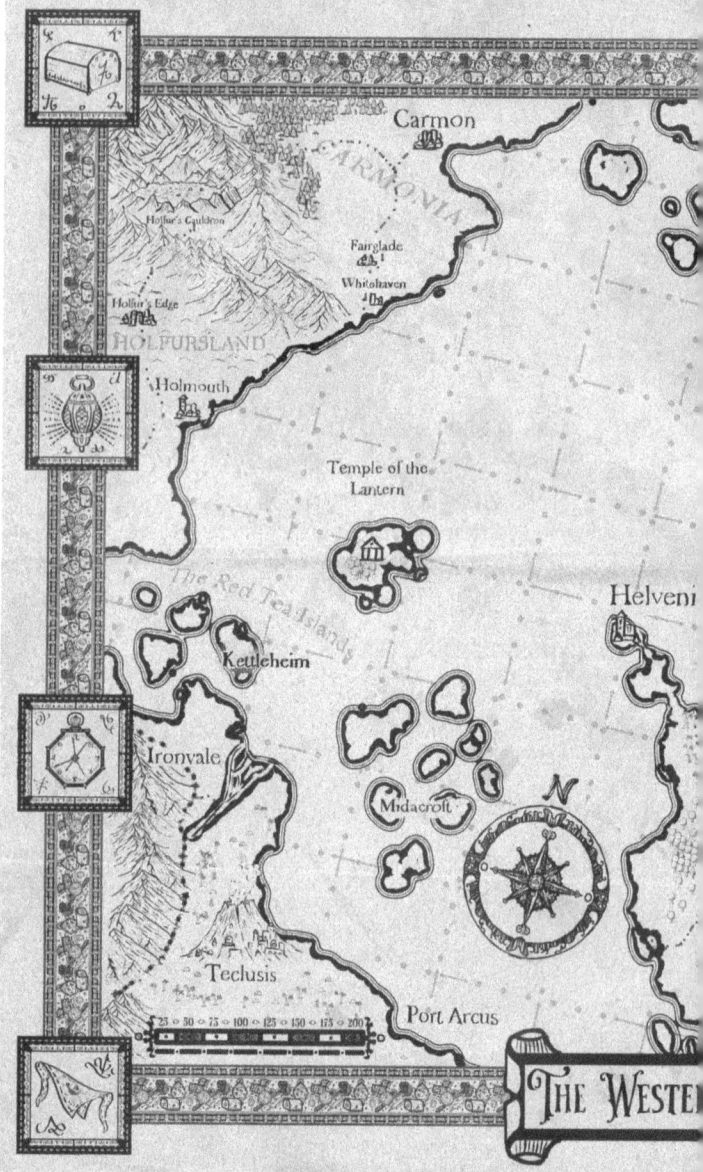

Mount Reckless

Froghester

Fort Rubbish

Avonmont

Haltide

Albunath

ALBUNATH

Old Knoll

Wellington

Morfindale

APELLION

REPUBLIC OF KATHARAN

The Free City
Of Kathar

...IELD WORLD

PROLOGUE

The Glass Dagger Corner Club stood at the intersection of hither and thither, between *lost* and *not-quite-there-yet*. It served travellers of modest wealth and repute, tolerated the boasting adventurers, but specialised in sheltering those who stumbled over the threshold.

Eight of whom were currently seated at separate tables, some near the windows as though they couldn't bear to be far from the road. The rest had scattered to the darkest corners the tavern had to offer. The bartender lifted their head, catching the usual scents—despair, sorrow, unsurety. But the eight patrons who sat without drinking were also burdened by other traits.

Guilt. Resignation. Revenge.

There was a clink as the bartender collected the small glasses. The bottle was withdrawn from its hiding place amongst the deepest depths of the rack, lest it be served accidentally. Their fingers lingered on the label, torn and peeling after a century, considering.

The female dwarf near the window shifted, her fingers going to the golden flower in her hair, as her foot tapped to an unheard tune. Curiosity burned, and hers was the first glass delivered.

She jumped when they approached, eyeing the drink.

"On the house," they explained.

The human by the windows, his eyes on the distant mountains, accepted the shot without question, downing it with well-seasoned practice. They grinned.

The skinny, dark haired human watched them place the glass warily, their eyes shifting to the trembling amber liquid as though it were a loaded crossbow. The bartender left; they would drink it. They always did.

The fisherman had placed himself in the darkest corner, his hand resting atop a cloth-wrapped bundle. He accepted the drink feverishly, like a shipwrecked sailor finding a freshwater spring, but the dwarf at the next table murmured his thanks, the first to do so. The two humans near the fire were also served, the man taking his without a word. The woman was stately in her posture, holding her hands out to the flames crackling in the hearth.

And finally, the tiny gnome at the large centre table, his feet swinging above the alestrewn floorboards. The glass was set before him, and the bartender offered no explanation. The gnome apparently didn't need one, peering into his waistcoat.

Seconds ticked by. The bartender returned to their kegs.

The gnome nodded, as though to himself, and picked up the liquor. One by one, the patrons drank. Looks were exchanged. And like migratory birds in the fall, they approached the gnome at the table, finding seats beside each other and comfort in the woodgrain of the well-worn tabletop.

Silence wrapped itself around the Glass Dagger Corner Club. But the bartender grinned and turned away, allowing the pretence of privacy. The words would soon follow.

The polite dwarf began, his words emanating in the stillness like a hymn.

"The *Sweeping Vista* had just docked in Kettleheim..."

BREWING STORM
ASHLEY BRAVINGTON

The gangway creaked as Khamid Saltstone stepped from the *Sweeping Vista* onto the harbour's wharf, fine salt air blowing against his beard, as the gulls sang at the sailors and dockworkers going about their business. The vessel had been at sea for some weeks, and had begun to near the end of the crew's preferred provisions; returning to port was a welcome exercise for all aboard. No one wanted to be left eating emergency hardtack rations, which could double as cannon ammunition in a pinch.

Khamid weaved his way through the crowd of industry surging around the ship, his job completed and leave granted ahead of the rest of the crew. As ships' chaplain and boarding sergeant, the dwarf had enough duties across the voyage without needing to load and unload cargo as well.

Warehouses surrounded the area, the food stalls hidden in the pockets between offering the fresh produce of the sea for immediate consumption. Having lived off caught fish and rations for long enough, Khamid gave a friendly shake of his head towards those vendors already eyeing him as a potential customer, and sought a feast of a spiritual kind before the gastronomic.

A few streets into the port town, Khamid found what he was looking for. Walking the temple's stairs, Khamid found his soul being warmed by more than just the midday heat, as if the pillars radiated their own. The entrance gave way to a sun-dappled interior, with sunlight passing through the wooden mesh windows. Khamid bowed his head in reverence as he crossed the threshold and, with practised motions, made the sign of Callath. The priest, in his dark flowing robe, stepped towards Khamid, but slowed as the dwarf made the sign of the Goddess, halting entirely as Khamid made his way towards the priest.

The priest gave Khamid a warm smile. "Safe travels, dwarf. Is there something I can assist you with?"

"Only your permission for me to use Callath's temple while my ship is in port."

The priest frowned in mild confusion. "Permission to... ah yes, I see."

Khamid had rolled up his sleeve to display a cluster of metallic beaded bands, each inscribed with a different God's symbol.

"My apologies, brother dwarf, I had taken you for one of Callath's own when you entered. But a Brother of the Ten Thousand is always welcome within these walls. Please consider this an invitation to use this temple anytime you require it, but the common request made of the Ten Thousand applies."

Khamid nodded in acceptance. The Temple of the Ten Thousand was a compromise, allowing ship chaplains to attend to the needs of the crew, regardless of that crew's personal religious affiliations, by devoting time to each of their Gods, without favour, to prevent any feeling slighted. To the devout of the Ten Thousand, it also meant trading the depth of wisdom offered to the devout of a single Goddess for being able to draw upon the shallow breadth of an entire pantheon. It also meant that permission should be sought before using any temple dedicated to a single deity, and no other deity's name should be uttered within those walls.

"Your invitation is accepted with thanks. May the Ten Thousand be with you," Khamid replied.

The priest nodded in thanks and returned to his duties, as Khamid made his way to the individual prayer nooks set throughout the temple.

He stepped quietly past the paintings of Callath watching her children proudly, as they bore triumph out of struggle, as they cheated certain death. Other delicate brushwork showed the sick and injured, struggling to take their next breath as Callath watched from a distance, urging them on in their recovery. At his chosen nook, Khamid knelt before Callath's image, tugging at the knees of his pants to straighten the fabric. The carved relief showed Callath in a doorway, with a warm smile and her arms outstretched in welcome. Khamid took a small rabbitskin pouch from his belt, opened it, and clasped the small, furry keepsake within between his hands. The dwarf bowed his head and spoke to the Goddess of Death.

"Callath, matron of peace. Long have I been at sea but have not heard your voice on the winds. I pray for your blessing upon my crew, my captain, and the *Sweeping Vista*, for while they each have their own Gods, may it be your hands that see them safe until such time." Khamid hesitated for a moment. His ears felt a complete absence of sound. "I also ask for your blessing upon those who have since passed, that they are not forgotten from your mind."

Khamid kept his eyes closed. The deafening silence lasted for just a few moments longer before the quiet noise of other prayers and movement became noticeable again. The dwarf exhaled, and opened his hands. He caressed the small toy for a moment, before closing the pouch around it once more and hanging it from a loop on his belt.

The dwarf quietly eased himself to his feet, placed a small donation at the desk of the priest on his way past, and took leave of the temple. Gazing about, Khamid turned his back to the port and headed further into the town.

The day felt a little brighter than it did going in.

THE SAUSAGE VENDOR LOOKED UP, then slightly down, as Khamid approached the stall.

"Good day, fair dwarf. Looking for a taste of Ironvale?" he asked, naming the largest dwarven hold in the region. A reasonable assumption, given the trade between the landlocked dwarf hold and many settlements.

"Not Ironvale, my lad." Khamid chuckled. "I was hoping for mutton sausage, spiced with ember thyme if you have it."

"Ember thyme? Not much call for that in Kettleheim, I'm afraid... I can do mud bark for you though," the vendor admitted, after thinking for a moment.

Khamid gave the man a nod. "That'll do nicely. I won't say no to something that reminds me of my kin in Ironvale." They discussed the price for a moment before coin was exchanged, and food sizzled away merrily on the hotplate.

"The name's Nomeri. We don't see many patrons from the Midacroft Isles. The Red Tea Isles is often host to Holmouth ships though," the vendor told Khamid. He wouldn't have; there was a lot of turbulent sea between the harbour and Khamid's home nation. The eastern sea routes between Midacroft and the Red Tea Isles were often affected by the volcano at Teclusis in one form or another.

"I go where the wind sends our ship," Khamid said to Nomeri, as the spiced sausage passed from hotplate, to bread, to waiting dwarf hands. Taking a moment to inhale the spicy aroma, Khamid made the traditional mistake of not waiting for the meat to cool. Nomeri's snicker died down and, with the second bite a minute later, Khamid gazed toward the sky.

"Ejun's light, that's a fine sausage," Khamid said softly, praising the God of the Sun and getting an odd look from the sausage vendor. Khamid held up his wrist, shrugging back his sleeve to show off the metallic beaded bands.

"You should expect there to be more from Midacroft in the next few days. We are only the first of the fleet to arrive with goods. You might be turning sand into rubies soon," Khamid told the vendor with a wink. Nomeri's eyes widened slightly; more sailors wanting ember thyme and mud bark, and he, the only vendor that knew in advance.

"Thank you, Khamid, and the blessings of the Ten Thousand be with you!"

"And the Ten Thousand with you."

They passed some time discussing the local news of the town and tides—where to stay, what to do, what

9

other vessels were expected—when a commotion rounded the corner and swaggered down the street. A group of burly humans and orcs sauntered through the vendors, taking food, drink, and goods from wherever they pleased. Khamid looked around for the guards, as surely this behaviour was going to be quashed by the patrols of the city. But not a single shiny breastplate or helmet could be seen. The sausage vendor swallowed hard, and Khamid gazed down at the stall; the vendor's coin pouch had vanished away from its place on the counter, now hidden presumably somewhere in the rear depths of meat stock and fuel for the grill.

An orc and a human came up to the duo. "Great day isn't it, Nomi?" The man grinned. "Giv' us a couple of yer snags." The brute leaned over, taking up a handful of sausages in a cloth from the grill's cooling rack. The orc eyed Khamid up and down, before jostling the dwarf and snatching the mutton from his hand in the process. A moment of anger rose and fell in Khamid as the wisdom of Ayer, Goddess of the Ocean—plus his own practical experience of bar brawls and boarding actions over the years—filled Khamid with the folly of swimming against the undertow; and this group was certainly one that would pull him under if he swam alone.

Khamid watched as the two oafs lumbered back to their group and continued ambling down the street, taking what they wanted before turning the next corner out of sight. The sausage vendor breathed a sigh of relief. Khamid turned, giving him a cocked eyebrow in question.

"The Rat Tail pirates. Group of raiders that have a hideout nearby," he explained. "Bunch of thugs with the guards in their pocket. They leave sailors alone unless they're on the sea, but for us locals it's a different story. They never take enough to ruin us but just enough off the top for themselves, like we're sheep to claim the wool from."

"Corrupt guards?"

"More like brigands that managed to steal enough armour to all look the same."

Khamid nodded in commiseration; there were plenty of similar stories the world over. "Then the only responsible thing to do is ask for a replacement sausage or two," Khamid replied, placing down more coin. After all, it was hardly the man's fault that Khamid's meal was taken. Nomeri gave Khamid an appreciative smile as he prepared the new order.

Khamid shifted in place to lean against the cart as he waited, and in doing so, noticed an absence of something that ought to be against his belt. Reaching down, Khamid felt naught but a chill from the God of Chance, Pheton, running down his spine. Alas, it seemed Pheton's dice had turned up a poor roll—Khamid's *Khlak Thurg*, or 'Dwarven Thingy' was missing, a torn leather loop on his belt all that remained of what should have been there. The orc had nicked more than just Khamid's meat.

Khamid closed his eyes in prayer, muttering softly as he traced over the band of beads around his wrist to find Onos and offer up an acknowledgement of the God of Misfortune's touch upon the dwarf, as well as seeking to enact His will upon those who visited Onos' touch upon him. A cruel mirth caressed Khamid's soul for a fraction as Onos agreed to the petition.

Khamid opened his eyes to find the vendor giving him a concerned look as he placed the fresh mutton shafts in front of the dwarf.

"Are you alright there, friend dwarf?" he asked as Khamid blew on the meat to cool it.

"Yes. Fine. Where might one go to discuss the cost of retrieving something the Rat Tails procured?"

Nomeri shook his head. "I wouldn't know. I don't want to draw any more attention from those thugs than I need in my life. But if you speak to the barkeep of the Drunken Minstrel he might be able to help. He's a regular of mine and has complained in the past of the Rat Tails running up large tabs."

Khamid gave the man a nod, thanking him for the food and taking his leave.

KHAMID RETURNED to the wharf with various ideas floating through his head. The loss of his *Khlak Thurg* was something that, centuries ago, in his grandfather's time, would have been cause to exile oneself in shame. Which was ridiculous in these more modern times; it was well known—by dwarves at least—that dwarves all over would quietly exchange their Thingys for something more appropriate and relic-like if they had the opportunity. After all, if something was to be an heirloom it ought to be something sufficiently impressive. Khamid happened to like his Thingy for what it was.

He slowed his pace as he navigated the docks, picking his way between fishery nets and grunting humans shifting crates. The sailors on guard duty for the *Sweeping Vista* nodded in recognition as he approached.

"Hail, Saltstone! Back to berth so soon?" Yacen asked, as he and his fellow, Aldo, took their hands away from sheathed blades. Yacen and Aldo, similar enough in height and appearance to be brothers—despite joining the crew three years apart and an ocean's distance between them—were in high spirits despite landing the first guard watch in port. Luckily for the ship, the two were much much better boarders and sailors than they were gamblers.

"Can't rush enjoyment of the delights of land, lad, too much too soon and you'll be begging for Ydall's touch," Khamid replied, eliciting a laugh from the men about the Goddess of Tranquillity. He spoke often on the subject of moderation while at sea and in port. Not for any hidebound reason; drunk sailors simply had a habit of getting themselves into more trouble than they could handle and, as the ship's chaplain, it set a bad precedent when he waded into bar brawls to assist.

Khamid climbed the gangplank and stomped towards his quarters in the stern. Nodding acknowledgements to the few remaining on board, he was lost in thought. Information on the Rat Tails had proven difficult to locate, and Khamid had no intention of allowing his *Khlak Thurg* to simply be taken by some oafish thug. Entering his quarters, Khaid dragged out the locked wooden chest containing his belongings from its place under his hammock, and began making preparations.

Not long after, the creak of the cabin's door and a subsequent knock upon the frame made Khamid pause in his work. He turned to see a well-dressed elf, wearing a dark, shin-length jacket, with a crystal blue scarf wrapped around their shoulders at the doorway.

"Captain Cilirin." Khamid saluted, straightening up as they entered the cabin. "I thought you might have gone ashore already."

Captain Nasir Cilirin, an elf of at least four hundred years, shipmaster for most of that time and

Khamid's captain for the past thirty waved off his salute. "Soon, Saltstone, soon. But first I would like to know what has my chaplain riled up."

"Riled up, Capt'n?"

"You go ashore, spend less than two hours on dry land before you are back aboard the ship and you are *humming*. Something has you worked up."

"A chaplain's allowed to hum, Capt'n. You'd hear me hum most days during Hours."

Cilirin leaned against the dwarf's desk, folding their arms and giving Khamid a look that brooked no further 'Capt'n' evasions from the dwarf. "You were humming the *Gha'tralak*, Khamid. You are planning to do something either incredibly dangerous, violent, or stupid, and I would know why before I am summoned to the local prison. Or the morgue."

Khamid nodded, slowly. He hadn't even noticed that he was humming that ancient song promising violent retribution. Trust an elf to pick up the difference between that and his usual tune.

"You're right, Nasir. Ran into a pirate gang on land. Got my meal taken from me."

"So? We've come across pirates before in port. And surely you have enough coin to replace a few mouthfuls of food. What is so different about these dogs?" Cilirin asked, increasing the look with a raised eyebrow.

"Took me a few moments to realise after they were gone. They stole my *Khlak Thurg*."

The following silence stretched, before Cilirin finally closed their eyes and pinched the bridge of their nose. "Okay, so you have shown enough restraint to have not already ended up in a cell or on a slab. But what do you plan to do?"

Khamid let a warm smile creep from under his

beard; this was why he enjoyed sailing with the *Sweeping Vista*. Captain Cilirin understood. He shook his head.

"The crew won't need to get involved, I'm only planning to retrieve my *Khlak Thurg* and leave them wondering what happened."

Cilirin shook their head as they stood up. "Not good enough, Saltstone. Follow me." With that, the captain departed without looking back. Khamid closed his chest and made his way to obey.

CAPTAIN CILIRIN's quarters were sparsely appointed for a ship the size of the *Sweeping Vista*, but it could never be said that her captain skimped on quality. Hardwood chairs lined with sheep leather, cushioned with some sea creature hide that was dense when wet but dried soft and spongy, providing an amazingly luxurious seat. The captain carefully unwound the enchanted scarf from around their neck, folding the cloth to bring the image of the *Sweeping Vista* inlaid in the fabric on top. Khamid knew some of the crew rumoured that the captain had bargained for their ship from one of the elven gods, and the scarf was a token of that oath. Khamid knew an inspiring tale when he heard one and refused to correct any who spoke it. The captain was never seen on deck without the scarf draped across them, bellowing orders in the worst squalls and fearlessly navigating the thickest of fog without error. Placing the scarf to one side, Cilirin sat, and gestured for Khamid to follow suit across from them. The desk had several drawers and boxes bound to it, preventing things sliding around in violent weather. Currently, one box contained two glasses and a bottle of safflower wine.

Cilirin poured two measures from the bottle, placed one in front of Khamid, and reclined back in their own chair.

"So... describe these pirates, Saltstone."

"Mixed crew, human and orc. The group that I met numbered near two dozen, but only two up close," Khamid replied, taking a sip from his glass.

"So you need to look somewhere in town for them. Somewhere that might fence goods?"

Khamid shook his head, as the lazily flowing light liquid cleared much of the foul taste the day had left in his mouth. The salt-tinged wine was a favourite of the captain's homeland. "Unlikely that the *Khlak Thurg* would have net the thief enough gold to be drinking for long."

"So these raiders are most likely to have a safehouse, or hideout nearby?"

"Aye, I think that's the more likely outcome. The vendor was unable, unwilling possibly, to give me any information on where the Rat Tails would be."

Cilirin raised an eyebrow as they mulled over their own glass. "The Rat Tails."

"That's what the sausage man said. For a number like that surely they would have a hideout in the port itself. Maybe a warehouse or something. But—"

"Someone would have to be mad to try and attack them."

Khamid nodded in agreement. "That seems to be the local sentiment."

Cilirin studied Khamid for a moment before adding, "I am surprised you didn't head straight out and do it anyway, Saltstone."

Khamid shifted in his seat. "I nearly did, but if I ended up in Callath's parlour for doing something like that, I knew you'd have me raised just to berate me for it." Cilirin snorted into their glass. "But that aside, The Ten Thousand may bask in my revere but I would not presume their aid in assaulting a stronghold alone."

The captain appeared to be paying more attention to the drawer they had opened during his report, but the dwarf knew they were listening to every word. Khamid took another drink of the safflower wine. Cilirin withdrew a parchment from the drawer and placed it on the desk.

"Then what I had planned to ask of you just became much easier. Have a read of this."

Khamid set his glass down and turned the parchment to read. It was a bounty contract, offered by a group of merchants within Kettleheim. Five thousand gold and the right of salvage to anything held by the Rat Tails.

"There is no signature on the bottom of the notice," Khamid observed. "Do you think whoever wrote it will be able to pay?"

Cilirin shrugged. "It doesn't matter. If these pirates have the run of the town that you say they do, then putting a name to this would be suicide. In any case, if we were to remove the Rat Tails, there's unlikely to be any governing body capable of stopping us claiming salvage rights.

"I believe your *Khlak Thurg* has just become a concern for the crew."

NIGHT FELL. Khamid descended the gangplank with his main accomplices for the night. Yacen and Aldo had taken their cues from their chaplain well, their studded leathers oiled and blades dulled with a coating of tallow and charcoal dust, as the trio made their way amidst the crates and carts on the docks, stepping quietly until they reached the paved street proper. Joining the path, Khamid made a show of adjusting himself like some mercenary who had just finished allocating some of the night's ale to the sea. Weapons on show and prayer beads tucked behind his gauntlets, he sauntered into the more populated streets with his crew.

The three sailors had been in the Drunken Minstrel for nearly three hours. From his seat, Khamid could overhear several drunken tables that appeared to be full of Rat Tails, their conversations loud and raucous. From discussions of locals that appealed to them, to previous pirate raids and merchants attacked, they carried on to discuss gambling debts owed to each other and jokes about their mates. Largely irrelevant to Khamid, but he continued drinking and listening. Two of them were passed out in their chairs, snoring away as their mates continued. Motioning to the barkeeper, the chaplain's mug received a refill, and he placed a few extra gold into the barkeep's hand.

"Reckon my friends need another top up. Can you see to that for me?"

The orcish barkeep weighed the coins in his hand, eyes scanning the room behind Khamid. He grinned. "Well, it pays for another bottle of the sour brandy you've been plying them with all night. I'm sure they won't complain, friend." At this point of the night Khamid had spent not an insubstantial amount of coin quietly plying his 'friends' with alcohol.

"You've put an awful lot of trust in the barkeep, Khamid," Yacen said softly. "Are you sure it's wise?"

"Not to mention an awful lot of gold, what's the point in cards when you keep giving away your stake?" Aldo complained.

"The barkeep is as sick of the pirates as everyone else in the town. We've probably handed more coin to him tonight than he's seen from the Rat Tails in months. Besides, I want to ensure Glurgamoth's drunken wrath on these pirates," Khamid said, looking past Yacen. The younger human was sitting with his back to the table of Rat Tails Khamid had identified with the *Khlak Thurg* thief. Several other tables held Rat Tails members as well, based on the chatter back and forth between them. While Yacen couldn't see many of their foes without making it obvious, he had a good view of Captain Cilirin and the tables behind Khamid, full of the crew of the *Sweeping Vista*. It had taken most of the afternoon to pull together the crew from various establishments and vices, but those not engaged in drinking and gambling here were now back aboard the ship. Whether they would be reinforcements, or a last line of defence, remained to be seen.

Aldo shuffled a deck of cards and began laying them out for another hand. "So, we are after the orc, yes? How do you propose we get him away from the table?"

Khamid shook his head as he picked up his cards. "We don't. We follow them back to whatever bolthole they have in this town. The rest of the crew will follow along in time and surround the place. Once we have them, we'll attack and get them all at once, as per Cilirin's plan. Are you sure you're not cheating with that shuffling of yours?" This was the worst hand Khamid had seen in weeks.

"I am sure I have no idea what you mean," Aldo replied. "But you didn't answer my question. You just told me the captain's plan."

"If I can get the orc alone, I am going to get my *Khlak Thurg* back. I am not risking losing it in the—you sneaky *chultz!*" Khamid chuckled as Aldo turned over his own hand, a matching suit of cards smiling back against Khamid and Yacen's own poor hands.

Aldo was the very picture of innocence. "You always said that the crew needs to keep in practice, chaplain."

WHEN THE TIME came for the pirates to leave, Khamid slid from the table and followed the last stragglers out of the tavern with Yacen and Aldo by his side. There was no need to hurry; the pirates were in a good mood and loud as they staggered through the town. Aldo stopped at each crossroad to make a small mark indicating directions for the following groups, using a chalky substance that glowed under the night sky. He claimed it was made from powdered jellyfish. Khamid had no idea how this would work, and was sure trying to find out was going to give him a headache.

Near the harbour, Khamid and his sailors caught up with the pirates. Tucked under an archway, Yacen held up his hand and pointed to the group ahead.

The drunken group had stopped at an alley to relieve themselves. The orc that had taken Khamid's *Khlak Thurg* was further down the alley away from his mates, noisily emptying the contents of his stomach. The other pirates finished and continued into the warehouse neighbouring the alleyway, not noticing the absence.

Khamid stormed across the street to the mouth of the alley, gesturing for Yacen and Aldo to follow him. He was in no mood for trying to explain himself to the thug, and opted to let his knife speak of his displeasure while Aldo and Yacen guarded the mouth of the alley. Giving the squatting orc's shoulder a reassuring pat, Khamid slid his hand around and under the chin, lifting it far enough to ram the blade past the jawline. Holding tightly against the orc's attempts to wrestle away, Khamid waited until his victim's body caught up with the reality that he was dead, either choking on his lifeblood or from a knife tickling the far side of his spine. The thrashing slowed to a final twitching, and Khamid let the body down to the ground, getting a calm nod from Aldo that all was well.

Satisfied, Khamid held his hand over the orc's face for a moment and prayed to Callath to accept her new arrival with tenderness. Khamid may have been the cause, but that was no reason to disrespect a Goddess who loved the effort all of her children went to in order to avoid her. Heart pounding, he finished his prayers and searched the orc's pockets.

Then his coin pouch.

Then the inner lining of his shirt.

Thalurg bahat! The bastard didn't have it on him!

———

THE DWARF WIPED down his leather armour with what remained of the drunk's shirt rags, took a deep breath, and joined the two at the alleyway entrance.

"You've got that look, Khamid," Yacen observed.

"We wait for the crew to get into position, and the *Khlak Thurg* could be lost in the confusion," Khamid said, eyeing the warehouse. "I'm going in there now to find it. Wait here and signal the crew when in position."

Yacen and Aldo exchanged a look. "The whole night has been planned around this attack, and if it goes up in smoke like the Twisting Row then Cilirin will not be happy. You know the captain gave us explicit orders on what we should do if you tried this?" Aldo said softly.

"If this ends with the loss of my *Khlak Thurg* then I don't give a damn!" Khamid growled. "I don't dispute how important it is that it goes well, but if I lose what I came here for then I may as well step into the ocean into Ayer's embrace!"

Yacen placed a hand on Aldo's shoulder. "Let's not get into death oaths and last stands just yet. What Aldo is *trying* to say"—he shot Aldo a pointed look—"is that Cilirin gave us orders that, and I quote 'When Saltstone tries to assault the pirate's hideout without the rest of us, then you two follow his lead and don't let him get killed or burn the place down'."

Aldo rolled his eyes at Yacen. "There's never any showmanship with you."

Khamid opened his mouth. Then closed it. Then worked it back and forth like an unsecured ship's hatch in the breeze.

"Thank you?" Aldo prompted with a grin.

"Yes, thank you. Both of you."

"Right, with that settled... lead on, chaplain."

Aldo slipped around the warehouse block, while Khamid and Yacen spent a moment tightening their gear and checking over the other's to ensure sounds were muffled as best they could. The pirate's hideout was a warehouse at the end of a row of three human-sized story buildings, with a wall of stone and iron-fenced courtyard for wagons to be loaded.

"A solid enough building, but it appears Zikion's knowledge has led you to where you need to be, Khamid," Aldo whispered on his return, pointing down the alley. Khamid followed Aldo's finger to a shuttered window set into the second story of the warehouse, then down to the lean-to propped against the wall, a wagon wedged in behind some barrels alongside it. Khamid nodded as the trio set back down the alley, past the rapidly cooling orc corpse. Aldo clambered up the wagon first, with Yacen giving Khamid a hoist up atop the wagon before climbing aboard himself. Aldo set himself against the lean-to and beckoned for Khamid to go first.

"We'll follow your lead, Khamid."

Khamid nodded and gratefully took the boost on top of the lean-to, placing his fingers under the shutter of the window. To his relief, the shutter was not barred from the inside. He eased it to one side and clambered into the room as Yacen followed behind. As Aldo slipped in behind the others, a snuffling noise froze them in place.

Khamid turned on his heel to see a pirate stretching from his bed, turning towards the moonlight brightening the room from its perch in the night sky. The dwarf's hands crept towards each other to clasp where his prayer beads resided under his glove. Khamid looked at the pirate, fatigue wearing on his face as he yawned.

"*Sleep.*" Khamid spoke in a deep tone, feeling the holy power behind his command. The pirate blinked at Khamid's word, sitting up to look towards the trio. Before he was able, the power of the word took hold of

23

him, and the pirate slumped back into his bed, contentedly snoring.

Khamid opened the bedroom door and took in his
new surroundings; a common area with a hardwood
floor, low couches and tables covered in mess, and a
wide solid wood staircase leading down. Not as noticeable was a carpeted staircase to the next floor midway
across the room.

Khamid's *Khlak Thurg* wasn't likely to be in the
kitchen, and the chatter of drunken pirates could be
heard from the lower levels, so he motioned for Yacen
and Aldo to follow him, taking his chances on the next
floor. The trio kept to the edges of the room to provide
little opportunity for any creaking floorboards to sing
their song. Yacen's eyes flicked nervously at each closed
doorway, lingering on one opposite the dining hall before being prodded along by Aldo. The Hearth God
Ilios be praised, the Rat Tails kept their hideout clean,
for the stairwell carpet was well maintained and thick,
muffling the sound of the sailors' boots as they
ascended.

The top of the stairs led to another corridor of doors.
Khamid gently opened the first with no sound behind it,
revealing a bunk room for several pirates. Breathing low,
Khamid and Aldo listened carefully at each door,
raising one or multiple fingers at each as they went.
Yacen gripped his blade tightly as they picked their way
down the hallway, with room after room full of sleeping
pirates. There was little value in entertaining even the
empty rooms without Khamid knowing where a specific
pirate slept. With his original quarry now dead, Khamid
reasoned it seemed his best shot at finding his *Khlak
Thurg* was with a pirate leader, if only because they

were more likely to have their pick of the valuables stolen.

Yacen reached the end of the corridor first, and motioned to Khamid as he turned the corner. Set further down the wall from the other doors was a larger room, a more likely prospect. Yacen listened at the door, before slowly raising a single digit and nodded to Khamid. Aldo remained outside, constantly shifting his view from one end of the corridor to the other with a furrowed brow. Khamid gently eased the door open.

An oak desk gleaming with wax, a fur rug adorning the floor, and polished golden clock on the wall—this was the room to check. Khamid spied the sole occupant in her bed, a blade sheathed and propped within easy reach. The life of a pirate ever watchful. Khamid nodded in approval at the precaution.

The dwarf took precautions of his own, gently walking his fingers through the motions and the low whispers to invoke Ydall to blanket the room in peaceful silence of tranquillity. Absolute stillness fell over the room as he began his hunt, which started by taking the sheathed blade away from the pirate's bedside.

Khamid went through each desk drawer. Open, ruffle around, close. Open, ruffle, close. The dwarf resisted the urge to simply dump each drawer onto the ground. The silence spell allowed him to make as much racket within the room as he wanted, but experience had taught that the creaking of floorboards communicated to other parts of a building, and kept his footsteps light. The desk was stuffed with papers, most of them probably looted from raided ships and possibly valuable in their own right. He left them behind and padded to the foot of the bed, turning his attention to the pirate's chest.

Khamid offered thanks to Pheton as he found the chest unlocked. He propped the lid open with the pirate's blade and dug through the items; boots, belts, cummerbunds. He openly cursed, thankful for the spell keeping the words from being perceived, and pushed it all aside. Against the side of the chest were several pouches. He dug through them feverishly, and between the pouches of waxed canvas he found one smaller, made of rabbit leather. Scored with the markings of the Saltstone clan! Khamid picked up his pouch, and the weight of it in his hand made him sigh in relief.

Khamid repacked the chest to remove all traces of the burglary, thinking of getting back into position for the *Sweeping Vista* crew's assault. He withdrew the pirate's blade, and briefly considered replacing it by the bedside; it wasn't what he had come here for after all. On the other hand, if they were about to attack, then this would be one less fully armed pirate to deal with, so Ayer take them. The pirate sighed and rolled over in her sleep as Khamid flicked the chest lid down.

He turned towards the door with one thought searing through his mind.

I shouldn't have heard her sigh.

The chest lid slammed shut like a thunderclap.

Khamid's silence spell had run its course.

The pirate woke with a cry, reaching for a blade that wasn't there, and punching up with a fist towards a nonexistent assailant's throat. Khamid was through the doorway and down the hall before she had a chance to take stock that there was no present threat in her boudoir. Shouts of query and irritation came from the closed doors the trio passed, Khamid's *Khlak Thurg* in one hand and pilfered blade in the other. They hurtled down the stairs leading back to the first level, halting on the landing at the sight of several pirates coming up from the ground floor in various states of inebriation.

Yacen pointed at the doorway opposite the dining hall. "That way!"

Since going out the way they came would be a dangerous dice game to play with Onos, Khamid opted to race for the door as the shouts from above merged with those from below. Rather than slow down as he neared the door, Khamid held the pouch of his *Khlak Thurg* between his teeth and reached for a chair. No time to swing, he simply raised it with legs pointed forward, like some stunted quadrupedal lance, and tucked in his chin as he charged the door.

It was a small relief as the thin door shattered around him, shards of wood digging into his skin and catching in his beard. Yacen's direction had not failed them, but the momentum of the dwarf certainly did as he stumbled and tripped over a small table holding a bowl of aragi fruit, the fragile timber shearing apart from the double impact of chair and mildly idiotic dwarf. Aldo slowed down briefly to haul Khamid back to his feet.

"No time for a snack, Saltstone, we need to be out of here!"

Khamid took off at a hobbling limp. Pushing down the next hallway, the trio found another stairwell down to ground level, and Khamid began humming a prayer to the Goddess of Weather, Ghophine, to mask their location. Aldo frantically manipulated the latch of the outer door as the beads around Khamid's wrist shifted.

Moisture oozed through the walls and rose from the floor as the air shimmered and grew hazy. Aldo's hair rustled as though being blown by a phantom breeze and, in response, turned to give Khamid a look before being obscured by a thick, solid bank of fog.

"You know that makes locks much harder to pick, right?"

Yacen and Khamid paced slowly within the fog cloud, knowing the risk of being shot by pirates within was simply down to Pheton and Onos' grace, but more importantly, any pursuers would assume all three of them would be heading for the door as quickly as possible. Which was accurate, but the three had spent many a night on the *Sweeping Vista* in similar conditions. Khamid took the moment to remove his *Khlak Thurg* pouch from between his teeth, tucking it into his belt. Yacen had moved to the window and was carefully running his hand around its edges.

Khamid could hear the pirates getting closer now; a couple of crossbow bolts had whizzed through the fog at the door with a buzz like angry insects, much to Aldo's grunted annoyance. They were running out of time. Khamid crept closer to the edge of the fog, slowed his breathing and tried to focus. Three pirates stood on the landing above, five more on the stairs, with more of the hideout waking and arming. He turned to the side and found a wooden stool by the wall. He hurled it out of the fog. It clattered in the darkness as it fell and one cried in surprise. It was quickly followed by a voice from behind.

"The thief hasn't moved, keep your eyes on that fog!"

It seemed the pirate whose bedchambers Khamid had ransacked had joined the chase. And she was not pleased by his attempts to misguide her crew.

"Surround the fog and weapons at the ready! The dog can't hide there forever!"

No, no I couldn't, Khamid thought to himself. He was beginning to realise his options were running out. The dwarf and his friends could either surrender to the tender mercies of a pirate they had just robbed, or he could make a break for the wall. Under instruction, those few crossbow bolts were likely to become more accurate over time. Khamid paced inside the fog for a few moments, swinging the acquired blade. Khamid decided to do something that Captain Cilirin was going to have... words about. He walked his fingers around the sword's hilt and began to draw on Thumnir's—God of Hope—power.

"What would it take, Rat Tail, to see my safety out of here?" Khamid called.

"You break into my home, thief, you assault my crew, you sully my bedchamber and you expect to be able to just walk out of here paying for your insults like some merchant?" the pirate's leader called back incredulously.

"Sounds rude when you say it like that, but yes."

The pirate scoffed. "Then I'll settle for what you took to be returned, along with your head. Attached as a slave or on a spike."

Pity, Khamid thought.

"Well, thief? Are you going to accept the iron collar or are we nailing your head to the walls?"

Khamid completed the motions to call on Thumnir, and gripped the blade tightly once more as a glossy film spread up his arm to cover his entire body. No time to think about what was coming next, other than to have faith.

A crossbow bolt zipped through the fog over Khamid's head, interrupting the final incantation. The crash of breaking glass was joined by a yelp from Yacen as the window he was working on came free.

"Time to leave!" Khamid bellowed, and made a break for the window. Yacen was already halfway through.

"After them!" the pirate leader roared.

With the window freed from its frame, the fog cloud was quickly filling part of the street with its misty soup. Khamid was both grateful and irritated, as it obscured the pirates' vision of the escaping sailors but made it impossible to work out which way was best to flee. Khamid could barely see Yacen ahead of him and did his best to keep up. With distance, the fog thinned out and allowed Khamid to spy the archway where the sailors had made their original plan. Whatever hope Khamid had had for reinforcements was dashed, as only a single group of the *Sweeping Vista* crew milled about under the archway, scrambling to their feet and drawing weapons as they approached.

"Wind's at our back, lads, move it! Back to the Drunken Minstrel!" Khamid called.

But Yacen had reached the group first, and before Khamid could reach them, all took off towards the port towards the ship. Aldo caught up with the dwarf and watched Yacen take the crew.

"What's the plan, Saltstone?" Aldo asked between gulps of air.

"Back to the Minstrel. Don't know what Yacen is planning, but we're going to need more bodies to deal with the Rat Tails," Khamid said, throwing a look behind them at the building, now glowing with light from within as if it were some great beast waking. A great beast which spewed forth irate, drunken pirates yelling challenges and pointing in their direction with fingers, blades, and crossbows.

Khamid sighed. "On the other hand, we may not have the time. Just get out of their crossbow sights."

The two sprinted under the archway and further down the street. The Rat Tails followed with varying cries of battle and orders for the two to stop. Some pirates split off to chase Yacen and the *Sweeping Vista* crew, but Khamid didn't have the time to worry about them. They rushed down a narrow street being used as storage for barrels and crates.

Khamid pointed to a gap. "Under there, quick!"

Aldo clambered in and reached back to help pull Khamid through the gap. Trying to slow their breathing, they readied their weapons in case the deception failed. Aldo palmed his long dagger as Khamid pulled his boarding cutlass, paired with the stolen pirate blade.

The Rat Tail pirates piled down the street, pushing and shoving each other through the trail picked out between the crates. If any pirate had the thought to stop and check for people hidden in the alley, they were not given the time to voice it by their comrades as they spurred each other to move faster and find their leader's thieves.

"Sounds like you really picked a winner this time, Khamid," Aldo observed. "What is so important about that sword you stole?"

Khamid shrugged. "Pheton and Onos guide in mysterious ways. If I could have traded the sword for our freedom, then I'd have done so. Come on, let's get after them."

"All I'm saying is, maybe you didn't need to take the sword. You got your *Khlak Thurg* back, why did you need to take the sword too?"

"You make it sound like we weren't planning on starting a fight with these pirates anyway. Would you really rather be having this fight in hallways and bedrooms?" Khamid's eyes narrowed at his companion as they squeezed back between the crates and into the street.

"Hey, I do some of my best work in hallways and bedrooms," Aldo said, with mock indignation and a waggle of his eyebrows.

Khamid shook his head and kept close to the buildings as they followed the sound of pirate voices shouting ahead. Khamid recognised the streets and motioned for Aldo to follow him. The verbal back and forth grew in intensity as they neared the market lane where Khamid was accosted, and there was a larger group in the street than Khamid and Aldo expected. Rat Tails were converging out of nearby alleys with torches and weapons drawn, evidently frustrated with their prey of sailors constantly running. But a second group swelled from the residential rooms above storehouses; locals with clubs and fish knives. This group of townsfolk couldn't be called a mob to Khamid's eyes, because they didn't band together. Rather, they formed into small groups in front of their establishments, eyeing the Rat Tails and their neighbours with the look given between smaller drinking groups when a tavern brawl is brewing.

The Rat Tails weren't doing themselves any favours either.

"Tell us where that sea carrion went! I know they came this way!" the lead pirate yelled at the group in front of her.

"Bugger off! We've nothing to do with whatever spat you're having!" The local spokesperson bellowed back. With a chill, Khamid recognised the voice—the sausage vendor, Nomeri.

"If you're nothing to do with it, what's with the knives, eh? Not like you to be in the streets unless you've got some meat for us!" the pirate jeered back. "Or maybe you're hiding them inside! Maybe we ought to burn it down and see what comes scurrying out!"

Khamid's grip tightened on his blades.

"You've been bleeding this town dry for too long like some Helvenican lord, Rat Tail! Dive into the ocean and let Ayer take you!"

Khamid broke into a run down the lane, a prayer on his lips.

"You merchant dog! I'll show you who Ayer's claiming when I dump your body in the port!"

The rearmost Rat Tail had just begun to turn towards the sound of hurried feet as Khamid's prayer ended and the dwarf barrelled into him. Khamid's eyes glowed white as Ghophine's power soared through him and knocked down the nearest Rat Tails with a thunderous boom. Slashing left and right, Khamid hewed into the Rat Tails with prayers to the Goddess' of Weather and Ocean alike. Those further away from the assault had just enough time to rally their wits before being attacked by the merchant groups, Khamid's furious attack being enough of a driving force to break the standoff.

Step to the left, stab to the right. Khamid let a sloppy sword thrust through his guard to impale the air under his arm, only to lock it in place by looping his wrist underneath and punching the pirate in the face using the basket hilt of the cutlass in his other hand. Blood sprayed across the dwarf's face, and the melee continued. The battle swung back and forth as merchants and pirates fought. Aldo stepped in and out of the fight to use his knives to best effect, dragging injured merchants away where he could in the chaos.

Khamid blinked sweat away from his eyes as his opponent drew back, the space between them cleared, both breathing heavily. The clash of weapons faded as smaller fights broke away from the main body of pirates, and both sides were more cautious as the initial frenzy passed.

"You're the one that started all of this, dwarf. I'm going to rip you apart. The only thing left of you will be that beard to scrape the mud from my boots!" the pirate snarled, not sparing a glance of support for her fellows.

"You Rat Tails started this before noon," Khamid spat, anger filling his voice. "You took something that didn't belong to you, and now you're going to die for it."

There was movement around the two circling fighters, but neither was willing to break away to see what. Instead each slowly circled, the pirate glancing past Khamid's ear and smiling wickedly. "Looks like my friends have found us, dwarf. Maybe we'll find out exactly what we took from you and feed it to you before you die."

Other pirates were drawing away, retreating out of Khamid's vision. The look of dismay from the townsfolk made Khamid realise their situation wasn't looking great, as the pirate and Khamid circled once again, giving him a full view of what was behind him; a fresh band of pirates stormed from the far end of the lane. These were not half asleep, nor poorly armed with whatever they had by their beds. Well made swords glinted in their hands, their eyes alight with fire. The merchants formed a loose group alongside Khamid, and looked to him for guidance.

Khamid gripped his blades and readied himself for the charge. The pirates were in no rush, enjoying their overwhelming advantage and the fear of the townsfolk.

Two short bursts from a horn nearby made a few pirates turn their heads, but they were mostly ignored. Khamid's ears pricked at the sound, and took a few steps back as a second horn, closer than the first, sounded a single short note. Not much—not enough to spook the merchants—but they followed suit, keeping the dwarf between them and the pirates. A long sharp whistle zipped from the rear of the group, courtesy of Aldo, through the night air. The closer horn sounded again, one long blast.

It was Khamid's turn to smile as the pirates' sauntering advance halted. Nasir Cilirin emerged from a connecting street just behind Khamid and the merchants with a group of crew members. With their blue scarf draped around their shoulders and a long thin sabre gripped in one hand, Cilirin gave a look to the crew member holding a horn. The signal given, the crew member raised her horn and issued three short blasts that gave pause to the Rat Tails for a moment, before their leader's eyes widened slightly in alarm.

Time slowed to a crawl as the Rat Tails and *Sweeping Vista* crew eyed each other from opposing ends of the street. Khamid took up a position alongside Cilirin, as Aldo stepped into the crew ranks and accepted an offered crossbow. The moment passed as Khamid and Cilirin levelled their weapons in unison towards the Rat Tails.

With a roar, the two crews charged down the street. Crossbow bolts whistled through the air as the more nimble crew clambered over crates and ducked through market stalls. Khamid and Cilirin moved in unison as they clashed with the oncoming pirates, Cilirin's sabre lashing out to interrupt attacks and Khamid's paired blades using the openings provided to drive the pirates back. Using their momentum, captain and boarding sergeant formed the tip of the *Sweeping Vista*'s advance, with other crew filling in as they pushed into the melee. The Rat Tails had superior numbers, but they were used to tormenting merchants and traders. The *Vista*'s crew were used to repelling pirates, slavers, and other horrors from the deep sea, often in the middle of raging storms. The merchants may not have been fighters in the true sense, but they fought on with the manic strength and fury of those defending their homes and families.

"Kill them all! Burn this place to the ground!" the pirate leader screamed at her crew, slashing at any *Sweeping Vista* crew that came too close. Several small fires were already burning, and any pirates not close enough to the fight were doing their best to spread it. Khamid pushed harder and further towards the pirate leader, Cilirin getting cut off in the process. The dwarf punched one final pirate to get them out of his way, and stood before the increasingly erratic pirate chief.

"You *again*, dwarf! No! Stay back!" she snarled, slashing her axe at a pirate moving to intervene. "I will have my blade back and then you'll be put to it! You will die, and then your crew, and then this entire city!"

The sounds of the battle faded away from Khamid as he focused on the chief. He slowly shook his head and readied himself. "Is this really why you're burning down the town you pirates have harvested for so long? Over a sword?"

"Shut your mouth, you *bahat*! That sword belonged to my father, and I would butcher the Mad King to get it back!" The pirate chief leapt at Khamid, steel clashing amid a flurry of blows with each trying to get the upper hand. Khamid may have wielded two weapons, but the pirate's fury made up for only having one axe blade. As long as it was kept in motion, Khamid couldn't do more than knock it aside. Khamid could hear Cilirin giving battle orders nearby, but couldn't spare a glance to see how the fight was going—the pirate would not let up. The dwarf was driven one step back, then another, as he staggered and dropped to one knee. A cry of triumph erupted from the pirate chief as she raised her axe high over Khamid's head.

A flash of blue. Khamid looked up to see Cilirin grappling with the pirate chief, their own sabre dropped as the elf wrapped one hand around the wrist holding the axe and the other fighting for purchase with the pirate's free hand. The pirate chief snarled and gave Cilirin a vicious headbutt.

A splash of red. Nasir dropped with a groan and the chief raised her axe again, this time at the fallen captain.

"Hey, Tail, fetch!" Khamid bellowed, raising up the stolen blade in his hand and flinging it away from the fight. The pirate halted and her eyes followed her precious blade sailing away from the fight. Without thought, the pirate chief moved to run after it, as Khamid used the momentum of his throw to skid forward on his knee, his own cutlass raised towards the chief, scoring a long and terrible gash in her side. The pirate chief managed several steps from Khamid before her legs gave out. Grasping hands still reached for the blade mere metres away as lifeblood oozed from her side. With a last bubbling breath, the pirate stilled.

The combatants watched the pirate chief die. A simultaneous roar from the townsfolk mixed with a cry of disbelief from the Rat Tails. The *Sweeping Vista* crew was between the two sides, and watched their captain and chaplain for orders. Khamid looked to Cilirin on the ground, who gave the dwarf a wave of their hand as if to indicate *I am busy right now, Saltstone,* while stemming the blood from their nose.

Khamid stood up, giving the Rat Tails an appraising look. "Your leader is dead, and I would judge that your time lording over this town is over. Surrender now, and you'll be handed over to the town for trial. By Ambris' sight it will be fair. The Law God will see it so. Or you can take your chances fleeing tonight."

Several Rat Tails made a run for it immediately, but the majority simply looked between them and dropped their weapons. Aldo and a band of sailors took off after the runners.

Khamid motioned for the remaining sailors to take the surrendering Rat Tails. "We'll lock them in the *Sweeping Vista*'s brig for now." Then, he turned to address the townsfolk that were murmuring discontentedly amongst themselves.

"You've fought well tonight, for your homes and lives. But you are not in the right mindset to pass judgement on every single pirate tonight. Look to your neighbours, and let the judgement happen in a few days, under Ejun's warm light." Khamid met the eyes of several of the loudest mutterers, keeping eye contact until each broke off. Wandering amongst the remaining townsfolk, Khamid shared some words of encouragement and checked minor wounds they had taken.

Not everyone had seen the end of the battle. Khamid gave several orders for various townsfolk to summon priests and healers, as some wounds were beyond his ability to assist. With one battle over, another began. Khamid stopped at one bloodied injury, the sausage vendor Nomeri, with his wife sobbing over him.

"Ease up, dear, I'll be fine," Nomeri said, breathing hard and wincing in pain. "It'll wash out I promise. Ah, my dwarven friend! I am afraid that I still do not have any ember thyme for you."

Nomeri's wife slapped him on the shoulder between sobs, her eyes not leaving her husband. Khamid knelt beside the vendor and inspected his wound. "You are in bad shape, Nomeri, but the healers will be here soon and they will be able to take you into their care."

Nomeri nodded, closing his hand around his wife's. She looked at Khamid briefly before returning to her husband. The dwarf stood awkwardly, and went to find Cilirin.

KHAMID SIGHED as he walked through the streets the next morning, a canvas sack slung over one shoulder. This was never the plan; the townsfolk shouldn't have had their blood spilt because of him. The *Sweeping Vista*'s crew had claimed the former Rat Tail warehouse as their own and were busy taking inventory; the ship's quartermaster had spent the early hours tallying up everything and preparing shares for the crew. Khamid had asked the quartermaster to make his own share something portable. The sack was mainly coin, with some smaller articles of jewellery and cooking utensils.

Khamid stopped outside Nomeri's stall, took a deep breath and rapped on the door. The sound of movement led to the door being opened by a girl slightly taller than Khamid, with a complexion matching Nomeri's own. The girl looked at Khamid through red rimmed eyes and stood aside to permit him to enter. Khamid's heart sank, and he entered quietly.

Nomeri's wife sat at the head of the family table, staring into the middle distance. An acolyte of Callath sat alongside her. Khamid stopped short of the table as Nomeri's wife snapped her attention to him.

"You."

Khamid bowed his head. "I wanted to stop by to see ho—"

"My husband is dead because of you."

Khamid stopped speaking.

"Nomeri has been saying for years that the Rat Tails needed to be dealt with. That someone had to stand up to them. I begged him to hold his tongue, to keep his head down. We had a good life here in Kettleheim, and it wasn't always easy, but we had enough. Then you came along. Nomeri told me what happened that morning, that you were robbed by the Rat Tails like a thousand sailors before you. But you had to go and kick the wasp nest." Her voice grew in anger. "Nomeri saw you and your crew following the Rat Tails, and he decided to organise what you saw last night. Because of you, he finally decided to fight back. Because of you, I have lost one of the greatest joys of my life."

Nomeri's wife choked back a sob and turned away, ignoring the dwarf. Khamid let the woman's anger and sadness flow. He didn't disagree with what she had said. Instead, he placed the sack on the table with a pointed look to the acolyte, who nodded and made a gesture of Callath's blessing. With nothing left to be said, Khamid turned and made to leave. At the door, Khamid felt a hand against his arm. He turned to see Nomeri's daughter standing by him.

"My dad has been saying for years that all that was

needed to stand up against the Rat Tails was someone who cared," she said. "Did you care about us?"

Khamid hesitated.

"I do care what happened to your family, young one. But what happened with the Rat Tails was because something very dear to me was stolen by them, and I would've gone to any lengths to retrieve it. If it had not been taken, I could honestly say that none of this would have happened," he admitted.

The daughter gave him a hard stare. "Was it worth it? Was whatever was taken from you worth the trade of my father's life?"

Khamid could not answer that. Instead, he reached for his belt and slipped his cutlass scabbard free, holding it out to the girl. "If we knew the cost of our actions beforehand, we would never take any. Everyone needs to decide what is important to them, and what they should do to protect it."

Nomeri's daughter looked at the blade sadly, placing her hand on the hilt. "That is exactly what my dad would have said. He always wanted a better life for us. You really have done a lot to help." She took a deep breath. "Please do not take this the wrong way, but I hope to never see you again."

The girl closed the door gently behind Khamid as he stepped outside, pretending he didn't hear the soft sob as the door latched shut. Khamid strode through the streets with purpose. He had one more stop to make.

THE TEMPLE of Callath had survived the night's fury unscathed, the warm sun trickling through without a care for the violence and suffering. Khamid slowed as he ascended the temple stairs, and crossed the threshold at a more measured and reverential pace. The temple priest was looking tired, bags under his eyes from the long night just gone and sipping from a mug of aragi juice to keep awake. He nodded as Khamid entered, saw the dwarf's dark demeanour, and retreated.

Rather than the private prayer nooks, Khamid took the path to the temple's main chamber. Passing between the pews and under Callath's shawl, the dwarf knelt in front of the altar, clasped his hands together and prayed.

"Callath, matron of peace. I come before you a humble petitioner. Delivered into your care this past night was a loving husband and father, and I ask that you consider restoring Nomeri to life."

Khamid's eyes remained shut. The deafening silence which often came with prayer continued beyond what he expected. He felt compelled to fill the vacant air.

"He died because of my actions. Do not let another family break apart because of me. Please."

Do you find it a hard burden to bear, Khamid Saltstone, shouldering the blame for lost families all alone?

Khamid's eyes snapped open. He was floating amid a black void spotted with pinpricks of light, as if he had fallen into a clear night sky. The silence had not dropped; the voice he had heard made no attempt to bother with his ears.

Do you think I know so little of my children that I would blame you for their actions?

"Callath, I—"

Hush.

Khamid stopped speaking.

Nomeri's actions were none but his own. I have watched him for years in his struggle against the injus-

tice of piracy and knew his end would come through actions like this. You may have been the spark to ignite the kindling, but the man was ready to burn brightly into the night with or without you. Without your actions, the only thing that would have changed is how much blood spilled in the streets. You may not see, Khamid, but I am very proud of Nomeri's determination to stand up for his family.

"But you won't bring him back."

No, I shan't. Because that would cheapen his sacrifice. His wife, Dineke, will mourn, and she will hate you until the end of her days, and for that I am sorry, Khamid, but she will prosper in time. Nomeri's daughter, however... she will be one I watch for many years with even more pride. Her father was a principled man who staked his life on his beliefs, and she is very much her father's daughter. Your blade in her hands will help to deliver a message of encouragement to the world, not with a single grand sweep but in a thousand small slices. That is something Nomeri would be content with, as he watches by my side.

Khamid did not know what to say. The silence stretched longer again, but more comfortable than it was before. Whatever presence graced the dwarf, it had not left.

"Callath. I have an offering."

I would hope this isn't to bargain for Nomeri.

"No, dearest Callath, I would not dare to gainsay a goddess. I have an offering that I humbly ask for you to pass on." Khamid reached for his belt and pulled free his *Khlak Thurg* pouch, extending it out into the void.

Your Khlak Thurg? After everything you went through to get it back this last day?

"It has been a comfort to me for many years, but last

43

night made me realise that I have used it to anchor my-self to the past. A lot of good may have come from it, but I saw a dark reflection of myself in the pirate chief." Khamid paused. "Days ago the thought of losing it made me think I was unworthy to carry it... that by losing it, I was repeating the shame of what I had already lost, but now I see that I need to let go of that feeling."

To let go of the past? Does it no longer matter to you, Saltstone?

"Far from it. To accept what has happened, and that nothing will change it, I need to remember but not be anchored to it for the rest of my life."

The goddess was silent for a moment.

Then you have learnt the lesson of decades past.

The pouch floated away from Khamid, its tied leather thong unravelling. A little toy rabbit, ragged and beloved, glowed white against the darkness of the void, disappearing in a flash of light.

She will be most happy to see it once again, I will see that it gets to her.

Khamid's throat was tight. "Thank you, Callath. I am forever in your debt."

Nonsense, Khamid. There is no debt between us. You are one of my dear children and will always be so. I am so very proud of what you have accomplished, but now it is time for you to return.

The starry void darkened. Khamid closed his eyes and, when he reopened them, he was once again knelt in front of Callath's altar, the carved field of stars twink-ling in the morning sunlight.

"ENTER. AH, KHAMID."

Khamid opened the door to Nasir's quarters to find them seated with Aldo and Yacen already in attendance. Yacen with a report from the quartermaster, and Aldo with a list of pirate names. Captain Cilirin's nose was still swollen from the fight, but they had improved over the last few days while the *Sweeping Vista*'s crew made efforts to reunite anything important claimed by the Rat Tails with the townsfolk, taking over law enforcement until the town's merchants could establish something more permanent.

"Thank you, captain. I wanted to speak to the three of you together," Khamid said, joining the trio around the table, sinking into the hardwood chair. "I am leaving the ship."

Yacen and Aldo's heads jerked in surprise, Cilirin merely raising an eyebrow. Khamid raised his hands in placation. "Not immediately, but either the next port the *Sweeping Vista* docks at, or by the next Midacroft Isle ship that berths here if our business is not complete."

Cilirin gave Khamid a long look. "Are you dissatisfied with the crew? After their performance the other night I would not have thought there was much room for complaint."

Khamid shook his head. "Not at all, captain, far from it. But I realised how much I have been focused on my past, and I think it is time for me to explore on my own once again. The crew, and your command, will be something I look back on with fondness."

Cilirin accepted the explanation without further comment. Aldo and Yacen shared a glance.

"You're going to be missed, Khamid. It won't be easy to find a chaplain and a boarding sergeant to replace your roles," Yacen said. Aldo nodded in agreement.

"You will be missed as well, friends," Khamid smiled, giving Yacen a clap on the shoulder. Before he could stop them, Khamid was embraced by the two humans, who spoke over each other to offer their friendship and a final send off.

Khamid turned to leave when Cilirin raised their hand to stop him. "Khamid, your *Khlak Thurg* is missing."

Yacen groaned with his head in his hands, but Khamid chuckled. "My *Khlak Thurg* is where it belongs, and where it will do the most good once again. For the time being, I will have to be content with knowing that."

Cilirin stood and moved to open their footlocker. "If our chaplain is to move on without his *Khlak Thurg*, then it is only appropriate that he is gifted with a token of friendship, to remember these past thirty years." Cilirin pulled out a folded length of blue cloth to hand to Khamid.

The dwarf unfolded it to reveal Nasir's elvish scarf, with a design of the *Sweeping Vista* rolling across the waves stitched in gold. The fabric was light and strong in his hands, the subtle texture of an enchantment running through the weave.

Cilirin smiled as Khamid held it up. "We will drink once more before you go, Khamid, but it has been an honour and a pleasure having you on my ship. You will always be welcome here... amongst family."

THE TEETOTALLER
ALAN KENT

Mount Reckless overlooked the grey landscape of the Northern Wastes. Crowned by a head of snow and a robe of mist, the mountain stood oblivious to the unseasonal hot weather searing the land below.

A trail snaked up the mountain, pausing halfway to the summit where featureless granite gave way to a sudden splash of pastel colours. Here, a solitary structure stood, a rudimentary cube carved into the mountain itself. Its stone walls were a mess of blues, yellows and pinks, with an archway flanked by stained glass windows providing the only way inside. The building lay snuggled in a recess, sheltered from the Winge, the northerly wind that relentlessly buffeted the mountain. It howled as though offended by the brightly coloured carbuncle defiling the dark majesty of the mountain.

The archway led into a warren of rooms and chambers. In the centre lay the great hall, lined by slender columns, each bearing a network of abstract carvings bereft of any pattern, as though someone had attacked them with a hammer and chisel in a murderous rage.

Twenty figures lined the hall, all shaven-headed, all

clothed in scarlet and orange. Their bodies lunged, twisted and contorted their way through a series of combat stances, each manoeuvre overseen by a tall, lanky instructor—shorn-headed and draped in scarlet and orange like the rest. His face was long and thin, his pointed chin as clean-shaven as his skull. Even his eyebrows were completely shorn, leaving only a canopy of flesh propped up by a crooked nose. Beneath the flesh-brow, narrow water-blue eyes jumped between the combatants, a sheet of stained parchment clasped between his slender fingers. He barked instructions, though the fighters seemed not to notice; swiping, chopping, punching, and kicking the air in a lumbering display entirely bereft of any synchronicity.

A young man entered the hall, skulked towards the instructor and whispered briefly into his ear. The instructor nodded before dismissing the young man with a sharp hand gesture.

"Brethren," called the instructor in a nasal trill, "morning session is over. Proceed to the contemplation chamber for spiritual enlightenment. Three barrels have been provided for the occasion. Draw well from the Chalice this evening, and let the Haze flow through you."

The combatants bowed, filing—or, more accurately, staggering—out, one-by-one. The man watched until the hall was empty, then exited the room down a long corridor that ended before a heavy pine door. He knocked.

"Grandmaster?" called the instructor. "You sent for me?"

"Enter, Brother Crunge," came the soft-spoken response.

The door opened into a small room with a single window, empty except for a wicker mat on the stone floor. An elderly man stood in the centre, scowling behind folded arms. He stood a head shorter than Brother Crunge, similarly bald-headed, though his garments shone white as the beard reaching down to his waist. Chestnut eyes bulged within a round rosy-cheeked face, crowned by twin sprigs of black eyebrows.

"Brother Crunge," said the elderly man, his reedy voice barely above a whisper.

"Grandmaster," replied Brother Crunge with a bow. "How may I be of service?"

"Did the training go well?" Brother Crunge sensed tension in the Grandmaster's voice.

"Good, Grandmaster. The disciples, as always, prove themselves skilled warriors."

The Grandmaster huffed. "What of Master Dyom?"

"Grandmaster?"

"Is training not his responsibility?"

"Of course alas, he was overcome by a hangover this morning and could not perform his duties."

"And so he thought it appropriate to unload his burden onto you? A Designated One?"

Brother Crunge allowed his gaze to drift to his feet. "I thought only to help a brother in need, Grandmaster."

The Grandmaster shook his head. "We all have our place here, Brother Crunge. It seems though, that you have not learned yours."

"Grandmaster, I—"

"Silence! Let me remind you of your duties, Brother Crunge. Recite to me the Pledge of the Designated One."

Brother Crunge cleared his throat, recalling the lines he had recited so many times before.

"Whenever one becomes lost within the throes of the Haze, I shall be there to serve as his anchor. Wherever one staggers from the path, I shall be there to guide them home. Whenever one neglects the Round, I shall be there to ensure all pay their fair share."

The Grandmaster nodded. "Continue."

"My responsibilities are great and responsibility breeds sacrifice. Thus never may my lips draw from the Chalice so long as I live."

The Grandmaster clapped his hands. "Indeed, but how can one comprehend the power of the Haze when they may not sup from the Chalice?"

"They cannot."

"Very good! How then, can one school disciples of the Haze in matters they cannot comprehend?"

"Grandmaster," said Brother Crunge, waving the parchment he carried. "I assure you I followed Master Dyom's instructions faithfully. Not once did I impart my own wisdom."

The Grandmaster stroked his beard, stepping up to the solitary window in his chambers. "Master Dyom ought to know better."

Brother Crunge caught himself wringing his hands and forced them back down to his sides.

"I only wished to help a brother in need."

"So you said. Your willingness to do so is something to be admired, but I cannot overlook the fact you have overstepped your boundaries. I do not overlook Master Dyom's role in this either and he will be punished appropriately for what he has done."

The old man turned away from the window.

"Unfortunately, Brother Crunge, so will you."

Brother Crunge ran a hand across his smooth head. "Latrine duty for a month again?"

The Grandmaster shook his head. "No, Brother Crunge, this infringement warrants a far more grievous punishment." A smile crept across the Grandmaster's cracked lips. "What do you know of the god of war?"

"Who?"

The Grandmaster twirled a lock of beard through his ancient fingers. "You don't know His name?"

Brother Crunge shook his head. "No, Grandmaster. I need know of no god but Glurgamoth."

"Your devotion is admirable, but today you shall know the name of 'Zugote'."

Brother Crunge began wringing his hands again. "I don't understand, Grandmaster. Surely you're not asking to start worshipping another?"

"Blessed barrels, no, I would never endorse such blasphemy. I merely ask that you... co-operate in a rather delicate matter."

Brother Crunge's hand wringing grew faster, sweat dampening his palms. "What do you mean?"

"A few days ago, a fashionable lady made contact with the monastery—a loud, brash creature from one of the big cities in the south. Normally, we would have sent her on her way, but she proved as stubborn as she was talkative, refusing to leave until she received an audience with myself, and she was somehow able to convince two of my disciples to lead her here. Naturally, I scolded the disciples for letting her inside, but they remained insistent that she was able to compel them in a way they could not resist, as though she were some kind of sorcerer.

"The lady introduced herself as Grizelda Burgerslade, and claimed to be a well-known collector of magical artefacts. Whether true or not, she claimed to have uncovered the location of the Godhammer, a legendary

51

weapon wielded by the god Zugote Himself. To get to the point, she is looking to recruit a team to recover it for her. Namely us."

Brother Crunge rubbed his long, dimpled chin. "Surely this is a job more suited to an adventurer's guild? Why come to us?"

"I asked her that very question, but her skills in persuasion were matched by her skills in evasion. She refused to answer any question to the point where I was ready to send her on her way. That was until she revealed how much she was willing to pay for the hammer, enough to keep us supplied with Ostrogovian brandy for a whole year. I could do nought but agree, given the precarious state of our finances.

"Of course, it would be an insult to Glurgamoth to send my best men on a quest of such an avaricious, and potentially blasphemous, nature. That is why I have decided to send six apprentices off instead, the task will serve as part of their rite of passage. The six have since been chosen, all they need now a Designated One to ensure they do not stray from the path." The Grandmaster fell into silence, raising an eyebrow.

Brother Crunge stifled a sigh. "I will start packing, Grandmaster."

The Grandmaster clapped his hands. "I knew I could count on you, Brother Crunge. Now, listen carefully and I will tell you what we know of the Godhammer. The collector believes the artefact lies in an abandoned castle far to the south. Unfortunately, she does not know exactly where the castle lies, she only knows it is somewhere in a mountain range close to the town of Frogchester. It is there that you and the apprentices will travel to find the Godhammer. Once you get there, ask for directions to Fort Rubbish. Someone will likely have heard of it."

Brother Crunge glanced beyond the Grandmaster to the window. The misty grey of the sky beyond seemed suddenly much bigger, and more hostile.

"The castle is called Fort Rubbish?"

The Grandmaster shrugged. "One should never place too much emphasis on a name alone. It may be a mistranslation, or a local nickname? Do not concern yourself about it."

Brother Crunge exhaled. "This artefact, this hammer of the gods, is it well-defended?"

The Grandmaster nodded vigorously. "Undoubtedly. Do you think the gods would be so foolish as to leave their relics unguarded?"

Brother Crunge felt his stomach sink. "I should have known."

"Come again?"

"Oh, nothing. What will we find there, Grandmaster?"

The Grandmaster shrugged. "I do not know, but that should not concern you, Brother Crunge. A disciple of the Unsteady Fist must always be prepared for any challenge, regardless of how much they have been drinking."

Brother Crunge bowed. "Then I humbly request leave to begin preparations for the journey ahead, Grandmaster."

"Request granted. Go and prepare, but be quick about it. You leave at first light."

Brother Crunge locked his fingers together. The sweat on his hands was growing cold.

"Tomorrow?"

"That is what I said, is it not? Do not look so dismayed, this is a punishment after all. Now, off with you. Prepare for the pilgrimage and get an early night. You have a long journey ahead of you."

SLEEP DID NOT COME EASILY that night thanks to the raging Winge beyond the walls. Brother Crunge tossed and turned in bed, wrestling with thoughts of the journey ahead. His mind dwelled on Fort Rubbish, and what kind of horrors lurked in a place so far from civilisation. What of Glurgamoth? How would He react to one of his disciples embarking on a quest on behalf of another god? Images of a vengeful deity raining down terrible curses swamped his mind. Outside, the Winge grew louder.

"Oh, great Glurgamoth, lord of beverage, scourge of sobriety," whispered Brother Crunge. "Heed my call in this, my time of turmoil, as I prepare to commit blasphemous deeds in the name of another. I implore thee, refrain from taking my sinful endeavours personally, with the knowledge that the Grandmaster made me do it."

Brother Crunge shut his eyes to visions of being struck by lightning. For now, Glurgamoth's only response was silence. Deathly silence

Wait, silence? That can't be right.

Brother Crunge opened his eyes again to total blackness. The Winge had stopped blowing, unheard of here on the slopes of Mount Reckless. There was not a sound, not even the rustle of bedsheets nor the sound of his own breathing.

There was only silence. Silence and blackness, as though all sound and light in the world had died. Fear took hold and the urge to wring his hands arose, until he realised he could no longer feel his fingers.

He tried to sit up, but he couldn't move. He could see nothing, hear nothing, smell nothing, as though he was without form, floating through a deathly abyss.

He tried calling out, but the words did not come.

Am I dead?

Somewhere in the darkness, he sensed something stirring, as though he was being watched by predatory eyes.

"You are not dead," came a voice, though he could not hear the words. It was as though they came from within his own mind.

Who's there?

More silence, only that sense of being watched. Brother Crunge almost yearned to hear the voice again, if only to break the loneliness of the void. Even the banshee wail of the Winge seemed inviting.

"What are you afraid of?" called the mind-voice.

I am afraid of you. Have you come to kill me?

Was that laughter he could hear? It was like a cold chuckle, pulsing through his head as though it were burrowing into his brain.

"Kill you? No, at least not for now. It is good you are afraid of me though. You should be."

Who are you?

"You know who I am, you seek my hammer after all."

Zugote!

"Indeed. Tremble before Me, for I am indeed Zugote, Lord of Battle and Bloodshed. Across the land warriors pray every day to Me for good fortune on the battlefield, shedding blood in My name. Not all shall find the glory they seek, yet I remember the names of all

55

who invoke Me in their battle cries. Yet I know not of you, nor do I understand why you seek to possess My greatest weapon."

My Grandmaster wills it.

"Then you are nought but a slave. Listen well, slave —leave my weapon well alone, for I will not suffer such a servile wretch to bear arms in My name. Go and lick the boots of your beloved Grandmaster and tell him to bring Me someone worthy of My name."

I am no slave. I serve my master willingly, for he is a great leader and a mighty warrior.

Somewhere within the abyssal blackness there came a terrible shuddering sensation. Brother Crunge felt it thrumming within him, as though he were caught in the midst of some divine earthquake. "It is most unwise to lie to a god, slave. How is it that I, Zugote, God of War, know not of such a warrior?"

My Grandmaster has pledged allegiance to another, as have I.

"Another? Who? Tell Me now." The godly voice grew louder, piercing Brother Crunge's mind with a fire that threatened to set his soul aflame. "Tell Me to whom you have whored your souls, and I might refrain from smiting you for now."

We are but humble servants of Glurgamoth.

Demon laughter erupted once more. "Glurgamoth? The self-proclaimed god of drunkards and tavern brawlers? This bumbling fop is who you devote yourself to over Me?"

Great Zugote, please, I ask that you refrain from saying such things about my god.

"And what will you do if I do not?"

Erm...

"Never mind. I have more important matters to deal

with, but as for you, I offer you a chance to repent your foolish ways. You claim to serve a great warrior, so I shall assume that you are a soldier of some skill. It is, however, only proper that as a fighter, you should carry My divine banner into battle. I therefore demand that you turn away from the Drunken God, and embrace Me above all else."

I cannot. My devotion is to Glurgamoth, now and forever.

"You would worship a god of fools?"

I would. Not that I'm saying Glurgamoth is a fool.

"Interesting."

Brother Crunge awoke, drenched in sweat. He sat upright and glimpsed a red sunrise beyond the window. Outside, the Winge raged.

FROGCHESTER BECKONED, yet only one of the six apprentices was awake—Lurg, Bung, Vong, Flarg, and Mlarf had drawn mightily from the Chalice during the evening and had suffered Glurgamoth's Blessing as a consequence, the mightiest of hangovers. Brother Crunge had therefore been forced to drag the bleary-eyed youths, one by one, from the sweat-addled security of their bed sheets. What followed was a kerfuffle of shambling and groaning as clothes were pulled on and packs hoisted over shoulders.

The sixth apprentice was Frang. Although a willing participant in the previous night's binge, she had emerged bright and early, fresh-faced with a grin that told of one very definitely unblessed. A glimmer of pity sparked within Brother Crunge as he was reminded of nights spent partaking of the Chalice, where Frang always remained the last one standing, sober as a Designated One, to the point where even the masters struggled to keep up with her. Such persistent sobriety did nothing to endear her to them—it was no easy task teaching the ways of the Haze to one who seemed immune to its effects.

Frang was not much more popular with the apprentices either. Whilst they shuffled around in the cold, fantasising about warm beds and silence, Frang insisted on persistent small talk, framed within an obnoxiously cheerful disposition. There were few people more hated. Brother Crunge did not escape her chatter either.

"Is Frogchester big?"

"Are they friendly there?"

"Will it be dangerous?"

"Is it far away?"

"Why aren't any masters coming?"

"Fort Rubbish? Really?"

"Have you seen the Godhammer before?"

"Is it big?"

"Where are the best pubs in Frogchester?"

Brother Crunge deflected every question with a mix of monosyllabic words and wordlike grunts. He could think only of the trip down the mountain. It would be a dangerous trek at the best of times, never mind when accompanied by six greenhorn apprentices who had never known life beyond the monastery.

Dressed in a coat and hat of black bear fur, Brother Crunge took up his weapon, a maul the size of a small child. Its gleaming steel head was inscribed with the Pledge of the Designated One in the wild, weaving strokes of Slurscript, the secret language of the long-extinct Scribes of Glurgamoth, its oaken shaft bound in strips of black leather. Any other who wielded the weapon might have been impressed by its craftsmanship. Brother Crunge recalled how a fellow brother had whistled in admiration when setting eyes upon the weapon—"How sober the blacksmith must have been to produce such a thing!". He had, of course, spoken in hushed tones. Well-crafted as it was, Brother Crunge knew this maul was no token of merit. This was the Hammer of Shame. Where one warrior had whistled in admiration, a dozen more would look upon it and be reminded of his failure, his failure to make the grade as a warrior of the Unsteady Fist. He had trained, fought, and drank alongside his peers since childhood, but his skills had not satisfied the masters, deeming him unworthy of joining their ranks. Instead, he had been ordained a Designated One, a title that doomed him to a life of servitude, condemned to serve the fighters he had once fought alongside as equals. Never again would he partake of the Chalice, never again would he know the power of the Haze, never again would he even be allowed to use his own body as a weapon. He was condemned to hide behind a weapon, as all cowards did in the eyes of the Unsteady Fist.

He strapped the maul to his back, feeling it weigh him down like a millstone. Slinging an orange cloth pack over his shoulder, he tried to push aside the memories of the past, instead focusing on one man, Master Dyom, the one responsible for his predicament. Brother Crunge hoped with all his heart that he was having as bad a time as he was.

The expedition streamed out into the courtyard, six slack-shouldered apprentices, and one sour-faced Designated One. Though the walls of the courtyard offered some sanctuary from the Winge, the air still bore fangs, sinking its frost-teeth into any exposed flesh, and so everyone wrapped up as warmly as possible. Brother Crunge surveyed the sextet of hunched, shivering figures, cheeks reddened by the frigid air. Meanwhile, in an iron sky overhead, Brother Crunge felt the eyes of the gods upon him.

The courtyard was a flat expanse of stone, framed by a modest cluster of vegetable gardens, leading to the great doorway and beyond, where the mountain trail began. Here the party would be thrown before the mercy of the Winge as they wound their way down to ground level.

There was little else to be seen in the courtyard, save a long iron pole in the centre of the yard. It stood about the height of a human being, its dulled surface scarred by a mottling of red-orange rust. Yet it was this crude centrepiece that drew the attention of all assembled.

The sight of Master Dyom's naked buttocks daubed in lemon yellow paint was enough to brighten Brother Crunge's day ever so slightly. Stripped of all garments, he had been tied to the iron pole, and could only stare silently ahead, listening to the procession of shuffling feet passing behind him. Brother Crunge was the last to pass. Despite his seething resentment towards Dyom, he could not help but admire the master's aura of dignity, at least as much as one naked with brightly painted hindquarters could remain dignified.

"Master Dyom," called Brother Crunge, stifling a smile. "Sent to the punishment post I see. My condolences on your predicament."

Master Dyom bowed his head. "Thank you for your concern, brother, but your sympathies are not needed. I find this strangely comforting. To be reduced to my most primal form, the wind as my companion, the sky as my shelter, clothed only in the mountain mist. I reflect that perhaps we were wrong about the Haze, Brother Crunge. Perhaps it is all just an illusion. Here I find a new reality and I feel enlightened. I feel exposed to the world, and for the first time, I feel at one with it. Perhaps this is how it feels to be a Designated One, without all the ridicule of course..."

Master Dyom trailed off. "Oh, no offence, Brother Crunge. I would suggest you disregard my words. If the Grandmaster should find out, I have no doubt he would chastise me most grievously for such blasphemous talk, even more so than now. You won't tell him I said that, will you?"

"Of course not," lied Brother Crunge. "Can I get you anything, Master Dyom? You look awfully cold."

"Cold? I'm absolutely freezing, but you don't have to do anything for me, Brother Crunge. It's called the punishment pole for a reason. I accept that I have sinned and I accept my punishment. I can only apologise for your situation, Brother Crunge, you're only here because of me. But, on the positive side, I think I rather like the cold. My goosebumps make me feel alive! Far better than sitting cross-legged in some stuffy chamber for hours on end, sweating like a pig, brazier soot in my lungs. I know I'm not the only one who feels that way. Disciples of the Unsteady Fist don't do very well in the heat, hence why we live up here."

"I am glad to see you're taking it well," said Brother Crunge through gritted teeth. "Alas, we must be on our way."

"Ah, yes! I hear you're off on some grand adventure in faraway lands. How exciting! I almost wish I was going with you. I'm sure the apprentices will prove themselves worthy."

"Farewell, Master Dyom," said Brother Crunge with a half-hearted wave. "May you never walk a straight line."

"You too, Brother Crunge. I wish you a good journey."

———

THE PARTY EMBARKED on the path down the mountain single file, each placing a hand on the shoulder of the one in front. They moved slowly, every step an effort against the wrath of the Winge. Left of the path loomed the grey-black granite of Mount Reckless, to the right an endless expanse of silver cloud. Brother Crunge, brought up the rear, forcing himself to stare ahead as he and the apprentices were buffeted from side to side. He watched the line of fur-hatted heads bobbing up and down in front of him, his thoughts dwelling on the souls lost to the mountain, blown to their deaths over the edge of the rocky precipice. He recalled a group of apprentices who had been lost on this very trail whilst on pilgrimage. Every single one lost to the Winge, all except the accompanying Designated One, who had immediately been drowned in a rain barrel for incompetence upon his return.

The party pressed on and the mighty strength of the Winge began to recede as they descended further and further. Still, they walked slowly and steadily until they breached the clouds, revealing the Northern Wastes below—a dirty quilt of orange and brown, pocked by scatterings of shimmering rock. Brother Crunge sensed the feeling of awe among the apprentices—most of whom were seeing the world beyond the walls for the first time.

There were audible sighs of relief when they reached the foot of the mountain. The icy claws of the Winge had fallen away to be replaced by the searing glare of the noon sun. Coats and hats were quickly packed away, and now they plodded on dressed only in suits of scarlet and orange.

"Well, brethren," called Brother Crunge. "The mountain is behind us, and there is an inn not far from here. What say we give thanks to Glurgamoth by making a pilgrimage?"

A cheer rose from the group. Shoulders straightened, bleary eyes widened, and for the first time since they departed the monastery, Brother Crunge found himself struggling to keep up.

THE WANDERER'S BLADE was little more than a wooden shack nestled within a small unfriendly hamlet. The party entered, finding only the innkeeper for company, a rotund man in a leather apron. The roundness of his head was broken by curly wisps of white hair protruding above either ear, while he watched the new arrivals with unblinking fishlike eyes.

"Greetings, innkeeper," said Brother Crunge, forcing a broad smile across his face. "We wish to partake of some refreshments."

The innkeeper responded with a roll of the eyes. "Good for you. Hope you find someone who'll serve you."

"Excuse me?" said Brother Crunge.

"No service to drunken brawlers. Sick of the sight of you people."

"Good sir, we have travelled a long way. Would you deny us respite?"

The innkeeper leaned forward, smiling a shark grin. "Indubitably, good sir. I wouldst most enthusiastically refrain from granting thee that which thou doth seek. Now piss off."

"Sir, I don't understand."

The barkeeper rolled his fish eyes again. "What's not to understand? No service. I'm sick of the sight of you lot, swanning around here like lords. Let me tell you this, you're nothing, all of you. Nothing but a bunch of troublemaking yobs."

"Good sir, we merely come to partake in pilgrimage. I thought you would be glad of the coin?"

"Yes, I would be glad of the coin. Too bad I always spend more than I make with you around. Every time you come here, you wreck the place and drive all my regulars away. They don't want to share space with a bunch of crazy monks who try to pick a fight with anything that moves."

"That is unfair," said Brother Crunge. "We only seek to fight when we are suitably inebriated."

By now the barkeeper was flashing his teeth. "Oh, I get it. You only fight when you're drunk. That's all right then."

"Drinking and fighting is our way. The way of Glurgamoth."

"Might be your way, but it isn't mine. Find somewhere else to drink, you're all barred, all of you. That includes the rest of your lunatic friends up the mountain."

"But where else can we go? There's nothing for miles."

"Do you honestly think I care? Get out, all of you, and don't come back."

They were barely out the door when Apprentice Vong erupted, "Good work, Designated One. If you can't find us a place to drink, then what use are you to us?"

"Don't be so naive, apprentice," said Brother Crunge. "This is but a minor setback."

"Don't patronise me! You're just making excuses for your incompetence. But then I suppose that's how you became a Designated One, isn't it? Through failure."

Frang stepped in, pushing Vong away as he advanced on Brother Crunge. "Stop," she said. "The Designated One is doing his best. Now is not the time to fight."

Vong laughed, patting Frang on the head before she batted his hand away.

"Well, well, well," said Vong. "Looks like the Designated One has himself a bootlicker. Perhaps you can find us somewhere to drink, bootlicker?"

"Mind your attitude, boy," said Brother Crunge. "Mind your attitude and swallow your pride. You may think yourself superior to me, but mind that I have knowledge—knowledge and experience that might just help you keep your head on your shoulders."

"I don't need advice from cowards who hide behind weapons." Vong almost spat the words out. "I am more than capable of taking care of myself."

Brother Crunge smiled. "Is that so? Tell me, what exactly do you know of the world beyond the walls? Do you know of that which awaits us on our travels?"

"I know enough," snarled Vong.

"Perhaps I should leave you to it then, oh wise warrior."

Vong sneered. "Don't talk to me like that, Designated One."

"Boy, you know nothing of the world." He turned to face the rest of the group. "None of you do. You might be able to smash through a pile of planks with a single swipe,you might be able to stand on your heads as long as you please, you might be able to shrug off a hammerblow, but none of that will save you from a knife in the back. I've seen battle-hardened wardogs lose their lives to rat-nosed cowards when they turned away for just a moment. I've seen proud fools like yourselves lose their heads just because they ridiculed the wrong person. So, let's try to humble ourselves a little shall we?"

"Brother Crunge is right," said Frang. "Are we not all children of Glurgamoth? Yet here we bicker like sober children. The more we argue, the less time we spend drinking and beating the living daylights out of each other. Is that really who we are? Is that really who we want to be?"

"Shut your mouth, bootlicker," said Bung, smashing his fists together. "You have no understanding of the Haze, just like the Designated One. You drink like a fish, yet you never even get a little bit tipsy. If Glurgamoth sees fit to deprive you of the Haze, surely it is a sign of His displeasure with you."

"Enough with this blasphemy!" snapped Brother Crunge. "You would mock fellow disciples of Glurgamoth? How can we expect to fulfil our quest if we see fit to defy Him when we need Him most?"

"Why would Glurgamoth give a damn about our quest?" said Mlarf. "Are we not on a mission to retrieve a relic of another god? That is where the blasphemy lies. Why do you lead us astray, Designated One?"

"Silence, apprentice! We are beholden to the

Grandmaster. He may not be a god, but as our leader and guide he is the mouthpiece of our lord and server. To disobey the will of the Grandmaster is to disobey the will of Glurgamoth himself."

"We already know this," said Mlarf. "Surprising as it may sound, we do pay attention during the sermons, you know."

Brother Crunge smirked. "It does surprise me, Apprentice Mlarf, as your actions suggest otherwise. But enough with this senseless squabbling. Let us press on to Frogchester."

"We don't take orders from you, servant," said Vong.

"No, you don't," said Brother Crunge, "but do you not take orders from the Grandmaster, who has sent us forth on this quest?"

Vong huffed loudly, but said no more.

THEY MOVED south across the tundra, encountering no sign of human existence over the next two days. Behind them, the misty black cone of Mount Reckless grew smaller and smaller, before vanishing beneath the horizon. As Brother Crunge turned back to see only sky in the mountain's wake, the realisation that he was further away from home than he had ever been in his life struck him in the face like a thrown bottle.

By day, they traversed rocky terrain, sweating under a sun that grew in strength the further south they trekked. At night, they camped among the rocks and rubble, though in these summer months the nights did not last long, and a lack of sleep soon added to the grumblings of the apprentices.

"We have to get up already?"

"We are surely lost, out here in the middle of nowhere!"

"Ration the ale? What kind of monster are you?"

"I need to fight someone soon or I'm going to go mad!"

"Trust in Glurgamoth, brethren, remember He wants to see a good fight as much as we do."

"Shut up, Frang."

They pressed on until the barren tundra wastes gradually yielded to grassy fields and bright scatterings of flowers and foliage. The apprentices walked agape, pointing excitedly as they set eyes upon the first trees they had ever seen in their lives. Hardy stands of oak, pine, and silver birch grew more prevalent, until the party found themselves walking beneath the green ceiling of a forest canopy.

The forest continued to grow more dense, as did the chorus of animal noises. Every squeak, squawk, or growl was enough to startle the apprentices—even the crack of a twig or the rustle of a bush was enough to invoke a gasp of fear. The sky gods seemed not to empathise with the party's situation, sending forth a sudden shower of ice cold rain. They walked on, now soaking wet, the rainstorm refusing to relent throughout the day until the sun set unseen behind the clouds. The remainder of an unhappy day was spent pitching tents even as the rain persisted.

The party spent the night bound in their bedrolls, listening to the sound of raindrops hammering against the tents, punctuated by the occasional crash of thunder. The storm at least had the courtesy to stop as they emerged from the aftermath of a sleep-deprived maelstrom. As they packed up the tents and stamped out the campfire, an almighty scream arose. They turned to see

Lurg flapping at his head as an angry honking beast threw itself at him in a blurred frenzy.

"What's the matter?" called Brother Crunge. "Never seen a duck before?"

Once the bird had been driven off, they pressed on through seemingly endless forest, pausing only to fill their flasks at a pond, where Brother Crunge had to explain to an extremely disappointed audience that the pond was in fact only water. Vong wasted no opportunity to grumble once more.

"Designated One, we have walked for days upon days, and you have yet to find us anything but water to drink. I'm sure I need not remind you that there are six of us and only one of you." Vong flashed a smirk at Frang. "Though I'm sure your little bootlicker has your back."

"Enough of this!" said Frang as she lunged at Vong. The other apprentices perked up at this sudden bout of entertainment, as the pair rolled over in a tangle of fisticuffs but cheers quickly turned to boos as Brother Crunge stepped in to break them up.

"Foolish children, how easily you lose your minds," he said. "We fight among ourselves so readily, how can we possibly hope to stand against the horrors that await us in Fort Rubbish?"

"You've made your point, Designated One," said Vong, as he dusted himself down, "but we will also fail if your incompetence deprives us of the Haze much longer."

A murmur of agreement trickled through the party.

They resumed the journey, their food supplies growing as empty as their hip flasks. Brother Crunge sensed the discontent in the air, the hairs standing on the back of his neck. The apprentices were young and headstrong, but Brother Crunge silently reminded himself that they were also extremely dangerous, each one a vicious killing machine. He did not relish spending another night in the forest. A sleeping target was an easy target.

Brother Crunge was therefore quite relieved when the party found themselves before the gates of Frogchester.

THE TOWN RESTED atop a gentle hill, ringed by a tall wooden palisade. Within the walls, Frogchester revealed itself as a sprawl of thatched cottages, ornate longhouses, and even the occasional burial mound. The cold air buzzed with the stinging melange of chimney smoke and animal dung. The streets were sparse, the emptiness broken only by the sudden appearance of a filthy-faced farmer swaggering through accompanied by a small herd of shaggy-haired cattle. He glowered at the apprentices silently, a wad of spit at Brother Crunge's feet his only greeting. The locals did not prove any friendlier, asking for directions around town resulted only in a tirade of insults, the locals mocking the party for their 'weird accents', their 'ridiculous red and orange pyjamas', and their 'glimmering egg-heads'.

Nevertheless, Brother Crunge, and the party were rewarded when they were pointed in the direction of the Placid Griffin tavern by a dirty-faced peasant girl, gesturing towards a heap of stone and thatch that squatted on a lonely spread of waste ground, as though ostracised by the other buildings in town.

"Watch yourself there," said the farm girl. "Place

gets a lot of weirdos." She looked the party up and down. "You lot would probably feel right at home."

"Weirdos?" asked Brother Crunge.

The girl shrugged. "Uncivilised yobs, barbarians. Outcasts and criminals, that kind of thing. Oh, and worst of all, adventurers."

"What's so bad about adventurers?"

The girl coughed. "What's good about them? They're a bunch of workshy crooks—don't know the meaning of an honest living. They go around in gangs looking for loot like robbers, they don't think twice about plundering temples and graves. They'd strip a corpse to the bone if they saw something shiny on it. They also smell really, really bad since they like hanging about in caves and stuff."

Brother Crunge sniffed the cow-riddled air. "Surprised you people would notice."

"What?"

"Nothing."

"These adventurers, do you know if they're any good in a fight?" asked Bung.

The girl raised an eyebrow. "What? Well, I suppose they are. You honestly never seen one? They're all armed to the teeth, and they like to yap on about all the monsters they've killed and the treasure they've found. I think most of the time they're full of shit, but I wouldn't go messing with them either way. At least when they're not blind drunk, which they usually are."

A chorus of cheers went up from the party as Brother Crunge took several slaps on the back. The pilgrimage could begin.

"Oh my. This might not have been such a good idea."

As Brother Crunge entered the Placid Griffin, he was reminded of all the drinking establishments he had visited throughout his life. He had reached the stage where he believed he had seen it all. Taverns typically bore a generous helping of broad-armed grunts, drinking themselves into belligerence. They were often big, they were often imposing, but they seldom offered much challenge to a gang of shaven-headed maniacs trained in the ways of the drunken brawler almost since birth. Sometimes, Glurgamoth would bless them with a more worthy challenge; bare knuckle boxers, stick-wielding hooligans, even the occasional swordsman, but —by and large—he had always seen the disciples come out on top,

By Glurgamoth, he thought. *It's as though we've wandered into an army barracks.*

Everyone in the place was armed; everyone, and not with the sticks and stolen bread knives he was accustomed to. At one table, he spied a broad shouldered man resting his arm on a broadsword that was almost as tall as he was. His armour bore as many scars as his great block of a head. The tall wiry woman he drank with was dressed in a leather jerkin lined with yellow fur. The longbow she wore seemed to thrum with some mystical energy, while the jet black arrows in her quiver screamed '*murder-death-kill*'.

Another table featured a stubbly hulk with hair black as soot. He leaned back lazily in his chair while he and his colleague tried to make conversation through the white noise of the tavern. Brother Crunge wondered if he would be quite laid back were he not almost completely clad in steel plate armour. His colleague bore no armour, dressed instead in flowing silken robes. In one hand he held a tankard, the other clamped tight around a gnarled wooden stave.

Brother Crunge felt something brush past his legs, and looked down to see a hobbledehoy shuffle by clad in chain mail, his iron helmet glinting by the lamplight. The hobbledehoy waved a greeting to a wild-eyed woman dressed in furs, a huge battle axe strapped to her back.

"Brethren," called Mlarf. "Behold! Here we have found a worthy test of our skills."

"Indeed," said Vong, bearing a rare smile, "but let us first imbue ourselves with the power of the Haze through the ritual of the Round. Frang! You're buying."

"Why do I have to get the first one?"

"Because I said it first. Don't worry your little head, we'll all take our turn. I'm sure our esteemed Designated One shall see to that, will he not?"

Brother Crunge raised a hand. "Brethren, let us not be so hasty. Look at all those weapons. We should tread carefully in such a place. We don't know what these adventurers are capable of."

"Gutless coward!" snapped Vong. "We are disciples of the Unsteady Fist, masters of the Haze. We never refuse a fight!"

"Do you remember what I said before about Designated Ones, boy? This sort of thing is exactly why we exist—to prevent headstrong fools from getting themselves killed. You who are but apprentices, you would claim mastery over the Haze? Not even the mightiest of our order would make such a claim. The Haze is the manifestation of the power of Glurgamoth. It is something to be respected, not conquered. Do you expect to master the power of a god, child? The Haze is a berserker, a powerful ally in the field of battle, but one

73

to be wary of, lest it takes your head off in the throes of battle frenzy."

Vong shrugged. "Be silent now, Designated One, you've made your point. Remember though, it has been days since we last fought. Glurgamoth will not tolerate such inaction for much longer."

"Then if you are so eager for action, perhaps you should accompany me to the bar?" Brother Crunge handed Vong a threadbare coin purse. "While you gather in the first Round, I will try to ingratiate myself a little more with the locals, preferably without punching anyone in the face. Perhaps that way, I can find out more about Fort Rubbish. The rest of you, have a seat. I have a feeling this will be a long night."

The barman raised the brow of his one good eye as Brother Crunge and Vong approached the bar. He was a great chunk of a man, more bouncer than barman. The network of scars on his broad arms mingled with a swathe of tattoos, while his balding skull bore a purple burn reaching down to his nose, a leather eyepatch concealing his bad eye.

He gave a slight bow, in which Brother Crunge detected a trace of mockery. "Hugo Thrusk," he growled, revealing brown, broken teeth. "Owner and proprietor of the Placid Griffin. And who, or what, are you supposed to be?"

"We are warriors of the Unsteady Fist, disciples of the Haze," said Vong.

Hugo collected a stray tankard on the counter and began cleaning it with a stained rag. "Disciples of what?"

Vong's eyes widened. "You mock us?"

Hugo shrugged. "Maybe. Depends on how much of an idiot you are."

"We are the children of Glurgamoth, masters of unarmed combat. We channel our powers through the medium of the Chalice."

"What?" Hugo continued rubbing the same tankard.

"Through alcohol," said Vong, his voice growing louder.

Hugo set the tankard aside. "You're drunken brawlers? Why didn't you just say so in the first place instead of yammering on like that?"

"We're more than that," said Vong. "Much more."

"Whatever you say," said Hugo. "So what brings you into my humble establishment, oh mighty warriors of Glurgamoth? By the sound of your accent, I would guess you're a long way from home."

"Indeed, we are on an important quest," said Vong, puffing out his chest.

"Of course you are," said Hugo, rolling his eye, "and pray tell, mighty warrior, what does this important quest entail?"

"We are on a quest to retrieve an important artefact. A literal hammer of the gods, from the ruins of Fort Rubbish."

A smirk crossed Hugo's pouting lips. "A hammer of the gods? Oh, but of course, presumably a sacred artefact of daddy Glurgamoth?"

"The hammer does not belong to Glurgamoth. It is the Godhammer, a weapon of Zugote, God of War," said Brother Crunge.

Hugo placed his hands on his hips and stepped back from the counter.

"So you're disciples of Glurgamoth on a mystical quest to retrieve a magic hammer of Zugote?"

"It's complicated," said Brother Crunge.

Hugo picked up another tankard and began cleaning.

"Evidently! And you know for sure this marvellous magical hammer exists?"

"What?"

"It's a straightforward question,' said Hugo. "Do you know if the Godhammer is real?"

"Why wouldn't it be real?" said Brother Crunge.

"Well I sure haven't heard of it."

"Of course it exists, you ignoramus," said Vong. "Our Grandmaster would not send us out to find a myth."

The smile faded from Hugo's face as he shook his head like a disapproving parent.

"Friend, I've lived in Frogchester for over twenty years, and I like to think I've come to know the place well. As you've probably seen by now, this place is cattle country. I see them everywhere, I hear them everywhere, and worst of all, I smell them everywhere. I've come to know cattle very well, and I think that qualifies me to tell you that your story is as much a case of prime bullshit as I've ever come across in all my time here."

"What do you mean?" said Brother Crunge.

Hugo offered a sad smile. "Twenty years, my friend. Twenty years I've lived here, and in all that time, I've never ever heard anyone mention the name Fort Rubbish. Did the name not make you even just a little bit suspicious? Sounds like someone's having a joke with you."

Brother Crunge blinked slowly. "The name is irrelevant. I know our grandmaster would not lie to us."

"Then frankly, you're a gullible idiot," said Hugo. "Look around you. Look at the people who come into my tavern. Adventurers, just like you, adventurers in fancy armour with big shiny swords and axes. Like you, they all come in with stories, stories of treasures guarded by mighty beasts in some forgotten hole, treasures that will make them rich beyond their wildest dreams.

"I will make this wager with you. Half the people you see here will be dead within the year. The rest will end up begging on the streets. One or two might get lucky and find enough loose change to get them back home again. I know this because I used to be an adventurer like you. Then I took a dose of reality to the brain. I once dreamed of gold and glory. I sought fame and fortune, and all I got for my trouble was a missing eye and a headful of scars.

"Adventuring ends up two ways—the first way is if someone else gets there first, cleans the place out, and leaves the next lot empty-handed. On the other hand, if the treasure is still there, it's usually still there for a very good reason. Those are the adventurers who are never seen again.

"In all my life, I've only ever seen one person get rich from adventuring. One. Not one party, one person. In fact, he's sitting right over there." Hugo gestured towards a tall, slim man with cropped black hair and a curly moustache, seated alone. He wore no armour beyond the velvet and silk clothing on his back, no weapons beyond the numerous gold rings on his large hands. He seemed oblivious to his surroundings, opting instead to bury himself in a large book while sipping from a glass of water.

"Crispin the Weirdo," said Hugo, "comes in here every few weeks, always sits alone, and never talks to anyone. Always pays in gold though, more gold than the rest of these reprobates will ever see in their lives. If they ever realised they aren't fit to fasten the buckles on his winklepickers, they would give up their delusions of grandeur altogether and go home. Adventuring only leads to the grave, or the poorhouse if you're lucky. My advice is to take the hint and give up on this little quest of yours."

Vong slammed a fist down on the counter. "We are not mere adventurers!" he yelled. "We are disciples of the Unsteady Fist. We are on a spiritual quest. We do not seek the hammer for wealth."

Brother Crunge recalled the artefact collector and her sizeable reward, but remained silent.

"Well, disciple of the Unsteady Fist, if you're so intent on drunkenly brawling yourself into an early grave, how about a little wager? Behind this counter, I have a bottle of Viscovian Absinthe. It has a kick like a horse in high heels and even doubles as an effective latrine cleaner. Here is my offer. If you and your friends can empty the bottle, it's on the house, but if you lose, you owe me double. You game?"

"Brethren, think carefully on this," said Brother Crunge. "I really don't think this is a good idea."

Vong responded with a blazing glower.

"You would deprive us of the Haze, Designated One? Unwise."

"At least show some restraint," said Brother Crunge. "You are still young, and I fear this Viscovian Absinthe may prove too much."

Hugo set down a bottle of green liquid and seven glasses on the counter before popping the cork. "What say you, warrior?" he said, turning towards Vong. "Too much for you to handle?"

"Not at all," said Vong "It would be blasphemy to turn down a challenge like this." With a sneering glance in Brother Crunge's direction, he added, "we're not all cowards."

Brother Crunge placed a hand on the counter. "Might I suggest an alteration to the terms? What say, if we win, you tell us how to find Fort Rubbish?"

Hugo rolled his eyes. "Did you even listen to what I just told you? I've never even heard of the place, assuming it exists." He paused, his eyes turning towards Crispin, the lone adventurer, who was still engrossed in his book.

"Tell you what, if it really does exist, I know who could tell you about it. You empty that bottle and I'll introduce you to Crispin, how does that sound?"

Brother Crunge sighed, but he forced himself to nod. "We accept," he mumbled.

We will surely regret this.

"Excellent," said Hugo, "though you should know that if he has heard of Fort Rubbish, it's probably because he's taken your magic hammer for himself."

Vong scoffed. "What's to stop us from asking him right now?"

Hugo smirked. "Look, boy, I can see you're an arrogant little shit who's crying out to be put in his place. But if you listen to anything I tell you, anything at all, listen to me now when I tell you not to mess with Crispin the Weirdo, all right? I promise you, you will regret it."

Brother Crunge snatched the bottle. "Like I said, we accept your wager, tavernkeeper."

BROTHER CRUNGE WATCHED in silence as the apprentices gathered around a table and set to work on the bottle of Viscovian Absinthe. Shots were drained one after the other, each punctuated with numerous toasts to Glurgamoth. Finally, with a synchronised slamming of glass on wood, the apprentices raised a cheer.

"Tavernkeeper!" called Vong. "It is done. We have won your wager. Now it's time for you to hold up your end of the bargain."

Hugo whistled. "I'm almost impressed."

"Designated One," said Vong. "You do the talking. Leave us to revel in our victory."

Hugo cupped his hands over his mouth. "Oi, Crispin!"

The man in velvet and silk looked up from his book. "Leave me be, Hugo."

Hugo gestured towards Brother Crunge, who shuffled from side to side, hands wringing while offering a half-smile. "This fella wants to talk to you."

Crispin turned back towards his book. "Not interested."

"Good man," said Brother Crunge, "I will take but a moment of your time. My brethren and I and my brethren merely seek knowledge. To be more specific, we seek the way to Fort Rubbish."

Crispin looked up from the book, revealing amber eyes. He stared for several seconds before waving a hand at an empty seat.

"You'd better sit down."

Crispin's eyes followed Brother Crunge as he shuffled over to his table.

"I think formal introductions are in order," said Crispin, extending a hand. "Crispin de Byrne, though I'm probably better known as Crispin the Weirdo around here."

Brother Crunge took Crispin's hand in his own. It was surprisingly smooth and soft.

"Brother Crunge, disciple of the Unsteady Fist."

Crispin smiled. "Glurgamoth's finest? I know of you. From Mount Reckless in the Northern Wastes, correct?"

Brother Crunge nodded. "You're the first person I've met here who's heard of us."

Crispin smiled. "In my youth, I travelled far, far enough that I saw your mountain with my own eyes. I was something of a treasure hunter back in the day, you see."

"Yes, the tavernkeeper mentioned that you were an adventurer."

Crispin smiled, twirling his moustache between his fingers. "Hugo never was one to keep anything to himself. Such a shameless gossip, but I suppose one can expect nothing else from a tavernkeeper. Since you know about me, why don't you tell me more about yourself? Why are you so interested in Fort Rubbish?"

"We are travelling there at the request of our grandmaster."

Crispin leaned in, a predatory grin stretched across his face. "In search of treasure, no doubt."

Brother Crunge flinched. "Why do you say that?"

Crispin gestured towards the tome he had set aside on the table. "I like to think of myself as an accomplished reader, and you, my boy, are so very easy to read. You're here in the hope I might share some of my secrets with you, are you not?"

Brother Crunge rose from his seat. "Perhaps this was a mistake."

Crispin placed a hand on Brother Crunge's arm.

"Why? Do you think I'll try to beat you to Fort Rubbish and steal the treasure ahead of you?"

"Maybe."

Crispin laughed. "Didn't Hugo also mention that I am also happily retired? You have nothing to worry about. I have all the treasure I'll ever need, I'm no threat to your little expedition."

"With all due respect," said Brother Crunge. "I only have your word for that."

"I suppose that's true," said Crispin, rubbing his chin with long exaggerated strokes. "Well, good luck finding your way to Fort Rubbish."

"So you do know how to get there?"

"Perhaps I do, my boy, perhaps I do. It might surprise you to learn that I'm also willing to share that information."

"Well... good," said Brother Crunge. "But what is it you want in return?"

Crispin slowly shook his head. "Nothing. Nothing at all. Like I said, I have everything I need in life."

"Then why help me?"

Crispin sipped at his water. "I could lie and say it's all down to altruism. In truth, it's probably more to do with a sense of pity."

"Pity?"

Crispin leaned back in his chair, locking his hands behind his head. "You don't actually know what you'll find at Fort Rubbish, do you, Brother Crunge?"

"I know danger awaits us."

Crispin slowly shook his head. "Danger? My friend, you have no idea how much of an understatement that is. Allow me to enlighten you. If you and your friends go to Fort Rubbish, I guarantee you you will not return. It is true that the halls of Fort Rubbish are swarming with troggs, foul-smelling, vicious beasts every one of them. But they are not the real danger, no, for that would be the one they serve."

Brother Crunge leaned in, feigning a stoic expression even as fear began to build within. Beneath the table, his hands had wrung themselves into a slick sweat.

"Tell me of this leader. We of the Unsteady Fist are not afraid."

Crispin twirled his moustache. "F'thoom-Gurth is his name in the trogg language, though in the northern tongue, he is more commonly known as the 'Fiery Bastard'."

"What exactly is this Fiery Bastard?" asked Brother Crunge.

"No one is quite sure. Some say he is a fire demon, others say that he is a powerful wizard, skilled in the use of fire magic. Some even whisper that he is a forgotten god, ready to vent His wrath on anyone who dares venture to close. Whatever he is, the troggs seem to worship him, and they'll fight like madmen to defend him. Perhaps now you understand why few have heard of Fort Rubbish—at least, those who have lived to tell the tale. Even I, with all my years of experience, would not dare to venture within a dozen miles of that place."

"I don't care," said Brother Crunge. "We cannot turn back now. Can you show us the way there or not?"

Crispin placed a hand on Brother Crunge's shoulder.

"So brave," he said, "and yet so very foolish. I will show you the way, though I do so reluctantly, as I know I will be sending you to your doom. But if you insist on walking this path, I will not stop you."

Crispin reached into a leather bag at his feet and pulled out a dog-eared piece of parchment and a piece of charcoal. He began to scribble on its yellowed surface, all the while mumbling to himself.

"Turn left here, go along this path, take the second left, and presto!"

Crispin handed over the parchment with a sad-eyed smile. Brother Crunge nodded his gratitude, then began to read. Crispin drew long from his water glass, studying Brother Crunge's expression as he examined the makeshift map.

"This can't be right. Are you telling me Fort Rubbish is less than a day away from here?"

Crispin nodded.

"Yet no one knew it even existed."

"It's well-hidden within the mountains," said Crispin. "Most people here don't stray beyond the pastures. They prefer cattle to castles."

BROTHER CRUNGE RETURNED to the bar, where Hugo was waiting for him wearing a smirk.

"Looks like you two had a lot to talk about. Did you get what you needed?"

"All that and more," said Brother Crunge, waving Crispin's map. "We make for Fort Rubbish tomorrow at first light."

"I'm impressed, Glurgamoth-man. I honestly didn't think you could be that naive."

"What?"

Hugo's smirk widened into an all-out grin. "Come on, Glurgamoth-man, don't be so stupid. Crispin, the man who barely says a word to anyone, and you think you convinced him to sing like a bird?"

"You think he was lying?" said Brother Crunge.

"Depends. What else did he say?"

"He warned us against travelling to Fort Rubbish. He warned of terrible beasts roaming its corridors, guardians of a hideous creature of flame."

"Good way to keep you away. I'd wager tonight's takings that map is a dud. Wouldn't surprise me if that magic hammer already has pride of place in his trophy cabinet."

Brother Crunge turned to where the man in purple had been seated to find that the table was now empty. He shut his eyes tight, and exhaled.

A crashing sound snapped his eyes open again. The sound was followed by Vong screaming whilst sending an elf crashing to the ground with a fist to the jaw.

"The waters of the Chalice have awoken the Haze!" he bellowed. "Up brethren! Up into battle!" With a forward flip, Vong sent a second soul flying.

"The power of Glurgamoth is within us!" roared Bung, as he struck two dwarves either side of him with a leaping splits kick. Springing back, he drove his elbow into the ribs of a charging half-orc, forcing him to drop the iron mace in his green hairy hands.

"My tipsiness is my strength!" cried Mlarf, as she ducked a flying chair, before putting two sword-wielding grunts on their back with a sweeping low kick.

Flarg whooped a battle cry as she threw an axe-wielding dwarf against a wall, before delivering a vicious chop into the throat of a flailing mage.

Lurg vaulted a table, smashing two heads together in mid air before landing on an unconscious dwarf.

Frang remained seated at the table, head resting in her hands.

"I'm going to sit this one out," she said. "The Haze is not with me tonight."

The rest ignored her, victoriously surveying the writhing carpet of bodies, smiles carved across their faces.

"A productive session, brethren," said Vong, slapping Flarg in the back. "Glurgamoth shall surely be pleased."

"I agree," said Mlarf, "is anyone else feeling hungry? I need food. Tavernkeeper!"

"Get out," said Hugo, "get out and don't ever come back."

BROTHER CRUNGE SPENT the rest of the night ushering the apprentices to their campsite on the outskirts of town. Undaunted by their eviction, the apprentices sang all the way there, a slurred medley of drinking songs, pausing only to challenge any passersby who got too close to a fight. As the party reached the palisade gate, he was met by a young woman in a straw hat carrying a shepherd's crook. She stood and watched Brother Crunge, assisted by Frang, as they herded the apprentices through the gate one by one.

"I know the feeling," she said with a sad smile, before disappearing into the night.

The campsite lay nestled in a patch of tree cover, overlooking the faint lights of town. The bedrolls were prepared with much fumbling and flailing, but once done the apprentices flopped on their backs, falling silent almost immediately. Brother Crunge rested against a tree, and gave thanks to Glurgamoth that the day was over. One of the apprentices began to snore.

"Designated One," said Frang, as she roasted a rodent-shaped lump of meat over a campfire. "I heard what the tavernkeeper said about the hammer. Is it true? It doesn't exist?"

"Let's not think about that," said Brother Crunge. "He was but a hoodlum who took joy in our suffering."

"So what now?"

Brother Crunge rose to his feet, dusting himself down by the firelight. "What now? Now we carry on as usual. Nothing has changed. We make for Fort Rubbish at first light and retrieve the Godhammer, as our Grandmaster ordered. Once we've find it, we leave this place and never come back."

"I shall trust in your judgement, Designated One," said Frang. "I only hope the Haze finds me when the time comes."

"Trust in Glurgamoth, apprentice, and you will find your fight in life. For now, we rest. Danger lies ahead."

———

BROTHER CRUNGE OPENED HIS EYES, and saw only darkness. He tried to call out, but no sound came from his lips. There was only silence, the rustle of trees, the crackle of the campfire, the cries of unseen animals, all of it gone. He tried to get to his feet, but he could no longer feel them. In the darkness, he felt something watching him.

I have returned.

"Returned?" called a voice from within his head.

Great Zugote? Is that you?

"Mortal, I know you seek the Godhammer." The roaring voice sent a shockwave of pain through Brother Crunge's ethereal essence.

Who are you?

"Irrelevant. Listen to Me, mortal, turn back from

this futile quest of yours. Turn back or face the conse-quences. Terrible consequences."

Lord Glurgamoth?

Brother Crunge awoke to find Frang kneeling over him.

"Apologies for waking you, Designated One, but we have a big problem."

Sunlight streamed through the trees, and Brother Crunge could see that it was almost noon.

"It's late. Why didn't you wake me sooner?"

"I tried, but you wouldn't wake up. You were shiv-ering and shaking in your sleep."

Brother Crunge sprung to his feet. "I'm awake now. We need to get going. Where are the others?"

Frang cleared her throat. "Over there, Designated One." She pointed beyond the dying embers of the campfire, where the five remaining apprentices lay mo-tionless in their bedrolls. Brother Crunge's jaw dropped.

"What? How could this happen?"

Frang looked to the ground, sadness in her eyes.

"Dead? They're all dead? All of them?"

"What? No! They're not dead, Designated One, just hungover."

"Then awaken them, we must move. There is no time to waste."

Frang sucked her teeth. "That may not be possible, Designated One."

"What do you mean?"

"When I say they're hungover, I'm talking the mother of all hangovers. Never mind trekking through the mountains, they can't even raise their heads."

Brother Crunge sprang to his feet and strode over to the sleeping bodies. He drove his foot into the flank of Bung, who offered no response.

"Up!" called Brother Crunge as he levelled kicks at the other four. "Up and at the day, brethren. We have work to do."

"Go away," croaked Bung. "I am surely dying."

"I think I'm going to be sick," said Vong. "Leave me be, Designated One."

"The Viscovian Absinthe," said Brother Crunge. "Damn fools."

"I heard that," croaked Mlarf.

"Then hear this, apprentices. Your irresponsibility has needlessly burdened this mission. Are you so completely beyond control as to defy the will of Glurgamoth? Warriors you call yourself? Pah! Show a little discipline and cast aside those blankets! Rise up, brethren! Up on your feet at once, all of you! Up in the name of Glurgamoth!"

"Begone, Designated One, and leave us to our rest," mumbled Vong.

"My head feels like it will explode," groaned Bung.

"This is hopeless," said Brother Crunge, turning towards Frang. "They fought a whole tavern and were bested by a humble bottle of Viscovian Absinthe."

"I must admit, I drank a good amount of it myself, Designated One," said Frang.

"Is that so? How do you feel?"

"I feel fine, Designated One, alas the Haze did not find me."

"If only the same were true of these ignoramuses," said Brother Crunge, rubbing his brow. "I dare not leave them behind, but we need to move quickly if we are to gain the Godhammer. Although, we may have another issue."

"What kind of issue?"

"The issue of Lord Glurgamoth Himself."

"What do you mean?"

"Last night I was visited by an apparition, one warning of dire consequences if we do not abandon our quest. I fear it could only have been the Lord Glurgamoth Himself."

"An apparition? Designated One? I do not mean to question your judgement, but are you sure this was not just a dream?"

"Possibly," said Brother Crunge, "but I am sure it wasn't. It would make sense that Glurgamoth would be displeased."

"Why do you say that, Designated One?"

"Think about it, apprentice! We as brethren of the Unsteady Fist have pledged ourselves to honouring Glurgamoth in all we do. Yet here we stand, ready to retrieve the artefact of the war god. I cannot fathom why Glurgamoth would not be displeased."

"What is to be done then, Designated One? Should we return home?"

"Definitely not. What would happen if we arrived empty-handed before the Grandmaster? Our only fate would be the water barrel."

Brother Crunge looked to the sky and exhaled. "We shall carry on. After all, it is the will of the Grandmaster."

"I don't like this, Designated One," said Frang, looking back at the sleeping disciples, "but you're right. We should not defy the Grandmaster."

"Then we are agreed," said Brother Crunge. "Onward to Fort Rubbish."

"Just the two of us?"

Brother Crunge scowled at the shivering bodies scattered around camp. "What use are they to us now? Yet, it would be wise to seek out all the help we can get. I do not like the sound of this Fiery Bastard at all."

The smell of cow dung lingered.

"What use would a town of cowherds be to us? Unless you mean—"

Frang caught Brother Crunge grinning broadly.

"You can't mean the Placid Griffin? Have you forgotten we are no longer welcome there?"

Brother Crunge gestured towards the apprentices. "No, they are no longer welcome there. We did nothing to anger the barkeeper."

"If you say so," said Frang, "but I'm not sure he will see it that way."

———

BROOM IN HAND, Hugo watched Brother Crunge and Frang enter amidst a sea of broken furniture, stray tankards, and smashed pottery.

"Well, well, well" said Hugo, "back for more, are you? Where's the rest of you?"

"I'm afraid they couldn't make it today," said Brother Crunge, nudging aside a pewter tankard with his foot. "It seems your Viscovian Absinthe got the better of them."

"Ha! I knew it. I hope the hangovers hurt like hell, vicious little bastards. But if you're here for a fight, you're out of luck. The tavern is closed for repairs."

Brother Crunge placed a hand on Frang's shoulder. "I'd just like to point out that my colleague and I played no part in last night's antics. But as the Designated One, I would like to apologise on behalf of my brethren, and if there's anything we can do to make amends, we would be glad to assist."

The tavernkeeper's eye narrowed. "Are you serious? Well, yes there is one thing you could do to make things up to me." He attacked a scattering of pottery with the broom.

"Name it."

"You can pay for the damages you owe me."

"Oh." Brother Crunge's thoughts turned to the coin purse at his belt. It suddenly felt very light. "How much do we owe you?"

"One hundred and fifty groats, and not a penny less."

"One hundred and fifty groats? A little excessive, no?"

Hugo stopped sweeping, locking his eye on Brother Crunge. "Smashing up my tavern, a little excessive, no?"

"Fair point." Brother Crunge unclasped the coin purse from his belt and opened it over the counter, watching with sad eyes as silver and copper coins clattered across the surface. Hugo leered over the glittering pile and meticulously gathered up the money, counting everything down to the last copper.

"Okay," said Hugo. "That should do it."

Brother Crunge murmured softly as he replaced the remaining coins into the purse; a meagre dribble of half-groats.

"Well that won't buy much," said Hugo with a smirk. "I guess we're done here. Bye now, and thanks."

"Well, there was one more thing," said Brother Crunge.

Hugo's eye narrowed. "Out with it."

"We were hoping you could assist us in an important matter."

Hugo sniffed, folding his arms. "Did you now?"

"As you're aware, our colleagues are currently incapacitated. We were hoping you could perhaps point us in the direction of some of your more competent regulars to take their place?"

Hugo sneered, revealing rows of brown teeth between his puffy lips. "Looking to hire some mercenaries, Glurgamoth-man? How do you plan on paying them with only a handful of coppers?"

"The promise of exciting adventures in strange lands. The prospect of gold and glory of course."

Hugo uttered a deep chuckle that sounded as though he were gargling gravel. "Ha! I like your style. Even so, I'm still not going to help you."

"What? Why not?"

"What, the fact you got drunk and smashed up my bar isn't reason enough?"

"I told you I didn't drink last night," said Brother Crunge. "As a Designated One I am forbidden to do so."

"I don't care if you're the Chosen One," growled Hugo. "Last night, your friends showed up in my tavern, swanned around like they owned the place and proceeded to beat the living daylights out of my regulars. As a result, they're all now off nursing their injuries instead of drinking here, which means I'm not making any money. So maybe you can understand why I'm really not in the mood to do you any favours."

"But we paid for damages."

"So what? That doesn't mean I owe you, it just means we're even."

"May I remind you that neither of us raised a hand last night?" said Frang.

"So you keep saying," said Hugo. "You didn't make much effort to stop them either, so the way I see it, you're as guilty as them."

"There's nothing we can do to persuade you to help us?" said Brother Crunge.

Hugo ran a hand over his burned head. "There is one thing, but you don't have the money for it."

Brother Crunge turned to Frang. "Then it appears, apprentice, that you and I are alone."

Frang gasped. "Are we capable of this, Designated One?"

"I don't know," said Brother Crunge, wringing his hands. "I really don't know. All I know is that this may prove to be the greatest challenge we have ever faced. If it is to be our undoing, then so be it."

"Wait a minute, you idiots," said Hugo. "Why don't you just wait until they all sober up?"

"We have no time to lose," said Brother Crunge. "If, as you say, Crispin seeks the hammer for himself, then we must move now, and fast."

Brother Crunge raised the Hammer of Shame.

"Let us carve a bloody path through Fort Rubbish. Let us leave a trail of bodies the likes of which none has seen before. We shall fight until victory or we shall fight until death. And by the gods, they will sing songs of our exploits. Songs that will echo through the ages! We shall fight or we shall die! Possibly both—"

The sound of a bottle slamming down on the counter broke Brother Crunge's flow.

"That was quite the speech, Glurgamoth-man," said Hugo. "You might be about to die, but I admire your determination. Maybe I'm going soft in my old age, but it looks like I'll help you after all. I'm going to let you have this bottle of Borpingdon's Infernowhisky. Maybe it will help you on your quest, it probably won't. Just go easy on this stuff though. It makes Viscovian Absinthe look like sprout juice."

"Thank you, most kind," said Brother Crunge. "But, as I said before, I don't drink."

"I know. But at the very least it might help dull the pain when you end up getting yourself horribly killed."

Brother Crunge took the bottle and handed it to Frang, who nodded her gratitude to Hugo in response. Hugo waved her away.

"Now get lost, and good luck," he said. "Oh, and if you do somehow survive, don't forget to drop by on your way back. I'd love to hear how you try to spin this story."

THE ROUTE to Fort Rubbish wound through a forest path before emerging into a rabbit-infested clearing. Frang recoiled as she caught sight of the creatures bounding to-and-fro across the grass.

"Troggs?" she queried, pointing a shaky finger.

"No," said Brother Crunge. "Those are cats, don't worry, they won't harm you."

"Are you sure?"

"I think so. Never seen one before, but a trader at the monastery told me all about them. Let's move on."

Braving the rabbit gauntlet, they pressed onward, passing back into the forest. Here the sweet scent of the greenery subsided, giving way to the smell of smoke. The air grew drier and drier until they emerged into a lifeless wasteland, the trees degrading into charred black stumps, the grass and flowers of the forest floor giving way to a carpet of ash and blackened twigs. Barely a sound pervaded this wasteland, save the groan of a slow-moving breeze wafting through the forest graveyard.

"Careful," said Brother Crunge. "Watch your back."

"Looks like the Fiery Bastard has been busy," said Frang.

They passed slowly through the forest remnants, though they encountered nothing, whether plant, animal, or slavering fire demon. The path cut between a pair of slate stalagmites jolting out of the ground, like stone fingers clawing through the soil. They pushed on between on beyond into a valley, flanked by granite grey mountains bearing jagged peaks.

Frang pointed into the distance. "There it is!" she called. "That has to be it."

By then, the low-lying sun was touching the mountains, and Brother Crunge had to strain his eyes to make out the silhouette of a castle perched precariously at the summit of a steep cliff. They searched around for a place to camp for the night, finally settling on a modest grove of trees that sheltered them from view.

They spent the night taking turns to keep watch, and slept poorly, though nothing emerged from the dark and the night passed uneventfully.

Brother Crunge rose with the break of dawn to find Frang seated on a tree stump, staring stoically towards the horizon. She stirred as she caught sight of him on his feet, as though roused from a trance.

"Good morning, Designated One," she called. "Did you get any sleep?"

"No. You?"

"Not a wink. I keep thinking about what is to come. I've trained in the ways of the Unsteady Fist all my life, I've fought countless times. Yet this is the first time I truly fear for my life. In the past, whenever we fought, I knew I needed fear no foe. Even without being able to invoke the Haze, I knew that Glurgamoth was always by my side. But now, I wonder if He has truly forsaken us." Frang seized a pebble and tossed it into the air.

"Keep the faith, apprentice," said Brother Crunge, unsure of his own words. He motioned towards the castle ruin. "It's time to go."

As THEY DREW nearer towards Fort Rubbish, they beheld the castle in its true glory. Worn down from centuries of neglect, the building was slowly turning into an elaborate pile of rubble. Moss and vines assailed the crumbling stonework like some terrible disease, while six turrets rose above the walls like fungus sprouting from a corpse.

"Be careful," said Brother Crunge, "the place is falling apart."

"Look at the gatehouse," said Frang, gesturing towards the dark marks pockmarking the walls like black bruises.

"Burnmarks," he said. "On your guard, the Fiery Bastard and his minions are likely nearby."

They approached the gatehouse in silence, hearing only the hissing wind snaking through the battlements.

"Don't you find this odd, Designated One?" whispered Frang.

"What?"

"Here we stand, right before Fort Rubbish, and yet we've seen nothing worse than a herd of cats. Where are the troggs? Where is the Fiery Bastard?"

Brother Crunge fished a torch from his pack, using a flint and steel to set it ablaze. "Don't get complacent," he said as he handed a second torch to Frang. "They could easily be lying in wait for us."

"A trap?" Frang felt her blood freeze as she likewise struck steel at her own torch.

"It's a good possibility. A grand castle like this bears many shadows in which to hide. Just remember to watch your back."

They found themselves before the gate, a pair of rusted chains dangling either side of the frame. Passing through, they cut their way through a thick wall of cobwebs, and they were inside Fort Rubbish. The smell of damp and dirt lingered. They passed through the gatehouse and into the main atrium, the walls illuminated only by Brother Crunge's torch.

The wind grew quieter as the pair pushed deeper into the darkness, sending a chill down Brother Crunge's spine.

I never thought I would miss the whistle of the winds so, he thought. Memories turned to those of home, of the monastery, the mountain, the screaming Winge.

Shall I ever see home again? Would that the Grandmaster had sent me to the punishment post instead of this gods-forsaken rockpile.

"Designated One!"

Frang's call ripped him from his daydream. Brother Crunge turned towards the light of her torch. A doorway, its wooden frame scorched black. Brother Crunge's stomach tightened.

"Let's go," he said. "We must press on."

They advanced, kicking their way through ashes cast across the floor. The doorway opened into a corridor, stretching off either way into darkness.

"Which way?" asked Frang.

"Left," said Brother Crunge, without knowing why. "Pray that Glurgamoth guides us true."

They pushed into the corridor and were surprised to hear the rising echo of the wind again.

The corridor passed by a set of double doors, made from carved stone. "Stop!" hissed Brother Crunge.

"Through there?" whispered Frang.

Brother Crunge nodded. "Quietly."

"They might be troggs in there."

"They might be troggs anywhere," said Brother Crunge. "In we go."

Frang pushed against the doors, which responded with an almighty grinding sound that echoed down the corridor.

"Shhh! Stop pushing, that's enough."

Frang nodded. They squeezed through the opening, finding themselves in a chamber, a bold shaft of light falling upon a stone sarcophagus through a hole in the ceiling.

From behind the sarcophagus, a figure emerged, shrouded in shadow. Brother Crunge's hands were immediately upon the Hammer of Shame, while Frang's body contorted into a defensive stance. The figure stepped into the light and the pair's jaws dropped in unison.

Standing before them was a face they recognised, dressed in a white silk shirt and black pantaloons. A silver rapier hung from his belt.

"Good morning," said Crispin the Weirdo with a smile. "You came after all."

———

SOMEWHERE WITHIN HIS HEAD, Brother Crunge heard the sound of Hugo Thrusk laughing.

"Crispin? What are you doing here?" he asked.

Crispin's smile dropped. "I might ask you the same question."

"You know why," said Brother Crunge. "We're in search of treasure."

"I never did buy that story of yours," said Crispin, kicking his foot against the stone floor. "Pious brethren of the Unsteady Fist, out on a mighty quest for gold and glory?"

"What's not to believe?" said Brother Crunge.

Crispin chuckled a sour chord. "I don't know much about your kind, but I know there are only two things you care about—fighting and getting blind drunk. Money holds little value for you. So that leaves me wondering why you're really here. My guess is you know exactly what you're looking for, but I can't think of anything that would be of interest to a band of drunken brawler monks."

"Very well," said Brother Crunge. "If you must know, we seek a hammer."

Crispin twirled his moustache, looking up at the hole in the ceiling. "There are many hammers in this castle, friend, though none strike me as being particularly valuable. I'm not sure I believe you."

"Had a look around already, have you?" said Brother Crunge, folding his arms.

"Ha! Afraid I'll snatch your precious hammer away?"

"Perhaps," said Frang, "your reputation speaks for itself."

Crispin fished a snuff box from his pocket, opened it, and took a long sniff. He replaced the box with a wrinkle of the nose. "I'll take that as a compliment, but for what it's worth I don't intend to steal a single bead from this castle."

"And why should we believe that?" asked Brother Crunge.

Crispin smiled. "Simple. Why would I steal from my own home?"

"What?" said Brother Crunge.

Frang's eyes widened. "You live here?"

"Well, in a manner of speaking," said Crispin with a subtle shrug. "I'm more of a custodian."

"Custodian?"

"Custodian, warden, caretaker, overseer, call me what you will." Brother Crunge sensed impatience in his voice.

Crispin continued, "What I *can* say with certainty though is that Fort Rubbish and everything within its walls is under my protection."

"You don't say," said Brother Crunge. "And what do the troggs have to say about this?"

"Troggs?" Crispin's laughter echoed off the walls. "Ah yes, the troggs. There were troggs here, once. A dirty great tribe of them."

"What happened to them?"

Crispin shook his head. "They died."

"All of them?"

Crispin nodded. "Indeed."

"How?"

Crispin smiled, bearing impeccable teeth. "I killed them."

Brother Crunge tightened the grip on the Hammer of Shame. "You killed them all?"

"Every one."

"How?"

"That's not important."

Frang stepped closer to Crispin. "So now, do you intend us to suffer the same fate?"

"That depends on whether you give me a reason to kill you."

"What do you want us to do?"

"I want you to leave."

"We can't leave without the hammer," said Frang.

Crispin looked towards the stone sarcophagus. "So you plan to steal from me?"

"The hammer is the only thing we want," said Brother Crunge. "Nothing else."

"I would rather you stole nothing at all and left. Leave this place and never return. If you don't, I promise you I'll make you regret it."

Brother Crunge drew the Hammer of Shame. "I'm sorry, Crispin. We cannot leave without the Godhammer."

Crispin frowned. "The Godhammer? Are you joking?"

Frang moved to Brother Crunge's side and uncorked the bottle of Infernowhiskey, taking a long draw. "We are not joking. Surrender the Godhammer."

Crispin stared in disbelief. "Have you two completely lost your minds? You came all this way—for the Godhammer?"

"Indeed," said Brother Crunge. "Now, hand it over."

Crispin shook his head. "No. It belongs to me," he said, drawing his rapier. "Whatever I might think of it."

Crispin lunged at Frang, but the apprentice dodged, striking him in the face with an open palm. Crispin seemed not to react to the blow, immediately ducking a swing from Brother Crunge's hammer before driving a knee hard into his ribcage. The sting of the blow hit hard, and Brother Crunge dropped to his knee, though he mustered enough energy to drive the shaft of his weapon into Crispin's stomach. Crispin replied by driving the pommel of his weapon into the Designated One's face, and Brother Crunge felt the wet warmth of blood from his forehead.

Frang leaped forward with a scream, connecting with a flying kick that sent Crispin tumbling. He was immediately back on his feet, counter attacking with a vicious thrust. Brother Crunge parried the attack, striking with such force as to send the blade clattering from Crispin's hand. Brother Crunge drew the Hammer of Shame back and swung, striking Crispin square in the face. The custodian of Fort Rubbish dropped to the ground and did not stir.

Brother Crunge surveyed Crispin's lifeless body with a mixture of sadness and satisfaction. His attention turned to the sarcophagus as Frang slapped him on the shoulder.

"Well-fought, Designated One," she said. "Perhaps we've regained some favour with Glurgamoth after that." She turned towards the sarcophagus. "Back to the search now, eh? Shall we have a look in there?"

"Defile a tomb?" asked Brother Crunge. "Not the best idea, but the Godhammer could be anywhere. Fine, open the coffin."

The sarcophagus was a plain-looking thing, a featureless stone box set into the stone floor. Frang coiled her fingers around the edge of the lid and lifted.

"It won't budge, Designated One."

Brother Crunge joined in, pulling with all his might, but still the lid would not relent. They stepped back, frustration in their eyes. Brother Crunge took up the Hammer of Shame.

"Stand back," he said, and raised the weapon, ready to strike. Before he could bring the hammer down upon the sarcophagus, a second pair of hands were suddenly around the shaft, jerking the weapon free from Brother Crunge's grasp. There was a flash of limbs and Brother Crunge found himself on the ground. He looked up to see Crispin, looking back at him with bared teeth, the tip of his rapier pressed against Brother Crunge's chest. He pushed tighter and tighter, until suddenly Frang burst from the shadows, a flying kick aimed at Crispin's skull. Without turning away, Crispin raised an elbow, striking Frang full in the face to send her sprawling.

"Apprentice?" called Brother Crunge, but no response came.

Crispin looked down upon Brother Crunge with fierce eyes, the rapier still pointed at his heart. "You should have left when you had the chance," said Crispin, "but it seems blood will be shed this day after all."

Brother Crunge felt the point of the rapier blade pushing harder into his chest. Brother Crunge shut his eyes.

A loud crashing sound filled the chamber. Brother Crunge opened his eyes and Crispin was nowhere to be seen. He sprung to his feet, to be met by the sight of a flurry of bodies, punching, kicking and chopping down on Crispin.

Brother Crunge's eyes widened. "Apprentices! But... how did you find us?"

Vong struck Crispin with a roundhouse kick, swivelling around to face Brother Crunge. "Mlarf got a good look at that map of yours while your back was turned in the tavern. She has a good memory."

He paused as Flarg's flip sent Crispin flying through the air. Vong took aim, then struck Crispin with a forearm smash.

"What? Why did you do that?" asked Brother Crunge, massaging a lingering ache in his hip.

"Simple," said Bung. "You're untrustworthy, and we had to make sure you weren't stealing from us, or engaging in some other dastardly deed."

Brother Crunge leaped to his feet, grabbing the Hammer of Shame. "What makes you think I would do such a thing?"

"Don't take it personally," said Vong as he slammed his foot down on Crispin's skull. "We've been doing it every night since we left the mountain, at the Grandmaster's request I might add."

"The Grandmaster told you?" said Brother Crunge, aghast.

"Of course," said Vong. "We're all here because you broke the rules, aren't we? We were just making sure you didn't break any more."

Crispin spat blood as he rose to his knees. His once-white shirt was now grey with dust. The apprentices surrounded him, smirking, smiling, laughing.

"What say you, brethren?" said Vong. "Has he had enough yet?"

They jeered as Crispin rose to his feet, dusting himself down. He looked up, his moustachioed face contorted into a snarl.

"There are few things I despise more than thievery," said Crispin. "Bad manners is one."

Before the eyes of the apprentices, Crispin's body began to swell. Flesh burst free, ripping through clothing. At the same time his skin turned blood red, growing scales whilst a pair of batlike wings erupted from his back. The hair on his head receded to be replaced by a pair of horns, and his lower face lengthened into a muzzle, filled with dagger-shaped teeth.

By the time Crispin had grown to four times his original size, he emitted a deafening roar, and a plume of flame erupted from his nostrils.

"A dragon!" yelled Frang. "Crispin the Weirdo is a dragon!"

"Oh, you sweet summer child," said Crispin. "Did you really think F'thoom Gurth was but a legend? Behold the true form of the Fiery Bastard! "

"Take him down, brethren!" called Vong. "Today, we slay a dragon!"

His words were cut short by a tsunami of flame rolling forth the dragon's mouth. When the fire subsided, there were only five piles of ash where once there had been Lurg, Bung, Vong, Flarg, and Mlarf.

"No!" called Frang. "No! It cannot be! You murderer!"

"Good riddance to them," replied the dragon.

"I'll kill you!' roared Frang. Her body burned with rage, but she felt something else within. A sensation she had not experienced for many years, and yet it seemed as familiar as the rage and hatred burning through her blood..

"The Haze is within me!" she cried. "Dragon, your time has come!"

"Do it, Frang!" yelled Brother Crunge. "Slay the dragon, and fulfil your destiny!"

Frang leaped at the dragon. "For my brethren! For Glurgamo—"

The dragon breathed again, and there was a sixth pile of ash.

Brother Crunge watched, mouth agape. The smell of burned flesh was becoming overpowering.

"'Fulfil your destiny'," mocked Crispin. "Could you be any more cliched?"

The dragon lowered his head until Brother Crunge was staring directly into yellow reptilian eyes. A stray plume of smoke spouted from the dragon's nostrils. He reeked of sulphur.

"I've heard it all before," said Crispin. "Chosen ones, anointed heroes, children of destiny. I can see you thought highly of your understudy, but unlike the storybooks, the hero does not always slay the dragon."

"You monster," said Brother Crunge. "How could you do this?"

"You would have happily done the same thing to me had I not acted in self-defence. You who came to my house to rob me, to attack me, to set your band of hooligans upon me. You were going to kill me, when I had done you no harm. Yet you call me the monster?"

"You're the one who showed us the way to Fort Rubbish. Why?"

"Curiosity," said Crispin. "I knew you were no threat to me and I was curious. Curious about why you would associate with such an uncouth band of drunken thugs. You even acted as their spokesperson, when all they ever showed you was contempt. I see now that it's because you and I have something in common."

"And what might that be?" asked Brother Crunge.

"When I found myself unwittingly ordained as god to a band of troggs, I revelled in their worship. I lapped up their tributes and basked in their hymns of praise. Yet despite this, I incinerated every single one of them as easily as I incinerated your goons. You see, when the novelty of godhood wore off, I came to see the troggs for what they really were—worthless parasites. They did not worship me because they loved me, they wished only for me to protect them. They would not even let me leave the castle, for fear I might not be there at all times to defend the tribe. I had become their prisoner. I was not their god, I was their slave.

"The same is true for you, Brother Crunge. You embrace the ways of the Unsteady Fist, even as they mock you in return. You attend to every need of your so-called brethren with slavish devotion, and they reward you by spitting in your face. So I had to know if you would go so far as to risk your life for them by coming here. Not only did you come here, they sent you and your lackey on ahead like a canary into a coal mine."

"That's not quite how it happened..." muttered Brother Crunge.

The dragon gave a sharp flap of his wings. "Even so, you and I have something in common. I can see the hatred in your eyes. I know you're insulted I would make such a suggestion, but it's true. We are slaves, you and I. I who believed myself a god, and you, the loyal and obedient Designated One, pawn of Glurgamoth."

Brother Crunge tightened his grip around the Hammer of Shame. "I would rather be a good and faithful pawn of Glurgamoth than a demonic abomination like you."

The dragon huffed a plume of black smoke, filling Brother Crunge's nostrils with his sulphurous stench. "What do your scriptures say of the Designated Ones?"

Brother Crunge blinked. "Scriptures? What scriptures?"

"Exactly," said the dragon. Brother Crunge was convinced he could see a smirk within Crispin's lizardlike features "A cult that desires only to drink and fight has no need of them. There are no Designated Ones in Glurgamoth's world. You Designated Ones live your lives indentured to humans, not Glurgamoth."

Brother Crunge raised his hammer. "My Grandmaster is a good and wise teacher."

A flicker of flame licked the dragon's teeth. "Is that why he sent you here? To take the blame for Master Dyom's failings? Are you a scapegoat as well as being utterly servile?"

Brother Crunge's eyes widened. "How could you possibly know about that?"

The dragon hissed. "You know nothing about me. But let us not deviate from the subject. Tell me, Servile One, how will your good and wise Grandmaster receive you when you return to Mount Reckless alone? Will he welcome you with open arms?"

"I know what will happen," said Brother Crunge with a sigh. "I will be condemned to the water barrel, but if Glurgamoth wills it, then so be it."

"Glurgamoth wishes only drunkenness and violence upon his followers. Come on, Brother Crunge, have a bit of self-preservation."

"I will not take advice from a murderous demon-beast," snarled Brother Crunge, readying the Hammer of Shame. "It is time for you to die for your crimes."

"Are you going to fight me, Brother Crunge? Shall I end you with a mere breath, as I did your comrades? What will you do then, if you kill me?"

"Then I will return home, with the Godhammer."

"And you think this will earn you your life?"

"I do not know. If I am condemned upon my return, then so be it."

The dragon rolled his yellow eyes. "I just watched you fight like a warrior, fight for your life. Yet you would just cast aside your weapon and allow your own kind to drown you like a newborn puppy? I pity you, Brother Crunge, you truly are a well-trained dog. Yet you are a likeable dog, and I almost feel bad sending you on your way empty-handed. For that reason I'm going to give you the Godhammer."

Brother Crunge raised his weapon. "What trickery is this? You slaughtered my brethren, and now you expect me to believe you would just hand over the hammer?"

"Brother Crunge, the only reason I would have for deceiving you would be to kill you, and I could kill you so very easily. Now, wait here while I go and get it for you, and don't move from this spot! I think I left it on the refuse pile somewhere.

The dragon took off down the corridor with a swish of his tail, and a rhythm of thunderous footsteps echoed down the corridor, growing quieter and quieter until there was silence. A brief time later, the footsteps arose once more, growing louder and louder, until the terrible silhouette of the dragon stood in the doorway, scarlet and sulphurous.

"Here," said the dragon, tossing a heavy-looking hammer at Brother Crunge. The Designated One recoiled in horror as the weapon flew towards him, and he instinctively reached out to catch it. The weapon landed in his open palms, and he scowled as the light from the ceiling fell upon the weapon.

"Do you mock me, dragon? What do you call this?"

The dragon huffed. "It's the Godhammer, you know, the thing you came all this way for. Now if you could get it out of here? It's cluttering the place up, you know the way out."

Brother Crunge's face was a mask of fury. "You won't buy me off with this... thing. Your time has come, dragon. The souls of my brethren cry out for vengeance."

The dragon shook his head. "Oh for goodness sake," he murmured, and with a swipe of his tail, Brother Crunge fell flat.

THERE WAS ONLY DARKNESS. Brother Crunge was back, back in the domain of the gods, the realm without form. He could do nothing but linger alone in the blackness. There were no sensations, no presence, no voices.

Hello?

Something stirred.

"Brother Crunge." His blood curdled as memories of this voice came back. The one who warned him.

"What did I tell you, Brother Crunge? Did I not warn you to turn back? Did you think My warnings were empty words?"

Lord Glurgamoth?

"Glurgamoth? I am not Glurgamoth, you fool. Cower before Me, for I am Zugote, God of War, and you will pay a terrible price for your defiance."

Great Zugote, was it not You who bade me retrieve Your sacred weapon, the Godhammer?

Brother Crunge sensed a tension in the darkness, as though some great beast was preparing to pounce.

"Godhammer?" Brother Crunge sensed a rising rage within the godly tones. "That mockery masquerading as an implement of war? You imply that thing belongs to Me? You will know true agony for implying such a thing."

I'm so confused and terrified.

No response.

Hello? Lord Zugote?

Not a stirring in the blackness.

"Brother Crunge." A second voice spoke, and yet it was equally familiar.

It's you? The one I spoke with at the monastery?

"You are correct, mortal, but by now you will have realised I am not Zugote. There was a reason for my deception. Oh, and by the way, congratulations on finding the Godhammer."

The realm melted back into silence

"You probably have questions at this juncture."

I'll say. Who exactly are you?

"The name's Glurgamoth. Pleased to meet you."

My Lord Glurgamoth! Please forgive my blasphemy. I only sought to carry out the will of my grandmaster, I ask that you spare me from your wrath!"

"Eh? What are you on about?"

The Godhammer, relic of the war god.

"You mean My Godhammer."

Say what?

"The Godhammer belongs to Me."

It does? Brother Crunge began to feel faint. *Okay, now I am very confused.*

"Then permit Me to enlighten you, Brother Crunge," said Glurgamoth. "As you are aware, a good old fistfight is one of the finest things in life. Now Zugote, who happens to be my older brother, is of the belief that hiding behind weapons is the true test of a warrior. Many a time I've had to listen to His endless yammering about swords and spears and shields and most of all, about that damned magic axe He always carries around with Him.

"Normally, when He refuses to shut up, I drink myself into unconsciousness so that I don't have to listen to Him. Alas, one fateful day, I could only find enough to get me extremely tipsy, and in a fit of sozzled stupidity I made a rather idiotic bet with My dear hate-filled brother. I bet Him I could fashion a weapon superior to His own magic axe. If he won, I would give him my entire supply of Ambrosia XXXX, and if I won, I would take his magic axe as my own. After he had finished laughing, he agreed immediately. It was only after I sobered up that I realised what I had done—I know bugger all about blacksmithing. But I was never one to shirk a challenge and set to work in the forge. I laboured for forty days and my efforts resulted in the weapon you know today as the Godhammer. Of course, when I presented the weapon to Zugote, He simply laughed in My face, claiming it was not worthy of even a limbless peasant, and proclaimed Himself the winner of the bet.

"Deprived of my favourite tipple, I sank into despair, until—in a fit of sobriety—I devised a plan to get my revenge on Zugote. It was genius, at least I thought so at the time. When I lost the bet, I had taken the Godhammer and cast it into the world of mortals, never wanting to see it again. It dawned on me that if I were to spread a few rumours that the weapon in fact belonged to Zugote, this would surely reflect badly on Him to be associated with the weapon he had so mercilessly mocked. The plan was a success at first, as tales of Zugote's 'lost artefact' took hold, to the point where the hammer took pride of place as the centrepiece of a shrine to Zugote, not far from Frogchester. Unfortunately, the shrine was looted by a gang of troggs and the hammer was stolen away to a castle out in the middle of nowhere. The troggs presented it to their dragon-god as tribute. The dragon-god, being a bit smarter than the troggs, realised at once that it was useless junk and threw it on the refuse pile when the troggs weren't looking.

"This left me with a headache. How could I continue to besmirch Zugote's reputation with the Godhammer festering in some dark unseen corner? I had to get the hammer back, and so I contacted your order under the guise of a collector, in the hope that you might retrieve the weapon."

Why ask us? Why not use worshippers of Zugote?

"Because Zugote is an egomaniac who loves being praised, and pays very close attention to His followers. By contrast, He views Me with utter contempt and takes nothing whatsoever to do with anyone who worships Me. I could hardly expect to keep things under wraps once his followers got involved."

Surely he would have found out eventually?

"Of course, but only after His supposed hammer became common knowledge. His humiliation would have been truly delicious."

And yet he found out anyway.

"Yes. My plan was undone when King Larry's army won a resounding victory at the Battle of Grumblehork. In the midst of their victory, one soldier, who just happened to be a mercenary from Frogchester, gave thanks to Zugote for sending forth the Godhammer. Naturally, Zugote became suspicious, and after beating a confession out of me, he realised what I'd done."

Brother Crunge stared blankly, in as much as a formless entity was capable of doing so.

My Lord, how could you not have anticipated this would happen?

Glurgamoth sighed. "I was sober, okay? I couldn't think straight. I admit it, it was a terrible plan from the start."

So what now? asked Brother Crunge.

"What now? Now you take that damn hammer

back to Mount Reckless and be done with it. Bury it, put it in a box, I care not what you do with it. Just keep it out of my sight."

My Lord Glurgamoth, I fear I cannot. I will be executed as soon as I set foot back in the monastery.

"Oh, yes, that's right, you let all your friends die, didn't you? Well, I suppose you can't go back. It makes you a wanderer now, doesn't it. In that case, I dub thee Warden of the Godhammer. Go forth, loyal wanderer, travel the lands in My name, and keep that thing as far away from Me as possible."

As You command, Lord Glurgamoth.

"Splendid. Bear my weapon well, Brother Crunge. The Godhammer is an unstoppable force in the right hands."

Really?

"Indeed. When used in anger, it can strike down any enemy with the force of a hundred hammerblows."

Will it help defend me against Zugote?

Glurgamoth scoffed. "Why, thinking of challenging Him to a fight?"

No, I'm just a bit concerned that he seems to be out for my blood.

"Oh, don't worry about that. Zugote hates everyone. He is the god of war after all. Trust me, this time next week he'll have forgotten all about you."

You're sure?

"Possibly. Now be off with you."

———

Hugo sneered at the weapon resting contentedly on the counter. "That's what you came all this way for?"

The Godhammer was not so much a hammer as it

was a lump of rock mounted on a stick. The wooden handle still bore scabs of bark, while a solitary leaf dangled from the base. The head was a shapeless chunk, its surface dull and unpolished. A phrase was carved, or rather scrawled, into its uneven surface. It simply read, 'Hammer of the Gods'.

"Looks can be deceptive," said Brother Crunge, as he sipped from a tankard of ale.

"I thought you didn't drink?"

Brother Crunge set down the tankard. "I felt the occasion warranted it."

"Whatever you say, Glurgamoth-Man. So, what are you going to do now that you can't go back home?"

Brother Crunge savoured the sharp tang of the booze on his tongue. It was a sensation he had not experienced in decades. "I'll travel, I suppose. I'll wander the cities, see the world, meet new people."

"Don't bother," scowled Hugo. "People are awful."

Brother Crunge sighed. "That's a shame."

"Well, whatever happens, I hope your amazing magical hammer serves you well, though I'm still lost as to what's so special about it."

Brother Crunge grimaced. "Why this is a weapon of unimaginable power. When used in anger, it can strike down any enemy with the force of a hundred hammerblows."

Hugo sniffed. "Very nice."

"Not really," said Brother Crunge. "Watch this."

Brother Crunge handed the weapon to a bleary-eyed patron seated next to him at the bar.

"Excuse me, my good man. Could I trouble you to hold this for me?" said Brother Crunge with a broad smile.

The patron took hold of the weapon, his reddened face twisted in confusion.

"Thank you, kind sir," said Brother Crunge. "May I say you are as kind and accommodating as your wife was when I entertained her last night."

The patron's dour expression curled into a snarl. "What did you say?"

"You heard," said Brother Crunge. "Now are you going to hit me with that hammer or not?"

The patron sprung, hammer poised. Drawing the weapon back, he was suddenly overcome by the weight of the weapon and he fell backwards, crashing through the floor.

Brother Crunge turned to Hugo. "Now you see. When used in anger, the hammer strikes with the power of a hundred hammerblows, but at the same time, it becomes a hundred times heavier. The Godhammer is an unstoppable force in the right hands, but mortal hands are not the right hands. It's called the Godhammer for a reason. It is a hammer that can only be used by a god."

Hugo rubbed his stubbly chin, setting eyes on Brother Crunge's empty tankard. "Interesting. Another ale?"

"No," said Brother Crunge, hoisting his pack over his shoulder. "It's time for me to go. The world beckons."

"Right," said Hugo, hand outstretched. "That'll be two hundred groats, please."

Brother Crunge's eyes widened in disbelief. "What? I only had the one ale."

"True," said Hugo, "but you owe me for the floor."

THE TIMEPIECE
JONATHAN MALONEY

B andy Fitzgibbon was a gnome much like any other who had grown up on the Twisting Row; the line of shops of tinkerers and inventors. A long chaotic winding snake of road lined with shops—quiet and loud—that marked who worked within.

The Twisting Row was divided into two kinds of people; the inventors, who made new and interesting objects out of metal and magic, blended with technological innovation; some practical, some less so—often explosive. They were workshops of noise, of embellishment, where the building was a living thing pumping out smoke, shouts, and volcanic retorts in often equal measures. They were heavily reinforced but often had lightweight roofs, so when the blast wave came it went *up* and not *out* and thus protected the neighbours. This happened often enough. Gnomes were like that.

The inventors were the celebrated masters of the Row of Helvenica, a city of industry and trade, where rich merchants looked for the latest device to peddle on their ships to other nations, born out of the Row, sponsored by the wealthy in the hope of acquiring that which would change the world and line their pockets. The looping, ascending road of reckless invention, coupled with boundless ambition, a boiling pot that every so often detonated with either a new, brilliant idea of creation, or in a more conventional—but no less spectacular—fashion.

The second kind of people on the row were the ones who cleaned up the mess.

Bandy was one of the latter. Where other workshops were loud, his was quiet—save for one pervasive sound. Where other buildings bounced around and thundered with the rapid tread of wide booted feet and the cries of very loud and excited voices, his was still. Light poured in through high windows, set to gold amidst the sparkling motes of hanging dust, and always in the background the firm, inexorable sound of time itself.

Tick tock. Tick Tock. Tick tock.

A thousand timepieces, all moving in perfect order, without fuss and without dissent; not a single one of them out of tune, all ticking in sync with the rest, to create what was less of a sound and more of a heartbeat.

Bandy Fitzgibbon did not create clocks, he repaired them. And all kinds of them as well; though his talent lay firmly in the mechanical foremost. He prided himself on his ability to take any sort of timepiece and unravel it, dismantle it, find the flaw of time and recreate it, to add that clear, clean sound to the rest of its fellows until it was returned to its owner, and in so doing... a touch of order was restored to an unquiet, chaotic world.

Bandy was an unusual sort of gnome. He did not

have the appearance of the unordinary—he was short, as a gnome was wont to be. His feet were large and kept in well made boots, like a gnome tended to find themselves; he had dexterous fingers, large brown eyes and curly brown hair, a most humble colour compared to the rainbow explosivity of his fellow gnomes, but not so notgnomish as to warrant a reaction or a second look. Where Bandy differed was his quiet and his lack of ambition, which, considering where he came from, was most unusual indeed.

Bandy was the last in a long line of Fitzgibbon, and the only son of the most *famous* Fitzgibbon; Burly Fitzgibbon, the Twister of Time himself, the Keeper of the Watch. An inventor both mysterious and ecstatic, he had spent a lifetime creating, changing, and adapting various kinds of clocks of all kinds.

They were not ordinary clocks, not by any means. The Fitzgibbon pieces were kept by kings and queens, by high merchant lords, by the deeping kindred and other fabulously wealthy and powerful entities. They told the time, true enough much like any other clock; they often told the time in various parts of the world at the same time, for whatever peculiar reason. But they did far more than that. A Fitzgibbon special clock did not just tell the time, it told what was to be; never in certain terms, never in absolutes, but in ways peculiar and unique.

There was a clock in the city square of Teclusis, whose hands counted not the time, but indicated the readiness of the nearby mountain to explode into a pillar of fire and ash, when the forces beneath it would finally decide they'd had enough of things, and were going to stretch. Others similarly predicted specific future events; most were far more mundane, such as the changing of tides, the best time to plant seeds and crops for the most fulfilling haul. One was even used for predicting the best time to have or to *avoid* having relations for the purpose of having a child, and not just any child, but a child of particular health, charisma, and personality. The Kingmaker clock had been the cause of assassination and war in its time, but now its location was a well kept secret.

Burly Fitzgibbon, however, had grown rich from these ventures. Closely guarded were his secrets of making, and he had given no answers as to how he managed such unique devices. There were even attempts to kidnap him, to make him a prisoner of clockmaking to create other pieces to predict futures perfectly, but Burly had always been one turn of the hands ahead of everyone else. He had grown rich, travelled the world, been lauded and praised, and bathed in the platitudes. And in so doing, had utterly neglected his wife and newborn son.

His wife had departed after years spent away, leaving her son behind and setting off to find somewhere that only made use of a sundial for the telling of time. Bandy had stayed. Stayed and become part of the furniture, tending to the clocks, repairing them, carefully making sure the timing was precise as precise could be on each of them. And occasionally his father would come back, a whirlwind of creativity and good cheer, wearing expensive clothes and carrying sacks of gold and other wealth, patting his son on the back and forgetting what his name was as he did so. A plastered smile of a salesman on his face that would look around at the workshop and wonder what it was he was forgetting, until remembering that his wife had left him years ago, and it had been half a decade since he had seen his only child; the only one that he knew of, anyway.

And then, one day, Bandy realised it had been ten years since he had seen his father. It had been years since anyone had come into the shop to ask about him or attempt to commission his father. And just like that, Bandy had come to realise that his father was never coming home again. So he had wound the clocks and listened to the click of seconds and when all of them were in line with each other and all was well once more, he carried on. Just like he always had. It was easier to miss a father who had never been there than he thought.

He was a known crafter by this point, excellent at repair beyond the measure of most. Not just clocks from his father's workshop but others as well. Bandy had spent all his life learning the tools, the mechanisms, and creating new and more precise methods. Nodding his head to requests made of him, before speaking in his quiet voice that barely rose above the ticking. He was well sought after, even if people left his workshop feeling like their thoughts were somehow being crushed inside their skull by that perfect, relentless ticking, inexorable as a hammer wielded by a dwarf with a vision and an ancestor's guidance.

That quiet little shop, tucked into a corner of the Row that no one came to unless they were looking for it. Sturdy enough that even the explosions did not cause too much rattling, besides the wobble of a window pane. Even those Bandy had come to anticipate and expect, and he would sometimes count between them idly, waiting for the next one, as he worked with gears and pieces so small that they could be balanced upon the point of a pin, where even breathing too hard would send them scattered into the ether never to be seen again. This was where Bandy lived, worked, and remained alone, with naught but the ticking of clocks to keep him company—as it had been, as it was, and as it would have always been.

At least, until the timepiece showed up.

It had not been any sort of special or auspicious day. Bandy made his breakfast. Nothing special, nothing rare—boiled egg, toasted bread, and freshly pressed juice from the aragi fruit tree that grew in the little garden behind his shop. The sour, pale green juice was invigorating and cleared the mind—it made it easier to let his heartbeat settle into the soothing rhythm of the ticks. Bandy did not at all understand his customer's complaints about the uniform clocks keeping time together; it felt entirely natural to him, to the point that being without it was akin to feeling suffocated. He wondered often if there was something wrong with such people—he assumed as much, since they all too often seemed to mistreat or even *break* their clocks and watches. Clearly they had no proper appreciation of time, but he did not mind; it kept him busy, and kept him in a job, and allowed him to restore them to their proper, working order, as time itself intended. A little more order to the world, as it should be.

All of this was shattered when the bell chime of the workshop door rang. Earlier than was usual—as most of the clients arrived at midday rather than so close to dawn—and the discordance made Bandy frown—or at least frown deeper than usual; his need to concentrate upon his work had set a permanent beetling to his brows. Departing from the humble, yet anticipated, breakfast, Bandy had made his way to the front of his workshop.

The courier was a human, a young man wearing the blue and white of his service, his heavy pack festooned with letters and other small packages of business, of affection, of the mundane and more that made up such messages, passed from soul to soul throughout Helvenica via this unassuming individual. His gaze darted this way and that, sweat upon his brow, but he did not appear to be out of breath.

"Bandy Fitzgibbon, sir? I have a package for you." He said it hurriedly, gesturing to a wooden box set upon the counter. Bandy climbed up the steps to it—like most workshops, there were two service desks for customers. One was at a much lower height, for normal people like Bandy and other races of a less than beanpole stature, and the other was to accommodate the looming giants of the taller races, to better prevent them from tripping up and injuring themselves with their seemingly common inability to look down.

The wooden box was utilitarian. Lacquered and sturdy, bound in black iron. It would have seemed entirely boring save for the lock upon it, which had no keyhole but a collection of bare gears instead. This immediately captured Bandy's attention. He could immediately see how to manipulate it, how to possibly open it—because it was work that he recognised.

"Who sent this?" he asked, but he did not need to.

"My missive has no name, sir," the courier stated nervously, even as Bandy nodded. "There was a letter as well, sir. Perhaps that will clear it up." He held out a wax sealed envelope—yellowing, old, but the seal remained. Bandy eyed him a moment, squinting up with his near-sighted vision, then adjusted the lenses of his eyepieces and nodded. He pulled two coins from his pocket, as was custom, and handed them over in exchange. As he took the letter, he felt the age of it—old paper, rendered smooth by time and contact. The courier was already hurrying out.

He paid the man no mind, staring instead between the box and the letter, until one crossed an imaginary line in Bandy's mind first. He turned from the box and broke the seal, pulling the letter open.

The message inside was remarkably simple. This was quite the departure from the normally verbose Burly—who would write letters when Bandy was small and still had hope of seeing his father—that were full of amusing stories he did not quite understand but would have made sense to an adult. Instead, there was a short phrase, written in a hurried hand that—even after all these years of no contact at all—Bandy still recognised.

Do not open it. B.F.

B.F. Burly Fitzgibbon. And that was it. Bandy turned the letter this way and that, expecting more. Expecting something. Certainly a whole lot more than entirely nothing. But nothing was what he had and all he was getting. The box sat there obstinately, entirely non threatening and yet somehow ominous, but that was entirely buried in the feeling that Bandy felt building up inside him; a most un-Bandy sort of feeling that threatened to drown him in rising wrath and frustration, as feelings long buried bubbled up to the surface.

That was all? After all this time, that was it? Bandy would have accepted a scathing admonition, a plea for forgiveness. *Something.* His fist closed around the letter, crushing it. He was angry, uncharacteristically so, and especially at himself; he had never placed expectation upon his father, or so he had thought. This welling upset put truth to that falsehood, and he was disappointed in himself for it. He glowered at the locked box with its spitefully formed clockwork padlock, and put a hand upon it, to pick it up and cast it into his workshop's depths behind him, after which he would rip the crumpled letter to pieces. But as soon as he placed a hand on the box he felt it.

TOCK.

The sensation travelled up his arm and into his head, rattled around in his skull and exited promptly out of his left ear. He wobbled in place a moment, thoroughly and completely disjointed, before he carefully put the box down and stared at it.

There was no question of *what* it was; it was the tick of a clock badly out of time, a jarring note of wrongness. But he had felt it through a locked, sealed box.

The box was heavy, but not nearly so large or heavy as to give *that* sensation. That was the sort of feeling one got standing by a great city clock, with hands thirty feet long and cogs the size of ships. He could still feel the vibration in his fingertips and toes. What was in that box? His anger at his father lingered, but now it was transforming instead into a sort of frustrated mystification. What had his father sent to him? And why?

This conundrum continued until it was interrupted by the ringing of the doorbell, the second such happening in one day. This was most unusual for Bandy, and he nearly startled out of his boots as he snapped his head up. Even so, the bell continued to ring several times over, which only added to the discordance—whomever had just entered, they had not done so alone.

Three very tall, very grim, and very obnoxiously

127

armed humans entered. First two, and then—after a brief pause—the other. But in the depth of that pause entered a woman. She was fabulously dressed and, despite her advanced years, held a lingering beauty to her —beauty entirely marred by her expression, which was akin to soured milk in its appeal. Bandy knew full well who she was, not least because the emblem of her house was sewn into her gown, which looked like it would have paid for a decent sized house. Her dark hair had a white streak at each temple, and she strode in like she owned the place—which, considering her reputation, was something that was probably true more often than not when she entered an establishment.

Lady Etheria du La'Corre was five times widowed, fabulously rich, and had little patience for anyone beneath her—which meant practically everyone. Behind her lay a long line of dead husbands, unwanted children, and a list of assassinations longer than the Twisting Row itself, though not a one could be proven. Her husbands had all died one after another but the money and power had always been hers, rather than the reversal. The deaths themselves were all fairly mysterious and the cause of many whispers over the decades, but none of them too loudly. Lady Etheria may have once been bright eyed and innocent once, but those days were firmly past. The woman she was now held onto authority with a steely grip, and did so through whatever means necessary—without compunction one way or the other, protected from retribution not only by her gold, but her rumoured highly competent contract killers. And she was, at present, standing in Bandy's shop, glowering down at him via the length of a long, straight nose.

Caught between the inexorable difficulty of dealing

with his father's letter and a very impatient woman, Bandy was able to at least piece together that this was highly unusual. Nobility usually associated with the working classes and traders via representatives and servants, but never personally. And certainly not one as powerful as Lady Etheria.

He gathered himself. Bringing himself up to his full, diminutive height upon his step ladder, he inclined his head and straightened. "How may I be of service?"

Lady Etheria had both of her hands hidden in the voluminous sleeves of her gown. She removed them at this point, holding a small silver box in both hands that she placed upon the counter.

"I believe that you can help me with this." She spoke in a tight, haughty tone, the words sharp and short —as though each syllable cost her in some fashion. Bandy did not like her. The opinion clicked into place with the ease of a key in a well oiled lock, but he kept it from his face. He frowned at the situation and presentation instead, reaching for the box. The elderly woman swished out a folded fan from her sleeves, pinning his hand to the counter with remarkable speed. He opened his mouth to protest, but she silenced him with a bristling glare.

"Before you set your paws upon this, I would first make some things clear. The timepiece kept within is a gift from my father. It was commissioned especially for me from *your* father, and I am told it was the beginning of his good fortune. It is"—she paused, stiffened, and gathered herself—"it is very important to me. Are we clear?"

Bandy opened, closed his mouth, and then nodded. "Yes, my lady. Perfectly clear," he said as evenly as he could. The moment held, and then she lifted her folded fan, flicked it open with the precision of a cut throat razor, and fluttered it before her face as Bandy opened the box carefully.

The timepiece within was breathtaking. It was a small, beautifully wrought one of truesilver, with a carved sapphire making up much of the exterior casing. He handled it with care, opening the small, cunningly wrought latch on one side that exposed the interior. He recognised the work immediately; Burly's second most famous creation had been his timepieces that had never needed winding, timepieces that ticked with perfect accuracy for their entire lifespans. He had only made a few of them, and each of them had been marked with personalised initials. *E.laC* figured prominently on the clock face, but the hands were stopped and still. Bandy blinked.

"Your predecessor assured my father that it would never need winding," Lady Etheria said in an acidic tone. "Clearly he was mistaken. I wish to have that failure corrected."

Bandy tapped the face of the timepiece delicately, and then gave it the tiniest shake— a mere fraction of a movement—and felt something slip. There was a sound within, not a tick, not a tock, but a slithering sensation of something out of place. He exhaled, reassured, as he placed the piece down. He could fix this. A gentle manipulation of the locks and seals, and replacing the part that had lost its way. Nothing he had not done before.

"I can do that. It should only take a few days," he said with confidence. Bandy knew his skill in these matters. His workshop was a monument to it, as the steady tick, tick, tick of timepieces rang out.

Lady Etheria did not look pleased. Her lips twisted, then she held out a hand and snapped two fingers.

There was a scurrying sound and a hunched man with a harried expression scampered up, holding a scroll which he presented to Bandy and unrolled on the counter.

Bandy knew what it was, and was instantly affronted. A contract of surety? For himself? The nerve! Such contracts were often made use of between tradespeople, but they were particularly common between gnomes and other races. Bandy was no fool—he knew his people had a well deserved reputation of having a love for picking up this and that curiosity, of having an erratic emotional response to seeing a new and shiny thing that led them to treating property that was not theirs as their own. In short, his people were unjustly decried as thieves—when in truth they were merely curious. That, and lacking entirely the self control to restrain such impulses.

But not him. He had always behaved with the utmost respect towards the possessions of others—but he also could not deny that the many time pieces that were now in his workshop were ones he had found discarded, or in old junk stores, or even simply lost here and there. But to Bandy, this was all right and proper; they had belonged to someone else, and now they were his. To be more or less called a thief was more than a little degrading, and his expression clearly showed the distaste that he was unable to hide, something he could only put down to being rattled by his father's letter. That lingering anger, born out of deep seated, unrecognised resentment, clouded his normal professionalism.

Lady Etheria spotted it immediately. "You object to such measures? They are standard procedure." Her tone was frosty, and she placed a hand on the box, ready to remove both it and the timepiece.

Bandy shook his head, murmuring an apology, as he

took hold of the scroll and started to read through it. The wording of the contract was fairly standard, documenting the timepiece to be repaired, its features, and the fact it was the property of the Lady LaCorre—but the clauses gave Bandy pause. Words leapt out at him, such as 'punishment' and 'as deemed fit,' should the timepiece be lost, damaged, or stolen. With another person this might have been concerning, but with a woman with Lady Etheria's reputation it was downright terrifying. It was hardly a stretch to think such measures she might take would be both swift and fatal. He hesitated, shifting the scroll to catch the lamplight a little better, and his hand brushed the locked box that still sat upon the counter.

TOCK.

Again that sensation of being rattled roared through him. It wobbled him on the spot and sent all thoughts of the contract flying from his mind, leaving him quite shaken until Lady Etheria snapped at him.

"What are you doing?" She sounded genuinely angry by this point. His sudden movement had surprised her, and Lady Etheria was a woman who did not enjoy surprises. Rumour had it the last had been a surprise birthday party thrown for her by an errant nephew, who was rendered penniless and destitute within a week—which was considerably a better fate than most, who were usually not found at all.

He did not have the wit to argue at this point. He seized a quill from the inkwell and scribbled his name. The scuttling footman seized upon it in an instant, clutching it in both hands and tucking it into a folder with an oily smile.

Lady Etheria set her mouth in a grim line. "You have one week."

Her tone spoke volumes—she clearly did not enjoy having to do this, and her stock in Bandy was low after his somewhat erratic greeting. It was not just that however—despite his reputation for repair, Bandy was fully aware that he was not his father. A fact brought painfully to the fore once again as his eye settled on the box, even as the noblewoman and her entourage poured out of the store again, leaving him in silence with the heirloom timepiece of Lady Etheria, and the box.

Shortly afterwards, he was back in the depths of his workshop, his desk now made up of his morning attentions. To one side, his breakfast. Before him, the timepiece of Lady La'Corre. And to the other side, the box from his father, along with his letter. He had carried it with care but it had not made another obscenely jarring sound again—at least, not yet. But still slightly disjointed, he was struck by the difficulty of what to do next.

The growl of his stomach saved him, a tone of dissatisfaction that would not wait further. As he munched upon egg and toast, his eyes shifted from box to timepiece.

This was unusual for Bandy. When he set himself upon a task, it would completely consume his focus entirely. He had made an agreement, a contract had been signed, and that was surely the end of it in nearly any other circumstance—except for the damnable box. It *loomed* in his awareness, sucking in everything around it, dragging the eye as though it were compelled.

Bandy forced his attention from it, and ate his toast while considering the timepiece of Lady Etheria. Small, cunning tools were deployed as he washed down the egg with sharp, sour tasting aragi juice. Small latches were undone, cunning screws unwound, invisible hinges shifted, and the device opened. Bandy had to admit, it was one of his father's better pieces of work. He would have enjoyed going through it on any other day, even when he immediately noted the gear that had lost a single, delicate tooth which had caused it to cease function. This would not be difficult. A single replacement and a turn of a few key screws, and the timepiece would work as intended.

Thus it was a complete and total mystery to him why he found himself having set the timepiece aside, with its unbeating heart exposed to the wider world, as he sweat and swore his way through the lock of the box his father had sent.

There was no keyhole, but there *were* various visible gears and other various mechanisms in the lock itself. Bandy soon figured out it was a manner of lock related to clockwork, but it was of a like and kind he had never witnessed before. If the timepiece of Lady Etheria had merely been a clock, this device of his father's making was something so advanced as to be breathtaking, a masterwork of engineering to the point of bewilderment.

It soon became apparent that the entire box was some manner of device, with the lock itself burrowing so deeply Bandy was quite convinced that underneath the wood the entire interior was a singular mechanism. For *what* he had no idea... but it filled him with foreboding. There was an undeniable air of menace to the thing that went beyond the simple and infuriating message that had accompanied it, even the unnatural weight of it—and that tick that had rattled his very soul. Whatever it was, it was not enough to stop him. He soon needed to bring out a directed lamp with a wrought mirror and magnesium flare that could put direct light onto the lock. He had not yet made a mistake with it... but he definitely did not *want* to make a mistake.

He almost missed the opening catch—it was hidden to look like a false release but was the correct mechanism at a different levering point. Most of the most technical inspectors would have missed it, and even Bandy himself almost had; it was not usual for his father's work which—while designed around concealment—was not designed around this sort of deception. This was new.

He eased the lever and heard a loud *click*, followed by a series of mechanical sounds of winding gears and releasing valves as the box opened on its own.

It was akin to watching a flower unfold. A series of mechanical movements flickered as panels and hatches slid back, shifted, and the box transformed before Bandy's astonished eyes, revealing two things—a folded piece of paper, and a crude, boxy pocket watch, whose lid was held closed by a simple catch.

After all the ceremony of the opening, Bandy expected more. Precisely *what* he was expecting, he could not have said, but definitely... more. He reached out, and picked them both up.

As soon as he had the watch in his hand, another body shaking, mind twisting *TOCK* sensation rattled him, moving him from his work bench and sending him staggering about for a moment before the disorientation ended. Staring at the lumpy, weirdly heavy, pocket watch, he finally turned the catch and flicked the lid upwards. It sprang outwards with a disquieting eagerness, revealing the watch face within.

It was nothing at all like what Bandy had anticipated. Whereas the exterior was clearly steel and put together without grace or artistry, the dial was entirely different. There were no numbers surrounding the five different clock hands, all moving at different speeds, but symbols of unknown origin instead—symbols that shifted even under his gaze, forming hypnotic shapes. Something about them hurt if he stared at them too long, so he shifted to the quintuple watch hands instead.

They were all different lengths, all with different styling. The long hand was straight and simple, the shortest was zig-zagged and had a curling point.. But the part that made Bandy pause in his aimless, dizzied wandering was that the hands occasionally changed the direction they were moving.

This should have been impossible; in any other watch, it would be. But as he stared, various hands shifted from clockwise to counter clockwise and back again before his very eyes—all of them winding down to the lowermost hand at various speeds.

It made no sense, but as seconds ticked by, he felt an odd sense of foreboding travel up his arm from the pocket watch. It only grew worse before he dragged his eyes from it to the piece of paper in his left hand.

The handwriting was, again, instantly recognisable. Recognisable and far more prolific this time around than the last. His father wrote in that easy, flowing script that spoke to an absentmindedness, but this was sharper; there was a precision that usually lacked in anything but his watch making. As Bandy read he moved through his shop, away from the now open box and the priceless timepiece he had been entrusted by Lady Etheria.

To my son—and only my son, for I doubt entirely that another could have opened that lock. If you are reading this then you have successfully ignored my warning, and done as intended. You are a gnome of my own heart after all, however much you have denied it before.

Bandy nearly crumpled the piece of paper and hurled it away right then and there. Even as the thought occurred to him, however, the pocket watch in his hand *twitched* without moving and the hands started racing to the lowermost point. He blinked, and then slowly unclenched his fist. As he did so, one of the hands started shifting upwards instead, moving clockwise once again.

Perturbed by this oddity, he went back to reading. *Though this fact matters not. What matters now is what you hold—my greatest creation, and my most dangerous. You have come into possession of the Fatewatch. A somewhat garish name I understand, but not one entirely of my own choosing. I am sure by this point you have noticed it is no ordinary clock.* Bandy's expression soured considerably, glancing at the odd arrangement of hands. But he kept reading.

The purpose of the Fatewatch is not to tell the time, my son. It tells one of their fate. More specifically, it tells them how close they are to death, moment by moment, choice by choice, from one instant to the next.

Bandy stopped dead in his tracks. Sweat broke out on his brow as he looked down with a now trembling hand to the device that lurked in his clammy grip. The very concept of such a thing was ludicrous, but then again—was not this sort of thing his father's speciality? What he'd made all his life?

But nothing like this. Nothing to *this* degree, which made his other clocks seem positively mundane. The hands were ticking down to the lowest digit again.

He kept reading. *The hands are working to either the uppermost or the lowermost point. The upper point is safe—but the closer they are to the lowermost point, the closer one is to their death.* Bandy's heart skipped a beat, then hammered. The hands were all nearly pointing completely downward by this point. He started to pace about, as he kept reading desperately. *The good news of this is, sometimes all it takes to restore oneself to a state of safety is to move to a different location. The simplest of choices are often the most necessary.*

Bandy looked around the shop, blinking, before returning to the Fatewatch. This was foolish. It was madness. Everything was fine, there was no danger present —but he could not shake the feeling. The device in his hand grew heavier and heavier, and now all but one hand was pointed to the lowest symbol, which shifted faster and faster. Bandy started walking this way and that before he made his way to the front of his shop. He stopped when there was a faint *ping* from his right hand. He jerked his vision to the Fatewatch, and saw that all the hands were winding clockwise to the uppermost point. The heavy feeling faded. He exhaled. Shaking his head at himself, he chuckled weakly and went back to reading the letter.

I am afraid that the reason for this will soon become apparent once you are in a place of safety. The opening of the box triggered a timed spell that should take effect shortly. If you can, I would cover your ears at this point.

The crucial factor, Bandy would realise later, was where he stood. The frantic wandering as the Fatewatch had warned him had directed Bandy to stand on the other side of his counter in the front of his workshop —in particular, the spot where he treated humanoid sized clients. The wood was solid and reinforced with stone. By standing behind it, he created a shelter for himself that protected him when the lockbox exploded.

There was, as warned, a tremendous noise. A sound

that went beyond and became a concussive wave instead, blasting out hearing and creating instead a high pitched, shrieking ringing sensation. There was a flash of fire and of bright, searing light, joined by heat washing overhead, with the smell of sulphur and burning as the box detonated with enormous force. Every single clock, the years and years of Bandy's work, ruptured and burst, the windows blasting outwards as a wave of broken crystal, wooden fragments, and thousands of clock pieces, and gears, erupted outwards with terrific force.

And then... silence, aside from the catastrophic ringing in his ears.

Bandy stood as still as a statue. The tips of his hair were on fire, but he could not bring himself to mind. There were, at present, far more important things to address, but he could not quite recall them at the moment, as thoughts somewhat failed to properly manifest. The world was a ringing bell and he was right at the heart of it, as he stared around at his suddenly unfamiliar surroundings. His shop. His home.

It was gone.

He could see the sky where the upper floor had once been. Bits of debris still fell, each one carrying a memory he could not, at present, recall. The ticking had stopped. Bandy's world had changed so completely that he simply could not recognise the existence he was now lost in.

He could not recall how long he stood there, frozen in shock. It might have been minutes, it might have been hours, but as he finally dragged himself back to the state of being, he dropped his gaze down to the debris at his feet. His heart started beating again when he saw a shard of blue.

Absently, he stuffed the—still unfinished—letter into his work vest, and crouched down, scooping up the little blue piece of crystal. He turned it in his hand, to see only part of the initials inscribed into it—*E.la*. The 'C' was now gone. Along with the rest of the timepiece that only an hour or two ago he had been entrusted with.

Realisation slammed down his spine in a mixture of ice and lead. The badly misfiring parts of his brain that were, even now, screaming at the silence and the complete lack of ticking in what had once been his world tore his gaze towards the still held Fatewatch. The hands were turning downwards at a *blistering* pace. There was shouting outside. A whistle being blown. The world was waking up and it was shaking. Somewhere out there, Lady Etheria would be getting word. Somewhere out there, she would be flying into a towering, murderous rage. And somewhere out there, the assassins that she kept to deal with such matters would be using the power of the contract that Bandy had signed to be allowed to do whatever they deemed fit in punishment—including execution.

Leave. The thought was accompanied by another gentle *ping* sound, reverberating up his arm. The hands were winding upwards again. And so, Bandy did what he had done all his life, and listened to the tick of the clock.

He turned and staggered with the steps of a drunkard back the way he came. Stumbling through the crater of his workshop, he was in shock, but the ticking and tocking of twisting fate in his hand was his guide now; a voice in his head that steered his body while his thoughts were elsewhere. There was a mighty hole where the wall of his workshop had once stood. The aragi fruit tree was smouldering in the yard. The memory of the now vaporised glass of juice lost in the blast rose in his thoughts, but his feet were carrying him down the small backyard, to the alley behind his home, where he bounced off walls and tottered along as the world he knew burned behind him.

The alley branched. Briefly, he considered his choices. He vaguely thought of going right, before there was another ferocious *TOCK* sensation roaring up the length of his arm. He paused. Left, then? A softer, gentler *ping*.

A more rational gnome would have questioned this —certainly a less singed one—and most assuredly one whose brain was currently not rattling about in their ears. Bandy did not quite have the luxury at that point and, thus, he dutifully heeded the call of the clock and went left. A rewarding ping joined the journey onwards. He had done something right, in the midst of the world going so very wrong. A contribution had been made.

This was how the rudderless vessel that Bandy had become was then piloted, stumbling along the back alleys and streets in an effort to go *somewhere*. Anywhere. Later he could take it all apart and put it back together and try and make sense of it, but in that time of shock there was nothing but the *ping* and *tock* of the Fatewatch, and his nerveless legs dutifully obeying the call.

An indeterminate length of time later, Bandy was sitting on a shattered crate in a mouldering alleyway. His heart still pounded, and his breathing was ragged, forcing him to taste the vile scents of the refuse of that alley as well as smell it, but it had an odd effect of clearing his head. What was he going to *do*?

His father–his mad, stupid, dangerously brilliant

father—had just blown up his home. That was bad enough, but he had also destroyed the Lady's timepiece, while the ink on the contract that rendered his life forfeit was still wet. There was no world where this made sense even by a gnomish sense of logic, which worked in leaps and bounds while unfettered by rationality and flying high on the ambition of grandeur; Bandy was much more level headed than that. Clearly his father was not, but as far as demonstrations went, this whole thing felt rather excessive.

He had been afraid, so he had run. Nothing else for it really; but part of him wondered, if he went back now, would it be just a bad dream, and would everything be as it was before? He vaguely shifted as though in preparation to do exactly that, before the sensation came. *Tock.* Rolling up the nerves of his arm in a warning.

He stopped and stared down at the Fatewatch. It continued to look both innocent and vaguely nauseating, a sense of menace lurking about it that seemed far more understandable now. Bandy wondered if he should throw it away—simply toss it down the alleyway and take his chances—but there was no warning tone this time. He could not fool it. It knew there was no way he could do that.

He stared at it, seeing how it sat in his hand, his fingers curled so tightly around it that it felt like it was part of him—no, that was not right. *He* felt like part of *it* and the thought made his heart quaver. This thing, whatever it was, that his father had sent him—it felt both less and more like a clock than anything he had ever handled before, and it frightened him. It gave no tones, no sensations, even though its winding hands shifted back and forth as he watched—some going one way, and some the other, and if he stared too hard sometimes it looked like they were going in different directions at once.

The baying of dogs brought him back to the present with a painful immediacy. There were shouts too, and he remembered that the tracking of criminals from the scene of a crime was often done by hounds—particularly when those criminals were gnomes, for reasons that people never seemed to want to talk about. He bolted upright, so stiffly that he wobbled, and clutched the Fatewatch to himself. Where could he go?

The Fatewatch gave no clue or indication. It made no sound, not in his head or elsewhere, until he looked to the mouth of the alleyway. *Tock*. Not back the way he came. But there was no other way, except—he looked upwards. *Ping*.

He had almost climbed up the drainpipe and onto the roof when the shouts and howls came from directly below. Soldiers in the livery of House du La'Corre yelled excitedly as they spied their quarry. It appeared that Bandy had drawn the ire of Lady Etheria's considerable power, influence, and wrath in a manner unprecedented, and she had poured her many resources into her vengeance. There was no time to think any more. Only time to run.

Down across the roofs of Helvenica went Bandy Fitzgibbon. His legs rubbery, but driven on by his terror, sent forward by the frenzied howling of the hunting hounds. He slid down shingles, balanced along drain pipes, and at one point disturbed a hive of jewelled wasps—bright green, dazzling and meaner than a very mean thing—knocking it down into a crowded street far below and causing a cacophony of panic. Something whizzed by his ear, and then another—someone was firing a crossbow. Several someones, in fact, shot from the street below him, their aim hampered by furious green wasps with a grudge against whatever foolish being had decided to be alive and within a hundred yards at that moment.

All he had to inform his directions were split second decisions and the warning or encouragement the Fate-watch gave. He had considered taking a safer route across more open rooftops before the warning came and sent him down a narrow gutter instead, from whence had tumbled the aforementioned wasp horde. If he had, those very crossbow bolts would have neatly picked him off with ease.

This was not to say the way was easy. Or particularly safe. And as careful as Bandy was, and as skilled as he was as a craftsman, they were skills heavily unsuited to the current task, which is why at one point, when he was forced to jump to a balcony, he mistimed it completely and plunged through a shuttered window instead.

This would not have been quite such an issue if the dingy, decaying room was not currently occupied. However, it rather unfortunately was, and by a couple making use of a bed for purposes other than sleep. The burly looking fellow was not pleased by the interruption and, ignoring Bandy's winded explanation, seized the poor gnome by his collar, opened the door, and hurled Bandy through it. Once more Bandy found himself sailing through the air.

He was afforded a brief glimpse of his locale as this happened—there was a terrible smell in the air, of alcohol, blood and sweat, overlaid with salt and sourness. There was a fire, there was a bar, there was loudness of voices and music and more besides. A tavern. And not just any tavern; a tavern on the waterfront, a place

Bandy would normally never go, for reasons that were wholly apparent the moment he crashed right onto, and through, the gambling table of Blacknail Tavern, a place so close to the edge of violence at all times that they were practically a couple.

Coins scattered everywhere, sent flying by an errant gnome who had interrupted the game of Toecutter and there was a moment of pause in the tavern. Each man and woman who sat or stood around the shattered table, where No Toes Billy was on his greatest ever winning streak, now had to ask themselves—just how much of the mountain of silver, copper, and even gold could they get, if they tried hard enough?

Bandy tried to form an apology, but didn't even get his mouth open before the first punch was thrown, and the place exploded.

A few moments later, the soldiers of House du La'-Corre burst into the Blacknail in number with their tracking dogs, barely getting a grasp of the situation before the first was knocked out with a precisely swung stool, and the brawl descended into outright warfare.

Through the carnage, ignored now by the thrashing mob, crawled Bandy until he finally cleared out the front door of the place. He still clutched the Fatewatch doggedly in one hand as he went, staggering to his feet and stumbling along blindly, guided only by the pings and tocks of the device in his hand. Down a street. Up an alleyway. Down a dock and along a ramp. No one seemed to notice him and no one seemed to mind, as his battered body and shock-addled mind sent him careening along until at last, someone noticed him—noticeably because he had walked straight into them.

The man was wearing armour, and for a moment Bandy's heart quailed. But he peered down to Bandy while lifting the visor of his helmet, and gave a friendly grin that was at odds with the scars on his face—warmer by far than expected—and extended a hand to Bandy to help him back up. Without knowing what else to do, Bandy let himself be hoisted to his feet by a strong arm.

"Taking passage, are we?" the man asked cheerfully, with a nod of the chin. Bandy looked about and realised that as fate would have it—perhaps literally in his case—he had walked into the boarding line of a passenger ship in the final process of loading, already straining to be away.

The sky was clear and bright overhead, the waves sparkling and bright as they gently rolled over one another to dash themselves on the shoreline. Truth told, Bandy had never been on a ship before, and had never had the inkling to be on one. But now, opportunity beckoned. He nodded, hesitantly, staring blankly at the ship for a moment as the urge to remain in the only home he had ever known, and the desire to leave and survive clashed together.

The armoured man hoisted his pack and sword at his back, giving Bandy a curious look. "Looking a little worse for wear there, fellow. Better have your coin together when you get to the bosun, or they'll probably turn you away."

Bandy patted himself down. He did not find his coin pouch, but he did feel something shift under his touch in his vest—and reached in to pull out the singed, but still legible, letter from his father. Without knowing what else to do, he continued reading it, taking up from where he left off.

I hope you can forgive me for my incendiary 'gift'. But of all the plans that I came up with, only that one would have worked, according to the very device that you now no doubt hold. The knack of using the Fatewatch is something I have spent decades learning, and I still do not have the full grasp of it. But I do know now that the key to my survival is giving it to you.

I do not know what is about to happen to me, and I cannot tell you even in this letter. All I know is that if I am to live, I must give you this terrible creation that has guided me for all these years. Forgive me, my son, and find me; let the Fatewatch be your guide. Find me in the world, and I will explain everything.

Your Fool of a Father,

Burly Fitzgibbon.

Swaying where he stood, Bandy did not know what else to do. He was lost, he was afraid, he was alone. And now all he had were the tools remaining in his vest, his clothes and this letter—and the Fatewatch, which still ticked and tocked and waited in his hand.

"I don't have any money, Bandy said to himself, his voice subdued. All his wealth was now no doubt scattered along the Row; that which had not been scattered in the blast was now claimed in wrath by the Lady du La'Corre, as down payment on his lifeblood. Despair threatened to drag him down to the depths of the ocean that lay before him. And then, up his arm and directly to his head, came a soft sound—the *ping* of something done right. A weathered hand appeared before him at eye level, with a small cluster of silver coins.

"Take it, friend," the man said with an understanding tone. "I've seen that look before."

Bandy was shocked. This was a sort of generosity that he had never heard of before from one of the tall folk. He looked up with surprise writ large on his features. The man shrugged, his hand still held out. "You can tell me your story on the ship. That can be payment enough, I would wager." The grin returned. "Call me Caleb."

Bandy blinked, overwhelmed a few moments more before he carefully took the offered coins. "Bandy." He lowered his eyes and nodded with a flush on his cheeks. The tall warrior, Caleb, nodded, accepting and going quiet save for one brief glimpse over his shoulder back to the waterfront. "Very rowdy day for the city, it seems."

Bandy swallowed, and carefully put the letter back in his vest. Then, for the first time since picking it up, finally let go of the Fatewatch and also put it away, noting absently that releasing his grip on it seemed strangely difficult.

"You have no idea," he said wearily, feeling the ache in his body from his endeavours that day. Caleb grinned down at him, and nodded as though satisfied.

The bosun was a surly dwarf who did not care about the foolishness of city folks, and asked no questions as long as the coin was shining. Bandy was the last to step onto the ship and find himself a spot below decks, getting a spot near Caleb, who—after divesting himself of his pack and gear—sat with the eagerness of a child ready to be told a tale. Bandy, taking a deep breath, obliged him.

———

DAY AFTER DAY AT SEA, Bandy learned much. He learned about sea sickness first and foremost, and it remained with him for much of the journey. He learned that Caleb was an adventurer, an explorer, and mercenary who had spent years venturing into danger with the bright eyed innocence of a youth that had never left him. He was younger than Bandy thought, but acted younger still. He had crowed with laughter at Bandy's tale of misfortune, which had rankled, but had offered support and gratitude for sharing, which had been heartwarming. Bandy had said nothing of the Fatewatch. The first time he had thought to mention it, the warning *TOCK* that had bounced in his skull had been so loud it startled him into a stunned state.

But Caleb had mainly been kind, without having reason to be. Bandy had asked about him, between the bouts of heaving over the railing, trying to learn about this strange man whom fortune had cast towards him. He learned that Caleb had lived a life of danger and scars, of loss and good fortune in equal measure. For twelve turnings he had done the work that kept him moving across the world, setting down roots nowhere and exploring where he wished. It was a life Bandy could never have imagined and would never have envied before the world he knew had exploded. Caleb lived life seeking nothing but new experiences and new friends, moving on as they settled down.

From one corner of the continent to the next he had walked, ridden, swam, and even flown on one memorable occasion. And with a keen eye he had spotted a gnome in need, and had not hesitated. He had not wanted anything, which to Bandy in his career of exchange and mercantilism had been somewhat disconcerting, but as time went by, he had learned to accept it. Quite unlike the nobility and other wealthy humans he had encountered, Caleb had nothing that was his own aside from what he carried with him, and yet seemed happier than all of them. It was quite a shock to Bandy's way of thinking, but he had adjusted as best he could as time went by.

There were other travellers on the ship. Caleb seemed able to make friends with all of them, able to relate by experience to any of them—dwarf, elf, human, and all the rest. Bandy could not do the same, and so he lurked in the background, simply listening and learning. And all the while the Fatewatch ticked in his vest, the hands turning one way and then the other relentlessly. He found the observations were able to belay the seasickness of the rocking waves, and few troubled the silent gnome who spoke to no one, tucked away in the corners.

When he was able to be alone and without anyone observing, however, Bandy would examine the Fatewatch. Indeed, he often spent hours simply watching how the hands were moving, trying to keep track of all six of them at the same time as they shifted and warped. It was painful, the lack of precision and seemingly random way that each twisted in on itself at total odds with his decades of experience with simple, progressive shifting of time. To understand the Fatewatch involved understanding a completely different facet of time itself —and Bandy could not figure out what that could possibly mean.

Caleb found him upon the deck, as the sailors bustled and shifted about to keep the ship on an even keel. The waves were calmer, the well worn prow carving through the yet ever restless ocean, the sails flicking and booming overhead with the errant wind. Bandy was staring listlessly into the Fatewatch, but snapped it shut with a twitch of his fingers as he felt a presence behind him. Caleb had emerged from whatever dice game he had been playing below deck, to stand at the prow alongside the comparatively tiny gnome.

Without his armour and other gear, Caleb was still a

powerfully built figure at least twice Bandy's height. His hair was dark, his eyes clear, and his skin sun browned from his ventures. Without saying anything, he stretched and leaned on the rail, looking over the side. It was a habit he had, but only with Bandy; he waited for the gnome to speak, rather than the other way around. And he kept his eyes on the water, rather than looking at him. Bandy could not help but appreciate it, without truly understanding why. The man had a knack for making him feel at ease, despite being of the sort that Bandy normally would find threatening.

At that moment, however, a question was lurking in Bandy's mind that he had refrained from asking; at least with any sort of coherency. He took a deep breath, and placed his own hands on the rail—unlike the man beside him, he could barely manage to rest his chin upon it.

"There's a question I have been meaning to ask you, Mister Caleb," Bandy said in that small, quiet voice of his, barely louder than the rush of the water beneath them.

The man chuckled, bringing his hands together. "Caleb is enough, Bandy. But ask it, would you?"

Bandy's face screwed up as he struggled with the question. "Why?" It was a monumental failure on Bandy's behalf to get out all he wanted to inquire about, but Caleb was a man used to bridging communications.

He shrugged. "Why did I help you get on the ship?" Bandy nodded as Caleb went on. "I've done this for a few years now. Met all sorts of people, learned to recognise them. You find there are *types* of people when you look hard enough, and I don't mean the size, shape, and colour of them. I mean *who* they are. Not what." He did look at Bandy now, with his expression turning grave. "I've seen people that looked like you many times, I

151

have. They all had the same look... neither lost nor aimless, but lacking direction. They know what they need to do, but they don't know how." He watched Bandy a moment longer until the gnome tore his eyes away, then turned back to the water, shrugging once more. "You looked like any number of people on the path. Knowing where you needed to go, but needing the push to get you started. Was the same for me once upon a time, before I took up the sword and the road." He sounded wistful, his gaze clouding in memory, his scarred features softening. Bandy, however, bore an expression of great perplexity.

"I have no idea what that means," Bandy confessed.

Caleb's expression flowed into its natural grin and he winked. "It means I know an adventurer when I see one, and I'm looking at one now."

Bandy was taken aback. The very concept seemed nonsensical. "I am no warrior," he stated, the fact rather plain to see, but Caleb was dismissive.

"You can wield those tools of yours. You would not believe how often that can come in handy. Locks, traps, all sorts of things." He gave Bandy a speculative look. "And you are trying to find your father, aren't you? If you have nowhere to start looking, why not come with me? We can look together."

Bandy struggled with it, confused—and flattered. There were plenty of others on the ship that Bandy would have thought fit the bill far more readily than himself; other travellers and warriors. Caleb let him struggle with it in silence a moment, before gently patting the small figure's shoulder lightly.

"Take your time to think about it. We'll be in dock in a day or so. Plenty of time to mull it over." With that, he pushed from the rail, whistling to himself as he strolled below deck, leaving Bandy alone with his thoughts.

At first, his natural instinct was to decline outright. Caleb's tales spoke of danger and daring, of long, hard days and nights on the road. Bandy had never once had a mind for adventure and such an offer now sounded nothing short of madness—but there was more to it than that.

He reached into his coat, pulling out the letter his father gave him, and the Fatewatch also. He did not open it this time, only held it, feeling the strange sensations it imparted in his fingertips. Once again—for perhaps the hundredth time—he read the letter, and once again the conflicted feelings welled up in his heart. But as angry as his father had made him, he could not deny that he wanted to find him; maybe for no other reason than to give him a piece of his mind. It may have been anger, rather than a more pure motivation, but the end result was the same. Linked to that was knowing that the pursuit behind him was almost certainly ongoing; Lady du La'Corre would suffer no escape from her vengeance. It would not take much for her agents to track him down, especially since he had foolishly let his name be known easily enough without thinking of the consequences while still in a state of shock.

But this line of thought led into the more potent realisation that then crawled up into Bandy's brain, that Caleb had not *needed* to ask him. Indeed, as Bandy had already observed, there were far better choices to go along with than himself, and yet the man had made the offer, for whatever reason—had it been sympathy? Or worse, pity?

As he weighed it up, the ticking of the Fatewatch seemed to grow louder. He stared at the device for a time, then put the letter away, opened the Fatewatch up, and watched the twisting, turning hands. Feeling incredibly self conscious about the matter, he whispered a question. *"Do I go with Caleb?"*

A pause. And then, a soft *ping*, as the hands of the clock turned properly clockwise. The answer was given.

And so it was, when the ship arrived at landfall, man and gnome stepped from it together. Into a place that Bandy had never visited, with a companion he had only met a few tenday prior, and going on an adventure he had no idea how to handle. This sort of thing continued on for quite some time.

THE NEXT FEW months were something of a blur for Bandy. Caleb did the talking, the planning, and more besides—others joined them on their journey, a sort of loose congregation of fellow mercenaries and adventurers. Experts in the art of magic, or of the bow, or of the blade. There were ventures into old tombs and lost caverns, where Bandy's careful eye was needed to undo ancient, rusted locks—his tools for timepiece repair finding themselves being used in completely different ways that he would never have anticipated. Hijinks were had in catacombs and sewers, and Bandy was forced to learn how to keep out of the way when blades were drawn. He had thrown up after the first bloody fight when a group of bandits had set upon them on the roads, and again when they'd encountered some sort of hideous creature in the depths of a cave, which had a voice like thunder and a stench like a thousand year old privy pit. By the fourth such battle, he had acquired his own scars and the throwing up had ceased.

And through all of it, through every step, the Fate-watch had ticked, pinged and tocked him through it. Every single step of his journey, guided this way and that, by the ticking of the Fatewatch, kept hidden from them all except for Caleb.

For it had been Caleb who noticed that each night Bandy fell asleep staring fixedly at the face of the Fate-watch, the twisting hands turning in conflicting direc-tions this way and that as he tried to understand it. It was getting easier, in its way. Each time it got simpler to communicate to the Fatewatch, to *talk* to it. He had learned to use it with the traps, with the locks, and more besides—it had saved his life time and time again. And so he kept his distance from the rest of the party, and spoke seldom to anyone save Caleb. The quiet little gnome was ignored except when it mattered, and frankly Bandy preferred it that way. Each night he asked the question of the Fatewatch—was he going the right way in staying with them? And each time, it told him yes. And so he trusted it with his life entirely, and again and again, the Fatewatch pulled the group from danger. When they needed to know which road to take. When they needed to make a choice in who to trust. Each time Bandy had an insight that the others lacked that proved true. The Good Luck Charm, they started to call him, in lieu of actually remembering his name at times. But Caleb was worried.

He was smarter than the rest of them, and that in-sight he exhibited in their first meeting never wavered, until at last Caleb cornered Bandy on it. It had been eight months since the journey on the ship, and Bandy was at last learning to sleep properly without having nightmares of being caught by assassins wanting to claim the prize of his head. They had taken a job from a local lord to explore an ancient ruin in the depths of the mountains full of old secrets and mysteries, and claim any relics within in the name of his family that had once ruled there. The journey there had been simple enough, and surprisingly free of challenge. The rest of the group took heart in this and were cheered, but Caleb grew more wary as the journey ventured on. Something was weighing on him, and Bandy had thought it was that things were too easy before then. However, he was only partially right.

Bandy was tucked away in the roots of a tree, contemplating the Fatewatch in privacy. He could feel it now, closer than ever. The ticking and tocking of the winding hands moving in chaos and yet symphony. Each moment he stared at them he felt he was on the verge of some kind of grand epiphany, some magnificent understanding, and even if he could not reach it, the sense of anticipation was akin to an ecstasy in of itself. The sensation of the ticks flowed up his hands and into his mind, and even though they were not in that perfect rhythm that had once dictated his existence, he nevertheless found more and more comfort in them, even if they made things that once seemed normal become strange.

He was so absorbed he did not notice Caleb approach, but the big man was there with an expression far less jovial, much more careworn, and even strangely cautious as he stood with one hand resting on the tree where Bandy sat. "We need to talk, Bandy."

Bandy scrambled a bit, snapping the Fatewatch shut and putting it away. But Caleb had already seen it, even as he took a seat himself, amidst the darkening forest. "You've been spending a lot of time with that thing."

Bandy stammered a little, trying to ask what Caleb

meant with the stuttering stumble of a liar caught in the act, which made the man's expression shift to a grimace. "The timepiece, Bandy, if that's what it actually is. Whatever it is, it's worrying me. Where did you get it?"

Bandy hesitated. He still had not told him the truth of what the Fatewatch was. He had changed the subject each time and Caleb had not pushed the matter. But now he was throwing that aside and leaving Bandy cornered. Caleb had been kind to him, protected him— even saved his life more than once in the dizzying career Bandy now found himself. Should he tell him?

The Fatewatch let him know the answer. It ticked warningly, a softer tone rather than the sudden, a quiet but firm *tock* that tingled in his ears. But it was at war with the guilt in his heart, and for once the guilt won out. He shook his head, and started to speak. He told Caleb everything—who he was, and what he held. The entire story, from start to the finish, where they now sat, what he used the Fatewatch for—how it had helped Caleb, and the company he had formed, in their travels and adventures for all the months they had been working together. And Caleb listened patiently, asking questions carefully from time to time, nodding often as Bandy let the truth spill out.

When the torrent had run its course, Caleb was thoughtful, his expression speculative. "So far, the whole thing *sounds* all right, but I am still worried," he said grudgingly, with a broad shouldered shrug. "I know little of spellborn things, and that which is wrapped round with magic—which that clearly is." He exhaled as he came to a decision. "But I will not tell the others, even those that might know about such things. What you have there is precious, Bandy, and I would imagine anyone would want it if they knew what it could do."

Bandy swallowed, and nodded. The Fatewatch had been drowned out while he had been talking, but now it continually made a *tock, tock, tock* against his heart where he had placed it, each one a foreboding warning. Caleb pressed on as the tempering beat continued.

"So far, it has helped you, and that has helped us. I do not want to disturb that, especially right before we go off to do something as dangerous as we are about to do." A broad hand rubbed his stubbled jaw. "But I would ask you to be careful of it. Your father wrote a warning in that letter, where all this started. He told you not to open it, after all."

Bandy stirred, protesting. "It has steered us right so far. Every step of the way. We've managed so much because of it." He clutched at his vest as he said it.

Caleb saw the gesture, and held up both his hands placatingly. "I agree. Just..." he trailed off, for once not quite finding the words. He gave Bandy a long look, then sighed, his gaze lowering. "Just be careful, won't you? You spend too much time around that thing on your own. Maybe spend some time with the rest of the company? Get to know the others a little better? It will be good for you, I promise."

There was no warning tock or approving tick from the Fatewatch. After a moment, Bandy sagged, and nodded. Forcing a smile like he used to when he worked as a shopkeep, he responded, "I will try. I promise. After this job is over."

Caleb mulled this over, and seemed satisfied by it as he stood up once more. Holding out a hand to Bandy, who took it after a moment of hesitation, he hauled him to his feet. Caleb gave a grin then, the old familiar one that rang of sincerity and warmth before patting his friend on the shoulder, and Bandy relaxed. Everything was all right again.

For a little while.

THE NEXT DAY, everything changed.

The place was a maze, a labyrinth of puzzles and magical intricacy; old defences designed to protect something that was not meant to see the light of day once more. Secret doors and hidden passageways that the companions worked their way through, each time wondering if the price offered was enough.

They were hours into it, and each time they had been confronted by an obstacle, Bandy had been the one to overcome it. To turn left or right, as when he had first used it, was such a simple question compared to the intricacies he could now command out of the Fate-watch. Impossible conundrums were easily overcome as spell runes that Bandy did not understand, and did not need to, were shifted around and rearranged. The last one lay before him now. A massive room, ringed with glowing crystals, with a great iron bound door at the end. Everything seemed completely harmless, but there was a forbidding air of energy that lent caution. There had been enough puzzles before this part to easily explain that this was a trap, and the group had acted accordingly, taking extreme care.

A single rune-etched crystal lay before the door, set on a plinth. It was surrounded by a complex array of copper rings that could be shifted about with a touch. As the rest of the group waited, Bandy held the Fate-watch in one hand as he gently considered questions and waited for the tone. Touch this ring, turn it this way? *Tick.* Turn this one, touch the crystal? *Tock.* The rest of the companions waited patiently. The youthful mage named Ersi, with flame red hair and a thoughtful air. The elven archer Yeth'liu, who spoke little but saw much, lurking in the background. The two dwarven sisters, Hilda and Greti, who both adored Caleb and fought like lions with their armour and weapons, spending much of their time arguing with Yeth'liu in good natured rivalry. They all trusted Caleb—and since Caleb trusted Bandy, they trusted him too—waiting patiently and without complaint as the gnome worked with the same careful, patient air that he had used when working in his little shop, even humming to himself as he gently used his tools and his hands to manipulate the device and open the door.

"How much more, Bandy?" Caleb asked hopefully. He sat upon his pack to one side, hands clasped together, his expression attentive.

Bandy continued to work, but couldn't help but chuckle. "Nearly there. Couple more turns, I'm sure."

Caleb gave a sour grunt, but nodded. "I am going to have words with our employer after this. This was most certainly not worth the pay he was offering."

"If it was easy work we would not be the ones doing it, Caleb dear," Hilda said, in her musical voice that belied her powerful frame. She was idly polishing one of her axes, her keen eyes speculative. "Now let Bandy work."

Suitably chastised, Caleb quietened, and Bandy could not help but give another soft little chuckle. The man had been right. It had been good to get the secret out in the open, to talk to him and tell him what was really going on. One short night had gotten him to know his companions better, and he wondered now what he had been worried about all this time. He had friends. It was a new sensation, but one so comforting that when he thought back on his old life, he could not recognise it.

Another turn, another twist. The device clicked, and the crystal hummed, a note of passive assent, a musical tone like the gentle ringing of a bell. A thrum of anticipation went through the party, and the top of the crystal glowed brightly, lingering there. Holding the Fatewatch tighter, Bandy asked it one last question.

Should I touch it?

A pause. And then, very deliberately, a pinging *tick* that left no doubt in him. He exhaled, relieved, and turned to the others and grinned. "Got it." And with that, he placed his hand on the crystal, covering the glow.

There was a moment of pause. Bandy had expected the great door to start creaking open, but that was not what happened. Instead, the crystal he now had his hand on went dark, and all the others lining the walls started to glow. Rapidly growing brighter and brighter, as the humming changed in tone and became a whine. The chamber blazed as the light turned painful.

The air changed, charged with static. Bandy blinked, shocked, and managed to look at Caleb with a growing realisation of horror. The man saw it too and his eyes widened as he opened his mouth to shout.

It never came.

Whatever the spell was, whatever defence it was, it was sudden, swift, and absolute. A cascade of energy exploded outwards from every crystal. It was over in a flash, and at the end of that flash, where each of his companions had stood, there was now a falling outline of ashes, crumbling gently to the floor, drifting without wind. Between one instant and the next they had been wrought to nothing but memories. Nothing but names on the wind, unheard and unmade.

All of them except for Bandy. Who stood, blind in the dark, his hand on the crystal that had been both the lock and the thing that had saved him, while condemning his companions.

The world had changed once again for Bandy Fitzgibbon.

THIS TERRIBLE PARADISE
DAVE DEICKMAN

The sun had been swallowed by a burly head of thunderclouds; a great barrel of a storm pushed shoreward, to share the wrath of the ocean with the earth that so opposed the waves. The heavy scent of godly energy, of lightning charged and omnipotent, drilled at the animated surf. Aquatic and fish hunting birds fled the storm, allowing their prey to rejoice, fleeing towards the forests that mounted the headlands about a mile away, as an ominous darkness saturated the cerulean water.

When Sujin rose from the depths of the sea with a basket full of seaweed, kelp, and his fishing spear hooked to a redfish, he was surprised at how fast the world had changed in the time it took him to hold his breath.

"No, no," he muttered with dejected panic, in an almost chiding manner, eyes scanning the illuminated clouds, the rolling barrels that warned of a belligerent cyclone. Sujin knew he was in trouble. "Ayer and Ghophine, quit dancing."

The goddesses of the ocean and weather ignored

him, as they would; gods do not hear the demands of their creations.

All he had was his canoe, and it teetered on the verge of capsizing in the violent waves. The crests and crashes made climbing exhausting, the boat tossed about in the troughs. His fingers struggled to clench around the lip, even as he threw his bounty and spear in.

"Ydall!" Sujin shouted, whining, invoking the goddess of tranquillity, heaving his weight over into the belly of his boat. "Stop them!"

The mist sprayed his face as a wave broke, threatening to submerge the canoe. The shift of his weight, though unintentional as he fought for balance, lifted the canoe enough to save it from becoming a chalice of ocean water. He struggled for his splintered oar, working desperately to paddle towards shore, fighting the ocean. But the oceans ruled by Ayer and the winds of Ghophine had other plans, and he found himself at their mercy.

Struggling as he did, Sujin could not escape the violent swells. They lifted his canoe up and threw it against another wall of water. His items, though carefully packaged away, were tossed out. His basket of kelp and seaweed, his bucket of bait for the crab pots, even the succulent redfish he had planned to stuff with aromatics and roast for dinner had come off the spear, and all were cast overboard.

He howled at the sky, then focused on his survival.

His paddle dug into the water, but the currents pushed back as the rains pummelling him, blinding his view of the land. He would come out alive amidst Ayer and Ghophine's dance, or be turned into the embrace of Callath, the visage of death.

Fish leapt to the heavens, praising the mighty wrath

of the waves of their world, lightning dragging across the clouds the same way flint sparks steel, striking the ocean surface. Birds were grounded, then drowned, and Sujin knew he would be, too.

Praying would not save him, nor would paddling.

Sujin dropped his oar into his canoe, grit his teeth, and wrapped his arms around whatever he could to steel himself against the storm.

"You may not take me so easily!"

And the storm saw that as a challenge.

Salt water drained from his mouth, seafoam fizzing behind it, tasting putrid. Waves continued to punish him as though his beating had not lasted long enough. The roar of the ocean was mighty, and he could hear the waves end against stone, the sound so familiar to him that it reminded Sujin of home.

The taste of the seafoam, the salt residue left behind, especially upon his lips and moustache, the waves pressing against his body and lifting it into stone—these were enough to recognize life. His breathing was shallow and painful, and continued to pool water into his mouth. He could feel warmth on his face, however. A kiss from the sun. A blessing from Ejun should he ever recount one.

Though his eyes were closed, he knew he wasn't home. The warbling sound of the birds were foreign, not those he knew; long and colourful, proud—not these shrill shrieks. The water was warmer, and so was the air.

How far from Kettleheim am I?

Sujin opened his eyes.

It was agonising, a feat of strength to get them to cooperate, and pain raged as light speared him and rooted all the way into the back of his head. The light was brilliant, reflecting off of the calm ocean, but he was far more glad to see this than the darkness of death.

He rose, kneeling, hands planted against the jagged, water-carved rock protecting what he discerned to be shore with a soft, sandy beach several paces from him.

A cove, he realised. Circular, restricted from the ocean and studded by pointed rocks and spires. A bird nested on one of these spires, watching him for a moment before fluttering off to sea.

With a frown, he glanced at both sky and water. He might have been delivered from the storm, but certainly not comfortably. He supposed he was happy enough to be alive even if his body felt like a freshly cured blood-sausage.

Rising to his feet took more out of him than he had anticipated, and the water rushed to meet him as he failed to catch himself. This weakness was foreign to him, having lived most of his life on a boat, harvesting seaweed and kelp, fishing when times were tough, and stevedoring at Kettleheim's port when times were even tougher.

He had never been so battered by the ocean, beaten to a sheer fibre so close to death. It was almost unfathomable, but undoubtedly traumatising. He'd never felt so helpless in such a belligerent storm.

"Bloodshine mornings." Sujin groaned a crestfallen curse, finding his feet. Suddenly nauseous, he lost his feet once more when he hurled the contents of his water-logged stomach. His head throbbed and his throat was scoured raw by the saltwater. Suddenly, there was a sharp hum in his ear that left within seconds.

He groaned again, sloshing through the knee deep waves as he started towards the beach.

"Hello?"

A warble from a curious gull aloft in the breeze was his only response. The same bird from a moment ago.

"Bloodshine mornings..." he mumbled again, trudging through the water, his feet sinking into the sand. He took quick notice of palm trees that dotted the shoreline, accompanied by knots of foliage, the lonely boulders by a sandstone escarpment that secluded the beach. The shoreline appeared to not go anywhere. Though he was next to the ocean, he caught a faint whiff of marshland, or perhaps a bog or swamp.

"Where am I?" Sujin wondered aloud with frustration and awe, taking it all in from the waterline. His eyes panned across the vibrant and distinct layers of the sandstone wall, to the great leaves of monstera plants and ferns, the twisting brambles of shrubs and bushes. He turned around, gazing out into the ocean in full view of the emptiness.

How far have I been carried?

Mind both racing and blank, Sujin started towards the sand, looking to dry his clothes with hopes of finding fresh water and something to eat. As the waves began to recede from his feet, a twinkle caught his attention. Off to the side and to the right, a piece of glass reflected prisms in the sun.

His canoe. The glass were mere baubles for larger boats to see in the distance, tied to the bow, and the craft looked to be largely intact.

Ejun smiled upon him.

Sujin broke into a sprint, losing his balance along the way with a thirst more belligerent than a morning hangover. There were casks of water and wine chained to the canoe; he could see them. He could taste them, and elation debased his worries for a moment.

There, beside the casks, wedged in and stuck tight—his spear.

His boots!

Sujin yipped and howled joy as he clamped his hands onto the walls of the canoe, heaving it over the rocks and sliding it to shore, taking an inventory of what was still left every agonising step of the way. But as the joy wore and the endorphins waned, he began to groan as he dragged it; his body was stiff and tender, the sweat from his pores almost electrically painful, the bruises on his tattooed chest bullying his lungs not to draw a full breath.

When the canoe was far enough away from the tides, he fell to the sands with a long exhale. Moments passed as he laid as flat as possible to fill his lungs and stretch traumatised muscles, examining the near side of his canoe while he was there. Despite a mendable hole, and a crack that could be repaired later, the tool of his livelihood remained sound.

"Praise the rays." He bowed his head to the sun as he struggled to his feet again. His nerves resounded with echoes of pain, but the intensity was fleeting. "Boots."

They were still in the chest, albeit waterlogged, but that was a tankard of relief. These boots were too expensive to replace and too damn comfortable, if he was being honest with himself. Kettleheim's docks were notorious for their splinters and the subsequent trips to the healer. Some even considered them poisonous. He hated to think of having to walk them barefoot.

He now revered the sun and opened his arms in benediction, with the wincing to a minimum, and smiled. "Praise the rays." He felt delivered with a tale over ale in Kettleheim.

"Time to dry," he announced with rejuvenation, laughing. His voice carried across the crags of the escarpment and out to sea, hoping the gods that had put him here heard him.

"DIP ME IN ALE!" Sujin growled with astonished ferocity, his tongue like steel and his tone sharp. He reached for his nearly-dried clothes and boots near the fire, as a storm brewed in the sky. It came in a hurry from the last time he looked, or perhaps he had fallen asleep during its conjuration. "Another dance? At this time? Have you not been thoroughly entertained?"

Sujin was furious, already frustrated from discovering that he was trapped on an island, but the storm left a bitter taste in his mouth far worse than the seafoam he had inhaled on the rocks, and chastising the gods didn't seem so blasphemous at that moment.

He glared deftly at the sky as though he could do anything about it and pulled his canoe farther up the beach. The swells had reached his fire where he'd smoke-dried his clothes, beginning to drink the foliage on the shore, foam hissing and bubbling as it broke apart across the sands.

"I hear you!" he roared back against the raging thunder. Lightning sparked. "I see you! I'm off!"

Sujin ground his teeth as he started west towards an inlet he had seen earlier, with his clothes balled up and against his chest. A knife hung from a string around his neck. His spear and canoe would be fine.

He paused mid-step and reconsidered. There might

be fish along the inlet he could scuff up. He turned and went back, the rain soaking his dark hair and matting his knife-sawed bangs to his forehead, while the length behind clung to his neck.

The rain was cold, despite the day being rather humid and hot, and a driftwood fire was beginning to sound quite welcoming. Other than a few stalks of kelp that had wedged themselves in crevices in the canoe, he hadn't eaten, hoping that the inlet and the rocky overhang he had spotted would deliver.

He stopped again. The sack of wine. That was certainly coming too.

Spear, wine, boots, and clothes in hand, Sujin made his dash for the inlet. He followed the water that went inward, avoiding the barbs of urchins and shattered seashells scattered across the sand. The storm raged on, the winds pressing shoreward with threatening fangs in the swells. Lightning struck again with a blast of thunder.

But soon, the sand underfoot became gravel, then stone, and he found himself underneath a natural stone bridge where vines and roots coiled and tumbled down from the lush land above. Mushroom clusters collected upon the walls with velvety moss, and the water suddenly ended against a wavebreak formed by the island.

And there were bugs.

Mosquitoes and other pests whined about him, biting and antagonising, drawn in by the rain and the smell of fish carcasses picked apart by the birds. The stench was bothersome, but as he had expected.

But then he stopped his stride and, while about to slap at the annoying bugs, something caught his attention. His eyes devoured that which the island had hidden, receiving a sudden chill as payment for the view.

Here, as the sandstone rounded under the overhang and as the ocean was held back, were steps.

Dozens—hundreds—driving between a gap in the escarpment, carved by hand and heading up to the crown of the island.

"There must be saltwater in this wine..." Sujin reasoned with awe. Grottos were cut evenly along the length of the steps, and in them, frescos so indistinguishable that they could've been faces of gods and kings, or warnings of monsters and demons.

He began dressing underneath the bridge, out of the rain. His brown pants and azure shirt, orange sash where his wine-sack and belt pouches were harnessed, the epaulette made from fishing net and woven with seashells and worthless bronze coins he wore over his left shoulder, finally pulling on his boots—tall, light brown leather with copper plates over his shin and metatarsal.

After a healthy sip of wine, fishing spear in hand, he started for the steps, apprehensive at first until the rain became heavier and he was forced to retreat underneath the land bridge. The steps became slippery, then a deluge of rainwater river cascaded down them.

He didn't want to risk breaking his neck should the water take his feet, and Sujin resigned to wait, once more, for the gods to be done.

Without proper driftwood to make a fire, and soaking wet duff and kindle-fibres, he leant against the sandstone wall and continued to sip at his wine.

***

"WHAT IS ALL THIS?" Sujin whispered with wide-spanned wonder, as he tentatively crossed a wide plaza

171

where a mosaic had been placed painstakingly with tiny tiles. At his level, it just appeared ornate.

Fluted pillars encompassing the circular plaza marked a boundary between the swamps and jungles of the island, trying their best to push in. At the top of each pillar were carved statues of lanterns, with bizarre calligraphy where the flame had been impressed.

The plaza was entered at the top of the steps and exited at a great structure carved into the mountain. Cylindrical towers jutted along the slopes, some with purple windows to contrast the stone, or terraces and balconies overflowing with autonomous gardens that looked long forgotten. A row of rotundas were aligned centre to the plaza, with the largest one the entryway, and the smallest nearest the peak. Behind each rotunda, stone carved walls fanned off, ending at cliff faces with dedicated precision, and he had noticed then that the crag behind each set of rotunda and wall had been cut flat and deep, flush to the base of the next rotunda up.

There were no flags or banners, nothing to speak for proprietary occupation. Pirates were messy and that would've been seen quickly. It was like a castle or palace, a temple perhaps, or a monastery.

Sujin couldn't guess, but he had an overwhelming feeling that he shouldn't be here. It was almost a primal anxiety, like the moments before an ambush on the road, or spikefish watching prey from the coral reefs.

He whistled his admiration under the countenance of the sun, allowing the echo to let him feel not so alone, and found himself strangely reminded of when he worked as a labourer for a stonemason one winter. One season as a strong teenager was brutal enough; he discerned that this place had taken decades to build.

Is it elvish? Were dwarves involved? He knew both

to create beautiful architecture with painfully precise geometry, something to be admired over their long lifetimes and forever more.

But something about this place seemed different, out of order, as though this temple was caught somewhere between the maelstrom of arcane and divine.

But which god adored lanterns? he wondered, reaching for the addictive hackle leaves he kept in a small satchel inside of his belt pouch, shoving some behind his lip.

There was only forward to go, and go he would. He needed to repair his canoe and find food, and the sooner he got off this island, the happier he would be.

"Kettleheim," he said aloud with longing finality, catching himself suddenly reminiscing of the dark elf bar with the cuisine that flared his taste buds into total ecstasy.

Sujin held his spear deftly in one hand, so as to draw quickly, but not to alarm anyone that he was something more than a fisherman washed up on the shore.

He felt meditative, thoughts wandering but lost, save for a pallid stare. This place looked abandoned. Not a caretaker or a guardian idling by, which something of this magnitude would certainly have had. There were no animals, a cat to hunt the mice, or the mice themselves. There were no birds either, appearing as though to avoid this place on their path.

Sujin had heard of ruins deep out in the ocean, great temples from before time started counting, when mankind still held profound rites under radiant arcane moonlight; those stories also told how the temples were covered in so much guano that the walls appeared to be painted in lime.

Not here. Besides dust and wind erosion, it was pristine.

A chill swept across Sujin as he eyed the immense structure once more, knowing there was no option but to go in. His saliva appreciated as he sucked on the hackle leaf and he almost spat, but feared retribution of desecration.

So he swallowed the bitterness, which settled heavy in his stomach, and started forward, leaving the plaza with its marvelling mosaics and the fantastically straight fluted pillars. He ignored the dense foliage of the jungles that flanked the plaza until he reached the first step of the first rotunda. The foliage was now contained behind stone, megalithic walls, placed without mortar but with care, where wide railings of marble were etched in the strange calligraphy and ended by a stoic pair of stone lanterns, identical to the ones placed at the top of each of the pillars.

He inched his way forward, stepping lightly as he approached the portal, a triangle of a passage, where again, the writing appeared. This time, it was scribed in an iridescent paint that shimmered in the errant spears of light as the clouds came and went.

Sujin swallowed some more of the hackle leaf, feeling the chill of the minty bitterness hit harder than it should, and went in.

It was dark with looming shadows, which appeared darker in areas where it shouldn't, like the centre of the room. The floor was tiled—though ornate, it was not a mosaic—as it followed the circumference of the room and the walls were barren. Not even a torch sconce was mounted to these incredibly smooth walls. However, the dome of the rotunda was illuminated in a haunting purple glow, though the light did not reach down.

Across the round room, wide as it was long—and it was indeed long—another doorway led into the heart of the mountain. But it was dark, so belligerently dark that his mind saw faces in the gloom, filling him with apprehension and dread.

"Not without a light," he said with absolution, but was startled by how crisp and sharp his voice carried in these forlorn halls.

As his heart settled and his stomach soothed, Sujin crafted a crude torch from a branch, all the while praying that somebody would approach from the temple and greet him warmly. But that was not the case.

Sujin used a piece of his shirt and wrapped his kindling inside, hoping that the flame generated would be enough to light the stick, at least until he found a candle. Or a lantern. A temple adorned with them would surely have one within.

He groaned with apprehension, standing in the rotunda once more with light that could be barely counted as adequate and said into the dark passageway, "Hello?"

The only response was the echo of his own voice.

THE DARKNESS INFINITE, never ebbing, a total wax of blackness to where sunlight was something of a forgotten memory as time ticked onward and possibly backwards. Ever-encompassing. It flowed like a river from the pits of the underworld, or so Sujin thought as he cautiously felt his way through the passageways.

Blind.

The torch had died after he'd gotten lost, a wet spot of sap in the middle of the branch sipping the flame into extinction while he followed the maze of delicate carved halls. He had stopped as he noticed the light dying, his eyes almost wet with panic, as there was no turning back before it ran out. There were no markers save for featureless intersections, identical to the last, and he waited in the darkness for a long moment, wrestling with tumultuous thoughts as to what he should do.

Now, the head of his spear was Sujin's eyes, scraping across the stone floor in company to his apprehensive steps.

And there was silence.

Sujin could hear the thrumming of his racing heart in his ears, forcing the hair on his neck to stand erect. His mind conjured terrors from the edges of nightmares, but how much longer until he was within those edges? It was the only sound, beside the scraping of his spearhead and the heel of his boot.

Time was fluid, congested and then free flowing. He knew he had been lost in the darkness of this temple for hours but it felt like days, and the air inside was stagnant, disturbed only by his passage.

"Bloodshine mornings," he whispered, though it came out too loud and carried faster into the hallways. But there came a response. A voice. A harrowing moan, long winded.

Sujin froze, holding his spear close to him as he pressed his back to the wall.

Again, the moan. Sujin decided it was not human, not elf or dwarf, nothing belonging to any of the races he had met in his travels. This was something far more foul, and his mind couldn't even begin to picture it.

The moan went on longer than anything he had heard before, filling every corner of the passageways and tunnels, reflecting in here the same way light did in a seaside villa. A second rise in tone, as though it had gained breath without pausing. This time, deeper yet and he felt it rattle his bones.

Something had risen from its slumber and he had awoken it.

And it was definitely behind him.

Electricity cruised across every sinewy nerve and muscle strand. His bones felt a chill like no other from his own anxiety. He was shivering... quivering with insuperable terror and berating himself for foolishly bothering with this temple.

And without another thought, Sujin took off running.

He ran into the nothing with his bootfalls equal in volume to the moan, the grim voice inviting the gloom to grow darker, and so the voice grew closer—or so it had seemed.

Sujin was in full sprint now, passing intersections of which he could not see but sensed by way of sound and currents of wind all the while running into walls and curves. Many times he tumbled, ragdolling, rubbing his face across the coarse floor as it rushed up to take a bite at him too.

He had no idea if he were going up or down with obvious slopes, or if he was rounding the temple to end back up wherever this thing cried from. There was absolutely no light and it frustrated him beyond measure.

His lungs were on fire and sweat saturated his clothes, but his thoughts were only of survival.

I have to get out of here.

Damn repairing the canoe; he'd hold the hole closed with his boot and paddle his way to shore if he had to. Hell, he would lay across a piece of driftwood and kick his way there.

This temple was a foul, corrupted place and Sujin wanted nothing to do with it. He had half a mind to find the nearest paladin and alert them to cleanse this island. Let those so pious rain holy fire upon this dark temple and that within which cried so horribly.

But he wouldn't come back. Ejun, no, he would not, but he had to get out of here first.

There was considerable distance now. The moaning, though loud, reflected a chasm from him and he began slowing to a jog. His legs were burning with his lungs and throat, his face was agonisingly tender and he was sure he was bleeding from all the walls he had run into.

There was distance now. He took comfort as he strained to hear the voice in the darkness.

Sujin slumped against a wall, reached for his wine, and drank. "Can't fight what you can't see," he whispered ever so softly, just to calm himself in the dark loneliness.

AFTER CATCHING his breath and recollecting his thoughts, he continued on, trying to ignore the moaning from deep behind him. It was becoming as abrasive as gravel, feral almost. Ignoring it was a challenge, but one he needed to accomplish if only to retain any sanity.

The pathway was curving now—he could feel it, especially with his hand riding the wall, and the floor was sloped. Sujin was going up.

It baffled him that he had not found a single candle or torch, a lantern or lamp. His hand running across the wall had not discovered a sconce or even a small pocket where any kind of illumination could be cast from. It left him feeling the only explanation was magic. Perhaps the priests or paladins used some sort of night-eye or prismatic orb to navigate.

But why?

The confounding thoughts were as vexing as the incessant moaning and, truly, it didn't matter how they did.

Without another bitter thought to slow him, Sujin pressed onward, figuring he had rounded the mountain given the steps he had taken. He continued counting, weary and exhausted. The hunger of his stomach was proud once more, but there was nothing he could do besides suck on his hackle leaves and follow it with wine. He wished he had watered it as he did not want to be drunk in here.

As Sujin followed that arc around the next bend, he saw light. A tiny sliver on the wall, angled with particles of dust twinkling in its beam. It was so white it seemed holy.

"Light." The word seemed so foreign to Sujin now, a condition of reality that felt like a distant memory.

The mandibles of the darkness separated from around him. The light was intoxicating to look upon, and realising that it was actually there was equally astonishing. His eyes began to water, either from relief, or sheer agony as they had adjusted to the pitch.

He was almost free of this place now, free of its relentless labyrinth of obsidian aether. Free of all the images he thought he saw. That little beam of light was his liberation and he was running towards it now.

Sujin hit a wall again, almost going face first into it. It was a corner, a left-handed passage that ended at a doorway. His hands probed the door, feeling no splinters or worn edges, but a door handle and, down at the bottom, filtering in underneath in a tiny seam as though the door had almost fit the configuration of the frame... light.

His heart swelled with joy. He pulled the handle, and the triangular door gave, light filling the hallways behind him. As he turned back to look from where he came, his chest went cold, as strange calligraphy written almost ritualistically erratic across the corridor was revealed by the new light. It wasn't done like below; these were scrawled haphazardly with hysterical and belligerent madness.

In some places where obscure geometry was cut, in the bizarrest of shapes, a rusty dried substance had been pressed in with trawling lines, smearing across parts of the wall, and splotches stained on the floor before it. A chill swept down his spine and he stepped back with apprehension.

An incoherent invocation left his lips.

But as he looked forward through the door, he had discovered the ocean again. In his elation, or even relief, the roar of the ocean had returned to its usual background noise for the fisherman, and he was glad to hear it.

The sky was purple and red with scars of twilight drawn near. The sun was half submerged and the horizon burned like a wildfire with glassy waves of a calm evening.

He stepped through the doorway into one of the autonomous gardens lofted upon a towered rotunda, capped with a dome but otherwise open. Ferns and flowering shrubs crowded together into a beautiful garden. Vines curled around the pillars and were interwoven into the ceiling, flowering with blues and violets. A bird, long dead, was entangled in the bramble.

Sujin moved into the foliage, into a small clearing which the overzealous growth of the garden had not occupied, and gazed over the edge of the rotunda. He was higher than he had anticipated, missing several of the levels and other rotundas down below, finding himself to be at one of the highest tiers on the mountain.

If he were lower, he could have tried scaling down to safety, avoiding whatever it was down below howling in the darkness. A sudden spark of anxiety caused him to look over his shoulder, feeling watched, back to the doorway making sure nothing was standing there. A sense of dread spilled into him, like a tankard overflowed by a distracted barkeep. He saw nothing, but he felt someone.

"I should close that," he conferred with himself, then nodded approvingly. Sujin was apprehensive to step towards it again, as his mind feared something waiting there to reach out and grab him; but nothing did and his smouldering anxieties soothed once the door was wedged back into the frame.

He tried to see the mosaic for the clue to what this place could be, but it was hidden behind a dome, and quite far away if he were to guess. He couldn't even see the shore which he had washed up upon.

The clouds moved, the light changing. Something sparkled. He frowned, trying to decide if the sparkle was danger or just a symptom of his hypervigilance. He moved towards it, spear in hand, and used the tip of it to brush away a palm frond.

A sword. It was somewhere in length between a shortsword and a longsword, with a wider blade than he would expect, and a handle for two hands. Coloured glass spheres were strung off the back of the pommel. It was nothing special, and he didn't know how to fight

181

with a sword, but with the tight spaces down below in which he would inevitably have to traverse, a spear was too long to really do any damage.

He lifted the sword from the soil and examined its wire-stamped lamination, surprised to find it rust-free and considerably lightweight. However, the leather frog that would hold it had deteriorated in the weather.

"What other treasures are you hiding?" he asked the garden, beginning to move fronds and flowers, but finding nothing save for where the water pumped from down below fed the gardens. "Good enough for me."

He knelt, cupping his hand under the trickle, and drank. He sat up, letting hydration settle him. As he went for another drink, he saw it there; little purple knobs poking up from the soil. He frowned again, this time in disbelief. "No," he reasoned, as instant wealth attuned all of his thoughts. "Can't be!"

Brushing away the soil with his fingertip revealed gold lines in the mushrooms. The vibrant rich and royal purple, the gold lines with just the faintest hint of blue. Such a rare pattern of colour to find in nature, it had only to be one thing.

Prism-cap mushrooms! A whole harvest of them.

"Praise the Rays!" he shouted at the top of his lungs, followed by a sudden burst of laughter spreading across all corners of the temple complex. One of the rarest and most expensive mushrooms on the market, they were a key ingredient in dozens of wizard potions and sorceress rituals, not to mention an incendiary flavour enhancer. One of these could bring in more than his best crab pot catch and, as he looked across the ground, there were more than he could count.

He went to pluck one from the soil and paused.

"Ah, too good to be true. Don't get your hopes up, Sujin," he warned himself, and pulled the mushroom free.

At first he closed his eyes, wanting to savour that last moment of happiness after such a dismal day. He prayed that, even if these weren't prism-caps, they'd at least be edible.

An inhale, an influx of apprehension. He turned the cap over and opened his eyes.

Polychromatic spores hung in the air around the gills, glittering with a light of their own. His eyes watered as he held the mushroom up to the waning sunlight and watched how the head reflected the sun the same way as the glass baubles on his canoe.

Prism-caps. "Praise the Rays."

That first one went into his mouth, followed by a handful more. Sujin didn't even taste the spicy sweetness he swallowed so fast. He dumped out his prized fishing hooks from one of his belt pouches and hooked them to his harness, stuffing in mushrooms by the handful. But it wasn't enough for Sujin. He began weaving a bag from fronds, the way his grandmother had shown him, using vines to strengthen them. He hadn't wove since he was a child, under her strict eye and was surprised to see that he still remembered, laughing with himself along the way. One bag was woven, large enough for several more handfuls and he tied it shut.

"Could buy the biggest boat in the harbour with this... and a crew!"

Just need to survive. That resentful thought worked its way to the forefront of his mind. *Just need to survive.*

Despite the haunting reality of the passageway that led him here, Sujin found a small piece of serenity in the garden. He drank his fill of the water again, and rose when something else captured his attention, something he had missed while picking mushrooms.

A hole in the wall had been hidden behind a thrush of ferns—not from deterioration but design. He used the sword—the keenness surprised him—to hack away at the brush, discovering a narrow set of steps that ended at a wall flanking the mountain. He could see from a distance, amidst the fading sunlight, that there was another portal into the temple.

Behind the wall, in the safety of its own sanctuary, was a domed building with no obvious entryway despite the courtyard that surrounded it. Its top was glass, stained and of strange design, coloured a very dark purple with an abstract coil of gold connecting each fragment. Another garden punctuated the courtyard, but with large tree-like mushrooms. From what he could tell, there were others. Rounded structures with glass or metal rooftops, one spot reminded him of a redoubt—another looked to be a small castle within these vile walls.

The erratic writing on the walls behind him led him to believe something corrupt had fouled this place, or perhaps it was always dirty, as though exhibiting hubris in the worship of something profane.

The idea of the other rotundas and courtyards holding more of these little treasures excited him, but getting to them filled him with dread.

Sujin decided he would go there tomorrow. He had no choice now and, as for tonight, he would weave another bag, eat, and rest.

"Tomorrow's courage."

Suijin awoke to a terrible storm. The gales of a hellfire hurricane pressed against the temple mountain with the ocean's mist spraying even to his height, the wind buffeting the rotunda, ripping the bramble of vines down on top of him. The rain flew so fast that the droplets stung his exposed skin, even covered as he was under the bramble.

Sujin used his knife to free himself from the tangle, and hunched low as the wind threatened to pull him out and throw him to his death with its godly force.

Lightning struck the dome of the rotunda, then again, and a third time with a great cacophony of thunder so loud that he was momentarily dazed and deafened. His vision tunnelled with blackness on the peripherals, accumulated by helpless terror.

He looked up to see the metal of the dome super-heated and glowing red, like iron in the smith's furnace.

"Bloodshine!" he gasped in awe, never having seen anything like this and, though he had been caught in a belligerent storm that landed him on this island, Sujin would easily wager the harvest of prism-caps that this one was worse.

He needed better shelter, but he wouldn't go back the way he came. No way in all the Sun's kingdom.

The wind buffeted again, moaning ethereally from the depths of the ocean's girth. Fronds and flowers were ripped from their roots and thrown out across the temple and, as he looked through the dense storm, he could see the same happening to the nearest rotunda.

He heard a sudden crash, not thunder, but a collision.

There were voices over the wind now, and a deck bell toiling louder than the shrill wind; a ship run-aground. He looked all around from the rotunda but wouldn't see where. The bell was crisp and sharp, calling the crew to deck. He couldn't pinpoint its origin through the storm. The shouted words were indistinguishable, but anything living was better than what he had experienced.

The thought of safety flooded him faster than a boat with a hole, and he considered that he could possibly be robbed of his precious prism-caps, no matter who they were, but that was fine by him. Hell, he would probably even offer them as payment for a ride. They could even take this fancy old sword while they were at it.

He had to get to them, but he also had time. The ship would be stuck in the meantime with the storm, and the captain would likely wait until high tide to break free. The idea of people down below, no matter who they were or what nation they belonged to—not that that even mattered to Sujin were he not in a crisis—filled him with hope.

Sujin thought about going back the way he came but the more he dwelled, the more it was not an option. Not with that thing, and because he had no idea how he even reached this point. He found himself at the threshold of dismal thoughts and his imagination spawned terrors from the dark groves and ancient orchards of his mind, conjuring monsters and he wondered what else skulked deeper in this temple.

He wondered what else knew he was here.

The lightning flashed temporal lacerations across the sky and Sujin's heart sank. He would no longer stay here, he would get to that ship one way or another.

He would go forward.

Sujin grabbed his things, holding on tightly to his spear, shoving the sword behind his sash. His hand rested on the woven bags of prism-caps as he started for the stairs, bracing himself against the wind.

But the winds of Ghophine had intended to show him its strength and he was terribly impressed as he hesitated in stride.

Sujin was forced to crawl down the steps, like a toddler trying them for the first time, using the wall for protection. The rain fell like hail, pummeling him lower.

From his high perch, Sujin could see the fantastic swell of the ocean and the great waves forming as though to try and drown the mountain. Lightning struck the domes again, arcing between each of them almost laterally, as if they were transferring.

One of the rotundas, however, could not take the immense energy burnishing its metal dome, and collapsed. Stone toppled down, destroying one of the walls with it, and the thought occurred to Sujin of how strange it was that he should be here to witness that.

Perhaps the gods demanded a witness of the island's destruction. Or maybe it was pure coincidence. Maybe they were trying to kill him, so he could not go further. The will of the gods was a mystery to him.

They made the rules, they broke the rules, and they slayed the fools.

And Sujin felt like the fool now.

Lightning struck the rotunda he had just left once more, then again, three more times. He could see the roof had now melted and was dripping liquid metal as the heat became too great. It was enough to ignite the garden.

Sujin watched in awe even as the rain nearly blinded him as the gardens burned and found himself curiously smirking as he touched the pouch of prism-caps, "Burn it, I've already got the treasure."

Another strike of violent lightning wiped the smirk off of his face.

"Sorry!" he wailed to the sky.

He stayed low now, crawling along the wall in fear of both wind and lightning while grinding his teeth. Water pooled across the walkway, pouring into the courtyards below like a waterfall. Shadows danced upon each facet and facade, pirouetting as though the lightning would remind the sun who also created illumination and illusion.

Again, he heard the deck bell of that stalled ship and was reminded of his deliverance. He just needed to get there.

With a surge of courage—or perhaps bravado—Sujin hunched up to his feet, while still under the cover of the wall, and began moving faster towards the next portal at the end of this long walkway. The anxiety closed his throat, and breathing became a labor with his bruised ribs.

The wind pressed harder, the mist of the ocean spray rushing up and curling perpendicular as it travelled along the wall and over, as the rain drummed from the heavens against him.

He glanced back once to the rotunda, now totally engulfed in flames. A black spiral curled up and faded into the storm as the superheated metal dome burned the fresh foliage. When lightning struck again, he could've sworn he saw a figure standing there, staring at him, but it was gone when the lightning settled.

Panic grappled, breaking all rational thought, and the heightened sense of danger jabbed him in the spine like a needle. Sujin, without realising, took off running. He fought against the wind grasping every part of his body. It screamed into his ear like a banshee. Still, he ran, blinded by rain and fear, terrified of what that figure could possibly be.

This place fortified his superstitions, and he could not be reasoned with.

The wind screamed again and the lightning, issuing from the roiling clouds overhead, flashed with a blast of thunder. Sujin jumped as every inch of his body demanded release from danger, only to be caught by the wind and thrown from the wall.

He flailed, flying through the air, his voice locked in his throat and making not a sound as he landed on, and broke through, the nearby glass dome.

A GASP of air echoed in the dome as Sujin broke the surface of a pool of dark water, shocked to find himself alive and, as far as he knew, uninjured but certainly aching. Rain trickled in from the glass he had broken, the room only illuminated slightly by the lightning as the storm continued to rage. He could see the clouds trundling by.

However, he could in fact see. There was just enough light. There were no windows in this room except for the glass above, and in the centre was a small aisle with a footpath leading to a doorway lower than the level of the water. With each burst of godly lightning, he could make out more and more details.

At the centre of the aisle was a small pillar; an altar.

And on that altar, held in a fork, was a lantern.

Relief.

He swam closer, cresting the walls with all of his strength. He felt worse than when he awoke on these terrible elder shores. But now, he could have light. A lantern with a candle.

The lantern was odd in shape, octagonal with a pointed top and bottom. At the top, there was a chain with a knob made of some strange polished black stone, of which he assumed obsidian, but it felt heavier. At the bottom hung a ruby, whose clarity was so immaculate that a rainbow would shine through it even with the faint light. The chains that secured both obsidian and ruby were counter-woven with golden thread, snaking through each link and wrapping each loop.

It was long too—as long as his forearm.

The glass was a deep royal purple, held in place by beautiful steelwork touched in black patina. At the top and bottom, it was stamped with what appeared to be a floral or star pattern. One side was muted by lattice-work, while the rest bore the full fantastic purity of the glass. It was so smooth, made with delicate precision and care. He'd never seen glass like this before and, like the prism-caps, assumed it to be worth some money.

To him, it was worth more than money, that was for sure. Now he had light to navigate these wretched halls.

"Bet my kindling is soaked," he murmured, reaching for his belt pouch, fingers probing the contents within. His eyes lifted back to the hole he had broken in the roof and shivered visibly, not because it was cold, but because death was only a dice toss away for him.

Through the tight mesh of the pouch, Sujin felt dry fibres of wood, and relief flowed through him once more like the rain that trickled down from the top of the dome.

He was glad now that he had purchased these pouches with catfish-skin lining. Waterproof, that nomad said, and now he knew she wasn't lying. He set a small bundle on the altar, ignoring the calligraphy that surrounded the lantern perched upon a delicate fork.

Flint to steel, strike.

Sparks poured off the steel and into the kindling, which began smoking, another strike and Sujin began blowing until he had a knot of fire rapidly fading.

He opened the hatch panel of the lantern as the wind whistled and buffeted across the hole in the ceiling, accompanied by the cacophony of thunder as the lightning blasted with rage, and he lit the wick with the kindling.

Sujin watched eagerly as the candle began to take hold, shaking with anticipation to prove that the wick was still good. And it was.

The wick began to crackle as a tiny flame, a small needle-head of light holding, burning. From the flame came a snapping. It was ever so subtle, practically muted by the raging storm outside which seemed to shake the walls of the dome with each boom of thunder.

But instead of a small thread of smoke as Sujin had expected, a thin kaleidoscopic stream of flashing particles issued from the flame, and the candle—which was white—began to turn red as the fire warmed the wax. Sujin closed the hatch, confident that the flame would survive, and the light began to grow, as he muttered a little prayer, praising the rays.

The light radius began to expand and through the glass came a haunting purple light, something between ultraviolet and red but never maintaining a permanent hue. The polychromatic stream exuded from the star-punched holes in the top and bottom of the lantern around both gems, before fading off into eternity.

Sujin could feel the light fitting his face and though there was no heat, he felt warmth, security.

But that didn't last.

His eyes and attention were dragged away with unrelenting tension from the little flame as horrifying screams filled the dome. Painful and agonising, belligerent and woeful, screaming without pause of breath. And he screamed too, knees buckling out from underneath him.

The screaming was coming from all around now, and his eyes scanned but he could not process that which he was seeing. His eyes were damned and unreliable as, within the radius of this ghastly purple light—which reached to the walls of the dome and across the water—Sujin discovered he was no longer alone.

In congested assembly was a horde of screaming, flailing ghosts, their ethereal bodies made of the same light exuding from the lantern, and they wailed. Wailed in pain, faces empty except for an expression of pain and woeful agony, as though they had been called into an existence to which they no longer belonged. They contorted and twisted, shuttering in on themselves as though a current of lightning coursed through them. Some were slapping their chests though trying to restart their nonexistent hearts.

Their eyes were black, darker than the night, darker than tunnels he had walked, except for one. It—his—it looked like it was once a man, though his face was hidden behind a star-shaped mask; his eyes were like prisms of static and he did not scream. In fact, he held himself almost in elation as he stood tall, his head high as though joy washed over him, like a farmer seeing the first sprouts of a crop after a long drought.

Their outfits, a part of their ghostly countenance, appeared ancient, tattered though similar in design, and what he had almost expected to find donned on a cleric here. Some bore the marks of the murder that had removed them from the mortal engine. Their faces sunken and decayed, emaciated, brought back to life in the state from where they were buried in the earth.

However, the man in the mask wore nothing but a loin cloth, his feet bare except for the anklet and bracelets he wore, and a large, sundisc-like pendant with another necklace holding a curved knife. His body was tattooed in the calligraphy he had seen throughout this foul corrupted place, outside of the light and love of the gods. In the centre of his chest, over where his heart had once been, the lantern. The lantern was sunken into a crater over his sternum, a wound like his heart had been ripped out and his bones stitched back together in some post-mortem ritual. The lantern glistened as though matching luminosity to that which sat on the forks of the altar by some way of communicating, symbiotic magic.

They were tied together and the lantern on this ghastly man's chest began to bleed. It wasn't blood however, not in the physical sense of the mortal experience, but a gossamer plasma of prismatic light that dripped like molten rock spewing from the maw of a drooling volcano.

"Go away!" Sujin matched their shrieking, his heart bludgeoning his ribs with an intoxicating overdose of adrenaline.

The ghost started towards him in their agonising march, and Sujin began to swing his sword as though to ward them back. Their bitter howling deafened his ears and shook his world harder than the thunder.

But the ghosts approached, gazing at him with baleful contempt now that they had been brought to life, to be taunted by the air that filled Sujin's lungs, by that sweet honey which they could not taste. They surrounded him, some standing but others within mere inches of his face. He could see their once rotten teeth and their foetid tongues, gazing into their black eyes.

He could not look away from these ultraviolet apparitions; all he could do was tremble, beg, and cry.

Each time he met their eyes, he felt wrathful trauma, almost empathic, as though he was experiencing what brought them into this nether state of being.

This was clearly a temple to Callath, but none he had ever seen before, not like the altars in place to respect her role in the balance. This was total, monotheistic worship and fanatical.

He saw death by murder and ritual sacrifice. A woman who had been cut down when faced with the calling of her faith, the price set to the toll of her mortality. The pain Sujin felt suggested that she attempted to reconsider only to be cut down by another, while the ghost of a man to her side paid the toll willingly, feeling only joy.

Time moved forward but he saw in reverse.

He curled up into a ball as each ghost tormented him, trying with every count of structure to not look them in the eyes, but he was petrified by their incessant lamentations. The fear was so nauseatingly intense Sujin froze. His quivering recompiled into numbness but the faint electricity of his body tickled the fine hairs of his moustache, his only anchor to reality.

The ghosts took turns torturing him with selfish cruelty. Each set of despondent eyes of these ghosts passed in front of him and shared with him the incredible burden of their woe. What they did here in this terrible place had called something no mortal should be forced to endure. Their suffering was endless, but fueled by fanatical, religious zeal.

Their worship before the altar of the lantern was profound and profane, a total desecration of the world order hidden forever in these dark halls. All done for one purpose and each person served their purpose whether by will or by force.

Each person here used to... charge the lantern.

But why?

Eternity in seconds. Lifespans coming and going with no attributes of pausing. They kept cycling, each ghost trying to expose him and trying again. Each memory pressed into his foresight, focused on the lantern. The lantern in his hand. The lantern burning.

The man in the mask, this dark magician, paced behind these sacrificial sycophants in long gallant strides across water and stone, but his eyes were focused on the lantern, never breaking away.

Sujin sobbed hysterically, dejected and ready to die in misery, as he laid against the altar and finally closed his eyes.

SUJIN AWOKE TO MORE SCREAMING. In fact, the hysteria had never stopped, and in the wake of his dreams, he only saw the lantern. It lay on its side beside him, the candle still burning, never shrinking and now the ghosts had taken to circling him.

They followed a wide arc around the lantern, around him, wailing and sobbing in their haunting light. Some broke off to walk closer to him, others walked in against the flow of ghosts. The man in the mask walked a wider arc along the radius of light.

Sujin saw this and held the lantern over the water, threatening to submerge it. As it swung in his haste, ghosts faded and reappeared, but it wasn't as though a single ghost was left and entered existence in the light radius, but others appeared as though he were surrounded by spirits, visible only in the light; new ghosts screamed and demanded Sujin witness their truths and torture.

"Leave me alone," he demanded, as the ghosts began screaming more erratically. The man in the mask began to charge towards him, reaching for the knife on his neck.

He found a bit of strength, even as the ghosts began approaching him once more, realising fully and consciously that the lantern was their existence. He stood, holding the lantern, and as it swung on its chain in his grasp, the man in the mask, at the edge of the radius, disappeared and reappeared in the swing.

The man reached him and plunged his knife into Sujin's chest, gazing into his eyes with those static kaleidoscopes, searching for fleeting life. Those eyes, those burning, cruel misanthropic orbs.

But nothing happened. Sujin was unharmed, and now he realised that these ghosts could not physically hurt him as the man whose arm was elbow deep into his chest also learnt. He met the man with the mask's eyes once more and saw confusion, a perplexing conundrum as to how useless his situation was, that melted into a chagrined grimace.

However, Sujin smiled and almost chuckled, though his eyes regaled all the pain and trauma he was forced to endure. "Not so tough," he whispered half heartedly, almost victoriously, and he dunked the lantern in the water.

The ghosts evanesced from reality and he was left with a deafening silence. Darkness took the aisle again, but as he turned his tired and weary gaze to the water, he saw light. And his heart sank.

The lantern was totally submerged, water flooding the globe and the air bubbles had stopped babbling. But the candle burned.

Sujin let go of the chain, hoping the thing would sink, but it would not. And when it surfaced, so did the ghosts, screaming. Their plane of existence was now reduced by the way the lantern bobbed in the calm pool.

Sujin reached for the lantern, emboldened now that he knew they could not physically harm him. He intended to use the lantern to light his way out of this temple.

He hesitated, his hand stopped, now wondering what to do with it once he left this terrible place. Sujin's eyes panned across the room and the ghosts that kept him at the limits of his sanity. He felt agony—their agony. The lantern's existence was their own

Sujin decided he would go and see a cleric at the temple of Ejun in Kettleheim to cleanse his soul after this terrible experience. Maybe the cleric, too, could disenchant this lantern. He couldn't leave this thing to be found again.

He wanted no other to experience what he had, lest some treasure plunderer find themselves disappointed. Sujin realised he could just throw it into the ocean, where it would eventually wash to shore, and all the gods should damn him if it were discovered by a child.

That much he knew, and that much he would endure.

He lifted the lantern from the pool, smearing the walls of the room in that alluring sanguine red and ominous fantastic purple light. It appeared smoky now, with the way the water sizzled off of the warm glass, and the foreboding prismatic sparkles that issued from the flame of the candle protruding from the star-shaped holes.

The ghosts, in their pallid existence derived from their illicit faith, began circling him and the lantern again hypnotically. Their paths were erratic and mad, irregular and asymmetric as it was once before. The man in the mask returned, standing firmly in between Sujin and the whirling wall of ghosts with his arms crossed and glaring.

"How disappointing," Sujin said to him, as he stepped forward with an inhale of spiritual realignment, recentering by thoughts of warm sunlight and a smile from Ejun. The circle of ghosts moved with him but the man stayed still. His eyes, which were all that was visible of this man's former humanity, were volcanic and brooding. The same sparkling dust that filtered out from the candle pooled in his eyes in a way that almost resembled tears.

But that wasn't the case.

"I've waited ten thousand years for this moment," the man suddenly said, in a soft voice uncharacteristic of his body. The language that left his mouth was foreign and of a long forgotten tongue, but Sujin could understand him clearly.

Sujin was taken aback, surprised by the astral defiance of his man, and just how threatening he could be from this conjured image across the Divine.

"Who are you?" Sujin asked, pressed back up against the altar with fear. "What do you want?"

"Hycerax," answered the masked conjuration. "Let

us walk, but don't get lost," he taunted, turning his star-shaped face to the passage.

"Where will you lead me?"

"Lead?" Hycerax scoffed, "As you have learned, I am bound by the lantern with these blubbering apostates." He turned his glowering eyes towards the circle with disdain. "I, the only one of true faith, am forced to follow where you go." He bowed his head curtly. "So walk, else you will see things that will truly drive you mad."

Sujin swallowed, trying not to blink, trying his damndest to retain any ounce of strength and fortitude against the threats of this spectral menace.

"You give me freedom of choice, but it seems I do not have that."

Hycerax disregarded him, and said with venomous accusation, "I see what you are thinking, Sujin." Hearing his name spoken by that terrible tongue, only to be reiterated in words he understood, made him blanch. "You can't cleanse the Ghost Gaze lantern. No cleric in your world will understand it, and the mace of a paladin will merely bounce right off. No necromancer will continue to practise once they see what I offer. The magicians and wizards and warlords will shrink at its power."

"That feels like self-preservation," remarked the fisherman with a grimace. He let the lantern down and tried to stomp it with his boot.

"I just said you can't break it. Were you not listening?" The magician's hands slapped his thighs. "You're clearly not listening," he said, as Sujin tried the pommel of the sword, attempting to use its angled end to crack the glass, but it slipped right off.

"The gods will not allow this to continue to exist!"

he barked with frustration, as he tried cutting the lantern, sawing the blade of the sword across the glass.

Hycerax laughed, a terrible and throaty belly laugh, as he threw his star-shaped head back. "The gods are as useless towards me as I am to you. They cannot commune death as I have, not even death herself. I imagine she is not the same goddess that I once knew."

"Once knew?" Sujin spat. "Gods do not change. They are."

Hycerax shook his head. "Gods very much change. We are a part of them, of their design. All life is in their image, the elves who grow cold for blood at mankind's desecration of their woods, the dwarves drawn to violent and paranoid greed by the gems of their mines, the leaves that turn in autumn and the flowers that wilt and die only to return the next spring. Forget you not, dear fisherman, the tides under moon and star? We change. Do you think a little boy, once picking clams out of the surf, showered in the love of his family and light of his pious tribe, desired to wear the Ascension Mask when it fell from the heavens?" He gestured to the mask he wore on his face. "Do you think a simple man would invoke Callath and her subjects to draw this temple out of the Ayer's oceanic prison? Gods change. And I can tell, they have grown weak and hedonistic in their desires for worship."

"You're mad."

A chuckle, simple and affirming amusement. "I was once one of these fools." He spread his arms, gesturing to the screaming, erratic ghosts. "I have clarity."

"Clarity," Sujin scoffed. He had heard enough and started forward, finally remembering the ship that had run aground in the storm. He took the lantern with him, and so followed the circle of ghosts and Hycerax walking beside him, as though his equal, with a condescending stride.

The hallways spilled open with contained light, the walls scrawled in the strange writing but otherwise featureless.

"Why didn't the water put the lantern out?"

"Its candle and glass are charged by the fire of destitute souls," Hycerax answered simply. "The geometry was strong."

"Then why did it go out before?"

"Because I added my soul."

"What does that mean?"

His voice turned brooding and cold with frustration. "Turn left up here."

"SCARED OF WHAT COMES AFTER DEATH?" Sujin asked coyly, feeling bold as Hycerax continued to guide him along the cold hallways scrawled with the language and now, bizarre and intricate arcane geometry etched by muscle and chisel. It was iridescent as the lantern's glimmer, rubbed with some kind of magic dust.

"Scared?" Hycerax retorted derisively. "How ignorant. Scared is for children under the storm's wrath. Terror is for those apostates who follow us, clinging to the light as they try to get one simple breath of honeyed air. It's the thinnest veil between here and there in this realm. There is nothing to describe what comes after death and what you will see, foolish fisherman."

"So you're a lich then, and you're scared of death."

"Insolent child!" Hycerax barked with abrasiveness on his ethereal tongue. "Shut your mouth."

"You can't make me, we both know this. Everyone is

scared of death, but your sins must have been great enough to try and prevent it. You fear being judged," Sujin said with a commanding air of absolution. He was almost proud of himself, figuring it a good dig under Hycerax's skin.

"Your assumptions are beyond frustrating." Hycerax ran his fingers through the long locks of braided hair on the back of his head. "You are a godless man in a heretical time."

"How easy for you to say," Sujin remarked, turning and facing the star-shaped countenance. "Your thoughts are as lame as a horse. I praise the Rays, I always have. You, Ghost, have forsaken all that is above us." He continued, "How does one invoke Callath to draw a temple out of the water? How does Ayer give it so freely?" Sujin tapped the wall with his sword, realising only then that his spear was lost in the pool. It was as good as gone in his opinion; no way he was going back into the dome.

"Because they fear that which watches above the firmament. I wear the mark." He gestured to the mask.

"And what's that? Another god?"

"Something older than gods."

Sujin blew a raspberry of disbelief, growing bolder by the moment. The realisation that these spirits could not harm him helped drive his new, brash attitude. "There is no elder god. You just circumvented the rule of order, probably had your followers build this place. Because you are a coward."

"Coward!" howled Hycerax, charging up against Sujin until they were face to face. If Hycerax could breathe, Sujin would have been able to smell the foetid breath that fouled his words. Their eyes met and Hycerax's were vitreous. Hourglasses of illustrious sand and sparkles.

"See what I have seen."

Sujin felt himself being drawn into them, and images so profound began to flood his mind. How despondent the world appeared through the eyes of Hycerax.

The light after death. The void and its iridescent oceans, ebbed with stars that formed similar geometry that marred these cold walls of the temple, waning and waxing with luminosity. The stars formed vertexes and beams of light intersected, running parallel or perpendicular to form incredibly fantastic and complex shapes of brilliant celestial design. The ocean—of aether, not water—rippled with the continuum of time and consciousness and he was but a drop in it.

As Sujin gazed upon it, suddenly crestfallen, he began to feel the unmistakable pains of drowning, as though he was trying to reach the surface but only swimming downward into the pressures of the ocean. How serene it looked, and yet Sujin was filled with something deeper than terror. How bright it was, not sunny in any case, yet full of light and colour the like which he had never dared to dream.

As he drowned, Sujin felt something feasting upon him, drinking his soul in a slow and constant sip. He almost began checking himself for parasites, but it felt internal; he would never see the straw syphoning that energy from it.

And yet, how empty, this terrible paradise.

Alone with nothing but thought and the forever motion of time; an everlasting prison. There was something else here—he could feel that too, gazing at him from the ethereal canvas above.

And then the stars would dim, eclipsed by creeping objects hanging in the firmament. The geometry moved to create different shapes, and he felt nothing but a grievous chill. The kind of chill that came with insurmountable depression where the beauty of life, where laughter and joy, was lost. The colours grew dull and pallid, wilting like a flower in its august twilight under the greyness before a cold fall rain that heralded the coming winter.

Sadness. Desolation.

Anxiety spooled Sujin and he reeled back, back to the present to this dark place, blinking, not realising that tears had wet his cheeks. His heart raced, his face flushed, and he was left with cold and miserable thoughts that he was sure even death would not free him from.

The ghosts that circled erratically became more animated, wailing hysterically in bitter frustration of how close they were to living, yet how far away they truly were. He had seen where each one had resided until the lighting of the lantern, trapped without rest by Hycerax's hubris.

Sujin set back against the wall and slumped down, burying his face in his arms as he sobbed, grief catching him in its swell. He cried not for Hycerax or his pitiful sycophants, but for the fear that this was where those lost had gone. Those dearest to him who died in battle, drowned in the ocean, or passed with age or illness. Was there really something older out there? A focal point to the living and unliving plane? And were there other worlds out there just like this one?

Or was this place a mere response to Hycerax's mortal attempt to outwit the gods for eternity?

The latter made the most sense to him. It had to.

Sujin couldn't accept that such a cold paradise was all that waited for the pious and defiant.

"You see it now," Hycerax said with sombre victory.

Sujin's smouldering eyes met his. "You created it, coward."

WITH ALL OF HIS STRENGTH, Sujin pressed against the great iron and wooden triangular door. It was painted black but marked with massively precise geometric shapes, all glowing in the lantern's light which was now clipped to his belt.

He threw his entire weight into it, finally putting his back to it, and planted his boots firmly. He howled, body and mind screaming, as the door began to move, face red with strain as Hycerax waited patiently.

The geometric shapes began to illuminate, glowing brighter than the lantern itself, as the door began to open. A gust of wind whipped through with the scent of the ocean's iodine breath. He heard the crash of the waves pounding against the walls of the island and with it, he saw sunlight.

It had been long hours wandering those disoriented passageways, finding routes around collapsed tunnels and defiant portcullises. He wasn't sure how long, but as he rounded the doorway, opened wide enough just for him to pass through, he saw that it was morning.

The room, the largest he had been in, unfolded before him. The back wall behind a great throne had collapsed, giving a full view of the ocean. The dawn's golden honey filtered through the early morning fog.

There were however, no other windows, and in the ceiling, purple glass fragments similar to that of the lantern were suspended. Each glistened with scrawled icons and sigils of the intricate geometry, creating its own light. Four massive fluted pillars held up the mountain, delicately carved with the calligraphy, top to bottom, not a space free except around the strange single shape cut into each.

There came a guttural moan—the same moan Sujin had heard previously—and he noticed sitting in the throne was a body... with a star-shaped mask. The mask, in the colours of this reality, was metal, coloured goldenrod like a healthy field of grain. Despite the ages that had passed, the mask was clean, dustless.

Hycerax's body, however, felt the passage of time and had long faded into a gaunt, emaciated husk. Skin darkened into leather, the flesh at the fingers peeling back to the remaining cartilage and bone, and a knife—his curved knife—plunged into his chest at the heart. He was still in the same loincloth, with the same anklets and bracelets, but his tattoos had faded with the life of his flesh. Ratty, decaying hair coiled around his shoulders and the lower points of the star.

The body shifted in the seat slightly, raising its head with what little strength it had, and let loose another harrowing cry. It tried to rise, but couldn't.

"You're a failed lich," Sujin remarked, hearing enough stories about liches from paladins and clerics burning their way through corrupted tombs to know what he was seeing. He smirked, turning to the ghost. "You failed and you are a coward."

"If that's how you wish to view it. Taunt me all you wish, I have learned from my mistake." Hycerax answered coldly from behind. "Callath saw the moment I added my soul to the candle as a blindsided moment in my guard. She chose not to exalt me with immortality, fearing I would call that which they fear, and I chose to let her watch in horror as I created the arcane mathematics and hymns to navigate out of death. Liches are weak magicians compared to me. Callath extinguished the candle the moment my soul entered the flame, but she cannot do it again. The gods are too divided now as are their worshippers. Step forward, fisherman."

"I'm going nowhere near that!" Sujin protested, pointing to the animated corpse grunting and growling from its place.

"Step forward!" Hycerax raged, inching closer, threatening to plunge Sujin back into that terrible place. The circle of ghosts were spinning now, spinning faster until they became individually indistinguishable. They were animated, spiralling in and out of the light radius, and even out of the level plane from which they had retained.

The circle was now a blurred sphere.

Sujin stepped back. His foot crossed into the threshold of the room, and a fierce gale of wind billowed. The dust in the floor was disturbed, revealing a line with inscription painted here at the threshold—here where the lantern had crossed.

Hycerax moved forward towards his decrepit body. He moved out of the light radius but still existed. Pieces of his spectral form dispersed and flew into the pillars. The shape on each pillar began to glimmer and glow, the pillar itself vibrating with life and freeing dust that had layered it over the long centuries.

The glass hanging from the ceiling began to swing on its chains, with their geometry, too, growing in brilliance. The sphere of ghosts dispersed, though Sujin could still catch glimpses of them trying to break into this realm in the form of abrupt purple flashes.

Hycerax continued on, never losing pace, hyperfocused on the convulsing body, as though it felt this ethereal presence and demanded it. It shifted and howled in total animation, magnetised and desiring realignment.

Hycerax sat in the throne, and mind and body rejoined without ceremony or glittery light, but his purple frame faded to just a faint outline around the body—then disappeared from this realm.

And Hycerax inhaled, the noise abrasive and raw.

Sujin was stunned and awed, equally horrified and fascinated as the body became more fluid and dexterous, as Hycerax's lungs inflated for the first time in ten millennia.

Hycerax rolled his neck, exhaled and laughed. His voice boomed in the curved walls of the room, vibrated across each pane of hanging glass, overpowering the wind. The sun began to rise behind his throne, sending spears of light into the room. Ejun was the first to witness this resurrection, and saw his faithful follower there too.

Sujin drew the sword from his sash and held it defiantly, angling it towards Hycerax.

Hycerax spoke, but it was in his own ancient language. Sujin could no longer understand. He was barking at Sujin, rising from the throne and drawing out the knife that was plunged into his heart. The old wound was glimmering, the same as when he was still just a ghost.

"Best sit back down," Sujin threatened, taking the sword in both hands and holding it like he had seen a fighter do once. He knew nothing about sword fighting —he wasn't even sure he could hurt Hycerax.

Hycerax issued something else from his corrupted mouth and in a blink, charged Sujin.

Before Sujin could react, the emaciated husk wrenched his shirt collar in his fist and tossed Sujin, as though he weighed nothing, reminding him that he could now be harmed.

Sujin sailed through the air, arms and legs flailing. The lantern swung violently as it hung off his belt and the purple lights flashed sporadically. He hit the back of the throne, a solid impact, snapping the weathered backrest with the force of his mass, and rolled all the way to the gaping hole in the temple.

He cried out in pain, laying flat on his back, writhing.

Hycerax was already after him, knife held high to end his life.

In an agonising hurry, Sujin rolled to his knees, but could not stand. Instead, he scooted back against the broken wall, watching and preparing for his life to end.

But as Hycerax crossed the backside of the platform, beyond the throne, he stopped. Not on his own agency, but by force, as though an invisible wall contained him. He stood, confused, and tried jabbing the knife through, but attached to his hand, it would not go.

He glanced down. Sujin followed his gaze and saw that the same line he had crossed at the threshold circled past here.

Sujin released a soft chuckle.

Hycerax roared with belligerence and started his assault on the invisible barrier once more, stabbing with his knife but to no avail. In frustration, he threw it, but it missed Sujin by an errant gust from the sea and, to Hycerax's grievance, Sujin let loose a belligerent and insulting laugh.

Hycerax was panicking now, enraged by Sujin's

laughter, flailing his fists against the barrier that kept him, shouting curses from his old tongue.

Sujin sat quietly, wrapping his arms around his knees, and wheezing in pain. He glanced over his shoulder, and saw that it was just broad ocean down below. He would've jumped, but there were rocks.

Visibly unthreatened, the unbothered silence Sujin now held antagonised Hycerax even more. He raged against his walls with fist, feet, shoulders, and head. He threw himself against the invisible barrier with a furnace of murder exuding from his smouldering gaze.

Hycerax was moving now, leaping with deft agility to land on the broken throne with his arms raised high over his head. His fingers were wiggling and his eyes, no longer the haunting kaleidoscopic orbs, were fixed on Sujin with misanthropic darkness.

Words profound and venomous spewed from the large star mask and with it, the symbols on the pillars began to glow, transferring energy into a sphere that formed over Hycerax's head.

The sorcerer was going to kill him with magic, and Sujin could do nothing but watch. He was too weak, too damaged to just get up and run.

The sphere of purple energy, that dismal purple and sanguine red and every hue in between, formed above his head. It was huge. It sparked with astral electricity and the ghosts bound to the lantern wailed with agony as they appeared in full form again.

Hycerax said one final sentence, of which Sujin was certain was a cruel farewell, and released the sphere.

Unable to look away, Sujin watched as the sphere hit the barrier and exploded. The released energy blew away the throne and the stone around it, sending Hycerax flying back as well.

The line broke, the pillars splintered, and the mountain moaned.

Hycerax rose from the platform, surrounded by rubble, unbothered by what had just happened. He hadn't even bothered to dust himself off, or examine a clearly dislocated shoulder and broken collar bone, as he began to approach with murderous intent and stark silence.

The way his body moved with sobering and slow determination was menacing. He was savouring this moment, Sujin knew; the first flavour since the breath of re-life would be the flavour of blood.

Hycerax drew closer with daunting, intimidating steps, his eyes hyper focused and piercing, unbreakable and unavoidable.

They no longer communicated by words, as a mortal death seemed to have been the only unifying compliment between them, but now, no longer a ghost and retaining his bleak physical immortality, Hycerax spoke his threats with the language of his body, and Sujin, far too weak to do anything about it, save for an act of antagonising defiance, smirked.

The grin on Sujin's face was brittle and humourless, but it was a taunt of strength that, even in his weakest of moments, Sujin would not give Hycerax the satisfaction.

Hycerax crossed the threshold of the line, the boundary of the barrier, and froze with a sudden gasp. His eyes were wide, wider than the holes in the mask, and they were fixed on Sujin.

His hand reached out for Sujin, but his feet had stopped, and that was when Sujin saw it—the dust at his fingertips. As the wind blew, more and more of Hycerax's ancient body began to blow away, and Sujin realised in that fundamental moment that whatever profane barrier kept Hycerax in, had kept his body alive all this time, and now that was gone and so was he.

Tears formed in Sujin's eyes once more, tears of relief. Tears that washed away the horror. He was caught somewhere between laughing and weeping, witnessing the wind-bound destruction of Hycerax's body.

"Another miscalculation?" Sujin asked the crumbling husk. His hand sank below the wrist, the wrist to the shoulder. Knees before the feet and eyes only looking on helplessly, and in profound horror, until they, too, washed away.

The mask clattered to the floor, and the ghosts sporadically fluttered in the light of the lantern. With renewed but brittle strength, Sujin reached for the mask.

He took it into his hands and rose, groaning with numbing agony, recalling what Hycerax had said. Power throbbed through his hands as he held the mask, a power that equally fascinated and horrified him. It was intoxicating, and his body demanded to fully feel that power just as the mask demanded to be worn.

Do you think a little boy once picking clams out of the surf, showered in the love of his family and light of his pious tribe desired to wear the Ascension Mask when it fell from the heavens?

Was this mask the source of his power, or the root of his corruption? The idea of power terrified Sujin; magic terrified him. Magic was reserved for the gods, in his belief, and everything he'd seen on this island only served to reinforce that.

It didn't matter to him how Hycerax's condition centred on the mask, and he wouldn't be tempted by it. Sujin threw it as hard as he could into the sea, watching where it landed until the waves consumed it.

THE PLAZA no longer held its beauty, the pristine walls, or architecture. The fluted pillars carried a morose humour about them and the domes invoked terror. The mosaic was a calamity of artistic zeal pooled from the heart of religious fanaticism.

The gardens on the rooftops and domed rotundas burned from the lightning storm, and Sujin wished that the oceans would drink this place again, but he would settle for the work of the jungles.

The lantern was with him. He could not leave it, not now since the island had been discovered by yet another. Whoever had crashed in last night's storm would follow the screaming ghosts and find it... if they were brave enough.

The lantern was now wrapped in his sash, the ghosts silenced from their howling which had grown increasingly terrible as they tried to relish in the sunlight, another forlorn experience they so desired.

He stood solemnly in the sun, relishing in utter silence save for the natural world in its glorious light, in spite of the destitute ghosts bound to the lantern and that which they had fouly created.

He inhaled peace and exhaled anguish. "Praise the Rays," he offered aloud as he reached for the lantern, still warm in the wrapping of the sash. He began to unravel it, to allow the ghosts to bathe in glorious life-giving light.

As the sash fell away and the lantern exposed its light to the world, so returned the ghosts. Now, they were silent, no longer sharing space with the dark magician who had placed them within glass and candle, but they paced, walking the edges of the radius as though compelled to. Some wept, while others looked on crest-fallen, but none felt the sun—none even noticed it.

"I'll free you," Sujin said with determination, though he melted over such an overwhelming task, working the sash back around the lantern.

It was there in the plaza that he discovered a handful of tall, lithe figures silhouetted by the morning sun, approaching from the same stairwell that had led him here. Elves.

One approached, a woman and the obvious captain.

Her narrow and hawkish eyes locked with his, and when she read what his eyes had to show, they softened.

"I'm Captain Red-Feather, independent contractor of the Devsa Mercantile Guild. What is this place?" she asked him, studying the rotundas and the immaculate constructs. Her keen eyes focused on the fires and the flared out dome tops, then back to him.

Sujin looked once more at the temple then faced her. His eyes were glossy once more, words held in his throat, stopped by his own confounded agency. He was about to speak when Red-Feather produced a pouch and extended it out to him.

"Hackle leaf?"

Sujin glanced at it then back up to her. "This is a corrupted place. It should be forgotten. We should leave."

"I told you I felt something!" one of the elvish sailors shouted, with an animated flail of his hands.

"Silence! I felt it too," Red-Feather barked over her shoulder. She tucked away the hackle leaf, looking to the walls once more, and to Sujin, who was visibly disturbed. "You look troubled," she said with unrelenting empathy. "You look like a man who laughs in the face of storms. One sailor to another, I can see that. I believe you, man-kin. The sea we know, but it's the land that holds the true terrors, and this place reeks of it." She observed the temple with visible disdain.

"It's a terrible place. It needs to be forgotten," Sujin begged.

"As it will." She sniffed the air. "Some things should be hidden from money," Red-Feather affirmed, referencing the palpable greed of the Mercantile Guild and their endeavours.

"Come, man-kin, there are harder things to drink onboard and whatever it is you carry there"—she pointed to the sash, wrapped under his arm—"take it to the priests when we reach Citadel de Arcana. It smells wretched."

Sujin turned to the sky, as a strange feeling of observation took hold of him—not like he was to observe, but that he was being watched. His heavy eyes turned towards the temple, following it up to the spires, and towers, and to the stone of the mountain, but he wasn't satisfied.

A cloud passed before the sun and a thought crossed his mind, a spectre of light, temporal and visceral. The hair on the nape of his neck stood erect and he sensed... rage.

His eyes, wide and straining, turned to the threshold of the temple, catching a shadow within the shadows, a black void, like a fluid pillar of darkness. Spots and pinpricks began to open, ebbing the darkness with vitreous gemstones, shimming prisms too brilliant to endure. Each one of them was like an eye staring back at him from a sentinel beyond the stars.

Sujin felt the rage, the catastrophic tension bending and binding him where he stood. It permeated and toiled throughout his body like an illness with the heat of a forge. He was helpless and terrified, too stone-struck to even mutter a word to call out to the elves who had rescued him, hoping that they were also to witness.

But if the elves had seen it—seen Callath standing there in the doorway to that palace of spiritual pestilence—they said nothing. Sujin was too scared to pull his eyes away from the goddess and her form. Too scared to even breathe, as though the anger issuing from her would unleash against him like a dagger cutting flesh.

He felt the starlike studs of the black veil begin to focus, turning its gaze away from him and to the lantern so neatly packed up like a treasure. The stench of hatred filled his nostrils, a static to tenderise his spine and then, Callath turned her back.

A message.

The lantern felt suddenly heavy, and Sujin suspected it would for centuries.

THE CASKET

KATE LONGSTONE

Solarna pushed back the shutters and opened the only window in the small attic room that had been her home for the last few months. A steady stream of cold air blew across her cheeks, removing the last remnants of a good night's sleep. The breeze carried a hint of moisture and, above the rooftops on the far side of the market square, she could see heavy clouds moving in from the east, which promised yet another day of spring rain for Fairglade.

Leaving her room, she made her way down two flights of narrow wooden stairs to the kitchen. Solarna was the only guest in the tavern, but as she had been staying there for some time and had often helped out when they were busy or short staffed, the owner and his wife were happy for her to share breakfast with their family on quiet days.

Breakfast that morning was a simple affair—a bowl of honey-sweetened porridge, followed by a slice of hot buttered toast.

"Do you have any work for me today, Algaron?" Solarna asked the tavern owner, more from habit than expectation.

"I'm afraid not," he replied, tapping the old tobacco from his pipe onto a piece of yellowed newspaper. "There have been few visitors to town recently, and with all this rain, I don't expect that to change any time soon."

Solarna sighed, knowing this would mean another day walking through the rain trying to find work. Finishing her second cup of tea, she helped Leticia, Algaron's wife, clear the table and wash the crockery, before returning to her room to collect her bag and coat.

Fairglade was a large town, the last major settlement on the Great Farm Road before it reached the port of Whitehaven. Its location meant it had a lively trade market between early spring and late autumn, with produce going from the Carmonian farms and towns to Holfursland, and coal, ore, and gems travelling the opposite way. She had arrived last year just as the late summer crops were being sold—the fourth town she had travelled to in her quest for regular employment, after leaving her position as a scribe in the prestigious library inside Carmon Castle.

Since arriving in Fairglade, Solarna had taken whatever short term work she could find—however menial and poorly paid—which, with the occasional work at the tavern, meant some weeks she managed to earn enough to pay for her room and food. However, the bag of gold coins given to her by the Duke of Carmonia as compensation when he had regretfully asked her to leave his employment, had been getting lighter. Now, although she was happy enough staying in the tavern, the lack of regular work meant she was considering moving on again.

SOLARNA PUSHED OPEN the large wooden doors of the Fairglade Library and stepped inside quickly, just as the morning rain turned into a downpour. The library was considerably smaller than the one at the castle, and had been the first place she looked for work when she arrived. The main librarian had been very kind but, although she had been impressed with Solarna's knowledge and previous experience as a scribe, had been unable to offer her any work. She had, though, agreed to let Solarna use the library for a few hours each week to continue her studies—even waiving the usual fee.

Solarna removed her damp coat and placed it on the stand next to the doorway. The loud drumming of rain on the windows above the main doors broke the usual silence inside the building. Spaced along the entrance hall were marble busts of early Fairglade mayors standing on circular plinths of stone. Double doors on each side led to two large rooms that occupied most of the ground floor. She walked past them towards the grand desk in the centre of the hall. On either side were stairs leading to an upper floor balcony, and the small rooms containing the more scholarly and specialised books that Solarna preferred.

As she approached, Solarna smiled at the grey-haired woman sitting behind the desk.

"Hello, Berenice. Has it been busy this morning?" she asked.

"No, only Old Tomas has been in today. Everyone else has been put off by the rain, I suppose," Berenice replied.

Solarna had just started to climb the staircase, when Berenice called out to her, "Oh, you might want to take a look at the notice board first."

Turning around, Solarna walked back to the entrance. On the left of the door was a notice board. Some of the messages pinned to the wood behind the glass had started to yellow with age, so it was easy to spot the pristine piece of paper which had recently been added. The sheet was covered in words, drawings, and symbols, within an ornately decorated border, apart from an enclosed box at the top of the page. Bold capital letters proclaimed:

TRANSLATOR REQUIRED

Underneath, amongst the elaborate markings, were four heavily stylised lines of text, each written in a different language to the common vernacular used for the heading. Despite the flourishes, Solarna instantly recognised the first two sentences as Dwarven and Elvish. The third line she thought could be Draconic, although she had only briefly touched upon this language while studying at the castle. The fourth and final phrase was in a script completely unknown to her.

"It's perfect!" she shouted to Berenice.

Walking hastily to the desk, she stopped when one set of double doors were pulled open by a man with a well-groomed white beard, wearing a shiny leather waistcoat.

"What's all the fuss about?" he asked.

"Sorry, Tomas," Solarna replied. "I've just seen an advert for a translator. Just the job I've been hoping for."

"Well, try not to make too much noise about it," Tomas said. As he returned to the reading room, he smiled at her, "Good luck, lass."

Trying to suppress a giggle, she made it to the desk before Berenice's smile forced it out of her. Composing herself, she quietly asked if she could take the note upstairs to copy. Granting permission, Berenice handed her a small silver key, indicating she should open the cover and take the note for herself.

After carefully removing the notice from behind the glass, and returning the key to Berenice, Solarna made her way upstairs to her favourite area of the library. Situated at the front of the building, it was the only room that had windows in two of the walls. Decorated with delicate iron work, they allowed plenty of natural light, which Solarna preferred when working.

She placed the advertisement on the large oak table and, taking a pen, ink and paper from the battered leather satchel she always carried, began to make a copy.

Solarna had always had an eye for detail. As she worked, she noticed that, although the heading was parallel to the top of the paper, the other lines of text were not, and would slope upwards or downwards, in an apparently random manner. Many of the pen strokes were thicker, thinner, or slanted differently to usual, and the letters they made contained flourishes and small illustrations. She copied everything exactly as it appeared on the sheet, as she had been taught to do by her tutor at the castle.

"Never assume you know better than the creator of a work how it should be presented," he had repeatedly told her in his soft Elvish tongue. "Every dot on the page could carry a significance you may not be aware of."

She smiled at the memory. Femian Vernys had already been master at the castle library for over a century when she began her studies, and she had been hugely surprised when he had selected her to be his pupil—it was a great honour not often bestowed upon someone from her humble background. Once they'd become better acquainted, she had queried why he'd chosen her, and had blushed when he replied that he had been impressed by her accuracy and attention to detail; traits seldom seen so developed in someone so young.

Satisfied that she had replicated the advert, Solarna took the original back to Berenice, then made her way to the library's language room. Although she had recognised some everyday words in the Dwarven and Elvish phrases, each line also contained words she was not familiar with. She soon found comprehensive dictionaries for the two standard languages, and placed them on a reading table, while she searched for books to help with the remaining text. An illustrated calligraphy guide confirmed her suspicion that the third line was Draconic, but yielded no possibilities for the fourth. Unfortunately, the library in Fairglade was not as extensive as its counterpart in Carmon, and the only books in Draconic she could find were a collection of poems written two centuries ago alongside their common translation, an illustrated recipe book, and a gardener's planting guide.

Taking the books to her desk, she picked up a blank sheet of paper and set to work. It did not take long for Solarna to establish rough translations for the first two lines, but she did spend time double checking, as the phrases written on the advert were grammatically incorrect; they read:

Locate my dwelling written here
Knock thrice noon Thumnir's Day

Forgoing lunch, Solarna worked on the Draconic line late into the afternoon. She struggled with the tome of poetry, which had been written by a low ranking royal, and whether due to their age, the skill of the original author, or the manner in which they had been translated, did not read well. She had not expected to be able to complete the translation, but luck had been on her side; one of the poems had concerned a young prince who had been set a task by his intended wife, to bring her a flower for each colour of the rainbow. The other volumes had surprisingly yielded the remaining words:

Bring rose wine mud bark sausages

Returning to the language room, Solarna spent another hour searching for anything resembling the final line of the advert... without success. When the rays of the descending sun broke through the clouds, making her squint, Solarna realised the library would soon be closing. Gathering her belongings, she made her way downstairs, where Berenice was still sitting at the desk; behind her the elaborate clock on the wall showed two minutes to six.

"I'm sorry, Berenice, were you waiting to leave?" Solarna asked.

"No, we never shut early, even if there's no one else here. I'm glad we have someone taking such an interest in the books, it makes a nice change." She smiled. "Did you find what you were looking for?"

"Yes... and no. I've translated most of the notice, but it doesn't make much sense. Do you know who placed the advert?"

"I'm afraid not. The note and payment were sent in a sealed package with a covering letter, but it was unsigned—it could have come from anyone."

Thanking Berenice for her help, and for allowing her to stay in the library for longer than usual, Solarna left to return to her room at the inn, her mind puzzling over the meaning of the strange note.

ALGARON HAD no work for her the following day, so Solarna returned to her room after breakfast to study the advert again. There were still two days until Thumnir's annual feast day, so she had a little time to try and solve the conundrums posed by the advert—who needed a translator and, more importantly, where could she find them?

She tied back the curtains to increase the amount of natural light in her room, even though it meant draughts of cold morning air. Seating herself at the small table opposite her bed, she had barely settled in the chair when her concentration was broken by the sounds of laughter outside. Looking down from the window into the rear courtyard, she saw the butcher's boy flirting with Algaron's daughter, having delivered the daily order of fresh meat to the tavern.

Whether it was the disturbance outside, or viewing the parchment from a different angle, but as she returned to her seat, the way the letters had been joined underneath the last Elvish word suddenly seemed to resemble a string of uncooked sausages. Scanning the rest of the line, the word for 'wine' appeared to have been embellished to form the shape of a bottle.

Completely side-tracked, Solarna spent the next half hour turning and tilting the paper, gazing at the page from different angles to search for further hidden symbols. In the end, she had identified over a dozen icons concealed within the lettering and border design, including a fish, a book, two crossed swords, and a pair of hands clasped in prayer. What she had *not* been able to establish was any meaning or reason for their inclusion, other than the whim of the creator. Nor was she any nearer to discovering who had posted the advert, and how to locate them.

Frustrated, and in need of some fresh air to clear her head, Solarna decided to return to the library, hoping to find some indication of the language used on the final line of the advert, as she was convinced this contained the missing information she needed.

In contrast to the previous morning, the weather was unusually fine for early spring, so she took a longer route to enjoy the warmth of the sun, walking along a street where food vendors displayed their goods outside their shops. There were rabbits and game birds hanging from rails above the butcher shop window, behind which choice cuts of meat and rings of sausages were carefully arranged. She smiled, waving at the young lad who had been at the tavern that morning, as he added fresh sawdust to the floor. Next door, the fishmonger had fillets, shellfish, and crustaceans resting on ice alongside whole fish. She was outside the wine merchants when a thought struck her—the three shops were represented in the same order as symbols on the advert. Retrieving the document from her satchel, she lined it up with the shops. A little up and to the right of the wine bottle was a book, just where the library was. The symbols weren't random doodles at all—the advert concealed a map!

Solarna continued to the library, and, after exchanging pleasantries with Berenice, went upstairs. Taking advantage of the elevated view, she was able to match several more symbols on the advert to prominent buildings in the town. There were a few icons still unaccounted for on the map, and Solarna decided to spend the following day walking through the town to try and identify them—hoping that one of them would indicate the location of the creator of the advert.

With her plans for tomorrow set, she spent a fruitless two hours in the language room looking for matches to the final line in the advert, before returning to her room at the tavern.

SOLARNA LOOKED at the map she had made from the hints given in the advert, checking that she hadn't made a mistake somewhere, as this *couldn't* be the right house. The cream paint on the walls had started to peel in places, several shutters at the front were hanging from their last remaining hinge, and the windows behind them were long overdue a thorough clean. The garden was another matter though. The flower beds lining the path to the front door were tidy and well planted. Neatly pruned bushes and shrubs filled either side of the garden, and the sound of birdsong resonated from the varied trees lining the garden borders.

This had to be it though—Solarna had eliminated all the other possibilities the previous day. The crossed swords had indicated a weaponsmith's shop, and the pair of hands had marked a small temple shrine dedicated to Holfur, used by the many visitors from Carmonia's neighbouring region on the other side of the White Mountains.

Placing the map in her pocket, Solarna approached the low iron gate. As she rested her hand on the latch, she noticed a jagged line within an oval carved into the top of the wooden gate post—the image she had identified as marking the location of the mysterious person looking for a translator.

The gate creaked as it opened, and she had to brush small pieces of rust away from her hand after she pushed it closed. Her feet crunched on the gravel as she approached the entrance. A shaft of sunlight illuminated the doorway, revealing the same symbol scratched into the stone lintel. Solarna took hold of the worn brass knocker, fashioned in the shape of a bird with outstretched wings, rapped twice in quick succession, and waited.

Solarna heard faint scuffled noises from inside the house, but as no one came to open the door, she knocked again.

"Don't be so impatient, I heard you the first time," a female voice called from inside. "I'll be with you shortly."

Solarna straightened her clothing. She wanted to make a good impression, and hoped that her attire did not look too worn. Leticia had helped her repair and freshen the best of her existing garments, but they were still items bought while she was working at the castle library.

Eventually, the door was opened by a woman with dark auburn hair pushed back from her face, wearing a plain dark green dress. Around her neck was a leather thong holding a number of animal and plant shaped charms. In one dirt-stained hand, she held a small garden fork and trowel.

"Hello. Can I help you?" she asked.

"I'm here about the translator job," Solarna stuttered. She had been expecting an old professor, similar to those who had frequented the library rooms in Carmon, not someone who looked like the gardener. "The one posted in the library."

"Oh. Is it Thumnir's day already? I hadn't realised. Do come in." She moved aside to let Solarna enter, and pointed to a door on the left of the hall. "If you would like to go into the study, we can talk there."

Solarna had to avoid a pair of old leather boots and a couple of plant pots that seemed to have been abandoned in the hallway, as she made her way to the indicated study.

A sharp burst of cold air greeted her as she opened the door and went inside. Her host placed the tools on top of the plant pots, quickly wiping her hands on an old cloth, before joining Solarna in the study. "Please take a seat in the chair by the fireplace. I know not everyone likes to feel the spring air as much as I do," she said, placing a small log onto the fire.

Solarna sat down, grateful for the warmth. Mindful that her satchel contained the wine and sausages, she placed it beside her so the chair would shield it from some of the heat.

"Would you like some tea?"

"Yes, please," Solarna replied.

"Lovely. Make yourself comfortable, I won't be long." She left the room, closing the door behind her.

While she waited, Solarna examined the room. There were large bookcases on each wall, crammed full of leather-bound volumes in a multitude of mismatched shades. Solarna approved of the way the large wooden table had been positioned below the room's only window, which was slightly open.

Her host returned bearing a tray laden with a china

teapot, matching cups and saucers, and a plate with several slices of fruit cake.

"I'm sorry if I appeared a little surprised when you knocked. There weren't any applicants the previous times I placed the advert, so I really wasn't expecting anyone this time either. I'm afraid I'm not that prepared."

She settled into the chair by the desk and leaned forward. "Perhaps I should start by introducing myself. My name is Tanitha Hopbeck, and I have dedicated my life to the compilation of all the history and lore relating to a subject very close to my heart. Many of the books containing this knowledge were written in languages not familiar to me; hence I have been searching for the last two years for a suitable translator to assist me."

She settled back in her chair and smiled at Solarna. "Now, please tell me a little about yourself, and why you would like this job."

The glow from the fire, and the welcome Tanitha had given her, helped Solarna relax a little. "My name is Solarna Nialice, and I'm originally from Carmonia. I studied in the library at Carmon Castle under Femian Vernys. I arrived in Fairglade last autumn, and I've been staying at the Summer Rose Tavern, helping out where I can, while I try to find work more suitable to my knowledge and experience."

"Femian Vernys!" Tanitha exclaimed. "You must have been a very promising student to have been assigned to him. But the library is very prestigious, and it is very unusual for a student not to finish their studies there, so... why did you leave?"

Solarna had been dreading this question, and had been unsure what she would say, but she felt a warmth and openness from Tanitha that suggested honesty would be best. "There was an incident with one of the Duke's sons," she began, shuddering a little at the memory. "Afterwards the Duke called me to his office. He was very kind, and said he knew it wasn't my fault, but he didn't want there to be another period of rumours and scandal surrounding his son. He decided it would be best if I left town straight away, and gave me some gold to help me get settled elsewhere. I have a reference from Femian, if you'd like to see it."

"No, the fact you could translate my note is proof enough to me that you have the abilities I require." Tanitha picked up a pile of papers from her desk, and began to flick through them, producing a copy of the advert. "Were you able to translate all the lines?" she asked.

"All except the last one," Solarna replied. "I'm afraid I don't recognise that language."

"I would have been surprised if you said you did." Tanitha smiled. "That was a little test of your honesty."

She replaced the sheet of paper on the pile and stood up. "These are the books and scrolls that I have collected over a lifetime," she said, gesturing to the packed bookcases all around the room. "Many of them are very rare and valuable, and as I said, written in languages I don't fully understand. Your job will be to translate them for me, without taking them from the house or speaking to anyone about them, as they contain some sensitive and highly sought after information. Do you understand?"

"Yes, I do," Solarna said quickly.

"Good. I'm afraid I can't pay you very much, but as you would be required to live here, your meals will be provided, and I think you will learn a great deal while you work, much of it that you wouldn't find anywhere else." Tanitha smiled. "Are those terms acceptable to you? If they are, I would be delighted to offer you the job."

"Thank you! Those terms are more than generous, and I'm happy to accept your offer," Solarna replied, then, remembering the items she had been asked to bring, asked, "But what about the wine and sausages?"

Tanitha laughed. "We can have those for dinner tonight, after you've returned with your belongings."

———

SOLARNA LEFT the market square and headed to the lane containing the butcher, fishmonger and wine merchant, to purchase the last of the items from Tanitha's weekly shopping list. The afternoon sun shone high in a near cloudless sky, and a welcome breeze whistled through the dark green leaves of the broad ash trees lining the road.

It was the last midweek of the month; a day Solarna could spend in Fairglade pursuing her own interests, providing the groceries were acquired. As usual, she had wanted to make the most of the opportunity, and had spent the morning in the Fairglade library, studying the effects of volcanoes on local wildlife, focusing on the area near Teclusis. She had taken time to catch up with Berenice over tea and scones before walking to the tavern to have lunch with Algaron and his family.

On the menu was one of her favourite meals, chicken spiced with mud thyme, and Solarna had even allowed herself the luxury of a small glass of safflower wine to accompany it. The family had been pleased to see her—Algaron had light-heartedly asked her if she would have time to help at the tavern during the upcoming festival, and his wife had given her a warm embrace as she left.

It had been fifteen months since she had moved in with Tanitha, and, although Solarna was kept busy, it was work she very much enjoyed. As well as the bookcases in the study, there were two rooms upstairs whose walls were lined with shelves full of books and pamphlets, with new additions arriving each month. The majority of the collection seemed to fall under four main categories—histories of the various countries and peoples of the Western Shield world, detailed studies of plants and animals, the mythology and beliefs of the realms, and various magic related spells, recipes and incantations. All of these subjects interested Solarna, and Tanitha had been right; she had learned a great deal while translating the myriad works.

Reminded of how she had first met Tanitha, Solarna added some mud bark sausages to her order in the butcher's shop before beginning the walk home. As the weather was particularly pleasant that afternoon, she decided to walk alongside the river that ran through Fairglade, in the hope of spotting one of the kingfishers that nested along the bank. Passing through the backstreet behind the shops, she heard footsteps coming from the adjoining path just ahead. She paused to wait, and two men entered the alley. After scanning the passageway, they walked towards her, stopping a few feet away.

"Good afternoon," said the taller of the two men, casually stroking his closely cropped beard. "You are the new apprentice of Tanitha Hopbeck, are you not?"

"I work for her," Solarna answered. "But I'm not her apprentice."

"Well, it matters little for the business I wish to discuss with you," he replied. He pulled a kerchief from the pocket of the dark purple robe he was wearing, and mopped his brow. "Please, tell me what you know about the casket."

Solarna glanced behind her, checking to see if there was anyone else in sight. There wasn't.

"I'm afraid I don't know anything about a casket," she said. "I haven't seen one in the house, and I don't recall Tanitha ever mentioning one to me either."

"I doubt it is in the house, my dear, she is far too shrewd for that. Perhaps she hasn't told you about it yet, but please be aware that I'm very interested in obtaining this casket you claim to know nothing about. If it should come into your possession, or its whereabouts become known to you, please let me know. I will reward you handsomely if you do." He stopped to wipe his brow once more. "However, should you decide not to help me with this endeavour, things may become a great deal unpleasant for both you... and your mistress." He smiled and motioned at his companion, who was leaning against the far wall. A large, heavily set man with dark blonde hair, wearing a long beard tied at either end with a leather thong, he casually drew a sword from his belt and began cleaning it with a soft cloth.

"You understand what I'm saying?" the first man asked.

Solarna nodded.

"Good, then we will leave you to continue your journey." He turned around, nodded to his accomplice, and they left by the same path from which they had arrived.

Solarna sank to the ground and waited for her breathing to return to normal. When it had, she walked back to the shops, wanting to get home as quickly as possible—all thoughts of the river gone from her mind.

———

SOLARNA WAS PUTTING the groceries away when Tanitha came into the kitchen quietly behind her.

"Did you have a good day?" she asked.

Solarna dropped the sausages she was holding, and her hands trembled as she stooped to pick the brown paper wrapped package from the stone floor.

"What's wrong?" Tanitha asked, "You're shaking like a leaf."

Solarna started to answer, but had to choke back a sob.

Tanitha put a comforting arm around her. "Leave the shopping for now," she said, her voice soft and reassuring. "Sit down, and I'll make us a drink."

Solarna had managed to calm her breathing by the time Tanitha placed a pot of tea on the table and sat down next to her. "Now, tell me what happened."

Solarna began relating her encounter that afternoon, and had just finished describing the two men who confronted her, when Tanitha interrupted.

"Rasden."

"What?" asked Solarna.

"Rasden Kaymar," said Tanitha, rising from her chair and beginning to pace around the kitchen. "That's the man who accosted you. The swordsman is Bulvar Hauss. He carries out most of... the more unpleasant tasks for Rasden."

Puzzled, Solarna asked, "But how do you know him?"

"He's been after the casket for years. At first he offered money, then, when I wouldn't agree, he started making threats, harming the animals I was looking after." She stopped pacing and sat back down, and Solarna could see tears forming in her eyes. "And then he attacked my assistant."

Tension gripped Solarna's body. "What happened to them?" she asked softly.

"He survived, but he couldn't work for me anymore. I gave him what money I could, and had a friend take him somewhere safe."

"What did Rasden do next?"

"I didn't wait to find out. I gathered what belongings I could carry, retrieved the casket from its hiding place, and fled. I moved from town to town, never stopping in one place for too long, until I arrived here. I thought I had heard the last of him, but it seems I was wrong."

Solarna started to pour the tea, giving Tanitha the chance to recover before speaking again. "So there *is* a casket," she said. "I haven't seen it in the house or heard you mention it before."

Tanith looked her in the eye and took a deep breath. "Yes, there is a casket. It is very old, and I am the latest in a long line of guardians chosen to look after it. You haven't seen it because it's not here. I hid it in a safe location. You haven't heard me talk about it to keep it secure, but also to protect you."

"So it is safe then."

"For now, but if Rasden knows I'm here, and is feeling bold enough to confront you in public, I fear what he may do next."

She was still shaken by the encounter earlier, and Tanitha's revelations had done nothing to reassure her, so Solarna did not want to hear what that might be. Instead she asked, "Why did he think I was your apprentice?"

Tanitha looked at her and smiled. "I had hoped to make you my apprentice in time. I think it is a role you are well suited for. It's traditional for each guardian to train the next one. The advert, and the translating I have given you, were both testing your aptitude, and preparing you for the role. Assuming you want it, of course."

"I would be most honoured to accept," Solarna said. She had been hoping an offer like this would be made; she liked Tanitha, the work was interesting and informative, and the house felt like home.

"Good. Now that's settled, we can decide how to deal with the threat of Rasden."

Tanitha rose from her chair. "Come with me. There's something I want to check."

Solarna followed her up two flights of stairs to the attic. It wasn't a room she had spent much time in—only visiting to collect books or documents from one of the many boxes piled on the floor.

Tanitha picked her way to the far wall, and slid a small wooden panel to one side, revealing two tiny shafts of light. She leaned forward to peer through the holes, then beckoned Solarna over.

"It is as I feared," Tanitha said. "There are two men outside watching the house. They're hiding amongst the trees. Can you see them?"

She moved out of the way so Solarna could take a look. There, positioned either side of the house, hiding behind dense shrubs, Solarna spotted them. Wearing dark clothing, it would have been near impossible to see them from the road.

Tanitha closed the panel, and then they checked

similar concealed viewing points in the other walls. Neither of them could see any other watchers, so Tanitha suggested they return to the study.

At the foot of the stairs, Tanitha stopped suddenly and tilted her head as though she was listening to something in the distance. Shaking her head she turned to look up at Solarna, took a deep breath and sighed. "Well, that changes things," she said. "It seems it's time to retrieve the casket. Perhaps that is why Rasden has appeared... maybe he knows more than I thought."

"Are you alright?" Solarna asked. "What just happened?"

"I'm fine. There is a bond formed between the guardian and the casket. It is difficult to explain, but it means I know now is the time to act. Follow me."

Tanitha went into the study. Taking one of the books from the shelf, she removed a piece of paper from inside the cover, and handed it to Solarna.

"This is a rough map showing part of Stonefall Forest, where it meets the foothills of the White Mountains, far to the north of Fairglade." She pointed to a symbol scrawled on the map. "This marks the location of an old ruined tower, once the home of Archmage Theonis. It was abandoned after he died in the fires that followed the Great Drought. Very few people even remember who he was, let alone where he lived. I hid the casket there."

"You want me to go there and get the casket?" Solarna asked.

"Yes. The journey will be hard, and you may need to pass through a number of obstacles to get to the casket, but I am confident you can do it." Tanitha placed her hand on Solarna's shoulder. "I have great faith in you."

Solarna took a deep breath. "When do you want me to go?"

"As soon as possible. Rasden knows where I live, that you work for me and is having the house watched. If he thinks you will tell me what happened today, we can assume he also expects, or even wants, me to flee again, either with or towards the casket."

Tanitha sat in the chair by the fire and laced her fingers together. "So that is what I'll do. I will set off in the afternoon, in a different direction, to lure away his men. That should leave the way clear for you to depart later, under the cover of darkness." Tanitha looked around the room. "There are a few things we need to do before we leave, but be ready to go tomorrow evening."

Solarna nodded her head in acceptance. Just as she was becoming settled, her life was yet again being thrown into turmoil, with another sudden departure into the unknown.

THEY SPENT the morning preparing dried food, before having lunch—the last meal they would have together for some time. The rations had been added to the packs containing spare clothes, and the other assorted items that she and Tanitha had decided would be useful on their journeys.

"You know which town to go to, and how to find me when you get there?" Tanitha checked again, as she adjusted the straps of her travel pack.

"Yes, I'll be there," Solarna replied, more confidently than she was feeling. They had gone through the details twice that morning, and even though she had never been to Whitehaven, she only had to follow the

White River to reach it. The difficult part would be retrieving the casket and staying clear of Rasden and his men.

Tanitha took an iron amulet attached to a leather thong from her pocket. "Take this," she said, offering it to Solarna. "If you encounter any dangerous animals on your journey, hold it in front of you, walk slowly making no sudden movements, and it should protect you from them."

Solarna took the amulet from Tanitha, who hugged her tightly. "Good luck," she said, "and remember, whatever happens, don't try to open the casket." Releasing her from the embrace, Tanitha opened the door and left the house. When she reached the gate, she made a show of looking up and down the road, before turning to wave goodbye to Solarna.

Solarna stood waving in the doorway for a few seconds, before returning inside and closing the door behind her. Hurrying up to the attic, she watched Tanitha, who walked briskly along the road leading to the coast. Shortly after Tanitha had disappeared from sight, both of the men emerged and followed the path she had taken. They stopped when they reached the turn that led to the centre of Fairglade. Solarna could see them gesticulating at each other, before they split up—one of them continuing in the direction Tanitha had taken, the other heading back into town. Satisfied that the first part of the plan was working, Solarna went downstairs.

She spent the remainder of the afternoon trying to rest, but her thoughts kept drifting back to the last time she had had to leave in a hurry, with just the possessions she could carry on her back. With Tanitha's assistance, she felt better prepared this time, but the scale of the task was daunting, and she hoped she was ready to undertake the challenges ahead of her. She cooked a substantial meal in the evening, partly to use up the perishable items in the larder, but also because she knew it would be a considerable time before she could get a decent meal again.

As the sun began to set, Solarna returned to the attic, and was surprised to see two figures concealed amongst the foliage. She noticed one of them was somewhat shorter than before, so she assumed the man who had gone into town had returned with a different colleague. Solarna decided to delay her departure. Waiting until the half-moon had climbed high into the summer night sky, she slipped out of the back door instead, setting off down the narrow lawn at the rear of the house.

Picking her way slowly through the garden, she tried not to disturb any of the birds and animals resting in the trees and bushes, in case it alerted the nearby watchers. Exiting by the wooden gate that marked the boundary of Tanitha's land, she ran for the edge of a wheat field, towards a small copse of trees. Staying under the cover of the interwoven branches, she waited until her heartbeat slowed and her breathing returned to normal. Then, once she was certain that no one was following, she moved on.

She walked through the night, crossing fields full of ripening crops and grazing land dotted with huddles of cows or sheep. The lights of Fairglade gradually faded into the distance behind her, disappearing entirely when the land dipped as she reached the banks of the White River and headed upstream.

SOLARNA MADE good progress following the river, as it meandered through the sparsely populated lowlands. She stayed each day in whatever shelter she could find, travelling through the night to avoid both the sweltering summer sun and the possibility of detection. After a few nights walking, tall grasses and reeds began to dominate the river edge as she entered the fens that occupied the land preceding Stonefall Forest. As the river narrowed, she switched to walking during the day to avoid becoming stuck in the more treacherous marsh areas, periodically spraying her skin with lemon water to keep the myriad swarms of flies, gnats, and mosquitos at bay.

Finally reaching the forest, she was grateful for the shade the tall ash trees provided, although the steepening banks of the narrowing river meant she had to regularly divert along the many game trails leading to and from the water.

When she reached the first of the waterfalls that gave the river its name, she turned away from the roaring cascade of water and started to climb up the chain of ravines and gullies that Tanitha had marked on the map.

The day was drawing to a close when Solarna reached the top of the waterfall. Stopping to rest on an outcrop, she was about to move deeper into the forest to set up camp for the night, when she heard the sound of voices below. Crouching down, she peered over the edge of the rock, and was startled to see a group of five men approaching, one of which was Bulvar. Quickly standing up, she dislodged some stones. Frozen in place, she watched them slowly cascade downwards, landing near the group beneath her.

Bulvar looked directly at her. "Solarna!" he shouted. "Wait there for us. We mean you no harm."

Solarna did not wait. She ran into the forest, only slowing to a brisk walking pace when she couldn't run any more. Her face and hands were scratched and bleeding from the branches and brambles she hadn't stopped to move aside, but she kept going. Using the moon to guide her in roughly the right direction, it was past midnight when she spotted an opening halfway up a rocky incline ahead. Needing a rest, she decided to investigate.

The area immediately outside was clear of vegetation, allowing moonlight to partially illuminate what appeared to be a small cave. Solarna approached cautiously, and a strong musky smell gradually filled her nostrils as she ventured inside. Standing just inside the entrance, she waited for her vision to adjust to the gloom. Ahead, she could suddenly see several sets of eyes staring at her. One pair moved closer to her, slowly revealing the pale grey form of a wolf.

Remembering the gift from Tanitha, she pulled the leather thong over her head. Dangling the amulet from her fist, she held it in front of her. After sniffing the charm for a few seconds, the wolf rubbed its muzzle against the back of her hand, and then walked around her, brushing its fur against her legs.

Solarna stood still, while the other animals in the pack followed the example of their leader, before returning to the back of the den. The presence of the animals calmed her. Feeling safe in their company, she moved near them, placed her bedroll on the ground, and lay down to sleep.

SOLARNA WOKE THE FOLLOWING MORNING, with vague recollections of a dream chasing rabbits through the forest. She felt her cheeks flush as shafts of sunlight brushed them. Stretching her arms, her hands met warm fur—the wolves had positioned themselves around her during the night. Careful not to disturb her sleeping companions too much, she got to her feet, and gingerly made her way to the side of the cave. Retrieving her water bottle from her pack, she moved to the entrance. She stepped outside and peered around, but to her relief, there was no sign of Bulvar and his men—the only indication of life was the cacophony of bird song celebrating the recent dawn.

Returning inside, she chose a piece of dried chicken and a hunk of bread for breakfast. The wolves began to stir from their rest, and Solarna broke off small pieces of the meat to share with them.

While she ate, Solarna pondered if Bulvar had been tracking her, or if he had somehow found out the location of the casket. Either way, she decided the best thing to do would be to get to the casket as soon as possible. Studying the map Tanitha had given to her, she estimated it would take another two days of brisk walking to reach the ruined tower.

As she was getting ready to leave, the wolves pushed past her, towards the mouth of the cave, their hackles rising. Solarna realised the birds had stopped singing, and the forest outside was strangely silent.

Then she heard a male voice, "She went this way."

The pack leader ran outside, followed closely by the rest of its brethren. Solarna went after them. At the foot of the incline, she could see Bulvar and his men. The wolves were rushing straight towards them. Taking her chance, Solarna turned away and fled up the slope. She could hear the howling of the wolves intertwined with shouts from the men behind her, but she did not look back. The sounds gradually faded away as she descended the other side of the rise.

Her flight last night had taken her away from the route she and Tanitha had originally planned. She had been meant to follow the river a while longer, crossing over an old stone bridge before heading higher into the foothills of the mountains. Now, in a bid to throw off her pursuers, Solarna decided to keep going in a more direct route through the denser part of the forest.

Regularly checking for any sign of pursuit, she kept moving throughout the morning. She ignored the more well-trodden paths and game trails she passed; eventually reaching a tributary of the White River. She walked along its bank, until she spotted a small stream of water trickling into the river from a narrow rocky ravine further along on the opposite side.

Removing her walking boots and socks, Solarna entered the river. Wading slowly into the middle of the river before turning upstream, she tried not to disturb the gravel bed. The water reached halfway up her calves at the deepest point, pleasantly cooling her feet as it rushed by. Reaching the gully, she continued barefoot, moving carefully from one algae-covered rock to another, until she reached the top, where a bubbling spring broke the surface of the stream. Kneeling, Solarna cupped her hands to take a drink; the cool water had a slightly mineral tang, but still tasted fresh and soothing. Her thirst quenched, she filled her flask before leaving the ravine, taking care not to disturb the multitude of paw and hoof prints that had been left by the denizens of the forest in the muddy bank.

Although the canopy of trees above her grew

thicker, there were still enough gaps in the leaves to allow her to navigate using the position of the sun. Whenever the trail split, she tried to take the narrower, less well travelled path, while still maintaining the same overall direction.

She stopped for a rest and something to eat as the sun began to set. The trees had started to be more spread apart, allowing Solarna to see more of the hilly terrain in front of her. There was no indication that Bulvar's group was nearby, but she didn't want to lose the precious advantage that the wolves had granted her, so she decided to continue walking through the night. The fear of being caught overriding any tiredness she felt.

SHE REACHED the outskirts of the fallen tower not long after dawn. Climbing the remains of a perimeter wall, she scanned the hilly terrain she had recently walked through, searching for anyone following her trail. Relaxing slightly when there was no one in sight, Solarna had a sparse breakfast before continuing into the ruins.

Entering what had once been the tower grounds, Solarna immediately noticed a significant increase in the density of the vegetation. Tanitha had said the area had been given a 'magical helping hand', to dissuade anybody passing nearby from getting too close to the casket's hiding place. Nearby crickets chirped, as she pushed her way through the banks of long grass and clumps of nettles, which filled the gaps between overgrown shrubs and bushes.

Reaching a small orchard, she grabbed apples, pears, and peaches from the overhanging branches as she passed by. Placing them, along with a sample of the abundant blackberries, raspberries, and wild strawberries growing nearby, in an improvised basket made from a spare shirt.

Eventually arriving at the remnants of the tower, Solarna was nearly overpowered by the scents of the climbing plants adorning the remaining walls. Yellow honeysuckle, white jasmine, and roses in a variety of pinks and reds, fought for space with long strands of ivy. The main building had been circular in design, but now only the jagged edges of the lower parts of the walls still stood upright. The ground floor entranceway had long since collapsed and been buried under rubble, so Solarna climbed the cracked stubs of the stone staircase spiralling around the outside of the tower, until she reached the doorway to the first floor. The stone arch was still intact, but the door itself had rotted away, leaving only the rusted hinges behind.

Before moving inside, she tried using her vantage point to look for anyone following her, but the trees were too dense—at least no one would be able to see her. She did notice, however, that she couldn't see the path she had taken to the tower; the plants she had bent or broken pushing her way through had reformed to their original positions.

Solarna went through the entrance, onto a small stone ledge which circled the inside. A few rotten beams jutted out, hinting at support for a long vanished wooden floor. She moved slowly around the edge until she reached the opposite side, where the remains of a stone stairway led to the ground floor. Descending slowly, she tested each of the cracked and broken steps to ensure they would take her weight. Her caution was rewarded on two occasions, when she stopped herself from falling as the crumbling masonry gave way beneath her feet.

Reaching the bottom, the stone floor was barely visible, covered in weeds and brambles. A few small trees and shrubs had even managed to take hold in the more open spaces. Solarna soon found the huge piece of masonry that Tanitha had told her obscured the entrance to the floors below ground level, but it took some time to clear away the flora and soil clinging to its edges, to reveal the area where a familiar oval design had been carved onto the stone.

Following the instructions that Tanitha had given her, Solarna dug soil from under the marking until she could place her hand completely inside and clench her fist. Taking a small leather pouch from her backpack, she retrieved a large seed from inside, and pushed it carefully into the earth at the base of the hollow she had made. The pouch also contained two unmarked, almost identical, tiny bottles. Picking up the one with the green top, Solarna measured three drops into the lid. Gingerly, she positioned the cap above the seed, and then tipped the liquid. Removing her hand, she resealed the bottle, gathered up her pack, and moved away from the stone's edge.

At first nothing happened... but then Solarna heard a sharp crack, followed by a low rumbling sound, as the edge of the stone started to rise, revealing a sapling sprouting upwards from where the seed had been planted a few seconds ago. She watched for the next few minutes as the tree grew several feet tall, holding the slab in its branches, forming a steep slope above a rectangular opening in the floor.

Once she was certain the tree had stopped its magical growth, Solarna moved to the edge of the hole and, using the branches to aid her, dropped onto the stone staircase below. The light entering from either side of the opening illuminated the room she was entering. Roots from the plants above dangled through the ceiling, brushing uncomfortably against her hair as she descended.

The steps ended in the centre of a large rectangular room. Storage racks lined either side, and standing against the far wall was a stack of small wooden barrels, which Solarna walked towards. She moved them one at a time until she was able to access the space behind the central keg. Pausing for a moment's rest, she sat down and leant back against the revealed wall. There was a warm glow coming from the bricks behind her back, which Solarna found oddly comforting and relaxing. Feeling the exertions of the previous days, she closed her eyes.

She woke with a start, thinking she was falling. Gradually realising she had dreamt she was flying, she slowly opened her eyes. The room was dark, only a pale glow visible at the top of the stairs. She listened, but the only sound was the scratching of tiny feet as a small rodent made its way across the shelves. Her legs ached, and her back was stiff, so she stood up and walked around, taking a few sips from her flask to soothe her dry throat. Still feeling tired and preferring to work with at least some light, she took out her roll and settled back to sleep.

When she next awoke, the light had returned, and she felt refreshed. After breakfasting on some of the fruit, she set to work looking for two pairs of depressions in the face of the wall. Finding them, she placed her fingers in the indentations, and was able to remove two bricks. This allowed her to take out those in between, exposing a hidden cavity containing a wooden box. Taking the casket from its hiding place, Solarna held it in her lap, enjoying the heat emanating from inside. She'd done it! She'd retrieved the casket. Brushing away the earth that encased it, she could make out markings on the outside, but as the light wasn't strong enough to identify them, she wrapped it in a spare shirt, and placed it carefully by her backpack.

Tanitha had requested that the room be restored, in case it was needed again. After meticulously replacing the bricks and barrels, Solarna picked up the casket and her pack, and climbed the stairs. Cautiously poking her head through the opening, she looked and listened for any signs of danger. Satisfied it was safe, she clambered out.

Sitting by the magically grown tree, she took the second bottle from the leather pouch, and—after removing its brown cap—let three drops of the liquid fall onto the base of its trunk. The rumbling returned as the limbs and branches began to shrink. While the second mixture reversed the effects of the first, Solarna removed the cloth from around the casket and examined it.

There was a curve to the top of the box, and the familiar oval symbol was repeated on the two small sides. Along the two longer sides inscriptions had been carved. Solarna recognised one of them as the line she hadn't been able to translate from the advert—the other seemed to be in the same language, but was not a phrase she had seen before. The most unusual thing though, was there was no obvious way to open the casket. Still intrigued by what it might contain, she wrapped it up again, placing it carefully at the bottom of her pack where it would be most secure.

Once the rumbling had finished, and the stone slab had resealed the entrance, there was a final snapping sound. Retrieving the seed and returning it to the pouch, Solarna filled in the hole, covering the symbol and edge as best as she could. Having collected what she had come for, she prepared for the next part of her journey.

SOLARNA TOOK her time walking back through the tower grounds, wanting to conserve her energy, in case she needed to be ready to run again. She stopped for lunch in the overgrown orchard, and studied her map. Worried it might fall into the wrong hands, Tanitha had deliberately kept details to a minimum, using unusual symbols to mark the key sites and waypoints. It had seemed sensible at the time, but now, Solarna realised, it didn't contain the information she needed to plot an alternative route to Whitehaven, where her mentor would be waiting. She would have to retrace her steps to get to the White River.

The sun was getting low in the sky when Solarna reached the remains of the perimeter wall. Wanting to survey the surrounding area, she had climbed to the top when a sharp piercing whistle shattered the silence. Ahead, Bulvar stepped out from behind some trees, and started walking purposefully towards her. Scrambling down, she jumped to the ground and turned to run, only to be confronted by another man emerging from a copse of trees, with a thin sword drawn, which he flicked towards her face. There was a sharp scratch on her cheek, as she twisted away from him and fled in the opposite direction, just managing to dodge between the man and the broken walls.

She had only managed a few more steps when a third man, holding a similar blade, came rushing directly in her path. Slightly more prepared, she managed to raise her right hand to protect her face, taking a cut on the palm. Realising all her escape routes would be covered by the three men, Solarna stopped running.

The two swordsmen positioned themselves a few feet from her on either flank, their blades lowered, but poised and ready to attack at any moment. Their leather jerkins had fresh blood stains, and bore scratch marks in places. Bulvar's clothing was similarly marked, and Solarna noticed fresh teeth marks on his bare arms as he halted in front of her.

Solarna, feeling the blood trickling down her cheek, raised her hand to wipe it away. She looked around. "Where are the other members of your party?"

"We ran into some problems with the local wildlife," Bulvar said, folding his arms tightly across his chest. "You've caused me quite a lot of trouble since we last met, Solarna."

"What do you want?" Solarna asked.

"Rasden wants you and the casket brought to him in Fairglade—unharmed, if possible." He paused and smiled at her. "Providing you cooperate of course."

"I was going to give the casket to him," Solarna responded, trying to appease the man.

"Please don't lie to me. If you really intended to give the casket to Rasden, why didn't you inform him before you left? And why sneak out of your house in the middle of the night, after your mentor lured my men away?"

He took a step towards her, placed one hand on his

sword hilt and held the other out to her. "Give me the casket."

Solarna removed her backpack, and, placing it on the ground in front of her, began removing items so she could get to the bottom. Lifting it out, she carefully removed the cloth. Then, as her hands were still slick with blood, she grasped the sides firmly and stood up. Hit by an overwhelming feeling that this was wrong, she stopped.

"What are you waiting for?" Bulvar snapped at her, and started to draw his sword.

Faced with no other choice, she reluctantly held out the casket to Bulvar.

He moved closer to take it from her. "Is that—"

He didn't finish his question. As the top of the casket flipped back towards Solarna, its contents radiated an intense light in his direction. Feeling the heat through the wooden casket sides, she watched in horror as blisters appeared on the exposed skin of his face and arms. Bulvar cried out in anguish as his clothes began to smoulder, his hair and beard shrivelling to black stumps. He fell to his knees, and then slumped to the ground.

There was a shout from her left. Solarna whirled around, still holding the open casket before her. The fighter, who was still some distance from her, stopped advancing as the swathe of bright light hit him. He clutched his hands to face, covering his eyes, yelling, "I can't see!"

Fearing an attack from behind, Solarna twisted around to face her final assailant, who was standing open-mouthed, as still as a statue, when the brilliant glow enveloped him. He dropped to the ground in silence, rubbing his eyes, trying somehow to remove its effects.

Bulvar was still crying out in pain as he writhed on the ground in front of her, as his allies crawled around aimlessly to either side. Solarna, beginning to recover from the shock, placed the casket on the ground and pushed the top down. There was no click or other indication that it had sealed shut, but she could no longer see the point at which it had opened—all that was visible were the strange markings and her dried bloody handprints on the sides.

Tentatively, she touched the casket with the back of her hand, and although she could feel a modest warmth, there was no trace of the intense heat and light that she had just witnessed emanating from inside. Replacing it securely at the bottom of her backpack, she hurriedly gathered her possessions from where she had scattered them during the fight, and tossed them on top of the casket.

Shouldering her backpack, she ran away from the carnage, ignoring the imploring pleas for help from the stricken men.

Struggling for breath, she halted, leaned against a boulder, and retched. Drained and exhausted, she staggered to a nearby tree and collapsed to the ground. Closing her eyes, she couldn't escape the images of what had just happened, and started sobbing, eventually falling asleep.

She was woken by wolves brushing against her, as they tried to sniff her backpack. Recognising them from her previous encounter, she relaxed. Seemingly satisfied, they moved off in the direction of the ruined tower, and she watched them fade into the twilight.

Shortly afterwards, Solarna heard brief cries of anguish in the distance. Strangely, she felt glad that the men's suffering had come to an end. Relieved, and feeling somewhat safer, she drifted back to sleep.

She awoke soon after dawn, and was comforted to see that the wolves had returned during the night and were curled up around her. There were fewer of them now, and many sported patches of fur matted with blood.

They stayed with her for the next two days as she made her way back to their cave; roaming nearby as she walked during the day, and sleeping next to her while she slept at night. Arriving late in the day, she decided to spend one last night in their company, and settled down for the night in the den.

Leaving the cave the following morning, Solarna soon came across the site of the fight between the wolves and Rasden's men, and spotted a dagger lying in the dirt between two male corpses. With all Bulvar's party now accounted for, she wasn't sure if she needed a weapon, but she plucked it from the ground anyway, and tucked it into her belt. Moving on, she set a brisk pace, eager to reach her rendezvous with Tanitha.

THANKFULLY, the journey from the tower to the outskirts of Whitehaven was largely uneventful. Only an encounter with a young bear, which she placated with the talisman and some of the fruit from the orchard, caused her any concern. She arrived two weeks later on a late summer morning, just as a light shower of rain began to fall.

The smell of salt and fish grew stronger as she headed to the fish market next to the harbour. Solarna soon found the stall with the yellow and white striped awning, situated as Tanitha said it would be, at the far end of the market. The proprietor, a broad shouldered man with little hair on his head but sporting a well-trimmed grey beard, was serving a trio of middle-aged ladies.

Waiting until the women had left, Solarna approached his stall.

"Are you Ellias?" she asked.

"That I am," he replied, puffing his chest out slightly. "Ellias Treffick, purveyor of the finest fish in Whitehaven. Guaranteed caught fresh yesterday by me and my sons. I can recommend the mackerel, if you're not after anything particular."

"I am looking for something specific, but it's not fish. I believe you might know where I can find Miss Findol." She smiled, hoping he recognised the name Tanitha would be using in Whitehaven.

"Indeed I do," he said. "She told me to expect you. She's staying in one of the old fisherman's cottages."

He proceeded to give her directions, and, after thanking him for his help, she purchased two mackerel fillets, before heading along the harbour wall towards a small row of white houses with brightly painted doors.

Walking past the buildings, Solarna could see that, as well as being a different colour, each door had a different fish shaped brass knocker. Taking the path of the penultimate house, she lifted the fish's tail and rapped twice on the green door. It was not long before the door opened inwards and Tanitha rushed forward to hug her.

"Solarna!" she exclaimed. "It's so good to see you again." Breaking the embrace, she ushered Solarna inside, closing the door behind her.

Solarna was led into the kitchen, where she gratefully removed her backpack and travelling boots before seating herself in front of the fire.

"Are you hungry?" Tanitha asked, placing a freshly filled kettle over the hearth to boil.

"Yes," said Solarna. "It's been a long time since I tasted fresh bread."

They talked of inconsequential things while Tanitha made sandwiches to go with the tea. She waited until Solarna had finished eating, before turning the conversation to her apprentice's recent journey.

"How did you get the scar?" Tanitha asked.

Solarna involuntarily touched the mark on her face. Memories of the encounter flooded back to her. "It was a sword... one of Bulvar's men." She started to sob.

Tanitha reached over and held her hand. "Take your time," she said. "Start at the beginning."

Solarna nodded, and started to tearfully recall what had happened. Tanitha listened intently, offering comfort to Solarna as she spoke, but interrupting to ask for more details or question a specific point.

When asked how the men had found out where she was, Solarna had been unable to answer. She was sure she had evaded the man keeping watch on the house, and hadn't noticed anyone on her trail until she reached the first waterfall. Tanitha frowned, but didn't say anymore on the matter.

Tanitha appeared pleased when Solarna described her encounter with the wolves; the fact she had used the amulet and passed unharmed seemed to hold some significance. It was only when she reached the point of the confrontation with Bulvar outside the tower that Tanitha looked troubled.

"The casket opened," she said, dropping her teacup onto the table. "How?"

"I don't know," Solarna replied. "It just opened, and then there was light and heat everywhere."

Her hands started shaking as the images of the day returned to her. "His skin was blistering... the air reeked of scorched hair." She gulped for air. "The cries of agony they made... they seemed to go on forever. It was horrible."

Tanitha took her hand, lightly squeezing it, and waited for her to recover before asking her to continue. Solarna hurried through the rest of the encounter, skipping the journey to Whitehaven entirely, as it had been so uneventful. When she had finished, Tanitha asked to see the casket.

Taking it from her pack, Solarna saw that the blood stains left by her hands on the sides looked paler and smaller than those on the top. She didn't mention this to her mentor, but noticed that Tanitha spent some time examining them, before pushing the casket back to her.

"I think it will be best if you continue to look after it," she said.

"Why?" Solarna asked. And as it now appeared to be the right time to raise all the questions that had been nagging at her over the last two weeks, she continued. "What's inside the casket?"

Tanitha took a deep breath. "An egg," she said softly. "A phoenix egg."

"The egg of a... what?" Solarna exclaimed. That was not what she had expected. "I thought they were just a myth. How did it get there?"

"I am the latest in a long line of guardians. Our duty is to protect the egg while it is sealed inside, and, when the time is right, help it hatch. Then we keep the casket safe, ready for when it is needed again for another egg." Tanitha lightly brushed the top with her hand. "The

257

casket was given to me by my mentor, shortly before her death. I studied and trained with her for many years in preparation to take over."

"And the egg has been in the casket all that time?"

"Even longer. The egg was placed into the casket by her predecessor. Like her, I have never seen a phoenix, although it is my dearest wish to do so before I die."

Solarna thought for a moment. "So the casket keeps the egg hot—I could feel it pouring out when it was opened. But how is it done?"

"The secret has been lost for hundreds of years," Tanitha explained, shaking her head slowly. "I know it was created by one of the first guardians, who found a way to magically seal the heat of lava inside. I have been trying to find out more, but have had no luck."

"So when will it hatch?" Solarna asked.

"I can't be sure exactly, but from all I've learnt and been told, once the casket has been opened, it is only a matter of weeks until it hatches."

"We just have to keep it safe until then I suppose," she said.

Tanitha shook her head again. "I'm afraid it's not that simple. The egg has to be taken somewhere very hot. There are a few places mentioned in the old books, but Holfur's Cauldron is the only place we can be certain to reach in time."

"Holfur's Cauldron?"

"An area in the Holfur Mountains where molten lava is exposed to the surface. It is said that Holfur created all the gems and ores there before scattering them deep within his mountains."

"And that's where we're going?"

"I'm afraid so. It's not ideal by any means, but the

extra heat from the molten rock is needed to help the egg hatch. We will leave in the morning."

Solarna looked at the pair of mackerels on the kitchen table. At least she would have one freshly cooked meal before they went.

"HAVE YOU EVER RIDDEN A HORSE BEFORE?" Tanitha asked, as they waited for the stable hand to bring the two mares they had hired.

"I remember clinging to my father when he took me for a ride when I was young," Solarna said, "but I didn't enjoy it, and we never did it again."

"Well, the little trick I taught you on the boat should help," said Tanitha.

They had left Whitehaven three days ago, travelling across the sea to Holmouth in a fishing boat crewed by Ellias and his two sons. The weather had been kind, and Solarna had spent most of the days on deck, sheltering from the sun under a piece of hastily rigged canvas, while Tanitha explained more of the role of the guardians and their relationships and responsibilities to the casket, egg, and phoenix.

Tanitha encouraged her to hold the casket each day; to develop the bond she said. There was no repeat of it opening, and when she had asked Tanitha why it had just happened once, her mentor was unusually reticent to reply, only saying that the casket had never opened while she had held it, so she couldn't answer.

Solarna learnt that as her link to the casket and the egg grew, she would find herself becoming more in tune with all the natural elements of the world. With practice, she would be able to tap into this power, and using incantations, hand gestures, and physical objects she crafted herself, she could persuade those elements to temporarily deviate from their current path or form.

This was what Tanitha was alluding to now, the gentle stroking of the horse and the speaking of soothing words before climbing into the saddle, would encourage her mount to be more responsive, and make her ride more comfortable.

"Solarna, are you ready?"

Tanitha's question jolted her back to the present, where the stable boy had returned with their rides. Taking the reins of her horse from him, she performed the ritual and mounted. Riding alongside Tanitha, they took the road that led away from Holmouth and the coast, and headed inland towards the mountains.

Pushing her empty plate into the centre of the table, Solarna pulled her half empty wine glass to her lips. The sweet red wine tasted especially delicious after a week of water from a flask.

They had arrived at Holfur's Edge that afternoon. The last settlement before the mountains, it consisted mainly of inns and traders, serving the needs of the adventurers and miners travelling to and from the mountains. After finding a stable that would care for their horses while they trekked into the mountains, Tanitha had located a small but cosy tavern where they could spend the night.

"What will happen when we get to Holfur's Cauldron?" Solarna asked.

Tanitha poured the remaining wine from the bottle into their glasses, and settled back into her chair.

"I was told, and I've since found several texts which seem to confirm this, that once the bond with the egg is established, its guardian is protected from the intense heat inside the casket. They also have a much greater tolerance to similar high temperatures occurring naturally—like molten rock. So when we get there, you simply open the casket, take hold of the egg, and place it into the lava."

"Me?" said Solarna, surprised at the proposal. "I thought you would be doing it. You are the guardian after all."

"Not anymore, Solarna. The casket opened for you, not me. You are the one the egg has bonded with. You are the new guardian." Tanitha drained the last of her wine, and looked at the empty glass. "I will never know what it feels like to bond with a phoenix."

They sat in silence for a while, before Solarna changed the subject.

"What about Rasden? Will he leave us alone once the phoenix has hatched?"

"It is possible," Tanitha replied. "I don't know how much he has discovered about the phoenix and its egg though, so it is impossible to predict what he will or will not do."

Solarna sighed; she had hoped they had seen the last of the man.

"However, Bulvar and his men won't be able to help him now, even if they didn't succumb to their wounds, or those friendly wolves. Their loss will have weakened Rasden considerably, as he relied on them to exert his authority. You have made the lives of many people significantly better by that act."

"Thank you," Solarna said, although she felt it had been very little of her doing.

Tanitha yawned and gave a light laugh. "All this wine is making me sleepy," she said. "We should head to bed. It will take many days to get through the mountains, and I would like to start early in the morning."

STOPPING on the crest of the ridge, Solarna looked down into the crater that was Holfur's Cauldron, the black rock slopes encircling a large mass of bubbling lava. The smell of sulphur that had been building as they approached now assaulted her nostrils, and although she could feel the heat, it did not affect her. She could not say the same for Tanitha, whose cheeks were glowing and was starting to sweat profusely.

Concerned, Solarna asked her, "Do you want to wait here?"

"No, I think I can get closer," Tanitha answered, wiping her brow. "I still have some resilience to the heat, and I would dearly love to see the egg hatch up close."

Pointing towards a spot where a small strip of rock protruded into the lava, Tanitha said, "That looks like the ideal place. Let's go."

"Tanitha!"

Turning, Solarna saw Rasden standing on the ridge. Raising his hand, he pointed in their direction, and a small bolt of dark fire shot from his hand, hitting the ground just in front of them.

"I want that casket!" he yelled, and started to scamper down the slope towards them.

Tanitha whispered urgently to her, "I'll try to stop Rasden. When I say, move away from me, then make for the outcrop. You know what to do." Tanitha shoved her, shouting, "Get away, Solarna! He only wants the casket!"

Taking momentum from the push, Solarna ran along the lava's edge, before suddenly diverting onto the encroachment. Reaching the edge, she removed her backpack, and fumbled inside for the casket. Across the crater, Tanitha was shielding behind a moving wall of vines, but as fast as they grew, Rasden hacked them away with a glowing blade of dark fire.

Removing the casket, Solarna held it in front of her, waiting for it to open.

From behind her, she heard Rasden shout, "No!"

Turning, she saw another bolt of fire coming towards her. She dodged just in time, as it flew past her, entering the lava with a loud hiss.

The casket wasn't opening, and Solarna began to panic when Rasden started heading towards her. A second later, the vines collapsed to the ground and shot towards Rasden, wrapping themselves around his ankles, causing him to stumble to the ground. Turning suddenly, he threw his knife at Tanitha, who dropped to her knees, clutching the blade embedded in her chest. The vines shrivelled away from Rasden's feet. Rising up, he started to sprint in Solarna's direction.

"Tanitha!" Solarna shrieked. Her chest tightened. She wanted to go to her friend, but she wouldn't let her actions be in vain. Urgently returning her attention to the casket, Solarna tried twisting and pulling it from different various angles, but it wouldn't open. Frustrated, she thought about smashing the casket on the rocks, but as she held it up she noticed although the top of the casket still showed stains of her blood, the sides did not. Solarna remembered one of the books Tanitha had asked her to translate mentioned cultures that used blood in their magic. Taking the dagger from her belt, she made a thin cut in each of her palms, and, dropping the blade, she grasped the casket again.

The top sprung open. Placing the casket on the ground, she reached inside and removed the egg. Her hands still bled, but as soon as the blood touched the pale blue-green mottled shell, it was absorbed.

Entranced by the beauty of the egg, time seemed to stand still until she heard Tanitha shout, "Solarna! Watch out!"

She looked behind her; Rasden had reached the encroachment.

In that moment, only the phoenix mattered to her. Turning away from her foe, she threw the egg into the lava. Her burden released, she spun to face Rasden, who was only a few steps away. Picking up the casket, she swung it at his face. He staggered back, raising his hands to his eyes in a futile effort to deflect the brightness.

Closing the casket, she tried to run past, but Rasden flung his arms out and grabbed hold of her.

Solarna struggled to escape but Rasden's grip was too strong, and it was all she could do to stop them both falling into the lava

Twisting and turning like dancers moving to an erratic beat, Solarna caught glimpses of the egg, sinking slowly beneath the surface of the lava before it disappeared completely. Moments later, small pieces of lava began shooting upwards from the spot where it had vanished, increasing in size and velocity.

Then, a massive plume of lava erupted and a fiery bird rose from its centre.

Solarna was transfixed by the beauty of the phoenix, whose feathers shone in a glorious mixture of orange and red, resembling a brightly burning flame. Above its golden beak, a dark black eye gazed straight at her, and she bowed her head in acknowledgement.

Rasden, perhaps sensing her distraction, lurched backwards, pulling them both closer to the edge. Brought back to her senses Solarna jabbed her foot into his shin, digging her heels into the stony ground to prevent him taking them both into the lava. The phoenix, with a great thrust of its wings, launched itself straight at them, hitting Rasden squarely in the back and scratching his face with its outstretched claws. Releasing his grip on her, Rasden raised his arms to defend himself from this new assailant. Solarna, seizing her chance, picked up her dagger and plunged it into Rasden's chest, pushing with all her might. His foot slipped on a loose rock, and Rasden emitted an anguished shriek as he tumbled backwards.

Solarna did not wait to see Rasden enter the lava; gathering her things, she rushed to where Tanitha lay unmoving on the ground, a large patch of blood soaking her shirt, her breathing soft and shallow.

Lifting her head, Tanitha grimaced as Solarna approached, but smiling, said quietly, "I saw the phoenix rise. She's so beautiful."

"She's still here," said Solarna, and, as if it had heard her words, the phoenix landed on a nearby rock.

Raising her hand to shield her eyes, Tanitha said, "It's so hot. I miss the shade of my garden."

Retrieving the leather pouch from her backpack, Solarna took the seed and placed it into a crack in the black rock, tipping several drops of liquid from the green capped bottle onto it. She returned to Tanitha's side, creating a pillow from her spare clothes as a mature tree grew rapidly behind them.

"Thank you, Solarna," Tanitha said, taking hold of her hand. "I want you to know that I have left written instructions with Ellias, stating that the house and all its contents should be passed to you if anything happens to me."

Solarna was shocked. "Did you know this was going to happen?" she asked.

"Not this exactly, but I feared my time as guardian was coming to an end." Tanitha coughed, and a small spittle of blood appeared on her chin.

"There is so much more I needed to tell you... wanted to show you. Being a guardian grants you many benefits, a longer life, and the ability for nature magic among them. I kept a diary, where I noted all the spells, potions, and artefacts I created. It will help guide you as you learn. It tells you where to find the most important texts and documents I've hidden for safekeeping. I left another note with Ellias telling you where to find it. The letter and diary are both written in the language used on the casket, to avoid anyone else reading them."

"But I don't understand that script," Solarna said, tears welling in her eyes.

"You'll be able to read them now." Tanitha coughed again; there was more blood this time. "Fetch my knife —it is time I passed the blood of the guardian to you."

Solarna handed her the knife. Tanitha made a cut in her palm, and asked Solarna to do the same, before grasping her hand. Solarna felt a tingling sensation as their blood began to mingle. The phoenix flew down next to Tanitha, laying the tip of its fiery wing on her forehead. The three of them remained connected, as the life ebbed slowly from Tanitha's body.

AFTER TANITHA'S DEATH, the tree withered and died, dropping leaves and branches to the ground. Solarna gathered the dead wood, and, using rocks from the crater, built a pyre for her friend and mentor, while the phoenix remained motionless by the body of its former guardian. As the sun lowered beyond the horizon, Solarna raised Tanitha's body to the top of the pyre, and the phoenix flew around it, the tips of its wings setting it ablaze.

Solarna knelt in vigil next to the phoenix throughout the night, until the flames finally died out. Rising as the sun dawned, she scattered the stones and ashes, and sang the lament her mother had taught her when her grandmother had died. Beside her, the phoenix echoed her song in its own final tribute.

Combining her belongings with those of her mentor in preparation for the return to Fairglade, Solarna found she could now read the strange writing on the casket's sides.

Guardian of the egg
Blessed by the phoenix

Placing it into her pack, she watched the phoenix rise into the sky and head into the mountains. Watching until it disappeared from view, Solarna left Holfur's Cauldron and began the long journey home.

GRIT AND GLIMMER
LUCINA NYX

"Y ou're an idiot," Pebble stated to the bottle of mead in their hands. "Why did you think moving to the wilderness and away from everyone would be a good idea?"

They had been sitting on the edge of their upturned boat for a few hours now, and the mead was starting to make Pebble feel drowsy.

"Out here all I have is the piercing wind, bugs with their incessant buzzing, and strange sounds in the middle of the night."

A frog nearby croaked.

"Well there are frogs too." Pebble looked out into the darkness of the river and yelled, "Thank you, my little mosquito eating pals!" After another moment of silence, there was another croak. A grin rippled across their face, but Pebble's gaze soon went flat. They swirled the bottle around for a few moments, noting with displeasure there were only a few mouthfuls left.

"I can't move back to town... I'm sure people will forever know me as Pebble, the dirty weirdo who only made it a few months by themselves."

They looked down into the bottle, and blew a low

note over its lip before downing the rest. Pebble stood up and threw the empty bottle into the still river, then crouched down and released a drawn out sigh.

"Why did I do that?" they mumbled. "Whatever, I'll get it tomorrow."

Standing back up, they stretched for a few moments, then dragged their feet to shuffle back towards the forest. Their cabin was easy enough to get back to; they had placed stone trails amongst the grass for nights like this, when they were too far gone to rely on familiar sights to lead the way in the dark.

Crunch...

Pebble spun on the spot, and it took them a moment to realise the sound was made by a small figure just below their line of sight. It was one of the small green goblins who lived in the caves not far from here.

"Pebble-Person drop glass," said the small figure, who was holding the previously thrown bottle out for Pebble to take.

"Y'know, if I wasn't so drunk I may have messed my pants," Pebble slurred while trying not to trip over their own feet. "I was going to get it in the morning, you didn't need to get soaked for me." Despite their grumbling, Pebble took the bottle and emptied the river water onto the grass.

"Pebble-Person having bad day," said the goblin in its wobbly voice. "Wanted next day to be not bad."

They straightened up a little. "Wait, were you listening to me talking to the bot— I mean, myself?"

"Yes." The goblin gave a thumbs up. "Gripp likes to listen to Pebble-Person talk."

Pebble frowned for a few moments, while Gripp continued to hold his thumb up and smile with his pointy teeth showing. "Okay well, I'm going to bed. Get home safe, Gripp."

Pebble gave a greatly exaggerated bow with one arm across their stomach and the other outstretched holding the bottle. In turn, Gripp did the same. Pebble properly smiled for the first time in what felt like a long time, and laughed softly as they wandered away. Ten long minutes of zigzagging and stumbling through trees later, Pebble saw the familiar deer drawn on the stump of what was once a large tree; they had finally made it home to their mess of a cabin. The fire in the pit outside had reduced to embers while Pebble was on their midnight field trip, but the air remained warmer here than in the maze of the forest. They lifted the latch on the front door and walked inside, kicking off their boots into a pile of fishing equipment by the door and stomped across the cabin to face-plant onto the bed.

THE NEXT MORNING Pebble woke up to the sounds of movement outside their cabin; shuffling, dragging, and metal against stone. They rolled over and onto the hard cabin floor with a thud, as the noise outside stopped. It resumed after a few moments with the snapping of sticks. Pebble pushed themself up off the floor and scurried like a drunk squirrel to the door. Through the keyhole, they spied Gripp building a fire, and another goblin with messy red hair filleting a fish with a small stone knife. Releasing a sigh, Pebble stepped outside and went to greet the visitors, only to be stunned by the intensity of the morning sun. A moment of silence ensued with the exchanging of brief glances.

"I don't suppose any of you have some tea or coffee

with you?" they said with a groan as they moved to a stool by the fire. Gripp turned and started to rummage through his large sack of possessions. Several minutes passed while the goblin emptied the contents of his bag, most of which were an assortment of shiny rocks and colourful shells. Eventually he pulled out a small, chipped clay teapot, along with a cloth pouch containing tea leaves.

The other goblin shuffled over to the fire holding several skewered fish, and handed one to Pebble with a toothy grin.

"Good to meet Pebble-Person again. Gripp say you are sad, so we decide to make food to share." She crouched down next to the fire. "Yowl like to catch and cook fish."

Pebble sat quietly by the fire, lost for words. Gripp and Yowl started chattering to each other in their own language as Gripp darted around preparing tea for the three. After flipping their fish a couple of times, Pebble finally worked up the courage to speak.

"Thank you," Pebble all but whispered. "I'm not really sure what I did to deserve this, but I appreciate it." Gripp gave them a thumbs up.

"You help Gripp out of rabbit trap, and out of hole."

"Don't forget time you got tangled in fishing net," Yowl interjected.

Gripp bellowed a laugh. "That too!"

"Gripp's lucky that goblin wasn't on the menu," Pebble said with a grin, recalling the days they'd come across the small, hapless creature. "But honestly, getting Gripp out traps and nets is just the right thing to do." They gazed over at the pair's haphazardly piled equipment—three flimsy spears, a few grubby sacks, and a soaked shirt.

"Hey, guys... is there another one of you around?"

"Only us, why you ask?" responded Yowl with a mouthful of fish.

"Well, you have three spears, so I figured there was an extra little green guy wandering around somewhere." Pebble looked back at the pair. "So why the need for three spears?"

"We break spear when fishing," Gripp said between licks of his fingers. "Or we lose them in river." The goblins gave each other a knowing nod.

"Have you considered using something stronger? Or y'know... tying a rope to the end of the spear so you don't lose it?"

"We only have what we find in forest," Gripp replied.

Pebble pondered for a few minutes while Gripp and Yowl hobbled around the camp, collecting food scraps. Finally, Pebble stood up with their hands on their hips.

"I have a proposition for you both."

Gripp and Yowl looked at each other, then back to them. "Proposition?" The pair asked in unison.

"Yes. It means I have a plan to help you with your fishing dilemma, but it will be easier if one of you can lend me a hand."

Before the goblins had a chance to respond, Pebble headed inside their cabin and grabbed the crossbow and quiver kept beside the front door. They paced over to the workbench that was set up against the back wall, and started rummaging through a box of odds and ends, before finding the spindle of thread that had previously been used as a fishing line. Pebble stepped outside and drew out a bolt from the quiver, loading the hefty crossbow.

"So... picture this. Instead of splashing about all day,

or having to drag around a net just to maybe get a fish or two, you shoot them with this." They turned to a nearby tree and fired, narrowly missing it. Gripp and Yowl laughed, running off to retrieve the bolt like a pair of loyal puppies. Yowl was still giggling when she returned with the stray bolt, holding it above Gripp's reach like a trophy.

"What if we miss fish as bad as Pebble-Person miss tree?" she asked as she handed it back. Pebble flushed red.

"I was getting to that part." They pulled out the thread. "I, uh, forgot to attach this to the bolt. But, yeah... tie this around the end of the bolt, shoot it, and then retrieve it. With enough practice you'll be able to sit in a boat and just wait for your chance to take a shot." The three stood there, staring at each other. Gripp eventually broke the silence.

"How can Gripp hold that? It almost as big as me." Yowl nodded along in agreement.

"Oh, good point." Pebble mumbled, staring out towards the nearby town. "I suppose some proper fishing gear could also work," they said, looking back at Gripp and Yowl. "But first, we need to make some money. D'you know about the colourful bugs in the caves upstream?"

Yowl grimaced. "Yes they taste bad, smell bad too." She pretended to spit on the ground multiple times.

Pebble held back a smile as best they could, and elaborated. "Those are the ones. If we can collect enough of them, or their scales, I can sell them to my old neighbour. She uses them to make dyes and paint."

Yowl looked sceptical. "We don't have to eat them?"

"Not a single bite. I'll even buy some meat to share with you when I'm back."

Without missing a beat, Gripp and Yowl started jumping around, chanting "Meat, meat, meat!"

After chugging their lukewarm tea, Pebble took a few small bites from their piece of fish and handed it to Gripp to finish off, heading inside to collect what was needed for the trip. They grabbed their weathered leather satchel and found a small wooden box that could hold the cave bugs. Then, they rounded up several empty bottles and wrapped them delicately in cloth, packing them neatly into the satchel. The last thing they grabbed on their way out was their trusty flask, still about half full.

By the time they were back outside, the goblins had assembled their belongings and were ready to set off. Pebble led the way down the dirt path towards the river, only taking small detours to check the snares they had set up the day before. None of them had been disturbed, but they figured they wouldn't be returning for a day or two, so Pebble took the time to dismantle them just in case. The trio found themselves on the rocky bank of the river around midday, and continued on under the pleasant spring sunlight; pleasant for the goblins at least. Pebble's stomach rolled and pitched, their head aching from the morning's hangover—which the great orb of fire in the sky was not helping.

A large trading vessel was making its way down the river, with a few people onboard waving to the trio. Pebble lazily lifted a hand in return, while the goblins jumped up and down, waving back furiously. After some time, the group had come across a series of rock pools that were adjacent to a dense and untamed section of thorn-covered bushes. Pebble, with their long legs, had no issues jumping across the stones to get by, but the teeny goblins knew their limitations, and decided to paddle through the river, around the rocks, and back to shore. While Pebble waited, they pulled the small wooden box out of their satchel and placed the rest of their possessions amongst the roots of a nearby tree, sitting to rest for a few minutes.

"Okay, I need a break, my head is *pounding*," Pebble groaned to Yowl as she approached, laying down and putting an arm over their eyes to block out the light of day. Gripp finally caught up and dumped his sodden bag close enough to Pebble that it splattered water up their leg. They sat up and glared for a moment, grimacing.

"Please try not to do that again, my floppy-eared friend." They went back to shielding their eyes. Gripp looked uneasy, but didn't say anything until Yowl prodded him forwards.

"Gripp sorry, Pebble-Person. We get berries for you while you sleep," he said sheepishly, then dashed into the underbrush, with Yowl not far behind.

PEBBLE WOKE to the sounds of Gripp and Yowl trudging through the bushes towards them.

"How did you go?" they asked while rubbing their eyes. Gripp and Yowl were beaming with excitement, and neatly piled their collection together at Pebble's feet.

"We find lots of purple berries for Pebble-Person." Gripp cheered, jumping up and down before tearing into one. Pebble propped themself up and inspected the pile before them, frowning; not only were they not purple, they weren't berries either—unless you classified fruit the size of your fist a berry. They picked up one of the pieces of fruit and held it out.

"This is a green-brown, not purple, and it's also... a pear. I've told you this before, Gripp, don't you remember?" Both goblins stopped eating and examined their food.

"It look purple to me," Gripp explained. Yowl nodded in agreement, continuing to eat.

"Fair enough," they sighed while pushing themself to their feet. "We can leave the rest of our stuff here. We're almost there."

Glancing up at the sky, Pebble realised they had slept much longer than intended. The silver lining, however, was that their splitting headache had finally ceased. Pebble collected their wooden box and motioned the goblins onwards. The rocky riverside had started to slope up, turning into a small cliff of trees, grass, and stone. The trio slipped into the shade of the treeline, away from the river's edge. The pear-induced sugar rush Gripp and Yowl were experiencing had filled them with more energy than Pebble was accustomed to. It wasn't much of an issue until they got caught in the middle of a sword-fight with sticks; after getting cracked in the back of the leg, Pebble broke up the play fighting, kneeling down to inspect the welt that had formed.

"There's no blood at least. Try to avoid innocent bystanders when you're fighting to the death with sticks, okay?"

"Sorry!" the goblins cried out in unison.

Pebble jumped back up and wandered over to the cliff edge to get their bearings. Holding onto a tree that was growing from a large crack in the stone, they peered over—the cave was almost directly below them. Gripp and Yowl had crawled up to the cliff edge nearby without Pebble noticing, and began whispering to each other in their own language.

Before Pebble had a chance to question what they were doing, Gripp scrambled down the rocks, with Yowl right behind him, giggling. Pebble cursed to themself but grinned at the carefree nature of their companions. They sprinted downhill, trying to beat the goblins to the bottom, but the wild grass grabbed at their feet. Pebble's foot snagged and they lurched forward, tumbling down the hill in a face first slide to the bottom. They reunited with the others with fresh grass stains on their clothes, and their usual messy black hair had more than a few prickles strewn through it. They would later find out that they had more bruises than they knew of at the time, but for now, all they noticed was intense itchiness. Yowl was cheering as Pebble approached.

"We beat Pebble-Person! Too slow! Too slow!" she taunted playfully. The rock climbers somehow still had energy to spare, and quickly began another epic duel with new sticks. Pebble sat with their back pressed against the stone entrance of the cave and watched the goblins play as they took off their boots.

When it was starting to seem like the play fighting would go on indefinitely, Pebble slowly rose and called to the pair. "Alright, kids, let's head on in while there's still light and get this done."

The goblins dropped their sticks and followed Pebble into the cave. It only took a few steps into the dim to hear the faint sounds of insects scuttling on the surfaces within. The noise roused memories; the first time they had ventured here years earlier, they slipped through a puddle filled with algae and had to limp all the way back to town. Their mother had always teased them about that day. The ground was puddle-free this time, and they were thankful.

A few of the brightly coloured insects scattered away from their approach, disappearing through a crack in the wall into the depths of the tunnel. While squeezing through a narrow passage, Pebble noticed something out of the corner of their eye.

The cave paintings were as vivid as they had been on their first visit years ago. This surprised Pebble; by now they thought the pictures would have faded at least a little. They approached the one that always stood out the most. It was a giant depiction of one of the insects, with messy writing underneath it. They reached out and softly ran a finger across one of the lines. Nothing. Not a speck of dust, dirt, or residue.

The goblins had gone on ahead and squeezed through the gaps in the wall without Pebble. Rushing to catch up, they lowered themself against the floor and pushed their way through. This hidden section of the cave was dimly lit by luminescent growth. Pebble didn't know what it was, but the goblins didn't eat it, so apparently they knew better than to disturb it. They tip-toed further inside to begin gathering the insects; Gripp and Yowl were crawling about, putting their findings into a single pile. Luck was on their side today, as there were more bug scales and shells spread about than usual. Pebble slowly wandered further into the cave while scooping up usable items, venturing only as far as there was light. They were never brave enough to go further into the darkness as they had heard enough stories from the mercenaries and adventurers that passed through town to be cautious of dangerous things that dwell where humans do not.

Gripp and Yowl suddenly lifted their heads. They

looked at each other, eyes wide. Gripp tugged on Pebble's shirt.

"Pebble-Person, we leave, we leave," he whispered, ears twitching. Pebble could see the fear in Gripp's eyes, and tried their best to peer into the darkness but couldn't make out anything. They decided to trust the goblins on this.

"I think we have enough. Let's head off," Pebble responded in a hushed voice. They crept out of the cave silently and started their trip back.

NIGHT HAD BEGUN to creep in by the time the trio arrived back at Pebble's boat. The goblins looked exhausted and Pebble had been feeling the same for hours.

"If you don't want to walk all the way home tonight, you're welcome to stay at my cabin," Pebble said with a yawn. "I'm going to float on over to town and get a room at the inn." They placed their belongings on the ground and laid down in the dirt for a few minutes, building up the energy required for the last part of the journey. They rolled their head to the side to look at the goblins, who had plopped down near them and leant on their packs.

"I've been meaning to ask for a while now..." Pebble shifted. "Do you know who did the cave paintings?"

"Gripp draw them," the goblin exclaimed proudly. "Gripp draw in lots of places."

Pebble rolled onto their side and propped their head up with an arm. "I guess that makes sense... There are not a lot of other goblins out here." They sat up abruptly. "Wait, so you also did the drawing of a deer on the stump by my house?"

"Yes, deer live near stump."

Yowl nodded in agreement.

"And the drawings of angry looking people on the boulders near the main road?"

"Yes, humans get angry when Gripp try to say hello," Yowl remarked, her ears drooping. Pebble lowered their gaze. The goblins that lived in these woods were friendly, yet frequently misunderstood by strangers. Despite this, they continued to reach out.

Hoping to cheer up their friends, Pebble put on a smile. "Well, I'm glad the people in town treat you nicely. I hear the fishermen like to trade with your clan."

Gripps' face lit up at the mention of the traders. "Yes! They give fish for pretty rocks."

"Oh. Good deal," they lied, while maintaining the fake smile; Gripp had once shown Pebble a small ruby he found while swimming in the river. "You should definitely ask for more fish next time though."

"Ok, Pebble-Person," Yowl said, and began to rip into the last of the pears alongside Gripp.

Pebble drew a circle in the dirt with a finger, lost in thought. "So what do you use for paint, or ink?" they asked, continuing to draw random shapes in the dirt.

"It just work. Like magic," Gripp managed between mouthfuls of fruit. He started rummaging through his pack to retrieve a small metal object, then stepped towards Pebble and held the fountain pen out. Pebble was surprised by the weight as they took it from their friend; for such a small object, it was heavy, and cold—very cold. Most of the pen was made from black metal and had multiple grooves carved in it for a comfortable hold. The nib was longer than pens Pebble had seen before, but it looked to be quite blunted. Several beautiful gems of varying colour were embedded in the end, along with unfamiliar words engraved down the sides. Pebble continued to inspect the pen, still sceptical that it was a magic object. Delicately, Pebble pressed the side of their hand against a small stone and began to write their name. Sure enough, an inky black substance appeared from the nib directly onto its surface, which appeared to dry in an instant. They sat there, wide-eyed and amazed by the display, then decided to test it on the side of their boot. The pen did not falter, and Pebble resisted the urge to draw on their hand next. If the ink hadn't washed off of rocks and trees after years, they figured a mindless scribble could end up looking like an exceptionally average looking tattoo.

"This is amazing, Gripp," Pebble muttered in awe, twirling the pen. "I want to hear all about how you got this when I get back."

Gripp gave a thumbs up and grinned. "Pebble-Person can have it."

"Wait, what?" they stuttered. "I can't just *take* this."

Gripp shook his head at the offer of its return. "Pebble-Person borrow it, do drawings," he insisted, pointing between the two of them. "Happy drawings. Happy Gripp."

Pebble looked away and smiled with their eyes closed, fighting back tears. Taking a few deep breaths to settle themselves, they turned back to Gripp.

"You're honestly too good to me. I'll draw a lot. I promise."

Yowl looked at Pebble with big soulful eyes. "Don't cry," she warbled, "or Yowl cry too."

Pebble choked out a laugh and rolled onto their back, hiding their misty eyes.

"Sure thing, Yowl," they chuckled, wiping their nose with the back of their hand. Pebble leaned back to rest their head on their bag, while rotating the pen and contemplating what they would draw with it.

PEBBLE WAS startled awake by the sounds of rocks crunching and Gripp grunting. Helpful as always, Gripp was trying his best to flip Pebble's little boat.

"Gimme a sec', Gripp," they groaned. "Let me help you."

Pebble pushed themself onto their feet and ventured over to help Gripp. With their combined efforts, they flipped it over and were able to carry it to the river. Pebble launched the boat into water and flopped into it with the enthusiasm of a dying fish. Sitting up, they swung their satchel towards the front of the boat and nudged it all the way forwards with their foot. Yowl waded into the river carrying two wooden oars, and passed them up to Pebble.

"We see you tomorrow, with meat?" she asked slyly, with a big toothy smile.

"Tomorrow night, or the next day at the latest. Get home safe, okay?" Pebble shifted themself into position at the rear end of the boat and pushed off with one of the oars. The goblins grabbed their bags and waved goodbye, trudging wearily towards the darkness of the woods.

After the laborious day they'd experienced, rowing was incredibly taxing. Thankfully they were drifting downstream, with most of the work being done for them by the river's current and a steady breeze. When they weren't correcting the boat's course, Pebble drifted in and out of daydreams, thinking about how great a hot pub meal and a pint was going to be. The bed that would accompany it also had them excited to find civilization—for once.

Small docks and fishing huts came into view after a couple more bends in the river as night fell. The few fishermen that were still out and about called out in a friendly manner. Pebble was too tired to return the energy, so they waved just well enough to be seen as sociable. It was as good a time as any to empty the flask they'd packed that morning. They carefully reached across the boat and retrieved it, unscrewing it with a flick. Pebble gave a tentative sniff and grumbled.

"Alright, booze, work your magic and wake me up a little." Three sips was all it took for Pebble's face to feel nice and warm. It was a comfortable feeling, between the gentle breeze of the night, the soft bobbing of the boat and sight of familiar faces. Drinking on an empty stomach had Pebble nodding off. They were completely oblivious to their surroundings and were roused by a sudden, familiar voice.

"Oi, kid, wake up! You're gonna smash into the pier!"

Pebble jolted upright, causing the boat to rock violently. They grabbed their oars and frantically worked them to stop their momentum. It worked—for the most part. The boat hit the thick wooden beam of the pier, but only hard enough to lurch Pebble forwards. Laughter echoed from further down the boardwalk. It was coming from Jeb, Pebble's elderly mentor.

"Come on, push a little harder. Or have you gotten soft in your time away?" he called out, looking at Pebble with a gentle smile.

"Gods forbid you help me out, old man," they grumbled. Pebble paddled with disgruntled energy, slowly navigating their way around a large trading vessel. Jeb was waiting by Pebble's usual disembarkment spot with rope in hand. He threw a small length to Pebble and—with little effort—swiftly tied the other end to a wooden post.

"I see you forgot to bring rope with you again," he said calmly. "What would you have done if I didn't happen to still be out and about?"

"Died in a catastrophic boating accident most likely," Pebble remarked blandly. "Honestly, I probably would have dragged my boat onto the grass again."

They finished tying the boat down, grabbed their belongings, and climbed out onto the pier. Jeb pulled Pebble into a warm embrace and squeezed them tightly.

"It's so good to see you again, it's been too long." He stepped back and clapped Pebble's shoulders with an affectionate smile plastered on his ageing face.

"It's good to see you too, Jeb. But I'm sorry to say that I won't be sticking around for long. I'm leaving again tomorrow." Pebble gestured towards the inn with a nod. "Come get a pint or two with me?"

"Hah! Absolutely, but the food's on me, kiddo." Jeb laughed heartily and began ambling onwards, leaning on his walking stick for support. Pebble followed along and let out an exasperated sigh.

"Still with the 'kiddo'? I'm twenty, not exactly a kid anymore."

Jeb chuckled. "Well, you never liked 'lad' or 'lass', so you're stuck with it 'til the day I die."

Pebble lightly slapped him on the back and grinned. "I suppose that's only another week or so then, hey, old boy?"

The pair were in high spirits as they walked into town. The streets were unusually busy for this time of night. Merchants from out of town were taking their carts back to their lodgings, and groups of well armed adventurers were sitting around their wagons on the wider streets.

"Hey, uh, Jeb, what's with—"

"There's a huge bounty out for some group of outlaws that are supposedly hiding out in the mountains to the east." He jerked a finger towards the nearest group of adventurers. "So in turn, groups like these are out to try and make some coin. Just a bunch of hooligans if you ask me. I'm glad you didn't choose that lifestyle." He scowled.

"We both know my weapon skills, well uh... suck. So it's not like it was ever a choice."

Jeb's glare broke into an expression of mild amusement. "Your words, not mine, kiddo."

The inn was overflowing with people when they arrived. Makeshift tables had been set up around the sides of the building and on the street, with each packed to capacity with all manner of individuals. Most were humans, but there were also at least a dozen dwarves and a few elves sprinkled throughout. Jeb sighed and turned to Pebble.

"Well, kiddo, I can't say I'm too thrilled about the prospects of getting knocked around just to get a bite to eat. I'd offer to cook something up for you at home, but we both know I'm a terrible chef." He prodded Pebble in the shin with his stick. "Come by my shop tomorrow, eh?"

"Sure thing, old man." Pebble nodded toward the noise. "Wish me luck."

Pebble climbed the stairs at the Gold Duck's threshold, squeezing past patrons who were either leaning against railings or trying to exit the building. Stepping inside, they immediately collided with a stout dwarf woman holding four tankards of ale.

"Watch where yer' goin', ye stringbean!" she shouted, splashing Pebble's legs with the overflowing ale.

"Crap, sorry about that," they apologised, weaving further inside. Pebble had never seen the place so packed before; at this time of night there were typically only a handful of people out for a post work drink, besides travellers who were staying upstairs. They craned their head around hoping to spot Cass, their only other friend in town and a barkeeper for the Gold Duck. It was a perfect relationship dynamic in Pebble's eyes—the only person they could stand, apart from Gripp and Jeb, also gave them a nice little discount on drinks.

Pebble fought their way up to the bar, Cass nowhere to be seen. They tried to flag down the nearest barkeep, but couldn't compete with the crowd of people trying to do the same.

Screw it, they thought to themself. They turned around, and went to push themself past two *impossibly* attractive and well armoured elves, but ended up stopping and gawking at them instead.

One elf seemed to tower over most other patrons, and had short, wavy lilac-purple hair, to compliment his boyishly handsome face. However, it was the girl to the right that Pebble stared at. They had never seen eyes so beautiful and green in their life. They seemed to glow, as if powered by luminescent mosses.

Maybe that's an elf thing, they wondered, *or maybe it's just the lighting.*

Regardless, Pebble was enraptured, trying to soak in all the details of this woman as quickly as their eyes would allow. Her peach pink hair fell in delicate waves to her chest, and seemed impossibly soft. Her radiant skin looked like it had rarely, if ever, been exposed to sunlight, complemented by form-fitted red leather armour with several strips of thin black metal. Pebble's ogling was abruptly cut short by two taps to the side of the face.

"Friend, you are blocking our way to the bar. Would you please step aside?" The lilac haired elf murmured in a voice that could melt butter. Pebble's face went red, and they nodded rapidly.

"Sorry, my lords," they squeaked, trying to step around the pair. The elves shared a glance, then smiled and laughed. Even that sounded like music to Pebble's ears.

"We are no lords, merely travellers," said the pink-haired elf. "I'm Leanore, and this is my companion, Zayle. Would you care to have a drink with us? It would be nice to learn the lay of the land from a local."

Pebble wondered why she assumed they were from around here and looked down at themself. Mud-stained shirt, barefoot, and overall looking quite dishevelled. They looked back up with an awkward smile at Leanore and Zayle.

"This is all a bit much right now," they said with a hint of panic in their voice. "If we see each other again, sure, but right now I need to find my friend." Pebble darted off immediately, not giving the beautiful strangers a chance to respond.

They moved across the inn as fast as they could, towards the stairs that lead to the next floor, trying their absolute best not to crash tackle an innocent bystander. They pushed themself flat against the wall when they made it to the bottom of the stairs, in an attempt to calm down and get their breath back.

The day was becoming too much for Pebble to handle—alcohol or not—and they knew it. Pushing themself off the wall, they moved around the stairs and headed towards the kitchen. With confidence, they strode up to the side of the bar and lifted the counter flap to let themself behind. The closest bartender turned to Pebble with an arm raised to stop them.

"Mate, you can't be back here!"

"Oh, calm down, you know me!" Pebble called back.

They stormed past the bartender then swung into the kitchen, and was immediately taken aback by how many workers were frantically preparing food. Pebble recognized Cass' fiery red hair in an instant—she was scrubbing dishes by the back windows. Nobody in the room gave more than a momentary glance at Pebble as they wove through the chaos. As they crept up behind her, they lifted Cass off the ground in a tight bear hug. She shrieked and flailed.

"Put me down, this is ridiculous, I'm trying to work!" Pebble dropped her and quickly stepped back to avoid the fury of Cass' signature right hook. As predicted, she spun around to hit Pebble, only managing to splash them with soapy water, and then launched herself at Pebble with her arms held out, forcing a long, tight hug. Cass looked up, moving her head out of Pebble's chest. "You disappear into the woods for months, and this is how you greet your best friend?" She scowled. Pebble smirked.

"Should I have swung through for five minutes on my way out of town then?"

Cass wiped her brow with the rag she kept tucked into her apron, going back to her work with a sigh.

"So, are you here to see me, or to try to get some free

booze?" she asked bluntly while scrubbing at a plate with vigour. Pebble leant down and rested their chin on her shoulder.

"Yes to both. Skip out on work, have some fun... live a little."

"Lose my job, get yelled at by Mum, don't count on it," she said in a mocking tone, then sighed in defeat.

"Look, help yourself to some stew from the pot by the hearth, grab a bottle of whatever from the cellar, and wait on the back steps for me. I can go home when I'm done with this mountain of dishes."

Pebble sized up the teetering tower of every kitchen utensil known to man.

"Yeah, this is why I have goblin friends to help me with the work. Good luck."

Cass looked incredulously at Pebble.

"*What?*"

"Sorry, Cass, food is calling to me," Pebble replied, dashing off with a bowl.

PEBBLE WAS FOUND DOZING on the bottom step at the back of the inn, with a bottle of wine in one hand, and an empty bowl on the ground beside them. Cass kneeled down and gently removed the bottle from Pebble's grasp.

"Pebbs, wake up," she said softly while patting them on the leg. Pebble stirred and sharply inhaled.

"Oh, hey," they said groggily, rubbing their eyes. Cass held out her hand and helped Pebble hoist themself onto their feet.

"Mum wont mind you spending the night, but we're

getting you out of those filthy clothes." Cass handed back the bottle.

"I sure hope you have something that fits me this time. I look like an overgrown child in your shirts," mumbled Pebble.

"You sure do," she teased. "And I adore it."

The pair started towards the back gate of the property, but Cass halted momentarily. From out of the corner of her eye, she spied a small inky black painting of a goblin on the stone foundation of the inn.

"Did you do that?"

"Yeah," Pebble replied. "I wanted to test my drawing skills, it's been a while."

"And you thought vandalism was a good place to start?" Cass' mood quickly heated.

"Nobody will care, it's not like any patrons are allowed out here."

"Urgh... alright, but if I get blamed for this, I'm sending a hunting party after you." Pebble laughed, then nodded in agreement. Cass unlatched the back gate and walked out into the back alley, with Pebble in tow. It seemed that most of the adventuring parties had retired for the evening.

Must be nice, they mused.

Cass finished locking the gate and took Pebble by the hand, leading them to her home on the other side of town. Dim lighting shone from inside most of the houses they passed, the racket from travellers likely keeping more than a few of the townsfolk awake. In silent protest, every building had its wooden shutters closed. The further they moved from the inn, the more varied the construction of the town became. From houses raised from stone foundations by the riverside with adjacent dirt roads, to much nicer, well crafted wooden homes with paved streets. The wealthier families tended to live in the latter area. Cass' grip on Pebble's hand tightened.

"Pebbs, did you want to stop by your old place on the way to mine?"

Pebble gave Cass a vacant expression.

"Why bother? I sold it for a reason." They took a sip from their bottle. "Unless you wanna try and commune with the dead or something, that could be fun." Pebble grinned.

"Yeah, great idea. That's how you get angry spirits and demons chasing after you." Cass laid the sarcasm on thick.

"They'd better know how to swim then," they quipped with an exaggerated shrug.

The pair continued at a steady pace until they arrived at the threshold of Cass' home. It was hard to see much on the property, other than the direct ground beneath them, by the flickering light from a lantern hung by the gate. Pebble snorted.

"I see your Dad still hasn't gotten around to trimming the trees. You're gonna break your neck walking through here someday."

"Don't get Mum started on the subject, unless you're prepared to hear her prattle on about it for hours," Cass huffed. "I tripped and fell into the garden a few weeks back, hence the lantern." She moved forward and led Pebble to the house, through the trees, arriving without any injuries. Pebble muffled a laugh with the back of their hand that held the wine bottle.

They whispered to Cass while kicking off their boots by the front door. "Look at you being my little protector. I'm no elf, but I can see at night with the help of the moonlight." Cass let go of Pebble's hand and raised the lantern up to her face. The glow from the tiny flame made her glare more intense than usual. She shuffled backwards into the darkness of the room while holding the look, but ended up playfully smiling as she turned to hang the lantern in a carved marble alcove. A dim light was cast into both the room and the adjacent hallway, throwing shadows from the dining room table and chairs onto the artwork on the walls. The depth unsettled Pebble, as the lighting caused the people in the paintings to look like faceless shadow creatures. Cass had disappeared down the hall to her room. Pebble tried to step quietly towards the rocking chair by the fireplace but the wooden floorboards creaked with each step, making a sound like one very drawn out groan, echoing throughout the house. They cringed as they lowered themself onto the old rocking chair. It, too, creaked in turn as Pebble leaned back and sat in silence, wondering if they should build up a fire. Cass' voice echoed from the other end of the house.

"Did you know that creeping around makes more noise than just doing the thing?"

"I figured your Mum was sleeping. I was trying to be considerate."

Cass waddled back into the room in her nightgown and tossed a clean shirt onto Pebble's head.

"Mum's old, she won't hear much."

"Fair enough."

Pebble peeled off their grass stained shirt and threw it to the floor beside them. Cass quickly averted her eyes, leaving the room to give Pebble privacy.

"Hey, Cass, are you gonna give me pants too? Or are you giving me permission to sit around half naked?"

A pair of pants flew into the room from the hallway, crumpling onto the floor.

"Absolutely not. Hurry up and get changed, I want to get a fire going and share some of that wine you brought."

Pebble changed into the fresh pair of pants and leaned into the hallway. Cass almost burst into laughter when she saw her tiny clothes on Pebble's tall frame.

"Oh, you look like the best kind of ridiculous."

Pebble groaned in turn. "I would have been fine with just a blanket."

"Sorry, no nudity allowed in this fine establishment, I'm afraid."

Cass grabbed the lantern from its alcove and sauntered into the kitchen, with Pebble trailing behind. This section of the house always felt the most foreign to Pebble; the house they'd grown up in only had two bedrooms, a section for bathing, and all meals were prepared in the hearth in the largest room of the house. Cass, however, lived in seeming luxury. Her kitchen was primarily made from stone, which her dad had painstakingly ground down and polished.

Pebble carefully hoisted themself up onto the large marble top counter so they could watch Cass potter about. Cass disappeared down into the cellar, leaving Pebble in the cool, dark room alone. While left unattended, they realised that it had been quite a while since they had been in such a calm, quiet and... *safe* location. Pebble put their head in their hands and took a deep breath, in an attempt to relax a little. It didn't really help though; their body was aching all over. The silence was broken by a call from the depths of the cellar.

"Are you hungry?"

"Sure, half of everything sounds good."

Cass took too long to respond. Pebble pushed off the

counter, back onto their feet, and squatted by the cellar's steps.

"Found anything for me yet?"

"Well, if you like cheese, cheese, and *more* cheese, I can accommodate you."

Pebble's soft laugh echoed down the steps.

"A gourmet meal that bards will sing songs of for years to come."

Cass leapt into view holding a cheese wheel the size of her head, while grinning like an idiot. She climbed the stairs and palmed off the cheese to Pebble, then unfurled a leather roll resting on the counter to reveal several knives and a pair of scissors. Cass pulled out the smallest knife, flipped it to rest against her forearm, and ushered Pebble back into the dining room. She arranged small pieces of wood into the fireplace, and soon had a steady flame growing with the help of her lantern. Pebble and Cass sprawled across the floor in front of the fireplace, hacking away at the cheese and passing Pebble's appropriated wine bottle back and forth. Cass chatted away, while Pebble continued to excavate the crumbling wheel of cheese.

"I've gotta say"—Pebble paused to stab the knife into the cheese—"I did not expect to return to a large gathering of well-armed strangers."

"We didn't entirely expect it either. Luckily for us, we had enough ale supplied in time for the bulk of the groups." Cass idly played with the bottle, gazing into the flames of the fireplace.

"Normally it would be exciting to meet all these new people, but given the circumstances I just..." She looked back to Pebble. "I just hope none of the adventurers get hurt."

"I mean, me too, but people chasing a bounty know

what they're in for. You don't learn how to use a weapon, roam around the countryside, and take bounties without anticipating the possibility of getting a fun little knife to the gut."

Cass grimaced. "You make it sound so casual."

"It is what it is," Pebble said with a shrug. "At least there's a few good-looking people in town now.' Cass gave a feigned look of shock, and threw a small chunk of cheese at Pebble in retaliation. Pebble caught it in their mouth and grinned, then swiped the wine bottle back.

"Well, I heard about your run in with the elf twins at the bar. It sounded like you panicked and ran away."

"Who told you that?" Pebble crossed their arms. "And besides, the only people I've ever really talked to are the ones who live here. What was I supposed to do? Ask about their opinion on their favourite time of day to go fishing?" Pebble flushed red, recalling the encounter.

"One of the other barkeeps told me while you were taking a nap outside. Just be yourself next time. Smile and wave." She paused. "Maybe wear some clean clothes."

"Whatever you say, little bird."

Cass pretended to reach over for the wine, and smacked Pebble on the forehead.

"I'll skin you with this cheese knife if you keep it up with that dumb nickname."

"I can call you 'cassowary' if you prefer? I've always said that it suits you. I hear that they're dangerous."

"Oh, like you're one to talk. You named yourself 'Pebble'." Cass was sulking now. Arms crossed and pouting.

"Yes, well... my old name didn't have that unique ring to it that 'Pebble' has. Pebbles are annoying, and the smaller ones get stuck in your boots. I try to embody that," they said proudly.

"You've got that part down for sure. You are quite annoying."

"I sure am, but you love me." Pebble yanked their bag towards them and pulled out the box of cave bugs. "Anyway, I have a gift for you. I figured you can use them for dye or painting."

Cass's face lit up with excitement as she received the box and examined the collection. "Thank you so much, this is actually really thoughtful of you."

"Well." Pebble scratched their head and laughed nervously, "I was sorta hoping you could either get me some fishing equipment, or give me some money for my efforts."

"So you want to sell me these, not give them to me out of the goodness of your heart?"

"Correct."

"Urgh, fine. You can have whatever I made at the inn last night."

"Did you not count it?"

"I only work there to socialise." Cass leant back. "I'm not exactly hurting for money here."

"That sounds like a nightmare." Pebble shuddered. "People aren't my strong suit."

"And that is exactly why you live like a caveman, and keep goblins for company."

"I sure do. They're better company than most humans if I'm being honest. I really don't understand why people try to attack them, these ones are basically just excitable children."

"Prejudice dies hard, I suppose," Cass said.

"I guess so..." They sat in silence, until Pebble remembered their gift from earlier in the day. "Gripp, my best goblin pal, is a huge help to me out there. He also let me borrow this." Pebble reached into a pocket of the bag, removing the ornate pen from its cloth sheath and holding it up into the light for Cass to see. The gems glowed blue, and refracted onto their faces.

"Huh. Haven't seen it do that before." Pebble wasn't bothered. "But anyways, it doesn't need ink, and I'm pretty sure it doesn't wash off."

"Doesn't need ink? Surely not." Cass leaned in closer to get a better look. "It looks like it has elven runes engraved on it. Pebbs, you can't read them, can you?"

"I figured they were decorative. I didn't think they translated to anything."

"Time for me to flex my superior reading skills, then." Cass took the pen and laid it on the ground, looking over it a few times, as if to make sure she was accessing the correct translation within her mind. After a few rotations, she nodded, seemingly satisfied.

"Okay, so, the runes on this side roughly translate to something along the lines of 'enhance'." She rolled it to its other side. "And these ones say 'create'."

Lost in thought while staring at the gems, Pebble drummed their fingers against the now empty bottle.

"What the heck does that even mean? Enhance and create?" Pebble asked.

"Dunno... maybe command words that affect the flow of the ink? Or the colour? If I made a magic pen, those would be useful features for me."

Cass peeled herself off the floor and disappeared back to her room. She returned with pieces of scrap paper and flopped them down next to Pebble.

"Only one way to find out. Write something down

and pick a word. Maybe enhance will improve your chicken scratch handwriting."

"Maybe it'll improve your drawings."

Cass smacked Pebble on the thigh, igniting laughter between the two of them.

"Okay, let's do this." Pebble scrawled their name down on one of the scraps while Cass watched, wide-eyed with excitement. She tried to smudge the ink but it dried immediately, the same as earlier that day when Pebble first tested it. They took a deep breath.

"Enhance?"

Nothing happened.

"Well, that was something alright," Cass commented. "Maybe the magic is just the ink itself.'

"Screw it. Create!"

Pebble felt their hand go numb as the gems lit up the room with brilliant blue beams of light. The writing started smoking and sputtering little fiery globs of ink, causing the paper to quickly go up in flames—taking out the other pieces with it. They both panicked and scrambled far away from the paper.

"What in the hells was that? That seems entirely counterproductive for a pen if it's just going to burn the surface it's on!" Cass shrieked from the entrance of the kitchen.

"Your guess is as good as mine!" hollered Pebble from behind the dining table. There was a long period of silence before they both hesitantly moved towards the remnants of the paper.

Only ash remained. Pebble shook their numb hand, hoping to get some feeling back. But it stayed dead and cold to the touch. Cass crouched down and cautiously picked up the pen, holding it between her index fingers.

"Fair warning," Pebble said. "My hand went numb when I said 'create'."

"What about when you said 'enhance'?"

Suddenly, Cass yelped as the pen lit up again—this time shining green. Her hands drooped, and she dropped the pen. But it didn't hit the ground—it stopped just above the floorboards, levitating on the spot. It began to spin rapidly.

'Cass! Move back!'

Pebble's desperate yell fell on deaf ears. Cass was curled into a ball and sobbing. Pebble rushed over to scoop her up, and carried her out of the room into the kitchen while the pen continued to spin. As Pebble set her down on the counter, they both heard a *pop*, accompanied by the sound of glass breaking. The eerie green light went out, and the house was dark again. Cass was still crying, her limp hands dangling. Pebble held her, stroking her hair with their one good hand.

"Just focus on breathing okay? You're safe, I've got you."

They weren't entirely sure on whether or not they were safe, but they said it anyway. Pebble touched her hands; ice cold, just like their right hand. Guilt began to set in. What if she never got feeling back? What if this was a curse? These thoughts set Pebble on the precipice of a massive spiral into self-hatred.

"Will you be alright if I go check out what happened?" Cass wiped her puffy eyes with her forearm and nodded. Pebble stuck their head around the corner of the doorway to peer into the room. They had never seen anything like it—the floor was coated in what looked to be some sort of sparkling dust. Relief washed over them when they saw that the pen had fallen to the floor and lay stagnant.

"Alright, I think it's over," they said, looking back to Cass. "How are your hands? Mine feels slightly less cold now."

Cass held out her arms for Pebble to see. Her hands still dangled limply. She looked up at Pebble with her tear-stained face, looking absolutely miserable.

"I can't feel them at all, Pebbs. What am I going to do?" Her bottom lip trembled and she struggled to speak. "I won't be able to do anything without them."

"Try not to worry about that just yet, it might take some time for our hands to heal." Pebble put on a brave face for Cass' sake and began looking for a broom.

They scoured the multiple cupboards in the room, eventually finding a decrepit straw broom. Trying to sweep with only one hand proved challenging to say the least, but they were just thankful it was only a small patch and not an entire room filled with the stuff. They leaned the broom up against the rocking chair when they finished, and stooped down to see what had become of the pen; one of the embedded gems looked to have shattered.

"Well, that explains the mess," they muttered to themself. Carefully, they slipped the pen into its cloth sheath and placed it back in their satchel. Feeling had begun to return to their hand, and they sighed with relief. They returned to the kitchen to check on Cass to find she was rocking back and forth with her eyes closed.

"How are you holding up?" they asked, reaching out to stroke her hair. Cass stopped rocking and looked up, eyes still bloodshot.

"My hands feel cold. I guess that's an improvement."

"Okay, that's reassuring, mine did the same before

the feeling started to come back." Pebble held up their numb hand and managed to lightly wiggle their index finger. It barely moved, but it was something. Cass let out a shaky sigh of relief.

"I'm exhausted. I want to try to sleep this off." She climbed down from the bench, and wearily walked to her room. Pebble followed her out, pausing to double-check that the wine bottle was empty, and scooped their bag up as they went. They went down the hall, passing two empty guest bedrooms and a dark sunroom full of books. Sounds of heavy snoring could be heard from behind the heavy door of Cass' parents room at the very end of the hallway. Cass stood in front of her closed bedroom door, with her head hung.

"Would you mind getting this for me?" she whispered, though Pebble would never admit how pitiful she sounded. They twisted the doorknob and gave it a firm push. Cass made a beeline for her bed and wiggled under the blankets. Unsure of what to do next, or if she would need more help, Pebble remained stationary by the door. The moonlight illuminated Cass' face. Her pale blue eyes fixated on Pebble, still swollen from crying.

"Get in here already," she huffed. "You're crazy if you think I'm spending the night alone."

Pebble stepped inside, closing the door behind them, and slipped into the bed beside her.

MORNINGS' warm embrace coaxed Pebble from their deep slumber. The curtains had been left open, leaving the sun to shine directly onto the pair in bed. Cass remained asleep, her head smooshed up against Pebble's shoulder and was gripping their hand between both of hers. Pebble squinted around the sunlit room in an attempt to get their bearings. They gently pulled their hand from Cass' grip and propped themself up, but the movement roused her from her sleep. She lay there blinking for a few moments, then looked up to Pebble, bleary eyed.

"Why are my hands so sweaty?" She froze. "Oh gods, I can feel them again!" The exclamation was followed by her jolting upright, pulling the sheets to their waists as she shook her hands.

"Mine seem to be fine as well." Pebble held out their hand for Cass to inspect. There didn't appear to be any signs of damage on either of their hands, nor any traces of magic that they could perceive. A yawning sigh of relief was shared between the two as they flopped onto their backs. Cass rolled onto her side and pinched the skin on Pebble's exposed stomach.

"Remind me to never use that pen again. I think I'm happy to stick with actual ink. Actual ink and working hands."

Pebble was lost in thought, staring at the ceiling, and didn't respond to Cass' statement. In response, Cass lightly tapped their face, then pinched their nose.

"What are you, a crab? You're so pinchy today," Pebble said, their voice nasal.

"You weren't giving me attention, so I chose violence." She released them with a flourish.

"As one does." Pebble massaged the offended area. "Breakfast?"

"Breakfast."

Cass launched herself over Pebble, landing nimbly on both feet at the side of the bed. She left the room, and the sounds of her footsteps faded as she wandered further down the hall. Pebble pulled their clothes from their bag and began to get changed. They could hear yelling from multiple voices outside, accompanied by the clanging of metal, but it was too distant to make much sense of it. Pebble chalked it up to rowdy adventurers, and made their way out to the kitchen. The windows in each room had been opened, letting the cool breeze flow freely through the house. They swung into the kitchen to find Cass and her mother preparing food and chatting away.

"Hey, Mum, how've you been?" Pebble asked the homely woman. She was the perfect likeness of Cass, just with twenty or so more years behind her. Cass' mum swooped in and gave Pebble a huge squeeze. They were immediately in pain, it felt like their entire torso had been bludgeoned with a sack of potatoes, and the hug was the sack being emptied onto them. Yesterday's tumble down the hill was now rearing its ugly head.

"Oh, how I missed having you around, how have you been?" she asked, then released Pebble. Pebble did their best to internalise the pain before they responded.

"I've been okay. Just swinging through to see Cass and buy some supplies." Pebble noticed Cass' smile before she turned to grab a plate.

"Well, now that you're both up and about, would either of you care to explain why there's a boot by my front door that looks like it was thrown into a fire?'

Cass and Pebble looked at each other in utter confusion.

Outside, sure enough, one of Pebble's boots had a gaping hole in the side.

"It sure as hell wasn't like that when I left it by the door last night." Pebble scratched their head.

"Pebbs..." Cass paused, waiting for Pebble to look at her. "Didn't you draw on your boot with the pen?"

Pebble froze.

"That's not the only thing I drew on."

They dashed back to Cass' room to grab their belongings and sprinted out of the house in the direction of the Gold Duck. Cass called after Pebble, but they were deaf to her cries. Groups of adventurers roamed the town on guard in loose formations. Nobody seemed to give more than an initial glance at Pebble, despite looking utterly tragic with their stained clothes and lack of shoes. As they got closer to the busier part of town, they noticed archers patrolling on the roofs of the tallest buildings. Pebble's sprint devolved into a strangled jog.

What in the hells is happening here?

A group of dwarves walked by, sporting greataxes and crossbows, and Pebble decided it was time to get answers. They called out and waved an arm to try to flag the group down.

"Why is everyone on edge? Did someone attack the town?" They panted for breath, and leant forward to rest their hands on their knees. From somewhere within the group, a burly woman with an intricately braided beard stepped forward.

"Ye livin' under a rock? Strange creatures crept into town, attackin' whoever they could find. We're out makin' sure we got 'em all."

Pebble was well and truly confused. "Creatures? Like what?"

"Like rock monsters and wooden humans. It sounds bizarre, but I ain't lyin'. They killed poor Willem in the middle of the night while he was takin' a piss."

Some of the dwarves murmured amongst themselves. Pebble straightened, trying to see any traces of these creatures, but had no such luck.

"Where did this happen?"

"One was by the tavern, a few more near the stables."

Pebble sprinted off without so much as a thank you or a farewell. "Bloody stringbean" was heard from behind them with accompanying armoured footsteps trailing away. They had begun to feel nauseated from the sudden exercise on an empty stomach, but managed to push through it all the way to the alley behind the inn. The back gate was open, and the sounds of a conversation behind the fence could vaguely be heard. Pebble stumbled over to the fence and supported themself against it, panting heavily while they fought off the urge to vomit. The talking stopped, and the street became quiet. There were sudden, hushed whispers. Before they even had the chance to move, three men flung themselves into the alley with their weapons drawn.

"Relax, guys," a melodic voice sung through the air. "It's just our friend from the bar."

Pebble moved into the centre of the alley and looked to the roof of the inn. Leanore was crouched down on the edge of the tiled roof, with a shortbow in one hand, bracing herself with the other. They realised one of the men that had burst into the alleyway was Zayle. The other two, however, were unfamiliar. Pebble nervously looked around the group with an anxious smile.

"So, uh, what brings you to this fine alley?" they asked casually.

"There was a creature made from stone, right here in this yard," Zayle responded smoothly, as he stepped towards Pebble. "What I don't understand is, how a monstrosity such as that could get back there without

306

damaging so much as a stray plant, let alone the fence or gate."

Pebble maintained their awkward smile and stepped around the group to get a look at the thing. The group eyed them off but remained where they were. Pebble peered into the yard and felt their stomach drop; a giant stone goblin lay on the ground before them. They moved in closer to get a better look of the creature, pacing around it several times.

"So what's your theory, friend?" Leanore called out after a time. "Our best guess is it was summoned here."

"Summoned? Like with magic or something?"

"Yes. It likely has something to do with the sigil drawn on the wall over there." She pointed to Pebble's drawing on the inn's wall from the night before. Its black lines had become scorch marks, as though it had been drawn with flames. A looming sense of dread built within Pebble.

Play it cool, they thought.

"I don't know much about magic, but that sounds like a good theory." Pebble paused, waiting for anyone else to respond. When they didn't, they continued, "I mean, anyone could have put this here, there are a heap of new faces in town."

Zayle stepped into the yard, and jumped onto the chest of the crumbling remains of the rock goblin. He began prodding its jaw with the bottom of his spear. "I'm honestly not sure if this is meant to be an ogre, or a troll of some sort. It's the ears that I'm most unfamiliar with."

"Well, if it's either of those things, it's certainly not from around here," Pebble replied.

Zayle pointed his spear at Pebble. "And how can you be so sure about that?"

"I've explored the forests in this area my entire life. There's only animals."

Zayle twirled his spear idly and locked eyes with Leanore. Pebble caught the subtle exchange between the elves, and kept up their seeming ignorance behind the facade of being uninformed. With cat-like agility, Leanore jumped down onto the wooden fence and balanced on top of it.

"Looks like we have another visitor," she said, gesturing to the other side of the tall fence. Pebble heard a small breathless voice greet Leanore from the alley.

"Oh, yes, hello. Is my friend over there?"

Cass had followed them into town, it seemed.

"If your friend wears dirty clothes and has a mop of bedraggled hair, you've come to the right place."

Cass slid across the gravel, and let out an exasperated sigh as she came into view.

"Gods, there you are, why did you run off without me?"

Pebble thought they had found their opportunity to slip out of here without further scrutiny. They looked her up and down, and gestured to her clothing.

"I think the better question is, why did you rush after me in heavy boots and a sundress?"

"They were the first things I could find. I'm not running barefoot and in trashed clothes like you," she huffed. "And why have rocks been moved into the yard?"

"Everyone's a critic," they replied, and started walking around the stone remains. "It's the body of some sort of a rock monster apparently. But I'm sure they have it under control, we'll clearly just be in the way and should move on. Goodbye, handsome strangers."

Pebble took Cass by the hand and hastily led her towards the river, out of the elves' line of sight. Pulling her behind one of the fishing huts, they peeked around the side of the building to see if they had been followed. Cass began to speak but was hushed immediately by a raised finger. A few minutes went by without any sign of being tailed before Pebble slumped down against the stone wall and covered their eyes with their hands.

"Why are you acting so weird? I didn't think a rock monster would shake you up this badly." Cass crouched down and pushed aside one of Pebble's hands. Tears had pooled under their palms and were now left to flow freely.

"You don't get it, little bird, there was more than one. I'm so sure this is my fault."

"How?"

"The drawing I did last night, the one at the inn... it's all burnt up now. And then suddenly there's this massive, *real* version of it, only metres away."

Cass bit her bottom lip. "Okay, but.." She trailed off as she scanned the forest line. "If that was the cause of it being there, you couldn't have known what would happen."

Pebble threw down their hands and turned to Cass, looking at her with bloodshot eyes.

"Cass. Have you stopped to consider the other things that have been drawn with this pen? Someone was killed last night." Pebble dug their fingernails into their thighs, inhaling deeply before continuing. "But if I'm being honest, I'm more concerned about the goblins. Gripp treated the forest as his personal canvas, and I need to go in there to make sure they're safe."

"Pebbs, you haven't fought a day in your life. If we

really did create monsters last night, I don't think it's safe to go alone."

Pebble chuckled and wiped their eyes with their shirt. "Cass, you couldn't fight your way out of a wet paper bag. I don't think you should follow me."

Cass smacked them on the shoulder. "I didn't mean me. Go grab one of the many adventurers in town to help you out. You were literally talking to some before you dragged me away."

"And risk murder-happy strangers turning on my friends just because they're different? Hells no. I'll figure something out myself." Pebble stood back up and slung their bag over their shoulder. "I'll come back to you as soon as I can. Please be safe."

"You better be safe as well. I'm banning you from dying."

"Alright, I'll be sure to pass that on to any monsters I encounter." Pebble gave Cass a tight hug, then sprinted towards the forest.

PEBBLE CRASHED through bushes and headed directly for the goblin commune. They scanned their surroundings, looking for any signs of danger, but the forest looked to be the same as always so far, though the sounds of Pebble tearing through the local plant life scared off more than a few birds and the occasional turkey. It didn't take long at all for them to run out of energy. Just as before, exercise on an empty stomach had a tendency to make them feel violently ill. They slowed their pace to a jog, then came to a complete stop when they found a boulder to sit on. But there was no time to completely stop and rest; their eyes darted around, trying to find anything out of the ordinary. There was still no sign of monster activity. Steadying their breath, they pushed off the boulder, continuing inland.

Clack clack clack.

Pebble had only taken a couple of steps before they heard the unusual noise. They dropped down low, anticipating an attack. Nothing came for them, but the sounds of wooden blocks hitting each other continued. Pebble moved from tree to tree, now wary of their footing. Pushing their back against a tree, they braced for the worst, then poked their head around to try to catch a glimpse of the noise. At first there appeared to be nothing, until they saw what looked to be four rounded planks of wood smacking against each other in a nearby bush.

"What am I even looking at here?" Pebble murmured. After some brief internal deliberation, they hesitantly tip-toed towards the planks. It didn't seem to react to their presence, and kept clacking away. Pebble reached down and picked up a long stick from the ground, then lightly prodded at the wood. To Pebble's surprise, it didn't react.

"Okay, weird moving wooden thing, don't hurt me and I won't use you as firewood."

They reached down and pulled it out of the bush as gently as they could. It was a large wooden bee, roughly the size of a fat house cat. Pebble stumbled away from the bee, expecting it to suddenly burst into flight and attack them. But it just kept weakly smacking its wings against each other and the grassy floor.

"I guess you're too heavy to fly now. That's sort of depressing," Pebble said, looking around for signs of a bee drawing. Behind them, the tree they'd hidden behind had a scorched bee outline burnt into it. The drawing was at about waist height, and the size of their head.

"Okay, well, you don't look like you can hurt anyone, so I'll figure out how to deal with you later." Pebble was unsure if this creature could even understand them, but they figured it couldn't hurt to try and communicate with it.

Leaving the wooden bee behind, they broke into a steady jog to try and make up for lost time.

But there were no further sightings of magically spawned creatures on the last leg of the journey. As they approached the walls of the commune, Pebble began to pick up the scent of smoke and meat. The goblins lived in a shallow cave, which had a long, winding wall made from loose stones that had been found around the forest and by the river. This wall only came up about a metre or so in height, but Pebble considered it to be an impressive feat, considering they carried most of the rocks by hand. Laughter echoed out of the cave, as did the sounds of sticks smacking together. Weathered canvas tents set up within the walls came into view, as Pebble ascended the pathway into the goblins' home. As they turned the final corner of the walled pathway, something cracked them in the shin, bringing them down onto one knee. Pebble yelped from the sudden and intense pain. Initially, they thought someone had tossed a brick at them, until they heard thudding on the ground behind them. A small stone rabbit hopped aimlessly down the trail, paying no further attention to Pebble's shins. Pebble briefly nursed the small egg that had formed on leg with tears in their eyes, until they were interrupted.

"Pebble-Person is back! Do you have meat?"

One of the younger goblins in the clan had come to

investigate the noise. He crouched down to look at Pebble's grazed skin. "You okay? Why do you cry?' He stared into Pebble's eyes, looking as though he had another barrage of questions at the ready.

"You're Lickrox right? I'll live, but help me up." The goblin nodded in response and held out a hand. Pebble pulled themself up with Lickrox's assistance and hobbled into the main section of the commune. They expected to see a bunch of goblins sitting around a campfire cooking food together, but instead found an assortment of large stone and wood tools, piled up in what looked to be a giant boat made from one smooth piece of rock. The boat had completely crushed one of the tents, and around the area, small animals made from stone milled about aimlessly. Pebble moved in closer, but was cut off by a chorus of cheers from the goblin clan.

"Pebble-Person, Pebble-Person, Pebble-Person!"

Pebble blinked in surprise, and looked around.

"Damn, I should come here more often," they said to the small crowd. "I don't have any meat though, sorry."

Three of the older, grey-skinned goblins groaned and went back to their tents. Gripp and Yowl bounded through the crowd toward Pebble, holding exceptionally well-made wooden swords.

"Look, look! Proper sword for fighting!" Gripp declared, jumping with excitement.

"Where did you get these from?" Pebble asked.

"They fall from tree last night. Same with bunny." Gripp held out a finger in the direction of the forest. Pebble pointed over to the boat and its pile of goods.

"And where did they come from?"

"They fall from wall."

"Did you by any chance draw on the wall with the pen you gave me?"

"Yes! Painting glow red and out came boat and spear."

"It looks like there's more than just spears."

"Yes! Rock food fall from wall, but they just taste like rock."

Pebble turned towards Yowl. "Do you have anything to add, or has Gripp covered everything?"

Yowl grinned and smacked Gripp in the back with her wooden sword.

"That everything! Why don't you have meat?"

"I ran into some trouble in town." Pebble walked over to the cave walls and inspected the scorched drawings.

Just like at the inn, each drawing had been burnt into the stone. Dozens upon dozens of varying items were haphazardly drawn on the walls, including one boat that looked like Pebble's, but a smidge smaller. Curiosity brimmed within Pebble's mind; it was time for an experiment. They held the pen up to an untouched part of the wall and drew a basic fish outline, then took three steps back.

"Create."

The ink sparked immediately, then glowed red with small flames spurting from it. This time, however, the pen only glowed a soft blue at the command word. Stone crumbed and cracked as an object began to form within the outline.

A chunk of stone fell to the ground with a hefty thud and started flopping about. A stone fish, acting exactly like a fish out of water would. To Pebble's surprise, their hand didn't go numb. They fully anticipated and braced for it, but it never came. Gasps of amazement came from the onlookers. Gripp, Yowl and Lickrox were wide-eyed.

"Do it again!" Lickrox squealed. Pebble laughed and indulged the request.

"I hope you like cats," they said, starting on the next outline. It was a little janky; Cass was always the artist of the two but it turned out decent—albeit a little chunky.

"Create!"

Once again, sparks and flames flared out of the linework, and a rough-looking fat cat fell to the ground. It looked around, then up at Pebble. Its mouth opened as though it was trying to make a sound, but nothing came from it. This time the goblins collectively gasped. Instinctively, Pebble knelt down and held out a hand to try and coax the cat over for a pat. To everyone's surprise, it stomped on over and bumped its head against their knuckles. It managed to scratch Pebble's skin with its coarse texture, but they were too captivated in the moment to care. It was time to test the pen's other feature.

"Alright, guys, step back. I'm going to make them bigger."

"Bigger!?" the three asked in unison.

"Yep. Enhance!"

The outlines of the fish and the cat spat out flames once again. Gems on the pen began to flicker green rays of light, as both of the stone constructs creaked and rattled, growing to almost double their original size. Pebble's hand started to tingle as though the blood flow had been cut off for a few minutes, but the feeling remained. Meanwhile, there was now a massive stone fish flailing about violently. They held their arms out wide and ushered the goblins to step back with them.

"Okay, there's tools in the boat right? Grab me the biggest ones you've got," they said with urgency. The three goblins ran off to rummage through the pile. However, the problem was solved by the giant cat; it pounced on the fish, smacking it repeatedly with clumsy stone paws. Unfortunately for the cat, as it destroyed the fish, it damaged itself in the process. They both shattered more and more with each blow until the fish stopped moving. By the time the cat was done beating on it, it had lost its entire right arm and cracks had begun to form through its body.

"Good kitty?" Pebble said, looking to the goblins to gauge their reactions. They were holding hammers and spears, staring cautiously at the cat.

"Will it eat us?" Gripp whispered. Yowl looked up at Pebble for their response.

"You smash cat for us?'"

Pebble turned to the cat and tried communicating with it.

"Sit?"

The cat dropped its hindquarters, looking at Pebble as though awaiting further orders. Pebble cocked their head and stared it down.

"Well, you're the first cat I've ever met that has actually listened to me... For that you get a name. I think I'm gonna call you Gravy."

Pebble heard Lickrox's small voice whisper behind them. "What is a Gravy?"

"It is yummy drippings," Gripp whispered back. Pebble dropped to the ground, laughing at the exchange while shaking their head.

"Gravy is the part where you have questions?" They stretched out their legs and looked out at the sky. "Have any other creatures come near this area? There was an attack on the town by things similar to these." Gripp shuffled on the spot.

"Angry rock men near road chase Gripp, but Gripp good at hiding."

"Okay. I think I can deal with them with the help of Gravy."

"You fight with drippings?" Lickrox asked Pebble, while looking to the others for clarification. Yowl smacked him on the back of the head in response.

"With big cat, dummy."

"Yes, with my big cat." Pebble sat back up. "Now, come on. Into the forest."

With renewed energy, Pebble pushed onwards to the main road. They didn't bother trying to move quietly; Gravy was smashing through the terrain with no regard for itself or the plants around it, though it was slow going as it had to hobble on its three legs, with cracks forming from its missing limb with each step. As the trees in the area had started becoming sparser, Pebble knew they were getting close and slowed their pace to match the cats. Through a clearing, they caught a glimpse of a shambling rock person moving between the trees with another two following close behind. Pebble reached up to pat Gravy on the back.

"Go get 'em."

Gravy ran in at full speed, crashing through the bushes, wobbling precariously as it went. The rock men responded to the noise by running at Gravy with their arms raised. With an astonishing pounce, Gravy crushed the nearest rock man with its rotund body. There was a crack as Gravy's good leg sheared away from its body. The remaining rock men broke Gravy down into rubble with a series of unrelenting punches and body slams. One lost a fist from the battle, but otherwise were unscathed. They spotted Pebble and stormed towards them, arms raised. A pang of panic shot through them and they sprinted in the opposite direction. Pulling out the pen, they ran to the nearest tree and began to draw.

"Create!"

They ran to a nearby boulder, ready to repeat the process. The line of ink on the tree smoked and briefly burnt, as the rough form of a dog splintered from the tree trunk and landed on its paws. It raised its head and wagged its tail, while looking around with seeming curiosity.

"I hate to do this to you so soon, but please try your best to kill those big guys for me." Pebble pointed to the incoming rock men. Without any hesitation, the wooden dog galloped towards the rock man that was missing a hand, launching itself directly into its chest. They smashed into a thick tree.

The sound of the impact resonated throughout the area as both creatures fell to the ground. Pebble's newest creation had a major dent on its snout and brow that had become a mess of splintered wood. It had fared better than its opponent, which had cracked in half after being knocked into the tree. Its upper body moved weakly, but wasn't in any shape to do anything further.

But the remaining rock monster didn't hesitate to continue the attack, and punched the dog on its rear end, sending a burst of wood chunks and splinters across the forest floor. Seeing this, Pebble scrambled to put pen to boulder, drawing another dog. As the newest creation formed, the wooden dog latched onto the rock man's leg. Just as the rock man raised its fist to deal a finishing blow, it was utterly decimated by the dog formed from the boulder. The area was coated in dust and debris from the battle, both dogs trotted towards Pebble and sat in front of them, patiently waiting for further orders.

"Uh, good boys?" they said nervously. "I don't have the most experience with dogs, but you sure get the job done." The stone dog licked their leg with a rough tongue that felt like a cheese grater being dragged against their skin, ripping off leg hair as it went. Pebble recoiled.

"Okay, no more licking!" The dog lowered its head and started backpedalling. "Don't be a baby, you did good." Pebble knelt down to inspect the wooden dog. It hadn't fared well after its battle; there were multiple chunks missing, along with other abrasions.

"I think you'll be okay for now, friend. Come. We're going back to check on some other friends." They gently patted the wooden dog, trying to avoid getting any splinters in the process. Pebble and their two strange dogs headed back to the goblins. A general sense of safety had begun to form within themself, now that they knew they could forge their own personal protectors from seemingly anything. This was especially welcome, as they had been running place to place since the moment they woke up. Two full days of roaming had taken a toll on them; they were in need of a very long rest, and soon.

"I wish I had some paper with me," Pebble said to the dogs between heavy breaths. "I really want to see if I can make a functioning bird or butterflies." Both dogs tilted their heads, as though trying to understand what they were saying. "Maybe I'll try it tomorrow. After I take the mother of all naps, and swipe some food from Cass when I see how she's doing."

The goblin wall had come into view, after what felt like an eternity of walking. Pebble stopped and sat against a tree, trying to recharge one last little burst of stamina before they had to wander the rocky pathway. Nearby, birds were chirping and watching the unusual group from the branches above. A tiny green parrot with a patchy red crest decided to investigate closer, and landed on the wooden dog's head. The dog didn't react to its new feathered hat, even when Pebble reached forward to interact with the bird.

Suddenly, their brief repose amongst the peaceful surroundings of the forest was cut short by a horrific screech that echoed from the goblin camp. Both dogs snapped to attention, leaning forward with their teeth bared. Pebble scrambled across the dirt, kicking into a sprint with the dogs following closely from behind. Further sounds of screaming and shouting intensified as Pebble tore their way along the path. They could now make out four figures within the camp. Pebble's stomach dropped.

Lilac and peach hair.

Leanore heard Pebble and their dogs, and turned to face them.

"I was wondering if you were going to show up," she called out. "You're a terrible liar by the way." The rest of her group turned to watch their approach. Fearing the worst, Pebble steadied their pace as they neared the entrance. An older goblin lay dead in the entrance of its tent, an arrow decorating its chest. Pebble spotted Gripp trying to protect Yowl by the stone boat, with a spear held up in defence.

"Why would you do this?' Pebble screamed, blind with fear and rage. "They did nothing to you!"

Zayle responded with a snort and spat on the ground.

"They needn't do anything to us. They're monsters, plain and simple."

Pebble was speechless. Leanore drew an arrow from the quiver on her back and jumped on top of a nearby barrel.

"So 'Pebble-Person', what other rare items do you have to share with us?" Leanore purred. "We know about Anduron's Pen, and if you have that you must have other possessions of his."

"I haven't heard that name before in my life. This is all I have!" Pebble cried. "Just take it and leave us alone, we don't want any trouble."

Leanore's expression turned dark.

"Don't lie to me!" She turned and fired an arrow at Gripp. He yelped, collapsing onto the ground. Yowl cried with anguish, pressing around the arrow in his chest, eyes wide and skin pale.

Pebble's heart hammered furiously, they couldn't remain passive any longer.

"Stop them from touching the goblins!" With the command, and a smack to their sides from their master, the dogs charged in and leapt at Zayle, and one of their human companions. Pebble's command caught the men off guard, and they were quickly knocked down. Before it had a chance to rip into Zayle, the stone dog took a thunderous blow to the back by one of the elves' lackeys. The warhammer did catastrophic damage to the stone beneath it, splitting the dog in two. Leanore sent three arrows flying, piercing into the side of the wooden dog, but it took no notice of the damage and tore into its foe's face. Pebble quickly realised that the dog's current capabilities wouldn't be enough to save them.

"Enhance!" they cried. Before Leanore could turn on them, they dropped to the ground and put the rocky wall between them and the elf. Their right hand had begun to go numb from the augmentation, but they couldn't stop their assault yet. Peaking over the top of the rocks, they saw their wooden creation expand in size and continue its attack. When it changed targets, its bloodstained face came into view. Pebble's stomach rolled, but they had to remain focused.

Okay, that's one down, they thought.

They drew another dog, this time on the dirt floor of the forest and much bigger in size. Pebble heard footsteps rushing towards them, and knew it was now or never.

"Create! Enhance!"

A gargantuan dog full of dirt, stones and roots erupted from the earth. It destroyed parts of the walls as it continued to expand in size. Through the chaos, Pebble spotted Leanore sprawled out on the dirt, while Zayle and the other human stepped past the destroyed wooden dog, bracing themself for the oncoming battle. Pebble pointed at the men and commanded their dirt creature to attack with a yell. It trudged towards its enemies, dirt trickling from its sides as it moved. Zayle threw his spear directly into the creature's head, but it merely slid onto the ground. The creature leapt at the men, destroying itself on impact, burying them from waist down.

Leanore had struggled upright and advanced on Pebble with her bow drawn. Pebble hobbled away with as much speed as they could manage; their right arm had gone completely numb from the constant summoning, leaving it dangling limply. Arrows peppered the ground around Pebble as they tried to flee, glancing over their shoulder; Leanore had blood flowing from her forehead and into her left eye. Her obscured vision was the only thing saving Pebble from certain death at that moment.

Another arrow whistled through the air, this time connecting and piercing through their right shoulder. It would have sent Pebble to their knees—if they hadn't lost most of the feeling in that area already. Leanore closed the distance and was almost upon Pebble.

"Any final words, brat?" she hissed. Carefully, Pebble started to draw a long, winding shape down their right arm as they moved. Pebble had no idea if it would work. They drew anyway.

"Yes, okay!" Pebble said. "I do have something to say. Just don't shoot me yet."

"Raise your hands! You wont get any sneaky, last ditch opportunities to create any more monsters!"

Pebble complied, and raised their left arm, pen in hand.

"Both of them!"

"You hit my shoulder, I can't." The two stared each other down, with Leanore's bowstring pulled taut, arrow nocked and ready to be released.

"Well?" she spat.

"I told my friend Cass something this morning." A flash of confusion, then anger crossed Leanore's face.

"Out with it then!" she yelled, pulling the bow string even tighter.

"I told her I would tell any monsters I encountered that I was banned from dying." Pebble's body tensed.

"Create!"

Leanore released the arrow as Pebble threw themself behind the wall. Pebble screamed as the snake began to peel itself from Pebble's skin, ripping and tearing as it formed, leaving a raised purple scar and blackened skin in its wake.

The snake didn't wait for their instructions, lunging at Leanore's throat the moment she appeared over the top of the wall. It tore the skin from her throat, leaving her to bleed out on the grass. It slithered over the top of the wall, then curled up at Pebble's feet, flicking its tongue and facing them. Pebble was light headed from blood loss and their creation. As their vision began to blur, the shapes of Zayle and his companion came into view.

"Get 'em," They slurred, forcing the word out. "Enhance."

Their arm seared with pain, and with that, they blacked out.

PEBBLE'S EYES FLEW OPEN, their mind racing to get them back into battle. They jerked upright and gasped for breath as their wounds numbly ached, left hand moving to cover the stinging scar on their forearm.

Despite the feeling of urgency, there was no fight here. Pebble blanched as they looked around and saw the bodies that surrounded them. They were beside a small stream, the rest of the forest seemingly still. Pebble was afraid that by moving they would dispel the quiet and return to the fight from moments ago. The arrow was still in their shoulder, but they moved forward inch by inch to reach the moving water, desperately feeding shaking handfuls to their mouth as their mind reeled. The sun was up, and their right arm was still numb, so Pebble estimated not much time had passed.

When they'd quenched their thirst, they turned back. The bodies had not moved, and they would not, for all of them were pale, yet stained with blood. Dead. There were so... many. For a moment Pebble was thankful their stomach was empty, as it rolled as violently as their train of thought. Did the goblins think they were dead too? Pebble was surprised to be clothed, but grimly wondered if the goblins refrained from scavenging the dead.

The pen! Pebble madly groped at their clothes in panic. *What if they— where is it?!*

The search was awkward with only their non-dominant arm, but they found the pen deep in a pocket. Pebble didn't recall putting it there, but everything that had happened was still a blur. Dread bubbled away in their mind as they looked back at the bodies.

Was Gripp in there?

Pebble's breath caught as they tightened their grip on the pen, pressing it against their blackened wound. It hurt—of course it hurt—but what else was there to do? If the elves weren't in that pile... Pebble looked down at their shaking arms, tears rolling off their lashes and onto their sprawled legs. Even if they were, how long would it be before someone else came for this pen?

"I couldn't save anyone..." Pebble whispered. Grief flooded their body as they forced themselves to their feet. They had to get away, had to take the pen far away, had to do *something*. The pen was attached to a name, an owner, it was known. Why on earth was it left *here*?!

Indignant, crippled, and wracked with grief, Pebble began to follow the stream to get their bearings. It didn't take long to recognize familiar landmarks, and they knew the bodies had been moved not far away from the general location of the fight. With some distance from the corpses, Pebble was able to think more clearly, and knew it was likely that the fight was over.

If not, Pebble thought, *the bodies would have been left to rot wherever they fell.* The thought twisted knives into their stomach. This pen was the reason the goblins were attacked... This pen was the reason Gripp died. Pebble felt their throat clench, slowing to a stop.

They couldn't go back to the town. Or their house. The goblins might be there. Pebble couldn't bring themselves to look anyone in the eye. Wandering the forest right now would be reckless, but what other shelter was there? Where in this forest would the goblins not find them? What sort of place did they avoid? Pebble thought deeply as they traced the raised scars on their arm with a thumb.

Abruptly, they remembered the cave. It was enclosed, discrete, and both Gripp and Yowl seemed uncomfortable soon after entering. It would have to work. If the depths were home to a monster, fighting it couldn't be worse than watching those they cared about murdered. Pebble continued forward, momentarily glad the numbness seemed to be mitigating their pain.

SUNSET STAINED the sky amber as Pebble slumped against the wall of the cave. They stared at the cave drawings with a sense of relief. The ink was still there. Knowing that they had not been animated made the cave feel safer, somehow. Pebble's numbness had started to fade; and a steady, throbbing pain emanated from their shoulder and forearm. To get any further into the cave they would have to squeeze through a crevice, and they couldn't with the arrow sticking out of them. They had thought of ripping it out while they walked, but there were plentiful tavern stories of hunters dying from the removal, while fine to walk around with one in. Snapping it with one arm was nigh impossible without using their own flesh as leverage. They needed to hold it still and then snap it, but waiting for their feeling to come back meant pain too. Pebble gripped the arrow where it met the skin, looking toward the narrow opening. They sidled toward the crevice until the arrow hit stone, bending as Pebble let out a small hiss. They gripped the arrow tighter, braced themself and pushed.

The arrow snapped and Pebble felt their consciousness roll with the contrast of pain and sudden relief, sinking to their knees in the cave's luminescent inner chamber. They laid there only for as long as it took to breathe deeply again, and then looked into the dim. With only the sound of their breathing to fill the dark, they were suddenly aware of a strange noise from deeper within the rocky walls. A quiet, rhythmic, scraping noise and accompanying thud. No matter how long Pebble remained afraid to move, it did not change.

Maybe it's not a creature?

The thought spurred Pebble on, and they slowly rose to their feet and moved into the dark. Higher off of the floor, the noise became even softer, drowned out by Pebble's resonating breath sounds and footsteps. With their hands outstretched, they shuffled forward until they felt cool stone. The void at their feet began to dissipate, and Pebble continued their shuffle toward the strange noise. The light beginning to illuminate the floor preceded an unnatural corner in the gloom, and they could see a room of light beyond it. The scraping sounds were echoing from in there, but didn't seem to be moving.

"Here goes..."

Pebble moved through the stone opening, squinting

as their eyes adjusted to the light. Though the space wasn't wide, it thankfully didn't pull on their injuries. As they turned away from the wall, Pebble held their breath.

A rock creature lay partially destroyed in a small trough. As Pebble watched, it used its one good arm and leg to attempt to stand, but it slid and thudded back to the ground. As if that wasn't strange enough, the light illuminating the room was coming from strange braziers behind the creature, which marked another doorway at the opposite end of this small room. Whatever was lit inside the braziers wasn't producing smoke, and did not flicker. Once Pebble confirmed the creature could not move, they approached it cautiously. It stilled on their approach, a gem on what they imagined to be its head glowing a faint blue that seemed too familiar. Pebble's heart thudded in their chest as they pulled the pen from their pocket. Each heavy beat of their heart sent waves of stabbing pain from their wounds. The creature did not make any attempt to move as Pebble confirmed the pen's gems glowed in the same way. They looked at the door, glanced back at the creature, then rushed forward, trembling hands pressing the door open.

The room was devoid of life. Papers littered every surface—including the floor—and a dark, rotting wooden shelf further back held what might have once been containers of some sort. Pebble stifled the heavy hurt that rose in their chest as their hope for answers was dashed, casting the pen back into their pocket despite their injuries' protest. The walls in here were adorned with more of the glowing gems, giving the still room an unsettling atmosphere. Pebble softly traced the fresh scars on their arm as they approached the nearest table and peered at the various papers. Most of them were texts, written in what might have been elvish runes, as well as separate notes in other strange glyphs. There were various incomplete maps, diagrams, even a picture of the creature outside—if it had retained all of its limbs.

A heavy breath finally escaped Pebble as they felt tears prick at their eyes.

This wasn't fair.

Their thumb pressed into the scars, seeking something familiar. *Whoever this person was, they made this pen and gave it to innocents. They were the reason the goblins suffered. This person had no right giving something so dangerous to the peaceful. Was it a game? An experiment?* Pebble's inner turmoil came to a halt as their restless searching revealed a map that seemed almost complete. There were runes on the corner of the paper, and they noticed now that they were on most of the papers.

A signature.

Pebble stuffed the map into their pocket, seething with indignant rage.

"I'll find you." They wiped at their eyes before tears could threaten to fall, their other hand curling around the pen in their pocket despite the pain.

"I'll find you and return this, tenfold."

THE GOLDEN BELLS
CRYSTAL ROLES

Like any tavern, The Belly of the Beast took time to wind up. The few day drinkers latched on early, drowning their coin while they waited and watched the polite daytime transactions; the lunch crowd, the above board meetings—it wasn't until dusk settled on the eaves that the beast rolled over to expose its underbelly, and that night was no different. Live music exploded from the beating heart of its taproom, people shouted along to their favourites or just to be heard by their compatriots, glasses shattered, and hearts broke.

"Do 'Queen Shinova'!"

"I bet *you'd* do Queen Shinova!"

"I bet Queen Shinova'd do *you*... with a dagger!"

"I think we should see other people."

Doc felt as if the shouted dagger had taken form and plunged into her heart; the blood roared in her ears, almost drowning out the half-giant staring awkwardly at her across the table. She stared back at him, her face frozen in place, as she tried to absorb his meaning.

"But... Finnick, th-the expedition... the gnomes' mission. They trusted us."

The half-giant shifted on the slightly-too-small seat, his eyes flicking to the door as he puffed out his cheeks. When he turned back to look at her, his eyes were almost kind. Almost.

"You're no longer required."

"No longer re... required?" The words tumbled out of her slackened jaw, as she tried desperately to get her mind to hold onto the meaning of his words. She had spent months on this expedition. The research, the books, the local lore gathered from their core sources—she had been the one that had managed to work out what the accursed thing was! Now she was... no longer required?

The half-giant lifted his shoulder in a shrug.

"That's how it is, babe." His toothy grin flashed, before slowly fading as her eyes blurred, the smell of sweat and beer closing in on her, sucking the air from her gasping lungs.

"Another round!" A perky voice announced, smiling at her elbow and shattering the spell holding her to her seat.

Doc's solid dwarven frame heaved a sob as she pushed back from the table, launching away from the blurred gnomish shape of her small—now slightly confused—best friend and the half-giant who had just set her adrift.

"What did you do?" She heard Hickory demand of the half-giant. Tankards were slammed on the table, and the gnome scurried behind her, trying to catch up.

"Doc... Doc, wait *up*!" Hickory cursed as she dodged through a sea of knees, but the dwarf did not slow down. She had one door in sight. One door that meant sanctuary.

Doc burst through the restroom doors. All females,

no matter their background, were given refuge under the flickering lamp light here. The tavern proper muted and dulled as the door swung shut behind her, and she fought to catch her breath. A blast of noise announced Hickory's arrival before the tavern receded again, giving the girls space to breathe.

Hickory stared—slightly up—at her best friend in the whole world. "What was that all about?"

Any composure Doc had gained by entering the watery sanctuary slipped away as tears spilled down her round cheeks.

"Finnick... he dumped me!" she wailed.

Hickory stood frozen; the only movement were her eyebrows shooting to her hairline. "Really? No, he wouldn't. He couldn't! What kind of idiot dumps the *head researcher* right before their party ventures into an unknown lair?"

Doc sobbed harder, bent in half with her arms wrapped around her middle, trying to hold herself in one piece before she shook apart.

The middle stall burst open as if kicked with great force. "A halfwit ignoramus! That's who!"

In one fluid movement, Hickory spun and released the gnarled wooden staff from the leather binds holding it to her back, levelling it at the newcomer's throat.

The elf swayed slightly, gently putting a finger on the brandished staff, pushing the gnome aside. She strode to Doc's side and swung an arm over the dwarf's shoulders.

"Honestly, is he really worth all those tears? If he can't see what absolute *royalty* he was datin', the fool don't deserve a second thought." She put her finger under Doc's chin and lifted it, smiling down at the tear stained face.

"There, that's better. Keep your head held high, sugarlumps, and the world won't touch ya." The elf nodded and smiled, throwing her shoulders back and lifting her own chin as she wobbled slightly. She turned to the mirror and started fluffing her dark ponytail that had gone a bit wobbly itself. "Besides, if you know all the things he doesn't, he will come crawlin' back, kissin' the very ground you walk upon," she declared. She rubbed something shiny on her lips and smacked them together, winking over her shoulder at them.

Doc smiled but then felt it drop. "Maybe, if he didn't have my notebook."

"You gave him your notebook?" Hickory groaned.

Doc looked at her defensively, "Well, he said he wanted to go over things before tomorrow..." she trailed off when she realised both of the girls were staring at her. She ground her teeth. "Look, I didn't know the son of an ogre's foot was about to stomp me into the ground!"

The elf's eyes narrowed. "Now, that's just not right, thievin' from an unsuspectin' dumplin' like your good self."

Doc felt her cheeks heat up, but she just looked at the ground miserably.

"This just won't do. Who is this fool that set up, not only the sting of setting ya adrift, but without your own notebook?" Doc avoided looking at her, and her eyes flitted to Hickory.

"A big, mulch-bitten, half-giant, worms-for-brains called Finnick." Hickory frowned, forcefully tucking her staff back into its bindings on her back. "He and Doc were sitting just to the right of the main doors before he crushed her heart."

The elf pressed a finger to her chin, her eyes unfocused as she thought quietly. Doc fought back more tears, lost once again in her own thoughts. Everything was in that book. Not just for this expedition, but everything she had learnt in Junlee's name. The goddess of wisdom and guidance, that book was Doc's portable altar to her.

"Everything was in that book? For the little foray your party was settin' to do tomorrow?" the elf asked suddenly, echoing Doc's own thoughts.

Doc nodded glumly.

A smile slowly spread across the elf's face. "Well then, we'll just have to get that one back for ya."

Doc snorted, about to tell her that was next to impossible, when she caught the hard look in the elf's eye.

"Name's Deidriallessa... Deidre, to my friends. Let's go get your little book of knowledge. No one should get to keep someone's innermost thinkin' without that someone's sayin' so!"

Doc looked at Hickory, who shrugged. "He would see us coming a mile away,"

"Ah yes, he knows to look for you two. Me? He don't know me from a bar of scrubbin'."

It was Hickory's turn to smile, and she raised her eyebrows at Doc. "I mean, she's right. Finnick has never seen her before, let alone knows we have anything to do with her. What's the harm in letting her try?"

And let her try, they did.

Hickory and Doc left the bathroom first. They headed over to a separate table that had direct line of sight to where Finnick was still seated, shifting every once in a while on the too small seat. His back was turned in their direction, and he was distracted, talking to a few others from their party. In fact, it seemed he wouldn't have noticed them even if they had plonked down at the same table; his focus was locked in a heated discussion with another of their party—his brother, Bazter. The sound was drowned out by the pulsing chaos of the tavern, but they watched as Finnick waved Doc's book around, seemingly trying to make a point, but his brother in arms and blood pushed up and away, storming to the bar.

Finnick threw the book down on the table as Hickory tapped Doc's elbow and gestured to the bar with her head. Doc nodded, signalling Hickory to go. The furious half-giant may give them a bit more insight, especially when talking to Hickory; the gnome always seemed to soothe Bazter, making it easier for him to use his words.

Doc watched as Hickory disappeared into the crowd and, when Deidre finally appeared, sauntering out of the restroom as if she owned the place, Doc grinned. Her new bathroom friend may have looked a little wobbly coming out, but when she spun around a server and then suddenly had a full tankard, Doc didn't even catch the sleight of hand. She leant forward, barely daring to breathe, as Deidre swished up to Finnick's table—just as they had described it to her.

"Aye, love! You're from that vale of Iron er, Ironvale, ain'tcha?" Doc's gaze was ripped away from Deidre's progress as a cheerful face sat down across from her. The human had obviously had one two many shots of courage, and thought it was a good idea to approach the dwarf sitting alone.

"*Thalurg bahat,*" Doc cursed to herself, slipping into her native tongue.

"Whatsat? Ferblog Blat?" The human squinted, working his slurred mouth to repeat back her words.

Doc gritted her teeth and forced a smile, staring past

his head to Deidre's progress. Whatever she had done, Finnick had stood up in a hurry, and was yelling and gesturing wildly. Deidre had her back pressed to the table and was shying away from his anger. Doc could not see the book.

She turned her most winning smile at the human in front of her. "No, no, not from Ironvale, unfortunately. I hail from *Ferblog Flats*." Doc kept her face perfectly straight, so as not to give away the fictitious place. Meanwhile, the human straightened up and smiled, confident in having worked out what she had cursed under her breath. He opened his mouth to speak again, but Doc cut in smoothly.

"Now, if you'll excuse me..." Doc stood as she held the forced smile in place, nodding at him politely, then turned on her heel.

At the back of the Belly of the Beast was a side door that would lead her outside, so she could make her way to the landmark Deidre had named their rendezvous. She and Hickory had been given strict instructions to make their way to the garden park, a bit past the town centre, near the old weathered well. They were to all meet here to discover if Deidre had succeeded or not. Doc smiled; she couldn't help but enjoy the cloak and dagger of it all.

BY THE TIME DEIDRE ARRIVED, Doc's smile was long gone—and so were the tips of her fingernails. She nearly jumped down the well when Deidre whispered from the shadows.

"Lil miss gnome missin'?"

Doc took a few quick breaths, trying to coax her

heart down from her throat when both of the girls heard a quiet humming coming towards them. Deidre dove around the well, peeping out in the direction of the noise.

Doc grinned in relief; she would know that tune anywhere. "Nope, definitely not missing."

"Not missing, just late!" Hickory skipped over to them. "Poor Bazter needed some venting time. Seems we aren't the only ones unhappy with Mr Finnick."

They all stared at each other, then broke out in relieved giggles.

Diedre sighed happily as she plopped down on the lip of the well, narrowly missing two golden bells that had bloomed from the moss adorning the structure. "Ya big ol' friend Finnick ain't the smartest in the bunch, huh? Your book was layin' out for all to see on the table, plain as day!"

Hickory laughed with her, and sat down a bit more gently on the other side of the blooms, tenderly twisting her fingers and making a third one grow up between them. "Nope, no one ever accused him of being the brains of the party. That was usually left to..." Her eyes flicked to Doc. Doc looked steadfastly at the well, ignoring her. Hickory shrugged, mostly to herself, and leaned closer to Deidre. "So..." She lowered her voice conspiratorially. "Did ya get it?"

Doc felt herself leaning forward too, her considerably shortened thumbnail back between her teeth.

Deidre held their gaze for a beat longer than necessary before brandishing the book. Doc felt her chest expand as she finally took in a deep, victorious breath.

"So, now that ya have all the information for this... heist? Trek? Exploration dig? You both just gonna wait til they come crawlin' back? Or...?" Deidre let the question hang as she looked between them.

Hickory turned to look at Doc. "Well, the way Bazter was talking, it sounded like Finnick was dead set on going without us. He even tried to tell him that Tiffen alone would be enough to get them through, even if he hadn't had scored your book. Tiffen!"

Doc felt her cheeks heat and she glared at the well. "Tiffen? She wouldn't know how to guide a rowdy bard to the local brothel." Her eyes opened a little wider as she looked at Hickory. "You don't think he and Tiffen..."

Hickory pursed her lips and looked away.

Doc felt what was left of her heart sink. "Oh."

"Look, even Bazter said she's got nothing on you!" Hickory hurried to fill in the silence.

Deidre sat up a little straighter, her eyes narrowed. "Already warmin' someone elses' camp mat? That's dirty." She tilted her head to the side as she locked eyes with Doc. "Your call, whatever you wanna do, hun, I'll back ya."

Doc looked back at her in surprise.

Deidre shrugged and lifted the book again. "I'm invested now. I wanna see this one through."

Doc grinned and looked over at Hickory.

Hickory nodded and smiled back. "Look, the whole point of this expedition was to help the gnomes out. We need to go find that sword that's... disappearing people." She gently coaxed the three golden bells from their stems on the side of the well, and placed them over an ear of each girl, finishing with herself. "Besides, I'm with you to the end, you know that, lovely."

Doc nodded, her chest filling with the support and love of her new crew—and the tantalising possibility of never-before-seen knowledge that lay waiting. She felt the warmth of her goddess wash along her skin as she made up her mind.

"They either crawl back to us to guide them, or we bring them to their knees by finding it first."

THE SUN WAS STILL CRESTING the foothills when Doc finally stopped them beside an unassuming hillock. Deidre looked slightly rougher this morning in the harsh dawn light, but she held true to her word in accompanying the two of them. This, however, made her pause.

"This is the place? You sure? It looks like a lil' gnome hole. What could possibly be in there?"

Hickory's laughter rang like music in the wind, fogging in the crisp morning air, and she beamed up at the sceptical elf. "You'd be surprised what you can find in a gnome's hole."

Doc chuckled. "What we're looking for is actually deep underground. This is just one of the entrances. The entrance, if I know my former party well enough, where they will decide to enter." She eyed the hillock and curled her lip. "Though, they may surprise me and head to the correct entrance... or even *completely* shock me and decide to turn around and seek us out for help." She shrugged, heading on a little further to a clump of trees and shrubberies in direct eyeline to the opening. The other girls followed, using the natural land as cover as much as they could, and settled in to wait to see which way their destiny lay.

Doc's prediction did not leave them waiting long. Boredom didn't even have time to set in before the sounds of a loud party arriving greeted their ears. They all sat up in their hiding places as Finnick and Tiffen came into view. Tiffen was giggling at something Finnick had said, and looked to be trying to walk so close to him she was just about in his pockets. Finnick, for his part, looked a little distracted, only answering the giggling human with short answers, his eyes darting around. Bazter trailed slightly behind, and scowled at their backs. He seemed to be muttering to himself, but from where the girls were poised they couldn't make out any words. Finally, he spoke loud enough for the duo ahead and the trio in the bushes to hear.

"This is dumb. Go back, make up with Doc, we're gonna get nowhere without her. She even has all the charges to blow this place!"

If glares could melt living matter, the one Tiffen shot behind her would have left the brother of her lover a bubbling puddle. Finnick's neck flushed red and he turned, stomping towards Bazter.

"We don't need Doc. We never needed Doc. We have this deal in the bag"—Doc felt her heart squeeze painfully—"besides, we won't need the charges."

Bazter's brow creased as he looked at his brother.

Finnick's glare returned hotter than before. "Just shut up and come on." He was almost spitting his words at Bazter at this point.

Bazter's entire body stiffened and his own neck went red, but he took a deep breath and said nothing. Beside her, Hickory shifted and grinned.

"Here! This is where we enter!" Tiffen announced loudly, breaking the tension. "Remember, 'curling *right* around, brings you to the heart of the ground. Only take right hand turns'! Got it?" Her singsong voice flitted across the cool morning air. Both Finnick and Bazter nodded, albeit Bazter a little more reluctantly.

Finnick and Tiffen picked up the pace, entering the

hillock without even a glance behind them. Bazter dragged his feet and took a deep breath before letting it out slowly, taking a final slow look around. His eyes searched, taking in everything they touched, passing over their little clump of trees. Doc pressed her lips together until they were thin white lines, fighting the urge to charge forward and stop her friend. However, before her legs could betray her and leap into action, Bazter heaved another sigh and plunged into the opening. Just like that, they were gone, leaving Doc to her decision.

"So, we go in ourselves!" Deidre declared. She looked at Doc and bit her lip. "Is it worth it? If they know the trick to the place is 'curling right around, brings you the heart of the ground', don't that mean they've got the place solved already?"

Doc smiled sadly. "They would have had part of the place solved... had they entered through the correct door. The entrance they chose should have been 'left to miss the cleft' and even then, not every left turn should be what they take. Going right may still get them there quickly, but our guide alluded to no help along that path, and there would be unnoted obstacles." Doc set her shoulders and gently moved the golden bell flower Hickory had placed and preserved in her hair to sit neatly behind her right ear.

"Move your flower to your right ear. If we get lost or disorientated, follow the golden bell scent."

The girls dutifully obeyed as Doc took the lead again. It seemed quite far from the other entrance, but Doc led them around the back of another similar looking gnome knoll and, sure enough, another opening came into view.

"This is it, point of no return. We go through that

opening, and we get that artefact or we die trying," Doc declared.

Hickory cracked a smile. "Really? Die trying? Isn't that a little, I don't know... dramatic? Come on now, we've got this, we're... we're the Golden Bells!" She twirled her fingers near her ear, and her bloom seemed to give off a soft glow as it tinkled sweetly.

Deidre came up beside her. "Golden Bells? Yeah, has a nice... ring to it."

Hickory trilled a joyous laugh as Doc let out a theatrical groan, pushing forward into the opening.

As the girls entered, it was just as Deidre had foretold—a gnome hole. Everything was brightly lit, the piles of clutter ranging from books, to piles of sewing and knitting with bright balls of yarn spilling about. Maps lined some walls while pictures and murals splashed over others. There were no corners, only round rooms brimming with oddities and discovery. Hickory squealed, stuck her arms out and did a big turn to take it all in.

"Just like back on the plains!" she declared happily.

Deidre hunched over, narrowly avoiding brushing her hair on the roof, and looked towards Doc. "So... the thing you're looking for... is buried somewhere in this here home? Do we have ta worry about the inhabitants comin' back any time soon?"

Before she'd even finished, Hickory was shaking her head, sending her long curly hair shivering in the warm light. "Oh no no, this is a place of respite. No one actually lives here."

Doc just smiled as Deidre's brow furrowed even further. "Gnomes are a rare breed. They love to explore every corner the world has to offer, collecting anything that catches their eye, trying new and exciting things, food, thoughts... but they're also *huge* home bodies. Wherever they roam, they still like to come back to nice homely homes. It just doesn't have to be *their* home. So they travel far and wide, establish gnome holes and the only price to stay there is to leave a little bit of your collection."

Hickory tilted her head to the side, running her finger along one of the precariously stacked towers of books, testing and pushing. The tower wavered, but held, as she retrieved a book with a triumphant yelp. "Really, all gnome holes are our homes. If it is for us, it is ours, is it not?" She grinned at Deidre before sitting where she stood, beginning to rifle through the pages of her newly acquired treasure.

Deidre cracked a smile. "That's actually... kinda nice."

Doc nodded and looked around with a wistful smile. "Imagine combining all of the holes together and just having... all this. The knowledge we would have at our fingertips—"

"Would take away the fun of exploring. If you already have everything, what's the use of going out to find more?" Hickory laughed, bounding up from her spot enthusiastically. "Besides! That's what the Twisting Row is for! They get all the really good stuff. Also, *make* most of the really good stuff." she grinned at Doc who nodded thoughtfully.

"I suppose so. You really can't go past gnome ingenuity, even if it does have a penchant for exploding. If you can think of it, it will probably be in some sort of production on the Row."

Deidre laughed. "So some of ya make, while others of ya take?"

Hickory shrugged and smiled up at Deidre. "Someone's got to bring back the ideas. Come on, the entrance will be around here somewhere." She tucked the book into her pack and skipped into the next room.

Deidre frowned again, gingerly edging around the precariously stacked piles. "I thought we already went through the entrance?"

Doc was already following Hickory, but turned and smiled over her shoulder. "One of the curiosities *this* particular gnome hole has collected... is a door to deeper curiosities."

It didn't take the girls long to find the doorway; Doc had come across a gnome who'd recently stayed in these parts and had—over a drink and some prized honey cakes—learnt a few of the tantalising secrets of the hillocks. Just as her source had excitedly described, she found a lone book on a shelf titled, *'On Opening Doors And Letting Yourself In'* by an R J Pickinstarff. A short tug later, and a hole in the floor opened invitingly.

Doc smiled at them and moved to dive in. Deidre grabbed her wrist.

"Woah woah woah, you can't be jumpin' into every hole that just happens to open for ya, ya gotta use that pretty head of yours. Check for traps."

Doc's lips pressed together tightly and her eyes narrowed, but she shrugged and moved back, letting Deidre crawl closer to inspect the hole. Hickory hummed happily to herself, and watched for almost a whole six seconds before slipping to another room to try and find something useful for the journey ahead. Doc stayed, watching their new friend, fascinated at the care this previously laid-back elf was showing; Deidre seemed to be going through some unwritten checklist, standing carefully she began circling the hole with her feet on each floor board, pressing on every exposed plank, and then going around the hole again on her hands and knees, her hands gently pressing under and around the lip of the hole. She had almost completed her second trip around when Doc heard a distinctive *click* and saw Deidre's whole body freeze.

"This is either gonna be amazin', or awful. Get ready for either!" she called.

Hickory peeped her head back into the room, hand already reaching back for her staff. Doc grasped her book tightly, feeling the warmth of Junlee sparkle up her arm.

Junlee...

"Wait!" Doc moved to Deidre and gently laid a hand on her shoulder. She slipped into her priestess voice and whispered, "May Junlee guide your hand in its quest for new knowledge in her name." The hand she held to her book heated up further, travelling through her body and down into Deidre. Deidre must have felt it too—that or decided Doc was crazy. Her eyes widened and she nodded a little.

Puffing her cheeks out, Deidre closed her eyes and appeared to murmur her own quiet prayer that sounded suspiciously like, "Please dontcha blow my hand off..." and released the switch that had clicked in at her touch. Doc gasped as a blinding flash flooded the room, the dark opening suddenly as bright as a sun—and then the floor began to shake. Deidre, blinded by the flash, backed away from the hole at a fast crawl, then flattened herself to the ground, legs and arms stuck out like a beached sea creature. The vague darkened shape of Hickory yelped and fell to her knees, her staff clattering to the side. Doc was thrown upwards, backwards, side-wards until she lost all sense of direction—she curled into a defensive ball, hands over her head in a vain effort of protection as the floor bucked and quivered under her.

Before long, the floor settled beneath them, leaving the girls sufficiently rattled.

Doc took a shaky breath and was the first to her feet. "Everyone okay? Deidre? Your hand still attached?"

Deidre flexed her fingers and wiggled them experimentally. "Seems to be!"

"Hickory, you still got your staff?" Hickory scrambled to her fallen weapon and wrapped it in her arms, snuggling her face into it.

"I'll never drop you again," she whispered to it soothingly, and Doc couldn't hide her relieved smile as her shoulders relaxed down from around her ears.

Excellent, everyone is still in one piece... so far, so good.

Now, to see what they'd found. She turned her gaze back to the hole, the hair standing up on the backs of her hands as she realised writing had appeared around the hole, raised as if from the wood itself. She edged closer and turned her head, following the writing around.

"'The wheel spins. What has died is renewed and lives, yet in death will rest again'." Doc flicked her newly recovered notebook open to a fresh page, her tongue poking out to the side as she etched the freshly formed words onto its parchment. They had a nice ring to them, an undeniable truth and quiet wisdom. She felt Junlee's warmth tingle where she touched her book in recognition.

"Huh... well ain't that strange." Deidre had come back over to look too, but was focused on the actual opening, drawing Doc's gaze. The opening had changed; instead of the dark, depthless hole Doc had almost jumped into, torch light now shone out and there

347

seemed to be a floor—though it looked more like a slide —connected to where they stood.

Hickory appeared beside them and gasped, bouncing on her toes. Before either of her friends knew what she was doing, she took a running start and landed perfectly on the slide, legs crossed, staff across her lap like an immovable rod holding her in place... and then she was gone. Doc and Deidre stared in a frozen, horrified silence, until the elated whooping of Hickory floated back to them. They looked at each other. Doc shrugged.

"Well, looks like this is it. Last one there's a rotten harpy egg!" she called, launching herself after Hickory. She heard Deidre let out a disbelieving laugh, but the elf's steps were light and close on her heels, as they followed Hickory's descent down the slide.

TWISTING AND TURNING, whipping them faster and faster until the torches on the walls blurred into one, the slide took them deeper into the bowels of the world.

Hickory's elated squeals changed tone slightly, before Doc heard a single, "Oh, pincerlegs!"

Before she could try to piece together what had happened, Doc was launched from the slide and landed in darkness. Not just a little darkness, but complete and utter pitch black, can't-see-your-book-in-front-of-your-face kind of darkness. It cloyed her senses; heavy, pushing in all around her... it was damp against her skin and left a taste at the back of her throat, as if an oil spill had been hit by lightning. She swallowed a few times uncomfortably, before she felt something shift under her. With a strangled yelp, she jumped to her feet, stumbling forward just as a soft *thump* landed in front of her. She heard Deidre groan and knew at least the elf had flown a little further forward than her. Which left—

"Oh, Hickory, did I land on you? I'm so sorry..." She blindly felt around in the general area she had jumped up from, her hand brushing an earthy floor before finding a pile of clothing which groaned softly.

"I'm up, I'm up," Hickory muttered as Doc's hand thumped onto her. Although, truth be told, none of them truly felt like they were awake. It did not seem to matter if their eyes were open or squeezed shut; they could not see anything in this new area. "Doc? Deidre? Where are you?! I can't see *anything!*" Hickory's voice was rising very high and sounding dangerously breathy. Doc reached forward again and tried to reassuringly pat her but either she or Hickory had moved, and she swatted nothing but air. At least wherever they were was roomy.

"We're here, don't pan—" Doc started in her best soothing priestess voice but was interrupted with another eruption of light. Barely recovered from the first one, Doc felt as if she had just turned her eyes to the sun. Dark dots danced in front of her eyes.

"Gods above and below!" Deidre cursed, somewhere to Doc's right. "Scourge it all! Hickory? Was that you? What did ya do that for?"

Doc blinked desperately. Whatever Hickory had done centred on the flower in her hair— it seemed to be shedding light all around her. The very air felt cleaner, less dense, as if the darkness had broken rather than just been shooed away with light.

Doc looked around now that her eyes had adjusted slightly. It was almost what she had been expecting from her first assessment—they had landed in a very roomy cavern. What she hadn't expected was the creature in the middle of the room. Now that they had stopped making so much noise themselves, Doc could hear the soft snores coming from the hairy beast. It would have been absolutely terrifying had it not been wearing—

Doc frowned.

"Is... is that thing wearing a nightcap?" Deidre hissed from Doc's right.

"I think so?"

Hickory giggled. "To be fair... it *is* asleep!"

"Shh," Doc and Deidre whispered as one, but Doc could hear the corners of Deidre's lips quirk up, and her own eyes were shining with barely contained laughter. Nothing that Doc had read had prepared her for a scary monster... in a nightcap. The gnomes had specified the time Doc's group should venture under the knoll— maybe they had left this behind? They had been talking rather fast and rather excitedly; she'd not gotten it all. Maybe they'd even mentioned it would be wearing something?

One thing Doc did notice, while all of this rushed through her chaotic brain, that despite their increased noise the creature had not stirred. It didn't even appear to notice it had company. Very odd for any creature, let alone a giant creature who was in pure darkness so, one would assume, would have heightened hearing? Seeing that it did not move, Doc took a moment to study it in a little more detail. With its long, cylindrical shape, the hairy appearance, the curve of its body—it looked very much like a fully grown Bixswallow. Female, if the size was any indication; they were much larger than their male counterparts, to have the surface area to carry their young.

Doc looked at Deidre and shrugged, then began creeping towards the creature. Deidre took her cue and started to creep around the other way to get on the other side of it. The creature was still completely oblivious, its snores echoing around the cavern. The only movement came from its back, twitching occasionally, and the rhythmic breathing. Doc had almost reached the creature when Hickory walked up right beside it, stuck her hand out, and planted it on the creature.

"Hickory, are you *trying* to die?" Doc demanded after a beat, her mace in her hand, ready to pounce. The creature did not stir as Hickory gently stroked it, but Doc kept her mace to hand.

"I had a theory." Hickory grinned triumphantly. She continued to pat the creature, slowly working up its body to where the cap sat. "I think this is keeping it asleep." She gestured at the bizarre nightcap.

"Yeah, and it coulda just wanted ta look pretty while it had a catnap! You coulda just started a world of beatdowns!" Deidre hissed.

Doc was already shaking her head. "No, it was a fair hypothesis. It hasn't stirred with any of the noise we've been making, Hickory's blinding light, nor the change in the air quality when that darkness shattered due to the aforementioned *blinding light*," Doc shot a look at Hickory who just smiled sheepishly.

Deidre snorted, but didn't argue further.

Doc shrugged and turned to look at the rest of the cavern. They were far underground, and the light emanating from Hickory's flower had completely destroyed whatever darkness had been hiding this place. To the right, part of an underground lake bounced the light up to ripple across the ceiling. Other than that, Doc could not see any other entrances or exits.

"So, anyone have any idea how to get out of..." Doc turned back to her party, just in time to see a mise-en-scène to freeze her blood; Hickory's hand slowly lifting the cap, Deidre's eyes opening wider, her arm stretching towards the gnome.

"Hickory, no!" Deidre's shout shattered the moment, and Doc lurched forward, her own arm reaching, but neither of the girls got to Hickory in time.

Hickory had the cap in her hand, and was already slipping it into her backpack when the beast stirred.

It was definitely the female of the species, and was way larger than Doc had first thought. It was truly a beautiful example of a Bixswallow—or, what others would term 'a giant, hairy worm'. Its back writhed as soft, squishy *pop* noises replaced the snores echoing around the cavern. Doc's mind flashed back to what she knew of the Bixswallow. The females were larger because... because...

It carried its children on its back. She watched in horror as pieces seemed to come loose from the creature and fall to the cavern floor. Each one looked like a smaller version of their mother. The ground shuddered as they moved, squirming in a giant crush together. Their tiny mouths opened and high pitched keening filled the air. As the girls watched dumbfounded, the little critters aimed one end—hopefully their heads—to the ground and the keening quietened as they began chewing at the dirt. Faster and faster, the ground was mulched up, and the little bodies pushed through, burrowing deeper into the munched dirt, until the ground looked like a pockmarked moon. Soon, there were only a few left with the girls, and the original beast that Hickory was standing alarmingly close to. Deidre took a step closer to Hickory, her hand still lifted. The giant, worm-like beast whipped its head towards the movement, its hairy back bristled and puffed out in all directions, the once smooth hair looking sharp and sticky.

"Eeeasy there, critter... just tryna get my friend..." Deidre stuck both her hands into the air as if in surrender and took a step forward.

Doc saw it all happen as if in slow motion; Deidre took that fateful step, a small critter popped its head out of the ground near her foot and let out a high pitched wail, Hickory bent over to peep into one of the holes left by the smaller critters, and the giant creature exploded in a rain of spiney bristles. Doc was, thankfully, out of range. Hickory's well timed bend down to examine a hole let them fly harmlessly over her head, and Deidre seemed to notice the movement right at the last second and dodged, but still caught one to the palm of her hand.

Doc learnt a whole new barrage of elven curse words that day.

She rushed forward to help Deidre, but the baby keened louder. It seemed to drive the giant creature into a frenzy, as it reared up and fluffed out its spikes again, ready to make a second attack.

"Woah, girl, shh, shh it's okay," Doc soothed. She raised her own hands, mirroring what Deidre had done, and started to sing a soft spell. The song that tumbled from her tongue was one of remembrance of Ishara, one of Junlee's three daughters. Ishara used to thrash through darkened nights, visited with knowledge and prophecy of man. It was a song Junlee would sing to soothe the tormented goddess, to get her through until first light. Doc swayed with Junlee's words, her hands in the air twisting and turning, making little patterns as her skin seemed to emit a soft glow, softening the harsh light Hickory was still casting around the cavern.

It was working.

The creature's bristles slowly folded back, and softened as it seemed to sway in time with Doc. The cries of the baby hushed, and turned to soft coos. As the girls watched, the giant creature tenderly bent forward, scruffed the last remaining baby with its mouth, and put it on her back, nestling it under the furry spikes. It seemed to take one last look at them before pushing its head to the ground, then unhinged its jaw, and burrowed.

With another night of terror over, Ishara welcomed the dawn's light, Doc's prayersong ending as the last of the Bixswallow's tail disappeared underground.

The girls all looked at each other.

"Well, that... was unexpected." Doc blew her cheeks out.

Deidre tenderly cradled her hand to her chest as she glared at Hickory. "What were you thinkin? That thing coulda killed all of us!"

Hickory's eyebrows shot up, but her voice was very small. "I was thinking the cap looked like it could be useful. I was trying to be quiet..." She turned her face to the floor. "I'm sorry."

"I mean, it could have gone worse. A lot worse. There was... mostly... no harm done." Doc tried to ease the tension a little, getting between Hickory's downcast look and Deidre's fierce stare. She turned to Deidre and took her hand, prying it away from her chest as gently as possible. "Here, let me have a look."

Deidre's palm was red and angry around the spine sticking out of it, a toxic black line starting to circle the wound. Upon closer inspection, it looked like the barb was covered in hair. Doc quickly found out that the 'hair' was a series of finer spikes coming off the main one, hooking and twisting in Deidre's flesh.

She whistled low. "That's gonna hurt like a dryhorn calving, but we need to get it out."

Deidre screwed up her face. "Can we not pull it out 'n say we did?" she asked half-heartedly, wincing as she tried flexing her palm.

Doc bit her lip. "I mean, sure, if you want to lose the hand..."

Deidre turned a sickly pale, highlighting a black line that had begun tracing up her arm from the wound. The black pulsed under her skin as it tracked up.

Doc winced. The poison would have to be drained.

"Look, I've got some nice, healing ointments in my backpack. We get that spine out, and we'll give that pretty little hand of yours a spa day." Doc looked up at Deidre with what she hoped was an encouraging grin. Deidre's lips twisted up in an answering smile, albeit a shaky one. Doc could feel the claminess of her hand. The elf's breathing was shallow and fast.

Doc bit her lip, and looked around for a safe place to sit her patient down. Hickory was quietly inspecting the holes left behind by the creatures, but none seemed to be present. She made a small noise to get the gnome's attention, but Hickory steadfastly kept her eyes down and hunched her shoulders a little.

Ah, that poison would have to be drained later, too.

Doc decided that where they were standing was as good a place as ever, and gently sat Deidre down.

"Alright, this is gonna hurt. I'm going to need you to concentrate on breathing. Can you do that?" Doc fished around in her backpack, and pulled out her medicine pack without taking her eyes from Deidre.

Deidre took a deep, steadying breath, and nodded. Doc grabbed some pieces of cloth and wrapped them around her own palms, so the fine hooks couldn't transfer to her own hands, then took hold of the spine.

She crouched next to Deidre, planting her feet.

"One... two... Hickory! No!" she yelled, her eyes darting past Deidre's right shoulder. Deidre spun right to look, half rising, just in time to see Hickory's head shoot up from studying the pockmarked ground, completely alarmed. As Deidre spun, Doc followed the flow of her movement, using Deidre's own momentum to aid her as she yanked backwards sharply, dislodging the offending spike.

Deidre let out an almighty howl, and Hickory flushed a pale shade of green up to the tips of her ears... but the spine was out. Doc hurriedly grabbed Deidre's hand and liberally applied some of her homebrewed salve.

"Good girl," she crooned, wrapping some fresh cloth around the wound. Deidre was shaking and sweating, but seemed to relax slightly.

"Now that was dirty," she said, and chuckled huskily.

As she wrapped, Doc whispered a prayer to Junlee, barely audible, and felt a warmth pulse out of her hands in response. Though she could not see it, she could momentarily feel the black line of noxious poison retreat back towards the wound, opening as if cauterised by a real cleansing fire.

Deidre bent her fingers experimentally. "Huh, feels better already."

"Now you see why we call her 'Doc'," Hickory laughed, the tension broke like a boil being lanced. Doc grinned fiercely.

"Are you okay to continue?" Hickory tilted her head to the side, staring at Deidre.

Deidre scowled, but flexed her fingers again. "Yeah...'slong as ya don't do anythin' that stupid again."

Hickory pursed her lips and looked at Doc.

Doc shrugged. "She should be fine, but maybe a little less 'getting our friends stabbed' as we go forward?"

Hickory beamed. "Excellent! 'cause... I just found our way forward."

The girls picked themselves up off the compact ground, and went over to where she stood next to the biggest hole left by the spiny creature.

Doc's eyes lit up. "Of course! That was a Bixswallow! They only ever burrow in spirals *leaning to the right*!"

Hickory laughed, recalling Tiffen's words from earlier that was meant for the entrance Doc picked. "'Curling right around, brings you to the heart of the ground'."

Doc nodded enthusiastically. "It didn't mean 'take the right turns' at all! It meant 'take the Bixswallow's tunnel that only curls around to the right'!"

Deidre's eyebrows raised but she was smiling. Hickory grinned too, and waited for Doc's thought to finish.

"So we... follow the Bixswallow's tunnel," Doc sighed as she stared at the hole the creature had left behind.

Hickory stuck her tongue out at the dwarf, but looked sideways at the elf. "All of the tunnels go clear through, there's a breeze if you put your face close enough. So we know it leads *somewhere*. That 'somewhere' is in the heart of the ground and leaning forever right... so it's just up to us to find out *where*."

"To be fair, it does seem to be the only way out of this cavern. It's either this, or we brave that river." Doc looked at the sparkling ripples reflecting off the roof thoughtfully. She felt the other two's gazes resting on her and she looked between them, heaving a sigh. "Right. So since *you've* been told no more stupid stuff, and *you* have an injured paw, I'm first in the marching order?" Hickory and Deidre were nodding before she'd even finished speaking.

Doc puffed out her cheeks. "Well, can't turn back now..." With a shrug, she sat down at the lip of the hole, and pushed off, sliding on into the spiralling tunnel.

THIS SLIDE WAS AN ENTIRELY different experience than their previous smooth, speedy, almost spotless entrance. The dark tunnel closed in on them, an unseen moist monster breathing inches from their faces, bumping and bouncing their way through; they could only grit their teeth and count the bruises they would end up with. They had to slide the whole way flat on their backs, twisting further into the ground. Not seeing what was ahead, while simultaneously staring at a dirt roof inches from their noses, added a whole new level of anxiety. Thankfully, the twists weren't too tight and they slipped right along. It seemed much longer than their abrupt entrance to the cavern, but eventually they were deposited ungraciously in a heap at the bottom.

Doc let out a soft *oof* as the small body of her gnome friend landed on her and let out a slightly larger grunt, as the elf awkwardly followed to collapse on top of them. Doc groaned as she disentangled their forms.

They really needed to work on their staggering.

She brushed herself off as she looked around. The ground here, too, was pockmarked and looked like just a stop in the progression of the beasts they had awoken, but the very fact that this opened out into more caverns suggested they were getting close to where they needed to be. If they needed to go further down, they could always follow the Bixswallow... but if they didn't have to, all the better to avoid running back into mumma critter and her deadly spines.

"So, just how do ya know this is the right way to what you're seekin'? It's pretty much guaranteed you didn't know about them critters." Deidre came up beside Doc, looking around uneasily.

"I might not have known about that critter specifically, but the ones who hired us to come down here did give me clues from the scraps they knew. They basically pointed us in the right direction, maybe left one or two aids to get us all the way, but every situation should be able to be worked out. We will get to where we need to go as long as we keep putting the correct ideas together." Doc smiled happily. She was always up for a good puzzle.

Deidre blinked. "Right. Of course. Makes perfect sense."

The excitement began to wear away to the beat of their trudging feet, after being underground for a few hours or so, dodging small traps, getting further and further into the underknoll caverns. Time felt like it was dragging, but slowly the scenery began to change. The tunnel walls turned from dirt to stone that, before too long, were slicked with moisture, chilling the air. The girls picked up the pace to try and fight the chill. Doc kept her eyes peeled for any other changes that might be lurking in the deepening darkness, but it was her ears that picked up the next clue. Metal. Slicing. Footsteps. Grunts.

There was someone up ahead. A lot of someones.

Doc flattened herself against the cool wall, shivering as the damp soaked into her top. She stuck her arm out so the other two would follow her lead. She turned wide eyes to them, finger on her lips she mouthed and mimicked 'tip toe' with her fingers.

The footsteps were louder now, so the girls did not hesitate to follow suit.

As quiet as she dared, Doc edged forward and peered around the corner. It took a moment to comprehend what she was seeing.

There were a bunch of creatures that looked to be in various stages of death—skin bluish green and rotting, bones at odd angles and the smell, even from this distance, stuck in the back of her throat, threatening to make her wretch. She felt her stomach lurch at the wrongness of these things being upright and walking. They were an affront. Life after death in form only, their minds, any knowledge they had, gone. She could feel Junlee's wrath burning with her own. These creatures, however, were not alone. In their midst appeared to be some very alive—very cornered—looking figures. Doc groaned as she squinted past the vile mockery of death and saw that these particular figures were all too familiar; Finnick, Tiffen, and Bazter.

Doc swore under her breath as she watched the monsters circling them. Finnick and Bazter stood back to back, slashing at anything bold enough to come directly for them, while Tiffen ducked and weaved to stay out of reach. She was throwing glowing spells, but looked to be almost spent. The half-giant brothers looked just as ragged as she as the monsters tightened their circle. Doc watched on in horror as, with a sickly squishing sound, one of the zombies ripped its own arm off and made to charge. Her eyes slid past the desperate group to the room they were in.

This was it. This was where the sword was being kept. She could see it a little way ahead, sitting on a pedestal invitingly. All of the monsters were being kept busy by her former party. A party who kicked her aside as if she meant nothing. Moved on as if she had no bearing on their fates. A party who quickly filled her place as if she was just a replaceable commodity.

Her eyes slid back to them uneasily. She saw Bazter take down the arm wielding zombie moments before it got close enough to be any real threat. Its weaponized arm fell forward onto Finnick, who yelled as it clawed at him, bright red slashes appearing down his own arm. Another zombie charged forward and caught Finnick while he was distracted, slashing at his side.

Doc could feel Deidre and Hickory's eyes boring into her back, waiting for her move. It was her decision. She had somehow become the default leader of the Golden Bells, and this was up to her—use her former party as fodder to get to the sword first, or save them. Her eyes lingered on the prize. She felt the charges in her rucksack. Quickly, and as quietly as possible, she passed them out to her two friends, keeping a couple for herself. With unspoken understanding they set the explosives up, as if choreographed for this moment. Whatever her decision, they would not let the terrors leave the caverns.

Doc's eyes flicked back to the sword.

We're so close.

Grinding her teeth, she stepped around the corner.

She stood out in the open, not even trying to slip into the shadows that Deidre and Hickory used to mask their steps as they followed her silently.

She heaved her mace over her shoulder and planted her feet, trying to appear as grandiose as her dwarven stature allowed.

"Oi, death heads! You're all abominations against Junlee's Wisdom and Guidance. I must ask you to leave,"

Her voice rang clear across the open cavern, and everyone froze, turning to stare in her direction.

"You heard me. Leave," Doc repeated stubbornly.

The zombies broke their circle around the others and shuffled—moving a lot faster than anything that dead and rotting had the right to be—towards the new threat. Out of the corner of her eye, Doc saw Hickory's form slowly changing into something bigger, deadlier and Deidre, hands on her twin spinning circle weapons at her hip, waiting for the perfect moment to pounce. Doc held a finger up and they paused.

Hold.

Let them get a little closer...

Go!

Hickory let out a roar, emerging from the shadows as a giant toothed pyre-tygre. Her red fur rippled in the light, sparks flicking off her shoulders, before she launched into the wake of the walking dead.

Deidre, spinning circle blades in each hand, danced out of the shadows, as though death herself reclaimed what defied her domain, as she spun and twisted, the shadows seemingly following her, wreathing her and allowing her to appear where she had not been moments before.

The girls were not the only ones to leap into action. It appeared Finnick, too, had faced his own choice, seeing his former lover and her companions stepping up to take the heat off himself and his crew. He, however, chose much differently. Using the distraction, he launched himself towards the sword.

Doc scowled, and ran towards him. A zombie lurched in front of her, and she let out a wordless cry, her fury channelling through her mace as it smashed into the side of the undead's head so hard its cheek caved in, its lower jaw clattering to the ground.

Bazter also saw Finnick's choice, and turned his back on his brother in disgust. He lowered his head and charged to the defence of the fiercely glowing pyre-tygre, issuing a bellow of challenge to the zombies closing in on her.

Tiffen stood still, torn by indecision and—because no choice is still a choice—chose to remain where she was.

Doc's head shot up at Finnick's pained cry. All the blood fled from her face as she witnessed the hand that had grabbed hold of him the moment before he managed to connect with the sword. It was deathly pale, seemingly blue in the dim light, fingernails grown into thick claws pressing against Finnick's skin as it hoisted him into the air with an unnatural strength. The hooded cowl and ragged black clothing covered much of the figure, but not the fact it, too, floated above the ground, no feet to be seen.

Doc felt the very air freeze around them. Her shallow, panicked breaths steamed in front of her, the air suddenly an icy hand closing around her chest, piercing pressure making every inhale a fight.

"Oh, I don't think so, boy," a voice crooned. It came from nowhere and everywhere at the same time, filling their ears and minds with whispered malice.

As if the voice's mere presence had summoned them, more zombies crawled out of the shadows close to where Finnick was being held, starting to surround him and their master. Before she could register what they were doing, Doc's stocky dwarven legs sped her towards the new threat to Finnick. She felt Junlee's indignant wrath warm her, cutting through the suddenly frigid air and giving her armour against the cold pull of death all around.

"Let him go!" she demanded.

The laughter welled up like a thick sludge in her mind. Doc ground her teeth together and narrowed her eyes, planting her feet as she gripped her mace with both hands.

"I said," she repeated, eerily calm. "Let. Him. Go." Her voice deepened, her skin glowing gold, her eyes flashing white hot.

The laughter paused.

"I have tamed death, girl, what makes you think you have any power here?"

"The knowledge you have is corrupted and skewed." The voice emanating from Doc was no longer her own. "You subvert everything you have learnt, and you shall not be suffered to live this undead existence."

Doc rose off the ground, her head thrown back, her arms and legs wide. As a concussive tremor rocked through their bodies, the others had to shield their eyes against a gleaming flash of brilliance that burst from Doc, lighting up the entire cavern. The radiance beamed through their closed eyelids as the space seemingly burned in time. Every zombie rising around the cavern stopped in its tracks and, like moths to a flame, turned their face towards Doc, burning hot as the sun. Mouths opened, garbled cries seeping out as some zombies burnt away, others falling to ashes where they stood.

Almost as soon as it started, it was over, and Doc's feet drifted back down to the ground.

The figure had turned to stare at her too. As much as a ragged floating cowl could, the figure looked shaken. Whatever the thing was, however, was stronger than the mini sun nova Doc had briefly become, and still stood tall. Well, not that tall.

A mimicry of a dwarf?

No, a gnome!

However, a gnome still taller than it had any right to be, levitating untouched. It uncurled its hand, and let Finnick drop to the floor.

Finnick began backpedalling before he even hit the ground, moving as fast as he could to get away from its reach, scurrying behind Doc.

Doc stood in front of him like a blazing beacon of hope. She could hear the others moving up closer, free of their previous fights, thanks to their dwarven cleric of Junlee. Hickory the pyre-tygre emerged on her right, crouching low on her haunches as she stared up at the spectacle. She spat out the disembodied zombie arm she had been carrying and growled low in warning, the spiral red pattern glowing with the heat of her anger. Doc noted Bazter step up beside Hickory, one of his large hands gently resting on her flank, the other gripping his war-axe so hard his knuckles shone white.

TALES OF ALE AND CHAINMAIL

Doc didn't see Deidre, but she was starting to learn that was one of the elf's specialties.

She felt the movement behind her, as Tiffen rushed to Finnick and helped him to his feet. Finnick cleared his throat uncomfortably and Tiffen made a noise somewhere between confusion and hurt, and out the corner of her eye Doc saw Finnick take a step away from her.

The cowled figure floated higher, looking down at them all.

"What now, priestess? You and your motley band are going to... what? Kill me? Take my very soul?" The unbridled laughter from the figure raised the finest hairs on her neck, but Doc just narrowed her eyes.

"You are already dead. It would just be bringing justice to the twisted knowledge you possess."

"Ah, but you're a devotee of Junlee herself, no? All of this? This sword, these creatures, me? This is knowledge so very few have. Does it not tempt you? Make you wonder? Crave to have it at your own fingertips?" The bluish skin shimmered in the low light as it turned its fingers over gently, almost hypnotically. Doc glared, but didn't say anything. The truth was, he had hit a nerve. She was a collector of knowledge. She wanted to know *everything* there was to know about everything, and what he was talking about was excruciatingly rare and hard to obtain.

She wanted it.

No one moved.

Again, Doc felt the weight of leadership settle on her shoulders.

She also felt her book burning a hole at her side. Her book of knowledge. Her portable link to Junlee, her comfort. She slipped her hand into her pocket to feel its warm guidance. Her fingers stroked the leather bindings out of habit.

"This is not knowledge to seek," a warm voice whispered in her ear.

Doc's brow furrowed. Wasn't all knowledge to be sought?

The warm voice breathed again. *"This knowledge is twisted and perverted. It is not true knowledge of life over death, it is patched together theories and unholy trysts that leave an undeath in the wake of what they do not know."*

Doc nodded slowly to herself. She looked at the mesmerising lich. For all that it thought it knew, it knew nothing.

"And what you don't know makes you weak," she whispered, continuing her thought out loud. Her voice echoed around the cavern as though she had shouted, and the creature that had been slowly moving towards her hesitated.

"I have forgotten more than you will even know!" it roared, and threw its arms out to the sides.

A thunderous clap rang out, leaving Doc's ears ringing as the full force of a fist of thunder punched into her, forcing her backwards, stealing her breath. All around, she could see her party pushed back, away from the lich. The aftertaste of ozone crackled in the air.

Doc felt the hairs raise at the nape of her neck as she realised they had only just begun to taste the lich's latent power.

Her brain raced.

There may have been six of them, but they were severely outmatched.

Hickory roared back at the figure in defiance. She charged, her shoulders glowing hotter and redder with each paw that hit the ground. She bunched her haunches and leapt, teeth out with sheer, unmatched power.

The figure raised a finger and pointed at her, mid leap, a ray of ice shooting from his finger tip. It lanced forward and sliced into her flank, pushing her off her trajectory, and she landed harmlessly to his side. But what he did not anticipate was Bazter, following Hickory's lead, the half-giant with his war-axe appearing out of nowhere from behind the enormous feline. He struck the lich with a bone shattering impact. A furious scream shattered the air as he jerked wildly, shaking Bazter off as the half-giant pulled his axe free. He landed near Hickory and spun, preparing for another attack. Hickory growled and turned, her breath panting in the painfully chilled air.

Tiffen let out a yell, racing forward, and the fight raged around them, but the lich began to rise higher and higher, out of the reach, rendering their weapons useless.

This left the sword wide open, a move Finnick did not miss. Again, he dove forward; this time the lich wasn't close enough to stop him. He grinned in triumph, holding it high in the air.

"I have your phylactery! You must obey *me*!"

The raspy laugh from the near-dead creature made them all pause.

Doc felt something nagging at the back of her brain. Phylacteries... What did she know about phylacteries? Could they even *be* swords? She stared at it. Yes, in theory. But, no, not this time; something wasn't adding up.

She cast her eyes around, looking for the missing piece.

The sword had been laid out on a pedestal. It had

been *made* to look important. It was what her sources had sighted as the main tool being used. That was the reason for the mysterious disappearances from the gnome knoll. Taking their lives—and if it was a phylactery—holding their souls.

She frowned.

No. That sword may be a bringer of death, but it was not the storer of it. If it could, the lich certainly wouldn't have left it out in the open.

She cast her eyes around, studiously ignoring Finnick's sudden look of panic as the lich floated closer to him.

Think, Doc, think.

The lich would never go far without his phylactery, but still wouldn't have it so plainly and easily found. Doc wondered what the sword really did that made it perfect bait.

No, can't think of that now. No distractions.

Shaking her head, she focused on the task at hand, her eyes desperately seeking something, anything, that looked even remotely like it could be his.

Apart from the sword's newly vacated pedestal, there was not much to draw the eye. Zombie bones and ash lay around in small, useless clumps and the shadows encircled the cavern, almost unnatural in their complete darkness. Doc's focus sharpened as she stared harder at that darkness, her mind flashing back to the Bixswallow cavern—it was too complete, too perfect. Not natural at all. Her eyes stopped on a particularly dark corner.

Doc started towards the corner as quietly as possible. She was not the best at sneaking around, certainly nothing like Deidre's dances with the shadows, but she felt she was capable enough to slip unnoticed to explore what was hidden while the others kept him busy. It was a good plan, and she would have been fine if she had looked at where she was stepping, rather than so intently at where she was headed. Her foot met a zombie's arm with a sickening squelch. It rolled under her foot, enough to unbalance her. Her body followed the momentum and she fell to the cavern floor.

Winded, Doc looked up desperately.

She could hear sounds of her friends trying to draw the lich's attention, roaring, slashing, cursing; but the lich had eyes only for her. It brought its hands in front of itself in a slow clap, each movement sending shockwaves around the cavern. All the noise stopped as Doc felt an invisible tightening around her, and what she assumed, also her friends' bodies. She couldn't move.

The lich wavered in the air, his eyes flicking from the prone dwarf, to where she had been headed. It glided forward, now the only sound from Finnick trailing behind him, looking somewhat startled that he was moving at all, the sword held out in front.

"Oh yes, you are the brains of this party, aren't you, little one?" the lich crooned as he stopped a few feet away from her. "Not so gullible and easily led as this one." It grabbed Finnick by the chin and gave him a little shake. Doc could hear the smirk in his voice as a shudder rippled through Finnick's body. "Such a pity you were overlooked. Discarded. Replaced." Each word dripped with poison and Doc scowled up at him. She felt the hold on her loosen and she desperately tried to get to her hands and knees to back away further. She did not like the look of that sword in Finnick's hands, nor the slight confusion creasing his face. She had enough knowledge to recognise the link between liches and 'harmless' objects found in their lair. If that sword had really been responsible for the collection of souls needed to maintain the lich, the lich's link to it would not be subtle.

Doc backed up slowly, keeping the lich in view at all times.

"Tsk tsk, brains you may have, but common sense? Lacking. Minion, teach her it's *rude* to go for other people's things."

Finnick jerked forward, his eyes widening. "Doc, this... it isn't me!" he stuttered.

Doc scrambled to her feet, and shakily held her mace in front of her. "Finnick, stop. It's the sword. Drop it."

Finnick's face changed in an instant, from slight bewilderment to roiling rage. "You'd like that, wouldn't you? Just drop it so you can have it!" he spat, his face and neck flushing a tell-tale red. "You want it for yourself! I saw how hungrily you searched for it... The smallest scrap of information sent you into a whirlwind. You're obsessed! You were going to take it all!"

"What? No! I didn't... I wanted to find what was doing this. Yes, study it, maybe... but you were always part of that!" Doc stared at him in horror. She had a strange, disconnected feeling, almost as if she was watching this from afar. Finnick was the same Finnick he had always been, but something had warped within him. The familiar face she used to stare up to, the strong arms that always felt like her safe space seemed like they belonged to someone else entirely. That same face now twisted with hate, his arms bulging with muscles ready to lash out—this cruel mockery of what they once were, to what they had become, hurt her more than the slice of any blade.

"Yes." The lich could barely contain his glee, floating closer to Finnick. "Yes, minion! This one, this

371

one would have taken it all had you not got to it first! Now, she uses honeyed words to manipulate you to her ends, how she *always* manipulated you to her ends. She wants to take what is rightfully yours. You reached it first, it is yours to claim!"

"Finnick, no! You're being controlled! My love, come back to me!" Doc stopped short as Tiffen interposed herself between the two, arms spread open, trying to reason with him.

Doc's face stiffened back into neutrality, her heart hardening. That's right. He was with Tiffen now. Or at least, *Tiffen* thought he was. But Tiffen's heartfelt appeal did not seem to have the effect she had hoped for.

Finnick's face registered only the annoyance that a flying gnat would cause as he thrust the sword forward. Tiffen gasped, throwing herself to the side just in time. Her quick reaction caused the sword to miss its intended target, instead sliding along the pale skin of her arm, oozing blood from the surface wound. Finnick growled, denied the heart blood the sword lusted for, and squared up to her.

"Doc, if you're gonna do something, now would be the time," Tiffen growled, bending into a defensive stance, her spear flicking up into her hands, an ozone of electricity emanating from her. Finnick dove to slash her again, catching her other arm but, with a thunderous clap, he jerked backwards as if struck by lightning. Tiffen grinned and spun, letting her spear follow his movement, making him dance further backwards. They began circling one another.

Doc knew she should run while he was distracted, but the deadly dance in front of her was captivating. So captivating, in fact, she almost missed the lich's abrupt change of tact. Brief movement out the corner of her eye was all the warning she got, instinctively pulling her head back and holding her breath, as a gnarled claw sliced past where her nose had been seconds before. The lich hissed.

"Doing your own dirty work now, huh?" Doc swung her mace at him, but he nimbly floated to the side.

"You are too righteous to know the true 'dirty' work I have done, what worthwhile knowledge *actually* demands. You swoop in and barely skim the surface, when all the while what you *truly* yearn for is deep, deep below."

"And what makes you so knowledgeable about my yearnings?" Doc grunted, ducking a spinning backhand from the creature.

The lich just smiled, which was worse than anything he could have said. Doc felt a shiver go up her spine. They began circling each other, a second deadly duet. She whispered quietly, appealing to Junlee, "Guide me to his weakness,"

"You will never find my weakness." The whispered words were not lost on the lich.

As if Junlee herself chose that moment to expose the twisted creature for the liar he was, Tiffen's blood curdling scream ripped through the cavern. All eyes turned to see her fall, Finnick standing over her. She stared up at him, wide eyed and shaking, the arm holding her spear twitching in the dirt a foot from her side. Time stopped.

Even the lich watched curiously.

"No, Finnick, please... my love." Tiffen's voice was barely a breath, but it roared through the cavern. Bazter watched with open-mouthed horror as his brother plunged the sword into the prone girl at his feet.

Hickory's scream and charge towards Finnick mingled with Deidre's wordless howl of fury as she spun out of the shadows, also sprinting straight for Finnick. Doc wanted to turn her eyes away from the horror, but it was as if a warm presence held her rooted in place. The presence did not feel malicious, just intense, forcing her to watch the final moments play out. She watched Tiffen jerk as Finnick unsheathed the sword from her body, and saw her blood defy gravity, droplets running *up* the blade, a silver essence coalescing into a glowing aura around it.

Deidre and Hickory tackled Finnick to the ground in perfect unison, sending the sword flying. As soon as the sword left his hands, Finnick fell to the ground. The blade landed at the lich's feet, taking the silvery essence with it. The aura seemed to shiver, turning to mist that rose up off the sword. As if running along an invisible pipe, the essence solidified into a twisting liquid, and flowed towards the very shadows Doc had been moving towards. The darkness lit for the briefest of moments, the silver catching something shiny; a thousand tiny shards of light illuminating an opening box.

The box peeked out of the darkness, its dark colour blinding her to its unassuming, many-sided shape—at first. It was the movement, the breaking apart of that shape, that drew Doc's gaze to it. Now it had a witness, it unfurled faster, a maw of jagged glass of keen, precise, edges; delicate as blooming petals but too sharp, too straight to be natural, snapping apart and reaching towards the incoming shimmering light. Finally, silvery strands touched the box, and strange music filtered into the air, a mournful melody wrapping around the cavern that whispered of love and betrayal.

If souls had a song, this was Tiffen's.

Doc felt her eyes well up, the bittersweet tune

moving her beyond words. As the box finished absorbing the essence, Doc's wet eyes were drawn back to the lich, whose outline now pulsed with an aura of silver.

Doc saw the lich's eyes flick towards the shadows, then back to her. She felt the warmth holding her in place flare hotter, as if in satisfaction, before letting her go. There it was—the weakness. There was the true artefact she had come for.

The moment hung like a crystalized teardrop. In a heartbeat, it fell, shattering in a spray of multicoloured action. Doc, wrapped in her god's warm gold light, took off towards the music box phylactery. The lich, still shimmering in the silver afterdew of Tiffen's soul, shot forward to stop her. Hickory exploded into glowing red teeth and claws mid leap towards the lich. Deidre, right beside her, seemed to summon the blackest shadows to draw back the lich to death's domain. Bazter melded into the grey stone ground, his heavy footfalls shuddering through the earth, threatening to bring the cavern down. The whole cavern trembled, dust and rocks drifting from the roof.

Doc saw it all during her frantic sprint, her desperate mind whipping back to the explosives set up at the entrance to the cavern—if they could help the cavern collapse, somehow trapping the lich, it could grant them the time to get away. If she could grab the box—maybe they could work out a way to free Tiffen. With this goal in mind, she put her head down, and pushed her screaming limbs harder.

The lich's inhuman scream sliced through the air as Hickory's newly sprouted claws found purchase. It gave Doc the edge she needed as she dove forward, her hands closing around the music box. The box was warm to the touch and hummed under her fingers; Tiffen's Lament still sang softly in her hands. Now that she was close enough, she could see a small figure spinning around the centre of the opened music box, as if weaving its deadly spell. The cleverly placed shards of glass mirrored its moves to infinity, encasing it in a glass prison of intricate complexity. It truly was an exquisitely elegant, simple design of something so complex.

Hickory's scream instead of her pyre tygre's growl, wrenched Doc back to reality. She looked up from where she was holding the box in time to see her best friend hit the ground—hard. Her form shifted back to her fragile gnome shape, unmoving. Doc felt her heart in her mouth.

Get up, Hickory. Move!

The lich turned its back on her crumpled form, its attention hastily switched to the crazed half-giant's newly-empowered blows.

Doc stood frozen, eyes locked on Hickory's broken form.

Please, not Hickory, not...

Hickory shifted slightly, peering up at the lich's back.

Doc wasn't the only one to see her movement.

"Hickory! The cap!" Deidre danced out of the shadows long enough to make an appeal to the gnome.

"The... wha...?" Hickory mumbled, having had half her senses knocked out of her as well as her form. She shifted slowly. Too slowly for Deidre.

"THE GODS BLESSED CAP FROM THE BEASTY MUMMA!" Deidre roared, dancing out of the lich's clasping claw, expertly keeping him facing away. As if her own words inspired her, she reached into her pocket and drew out the spine that had pierced her hand. With a half-crazed yell, she plunged it into the lich.

Doc felt taken out of time as she watched events line up; Hickory's face lighting up in recognition, the slow reach for the cap, the deadly battle Deidre and Bazter danced with the lich. Hickory leapt up, hands outstretched with the cap at the same time the lich began to turn.

"You... should... stay... DEAD!" it roared, raising a finger at the leaping gnome, a blackness gathering at its tip. The hat left Hickory's hands—Deidre followed the trajectory and grabbed it out of mid-air, then spun and pulled the cap over the lich's crown—just as the inky blankness left the lich's fingers.

His levitating form fell gently to the ground, his eyes slipping shut with the utmost serenity. Hickory's small body spasmed at a sickening angle as it was hit with the last spell the lich had aimed, throwing her into the stone wall with a sickening *crack*. There was no resistance as her form slid down the wall in a heap.

Doc froze in horror, not knowing if the box had started trembling on its own, or if her hands betrayed her. The box grew warmer and warmer in her grip, almost too hot to hold, demanding Doc's attention. Her eyes slid away from the broken form of her best friend to take in the now activated box. As Doc watched it, the undertones of Tiffen's Lament seemed to draw to a finale, the final bittersweet notes snapping at her very soul. Her heart skipped a beat as her brain fought to work out what was happening.

No.

A silver essence sought its way towards the box.

Oh no. No. Not this. Anything but this.

The box hummed with energy. Doc felt the bile rise in her throat.

Please. Junlee please, don't let this happen.

But there was nothing Junlee nor Doc could do. The sweet notes that started issuing from the box were Hickory's. She could almost hear the silver voiced gnome humming along; it was her song. Of course it was her song. It was everything that made up Hickory, and more. From the plains where she'd grown up, to the wonder and the merriment of each creature she came across, to her fiercest protection of them. First meeting Doc, saving her from the well she had fallen into, her nose in a book, with giggles and unrestrained kindness. The soultwined friendship that had blossomed and grown, through thick and thin. The small gnome had met life with curiosity and a silver song.

Doc felt her heart shatter into a thousand pieces.

No.

Hickory.

Doc's mind raced. She had the box.

This was not the end. This *couldn't* be the end.

Her eyes travelled to where the lich rested peacefully, and she stormed forward. Nothing else mattered. She would wake him and he would tell her how to get her friend back.

She was so focused on the lich she didn't see Deidre running to intercept her.

"No, no darlin', you can't..." Deidre's form loomed in front of the dwarf, putting her hands on her shoulders, trying to hold her, but Doc kept walking, forcing Deidre to step back. "Bazter... Bazter, help!" Soon, there were two forms blocking her way. The sheer mountain of the half-giant finally halted Doc's progress.

She glared up at him, pushing her hands out against him, the tears leaking from her eyes mirroring his.

"Let me go! He can get her back! HE HAS THE KNOWLEDGE!"

Bazter's face twisted and looked away, not meeting her eyes. He shut his own, but held firm. "No, Doc, no. She's gone...she's..." His voice cracked.

Deidre continued softly. "Darlin', even if he has the knowledge, he sure as the seven hells ain't gonna tell you. You wake him up and this is all for nought. Her sacrifice worthless. Don't make her havin' given her life for nothin'." Doc noticed Deidre's eyes shift to the box. "You know that has to be destroyed."

Bazter managed a nod, but little else.

Hickory's soft, cheerful song spiralled around them, dancing and teasing.

Doc stopped trying to push against them and stilled. Destroy the box? That had been her idea... before. In the beginning, they had responded to the gnome's call for aid, and she was prepared to destroy whatever was doing this under their knoll to ensure their safety. That's what the charges were for, after all. But now? Now the box had Hickory. Her very soul was at risk. There would be no destroying the box.

The charges.

Doc looked at her friends in a new light. No. They would not *let* her leave with it intact. They would try and stop her... maybe even try and destroy it themselves. Doc's grip tightened on Hickory's singing artefact.

"You're right, of course... he'd share nothing. I... we should go. We have no idea how long that nightcap will last, and we need to be gone well before he wakes up." She cast her eyes around the cavern.

One entrance.

Perfect.

Her plan started to come together, as her eyes fell on the prone shapes of their former party members. First was little Hickory. Doc felt as if she had been thunder-punched by the lich again—the gnome's crumpled body looked so small. So fragile. Unable to stare any longer, Doc's gaze quickly shifted to Tiffen's unmoving corpse. Even if she hadn't liked her the best, she would not have wished her death on her greatest enemy. Doc noticed the skin around Tiffen's mouth—the tips of her fingers, the pallor of her cheeks—had all started to turn deathly shades of blue. Doc grimaced as an unpleasant piece of knowledge clicked into place; Tiffen was becoming one of the zombies they had fought. Shivering, she turned to look at Finnick's still form. His cheeks shone with a rosy hue, and his chest rose and fell with each breath. Doc glared. Of course he would survive his greed. It was as if the universe was mocking her. Or... giving her an opportunity?

Before she could think about it, Doc felt her mouth moving, almost of its own accord. "We need to get out of here. Bazter, your brother still seems to be breathing, although if he has any hope of leaving, 'twill be upon your back, and Deidre..." Doc's brain whirred, but it all came together so perfectly. "Deidre, Hickory and Tiffen... they deserve a better resting place and fate than to become one of the lich's zombies to be beckoned and raised. Once Bazter has Finnick, you help him gather their b—" Doc's voice caught in her throat and she took a deep breath. "Their bodies." The bodies didn't matter anymore. She had their souls.

"I'll check the charges and make sure they're ready to blow."

Bazter and Deidre both nodded, and separated from their huddled group to attend to their assigned tasks.

Doc hurried over to the entrance, straight to where she knew the charges were primed and ready. She stared at them each in turn; gentle Bazter bending over his broken brother, and lovely, deadly Deidre who'd only wanted to help, the picture of tenderness as she carefully lifted Hickory's body into her arms.

"I'm sorry, my friends. But I can't let you stop me," she whispered.

She hit the trigger.

The perfectly set charges exploded, bringing the entrance to the lich's cavern under the knoll tumbling down. Doc hugged the music box to her chest as rock and stone collapsed around her, the dust roaring, deafening, and blinding her in the darkness. She cradled the artefact close, shielding Hickory's spirit, even as her goddess' light left her.

The cavern began to settle, and Doc blinked in the sudden stillness. It was done. She was out. She was alone. She looked at the artefact pressing into her chest. *No. Not quite alone. With you to the end. And this is not the end, my friend.*

As the dwarf began to trudge back up the long tunnels towards the surface, the Lullaby of the Golden Bells followed in her wake.

A LIAR'S BANE
THOMAS D MOORE

"**M**y Lord, I cannot recommend a person so much as Malik," the large man next to his wares explained. "He came to me with dreams of travelling, and making a name impressive enough to impress the local lord—yourself. For a chance to join his elite forces.

"We have had many mishaps along our journey. But Malik here, he managed to pre-empt all of them. May the Mad King take my hands, I'd swear he had some kind of future vision, if it wasn't such a heretical art."

Brythan, Lord of Albunath, looked at the scrawny young man. Whereas he was not much of a fighter him-self—in fact the closest thing he had ever come to fight was a particularly tough porkchop—compared to this black haired, young ruffian, he looked positively de-structive. The lord had known Reginald for a long time... heck, there was no merchant in the world as trusted as the large gentleman. Still, there was no way this poor excuse of a person that the merchant had brought before his lord was what he was claimed to be.

Brythan was already exhausted; he had seen so many of these useless guards today. Every merchant had come to 'provide aid' at the Lord's request. The handsome reward had nothing to do with it, or, at least, that was what they would claim. The regal being stroked his beard and waited. Even if this 'Malik' had somehow fooled Reginald, nothing got past his eyes. Not for a matter as grave as this.

The arrow flew from the right; the advisor already sending the signal. Vallie was what you would consider a perfect aide. Most thought her just another of Brythan's fancy, and that was the way she wanted it to remain. The lady of the Baylin household kept up her appearance perfectly, from the golden blonde hair, to the way her dress curved in just the right way that she would catch any man's eyes, but not for the reasons they should be focusing on. Very little was known about her, the interests she disclosed a front to play into the mistress story they produced. Her biggest and most dangerous asset was her shrewd mind. It was lucky she was loyal.

Lord Albunath had no clue which guard had loosed the arrow. That was important to the ruse, so said Vallie —a shrewd man would be watching the king's eyes, his actions. The beard stroke was already a gambit, but an important one. Give anyone smart enough to notice time to over analyse. When the arrow fell at their feet, it would reveal the type of person they were dealing with.

The guard didn't move. Brythan couldn't help but release a sigh. "You claim him to have the foresight of a heretic, but look at him... not even now has he fully comprehended that he could have died."

The guard shifted, falling to one knee, bowing to the lord. Brythan opened his mouth to say something about cowardice, but the guard got his words out first. The tones he used were like butter to the lord's ears. How could anyone have a voice so naturally calming?

"My lord, apologies if my actions have been perceived as an inability to act. I saw no reason to move, for neither my life, nor the life of the one I am charged with protecting, were in any danger. I sensed no bloodlust and, even when the arrow was loosed, there was no malice in this room."

The strange guard, Malik, continued to kneel, but the room was silent. Even the merchant had fallen when the arrow hit. This man though... he was different. The lord looked Malik up and down, evaluating something that he would never be able to see. That wasn't to be his job though.

The signal came—a simple cough from the lady-in-waiting at the back of the room.

"So you say, Sir Malik, however simple words are not enough. The next arrow won't miss, they will be aiming to kill. Do you accept?"

Malik stood and nodded, not a single emotion appearing upon his young face. He couldn't have been older than twenty, but even so, he had the eyes of someone with years of combat.

"Your lordship, a question before we continue. Am I allowed to harm the guards trying to hurt me?"

The lord nodded, sensing an ego that was likely about to be put in its place. "So long as they are fit for combat after, you may attack those that attack you."

The guard was out of Brythan's sight before the sentence was finished. He was fast—incredibly fast. By the time the Lord's head had shifted, he only caught a brief glimpse of the man as he entered the balcony where the guards were stationed.

A fight broke out above, yells echoing down. It was

clear even without seeing that this man was skilled, although how he would actually fare against six of the best guards the lord could afford was interesting to Brythan.

Silence followed. Anticipation grew. Brythan turned to Vallie, who looked just as confused as he did.

The silence was broken as a loud thunk sounded, then another, and a few more as if for dramatic effect. The lord turned, as the last of six bows fell to the ground. Malik jumped after them. He nodded, still with nothing behind his eyes; no bloodlust, no happiness, nothing. The only thing he did was produce a few throwing knives. It didn't take a close inspection to work out those were the last resort weapons given to each of the guards upstairs.

Malik fell to his knees. "They are all alive, as you commanded. No serious injuries, but they could probably use a moment's rest."

The Lord of Albunath couldn't believe what he was seeing. Absolute silence filled the room. Vallie walked forward to whisper in his ear; she had already sent someone to check above, and confirmed what the guardsman claimed was true. She elaborated no further, but, as no one was attempting to arrest the man, the guards were probably still alive... or no one wanted to take a chance fighting him.

Who was this man? Brythan couldn't help but wonder. Appearing out of nowhere and effortlessly taking down six of Albunath's finest marksmen. His dexterity was nothing to sneeze at either, climbing up to them like it was but a simple staircase separating him from his foes.

To appear just as they needed someone with his particular skills and loyalty was the most concerning of all though—it was like he had been training for this moment his entire life. The Lord's eyes narrowed; he did not need the advisor to whisper his worries in his ear.

"Do you know why we are looking for someone right now?" The large man questioned, leaning forward as if to warn the guard. If Malik showed any concern for how Brythan's demeanour had changed, he did not show it.

"My lord, the merchant Reginald and I arrived here three days ago, and, as he had unfortunately been feeling unwell, I was either by his side or guarding his goods. I cannot speak as to why you need someone, only that I can fulfil that role."

There was no emotion on his face; his tone seemed to carry it all instead. As the words brushed over the room, the Lord of Albunath's worries began to fade. By the time Malik had finished speaking, a decision had been made in his mind.

"You have shown skills far above what we were looking for. Between that, and Reginald vouching for you, it would be an insult not to hire you for the task. Congratulations. Come back tomorrow to get fitted for your guardsman's outfit."

The newly employed Malik bowed his head, not even questioning what the job was. This pleased Brythan, as a guard should only follow orders and not question them.

When they were gone, and the room empty except one, the lord turned to his most trusted advisor.

"Well?"

She nodded, taking a perch on the throne he sat on, the end of day ritual. If anyone walked in, they would only assume Brythan was indulging in his desires—the lord had yet to take a wife after all. None were as useful as an advisor disguised as a mistress. It had taken him a while to not get distracted himself, and he still wasn't entirely comfortable with how close she got.

"It's hard to say. On the one hand, it feels like he is perfect for what we need. On the other hand, he feels almost *too* perfect for our requirements. I'll send out my informants to get more information on this Malik.

"At this moment though, I will admit his words moved me." Vallie nibbled her thumb. "I feel like you have made the best choice."

THOSE FOOLS HAD MADE the worst choice.

Of course, it would have been hard to find someone better; no one was as prepared as Malik. That was the real trick—be smarter than everyone else.

He was—there was no doubt—but still, if he had made one mistake thus far, it was choosing to become a stone-faced guardsman. The role was so stifling. He hadn't laughed out loud in almost a year, and keeping his emotions in check was exhausting.

Long cons were always the best ones. A quick grab and run... well, any two bit thief could do that. No, it was the skilled who went for the giant prize at the end of a long piece of theatre. The ones who truly mastered the art could wait as all the pieces slotted perfectly in place. Had being a guardsman for a merchant who couldn't keep track of the coins in his own wallet for a year been fun? Admittedly sometimes, but there's only so many times you can make a man sleep while you went to steal the things he had just sold.

Most of the time had been hard work, planning 'bandits' to come allow Malik to play hero, paying off the real bandits to leave them alone. The cheese wheel incident.

He still had nightmares about that one.

It was necessary of course; like all the best laid plans, a good performance was required. It wouldn't be much longer now. The pieces were in place. Malik 'the guard' had passed every trial they put in front of him. The informants had found what he wanted them to easily enough. They were good at their job, that was for sure.

It was just a shame he was better.

Son of a humble guardsman, they would tell that advisor, a father who would take his anger out on the boy if he failed to learn to fight. But he had, and had learned to defend himself even better. Raised to serve, the truest honour of any guardsman. He would continue his own path until he found the perfect lord and the skills to protect him.

Vallie would swoon over him, as would that barrel with a crown that called himself lord. He knew they would; the story was perfect, not too heroic, a touch of tragedy, and a resolve that made Malik trustworthy. By the time he had returned to get fitted for his new job, they already had such expectation in their eyes.

It would be the honey on top of everything that was about to happen.

They had hired him for a single purpose. A week prior they had received a card—in Brythan's bedroom no less—while he slept. There were few with the audacity to pull off something like that, and only one had the skills to enact such a plan.

The Phantom of Scratton was an entity that few hadn't heard of, and even fewer didn't fear. No one knew who he was, only that once he sent a card, your treasure was as good as his. All of the greatest heists were committed by the Phantom, and the only evidence of who had committed it was a note that simply read 'Thank You'.

Malik kept walking through the halls, bowing to the men he had positioned to catch the Phantom. They were perfectly placed; no way in, no way out. Traps littered about to make sure the thief would alert everyone if he came unprepared in the night. The Lord and his advisor had given him leadership roles to catch the fiendish miscreant. The manor was impenetrable, a beacon of safety. No thief would be able to get in or out of this fortress.

Unless... It was the thief himself who had set everything up.

Malik did his best to suppress his smile. The guardsman he played was incapable of smiling, the only wrinkle in such a perfect plan. Gods be damned, it had been difficult to keep this character up. To be stone faced at all times when people were around. He had spent his nights camping with the merchant Reginald, unable to show any smugness as to how well the heist was going.

Still, it was required to enact the perfect plan. Everything had started over six months ago, sat in the Thief's Guild listening to rumours from his less successful colleagues. Well, colleagues might be a bit of a stretch; no-one could match the charm and talent as the Phantom of Scratton, after all.

Not that those lackeys knew who he was. To them, Malik went by another name—Ger. A simple thief, always trying to think up the next big, get rich quick scheme, always down on his luck. A nobody. It was the best way to get information, to be like those who looked up to him.

"I'm telling ya, no one coul' do it!" the drunk pick-pocketer whose name was unimportant to Malik, even if Ger was best friends with him, said.

"No one could get into that mansion and out unde-tected. Even tha Phantom would ge' caught."

Now Ger shouldn't have cared, but Malik took that pretty personally. There was no one better than him. This idiot could barely lift a pocket, how dare he accuse the Phantom of imperfection!

Ger stirred. "You should really be careful with your words. What would you do if the Phantom heard you?"

That made the man laugh. "Bah, he wouldn't ap-pear here with us commoners. Too up his own arse with self-importance. I'm telling ya, getting in that Lord's manor would be impossible, specially afta' he did that little card trick of 'is."

The bar actually cheered at that. The fast fingered and fat mouthed lummox had been getting louder.

Ger had excused himself not long after, making sure to add a little 'medicine' to his friend's drink unnoticed. The man wouldn't have a great time come the morning; the toilet would become his new best friend for a while. Still, the challenge had been issued loud and clear. It would have been insulting to not meet the expectations of his lesser and unworthy peers.

As it turned out, the Lord of Albunath had awful defences. The first time Malik had infiltrated the place, he was astonished at how easy it was to get into the trea-sure room; the Phantom had seen more defences in the

Republic of Katharan. It occurred to Malik that he hadn't been back to the city for a year, and that maybe, after this heist, he would find some entertainment over there. Without nobility, it was a fun and unique challenge, as everyone had access to resources that people in cities like Albunath could only dream of.

But it was unacceptable how lax Lord Brythan was. Malik had been set a challenge! For things to be this easy went against everything he stood for. Imagine if the Phantom stole from the Lord's manor now; the thieves would not be impressed, they would not sing his praises. No, this heist would require work.

It had taken months of forcing the Lord to increase his security. His greatest piece was convincing a team of builders to play a prank on the Lord's carriage, while also warning Brythan that bandits were in the area. No one had died, but still, the lord was more and more protected every time he ventured out.

It wasn't hard, of course; had Malik been a merchant, he could have sold a square wheel to a carriage driver. *The golden voice*, Malik had described it to one other, before the guy was taken for the punishment that Malik had rightfully deserved. It had been a gift from the heavens, one he had trained and mastered over the years.

The Phantom had learned by many years of watching and listening to liars. Honestly, even Malik didn't quite know why people were so easy to manipulate, but that would be for the great scholars of the future to work out. To him, it was his gift and his right.

He turned a corner, near the hall where he had convinced the fool and his mistress to hire him. There was no luck on that day, just more of getting his way. A normal man might have struggled against six armed

men, but it was simple when the group was still weakened from the drugs he had slipped them the night
before.

It made him laugh, thinking how quickly they had
been overpowered. Only one hadn't been unwell, but he
was already in the Phantom's pocket—not that the man
had known. He had been told that the guard, Malik,
would not hesitate to kill if threatened, and seeing his
five friends taken down in seconds was enough to convince him to lower his weapons. He was the one who
had made the shot at Malik's feet, the only calculated
risk in an otherwise perfect plan.

And now the castle was a fortress, designed to keep
the evil of the world out. Unfortunately, with Malik in
charge, he had already made a good enough side entrance for himself.

The rest of the plan had been underway for the past
three weeks. No one had yet realised that the treasury
gold was being slowly replaced with stone, no one had
checked, and had trusted the new guards' words when
he told them everything was in order. How could they
not, everyone always believed his words to be true.
They expected the Phantom Thief to strike on the night
the card said. The only thing Malik would really need
to do was place the 'Thank You' note.

It was a shame really. Malik had always wanted the
Phantom to appear on a windowsill, with a bag of gold,
taunting the target with how useless all their efforts had
been. There was always too much to steal though, he'd
never get out of the window he had set up for the
escape.

That was the genius of being left in control of the
castle's defences; sure he would be blamed for letting
the Phantom of Scratton escape, but so long as he

fought the thief and lost, he would be spared. A quick false injury, a little fake blood, and an apology to the lord, and Malik's life would be spared. They wouldn't even realise that they had been feeding and housing the thief until Malik didn't show up for work the next day, and by then the Phantom would be halfway to Katharan, laughing the whole way.

The plan was perfect, the stage was set. The night was tonight, everyone was on edge watching every window and guarding every door, not realising that the Phantom of Scratton was already walking the halls, giving the orders to follow.

MALIK WAITED IN THE TREASURY, nominating himself as the castle's last line of defence. It had been hilariously easy to convince the others. His best and brightest were standing outside the door, even if they didn't even hold a candle to the thief.

The plan was simple really. But a simple ending to a long con was always the best way to go. The guards would change, which would give Malik a few minutes to set up the scene for a fight like no other. Torn cloth, blood, and a knocked out guardsman who had fought valiantly to the end. The Phantom had managed to fly through the castle like the spirit people claimed him to be, taking an impossible amount of gold with him. Malik would be interrogated, but ultimately could not be blamed for doing his best. While the castle was searched, a window near the infirmary had been set up to allow the thief to climb up and fly off into the night.

Malik casually inspected the wares, looking for anything he had missed. He knew every box was full of pebbles, and every ornament a cheap imitation; the guardsmen who watched the treasury were hired for their strength, and alas they lacked the intelligence to see the differences. But something was calling to him... something he had missed.

It pulled at his senses, making him frown. He knew he would need to set off the next part of his plan soon; the guard change was just around the corner, and if he missed his window to start the 'fight' then someone might be able to tell that no one had entered the room. Malik had only allowed for one guard change, wanting to show off that the Phantom could take advantage of any situation. This city would never doubt his greatness ever again.

They may not financially recover either, but that didn't really concern Malik.

Five minutes before the guard shift, he finally spotted it. One of the paintings was just a little off, the only thing he didn't steal. Paintings were valuable, but easy to trace back to a seller. It hadn't been worth the extra hassle.

Peering behind it though *was* something worth the hassle; a safe. A hidden compartment in the seas of wealth. A treasure amongst treasure. Just the sight made Malik's heart glow. It was a test, a challenge, and a promise that no thief could ignore. It was like the cake at the end of the feast; no matter how full you were, you must always have room for that delectable dessert.

He put his ear to it and began to turn the dial. His heart jumped with anticipation with each click. What could they be hiding in here?

Click.

It had to be something extra precious to hide, the room was already full of treasure after all.

Click.

Whatever it was, it called to Malik, begging him to liberate it from the cold, dark void within. What kind of gentleman would he be if he didn't answer the call of a damsel in distress?

Click.

The door opened as if it awaited him. Time became irrelevant as he eyed his prize; a single box ordained with locks. Some delicate, some strong. It was a challenge within a challenge.

Oh, how the lord spoiled his thieves.

He took off the strong locks first, removing the larger confines and moving on to the delicate areas. These locks were old but beautiful, and slipping each piece off made the thief's fingers twitch. As the last of the chains fell, gold and jewels sliding away almost seductively, Malik pocketed them for later inspection. The thief slowly opened his prize.

Inside was a ring. A beautiful ring that sang in its simplicity. A single gold band, hiding strange carvings within. He knew them to be Elvish, but had never even considered learning their language. Their culture was not one of thieves and vagabonds, and their grudges lasted much longer than Malik intended to live.

But the cherry on top was the garnet. It glowed in the darkness like the light of the sun. Any normal man might question why a gem would glow in a darkened room, but Malik was entranced. He could hear it calling him, begging to be worn. He didn't even notice himself responding until he felt it brush down his left ring finger, almost as if the ring were proposing to him.

By then it was too late.

The moment the ring touched his finger, it moved, forcing its way down his hand. It grew to fit him as if it had been attached to him for years. Malik panicked, trying to force the ring off, but it wouldn't budge. In that moment, a burning began, causing the silent thief to scream. It was a deep heat, like the ring was searing his very soul. He swore he could hear laughter.

In the Phantom's mind he knew he should not scream—it wasn't time. But when no one came, it was clear that the changing of the guards was already happening, and he was falling behind schedule. Malik chose to worry about the ring later; he would claim it had attached to him in the fight. Lying was Malik's biggest strength after all. Maybe Brythan would be so thrilled that something survived, he would help Malik to remove the ring.

The thief pulled out the knife and started to clang it on metal. He had done this before, and knew how to get the sound just right. The changing guards started banging on the doors. "Why was it locked?" they would ask. Well obviously, the thief felt he could take Malik one on one easily, so he relocked the door behind him to make sure there were no intruders.

Malik had already prepared the cuts on his arms and legs. They unfortunately had to be real, as there would be doctors looking him over when the fight was done. A loud crash erupted as Malik threw himself to the floor. He hit the ground a little too hard, but it was fine. The bruising would mean nothing compared to all the riches he had acquired. At least it made his battle seem more authentic.

He waited with eyes closed as the door was slowly bashed in. Malik sighed inwardly. By the many gods, these guards were useless. The Phantom could have snuck out, stole a sandwich from a noble's hand, and then snuck back in in the time it was taking them to knock down a simple reinforced door.

When they finally came in, they were met by the remains of a hard fought 'battle' and the man, supposed to stop the thief, lying on the floor. Malik was a good actor; he had trained for moments such as this for a long time. Mostly through trial and error while on the streets. There had been many errors.

The game of being knocked unconscious was to make sure you found the perfect time to wake up. If he opened his eyes when they bashed through the door, it would look like he had been a princess waiting for her prince to come and save her. If he left it too late, they would pick him up and take him to the infirmary, and then there would be too many eyes on him to escape.

No, the perfect time was as the first guard came over to check Malik was still alive. It was dramatic. It would let them know he was okay. It would mean these lowly creatures wouldn't touch him.

Malik tried to stand, but very quickly realised he had hit his head harder than he thought. He stumbled and the guard who came to check on him quickly helped prop Malik up.

Well, there goes the no contact rule, he thought.

It was fine, his pockets were lined in such a way that simple contact wouldn't give away what was beneath. For as perfect a thief as he was, it was best to plan for the worst case scenarios. Malik was amazing at what he did, he was certainly no fool.

"The Phantom?" Malik asked. "Where is he? We must inform the lord. Take me to him."

The guard stopped moving for a second, a weird motion that Malik noticed immediately. The man very quickly snapped back to attention, and looked at the thief in front of him.

Malik felt his whole world begin to crumble as the guard began violently shaking him back and forth, yet still dragging him out of the room in the process. If the dizziness was bad before, it was painful now. Worst of all, he began to hear the fancy locks rattling inside his hidden pocket.

If either guard heard it, they made no move to take them. Instead, the guard pulling him towards the throne room was far more interested in making sure the thief was as disorientated as possible. In the few moments that he saw the other guard, he could tell this was not normal by the look of confusion in his eyes. In front of the lord, composure was the name of the game, and this madman was giving Malik a disadvantage he was not ready for.

They entered the audience chamber, and the guard finally stopped shaking Malik. The two knelt before their lord. Malik tried to do the same but was so disorientated he ended up falling face first onto the floor.

"Malik? Dear gods, man, what happened to you?"

"The Phantom attacked, my lord," Malik said, trying to fight off the wave of nausea. His guardsman persona was crumbling around him, as he struggled to find his balance.

Before he could, the man to his left shuffled a bit, but continued to kneel. With a breath or two, Malik managed to get a hold of himself. His cover wasn't blown yet; he could still recover.

He turned to the one who hadn't been shaking him. "I seem to be unable to stand at the moment, pick me up would you?" The same moment of stillness he had seen from the other guard came about. His eyes seemed to glaze over for a moment. Then he stood, and nodded at Malik.

The Phantom was not expecting the kick to the stomach, the second one even less. They didn't stop, even as Lord Brythan cried out. It was only when Malik finally scurried back and managed to get to his feet did the kicking stop.

Malik tasted blood. How long had it been since that had happened? Probably not since his attempt at a gladiator caper, but even then, that had been a little extra to the plan... and not even his blood! Not like this, this was simply not right.

Did they know?

He put his hands up. The other man just looked confused, like the last few moments were a blur to him. It was only when the Lord of Albunath let out a gasp did Malik remember the glowing pink ring on his finger.

Brythan didn't even glance at his advisor—just clicked his fingers, pointing at Malik. The guards knew the command; it meant trouble. They surrounded him, grabbing at him, forcing him into a corner. It happened so quickly and unexpectedly that Malik, as disorientated as he was, couldn't react fast enough to not get caught.

"My lord," he managed, trying not to break character. "What is going on? Please, let me go!"

He expected his words to carry the same persuasion it always had; Malik could always entrust his life to his words. It was only a misunderstanding—he would explain when his hands were free. They would understand, they would sympathise. No one was immune to the Phantom's charm.

The rotund lord stood up and walked over. Not a single emotion flared on the guardsman's face, watching his lord come towards him the same way a cat would watch their owner, curious but with no need to put much thought into it. Internally, Malik bit down his worry, fighting his latent urge to fight his way to freedom. Where did it all go wrong?

Malik closed his eyes, waiting for the judgement to be passed. It'd surely be painless if he never saw the death coming.

When he felt movement on his hair, curiosity took over. His eyes looked at the fat lord who was now patting his head, like you would do to praise a friendly animal. Malik felt his face heat. Rather than death, he was being treated as low as some creature. The Phantom of Scratton was better than some common dog.

The thief felt the hand leave his head, followed very quickly by a punch to the face. The man looked furious, with a hint of embarrassment.

"You will only speak to me when spoken to, are we understood?"

Malik could only nod as the lord returned to his seat, the advisor standing in the background trying her best to hold back laughter. Malik was just stunned—there was no planning for the madness currently unfolding and, worst of all, his words had failed him.

Vallie stepped forward. "So, Guardsman Malik, would you care to explain how that got onto your finger?"

The Phantom of Scratton knew a chance to lie when he heard it. He nodded. "I'm not entirely sure... one moment I was fighting the Phantom, and he threw a strange box at me. The next thing I remember was a burning sensation and this ring was stuck to my finger. That was when I got knocked out."

Vallie looked intrigued, and Malik was already

thinking about her next question. Sure enough, he was not surprised to hear. "The box was full of locks though? Not to mention it being behind a safe. It would be strange to be in the same room and not hear him attempting to unlock that."

"When I realised he was in the room, he was halfway through cracking the safe. His fingers are quite quick, ma'am." Malik would have saluted the advisor if he hadn't got two men to each arm. Certain ladies would have loved such attention.

A cough echoed and the guard who shook him stepped forward. "Ma'am, I know it is not my place to say something, but on the way to the throne room I couldn't stop this compulsion to shake him... these locks and a couple pieces of gold fell out of his pocket on the way."

Malik felt his blood freeze, and it took all his restraint not to check his pocket. It was fine, he was smart, he was resourceful, and he was the greatest liar this palace had ever seen.

He looked into Vallie's eyes, a pleading look, a desperate look, an all too well practised sight guaranteed to tug on the heartstrings of those who heard his words. The pale blue eyes of a conniving woman stared back, but he could see the cracks. Malik could read people like a book. It just took the right series of words to turn the most hardened gladiator to a blubbering mess. Most men would reach those words by accident; Malik just needed the right set up.

"Advisor. Your Lordship. Please, I'm being framed! The Phantom is using me as a distraction while he escapes. Send your men to find him. There is still time. You have to believe me!"

He could feel the magic in his words, grasping at the

emotions within his targets, but upon the last five words, something changed—twisted—he couldn't understand it. The knife in his gut, the burning on his finger, something was *wrong*.

The blue eyes he had watched so carefully glazed over for but a fraction of a second, and then turned to malice. She stood straight, pointing at her foe, the persona of the lord's maiden dropping away, finally showing the cunning woman beneath. Malik's heart may have fluttered a little if it wasn't frozen with fear.

"Strip him. I want to see what this man is hiding in his entirety."

Few events are more mortifying than a strip search of a guilty man. Layers of lies stripped away, his jacket, once a bastion of hidden thief tools and pockets sewn in by his own hand, thrown to one side, modifications laid as bare as his pale skin. To be in front of all these strangers in nothing but what a man was born with was a fate few would crave.

Everything was found—the men were not gentle. His true trade's tools, the coins he stole, his lucky coin he took on every mission. The 'Thank You' card he was meant to drop as he left the room was the worst one; it sealed his fate tighter than the suspenders that were clinging for dear life, trying to hold the lord's trousers up.

He could beg and plead that it was all a ruse, that the real Phantom had planted all this evidence to get away. On a normal day, he would have already, but everything was wrong. Malik had never suffered such humiliation. His lying hadn't failed him in years, not since his early days of thieving.

He lay there, left thankfully in his underwear—not that it had prevented them from a full search—and the mysterious pink ring. They had tried to remove it, but it hadn't budged. The guards had given up at a cough from the lord.

"So, this is the famous Phantom of Scratton?" Brython laughed. "Colour me unimpressed. Caught in his own trap it seems."

Vallie let out a chuckle, seemingly returning to the dainty mistress once more. "To be fair, my dear lord, I don't think this is his fault. Few could understand the mistake the little man made."

Mistake... MISTAKE? The Phantom of Scratton does not make mistakes. Tell me what mistake I made, Malik thought.

"Well, I guess now two mistakes!" Vallie yelled suddenly, but she seemed confused at the loudness of her own voice. The Lord of Albunath let out a laugh, poorly disguised as a cough. It fooled no one, especially not Vallie, who shot the large bulb of a man a look that made him sit up straight, one of the suspenders finally giving up the fight in the process. If it hadn't been clear before now who was really ruling this kingdom to everyone, the room became well informed then and there.

"First mistake. You put on the ring... Liarsbane." Vallie coughed. "Mistake two was admitting that you were the Phantom out loud."

Malik was stunned. Had he really said what he was thinking out loud... to the people he was robbing? He was tired—very tired—with a splitting headache forming long before the thief had entered the throne room. Between the shaking, the kicking, the strip search, and the insults, the man was at his limit.

A thousand questions entered his head, the headache continuing to grow. But as a jumbled mess of thoughts continued to spiral, one question pierced through his lips before he realised he was speaking. "Why are you yelling?"

The thief was kicked swiftly in his side from one of the guards. Right, he wasn't meant to be talking.

Vallie smiled, moving towards him like a bear prowled towards the salmon trapped on land after an intense chase. Every step had a purpose—to instil fear, and it was working well. The lord sat back, watching her hips swing seductively, dangerously. This was clearly his favourite moment of the night.

The woman extended a finger and lifted the chin of her captive. Their eyes met and Malik knew total defeat in that moment. She was practically glowing with mirth. Vallie was enjoying this, the theatrics she put on seeming to come from a place deep down. Was this who she really was? Someone as trained in acting as Malik was?

"Why, you told me to. Didn't you hear your own words? 'Yell me what mistake I made', you said. We all heard it, but the ring compelled me to act." She let the thief go with a flick of the chin, turning without a care for her safety, and returned to the lord, her voice ringing back to him.

"Liarsbane, the greatest curse that has ever befallen a thief! Created by the elves hundreds of years ago to destroy the liars of their lands, the destruction it has wrought is second to none.

"It allows the user to compel anyone to do anything. If you wanted money, all you need do is ask for it." She eyed the Phantom. Malik felt so simple, so useless; it only set flame to the anger within.

"I'm sure you're thinking that doesn't sound like a curse.. But maybe a simple tale will teach you all you need to understand so we can move forward.

"Do you know the tale of the Mad King Eridon?"

Malik blinked. Who didn't? The Mad King was a tyrant whose insanity led to a level of torture that few had seen before or since, and a rebellion that opened the way to the Republic of Katharan that Malik was desperately wishing he was standing half naked in.

"Did you know that Eridon was considered a sane king until he snapped overnight? He was destined to be one of the greatest that Katharan ever knew. The day before the disaster, he was leading the city into a new golden age." Malik could tell Vallie was enjoying herself. Every word she said was becoming more pronounced, more dramatic.

She came up to the thief. "But what would lead a man to become so cruel and insane that his name is used as a curse to this day. I'll give you one guess."

Malik gulped, the ring not only cruelly grasping his finger, but somehow the pit of his soul too. More annoyance began to build as Vallie saw what she wanted from him.

"I can tell by your eyes you have the right answer. But, my dear sweet Phantom, it was a fool such as yourself that toppled the kingdom. He knew the effect of the ring, knew the consequences, but assumed there was a trick to controlling the power. The then Lord of Albunath, Keiriom.

"He believed you just had to be very precise with your wording, so confident and greedy that lord that he didn't even test his theory. Just rode straight to Katharan for his meeting with King Eridon.

"They had sat in a private audience room together, the only reason we were spared the wrath of the republic, as they still have no idea of our involvement to this day. It took seven words to create a disaster and a revolution."

Vallie held up seven fingers, enunciating the next words with fire and passion of a performer in the middle of the biggest, most enjoyable performance of their life.

"Give. Me. All. Of. Your. Kingdom's. Lands.

"The spell took place, the king rose and said, 'as you command.' Keiriom went home thinking he had been successful.

"When the crate came in from Katharan, everyone was confused. All the lords and ladies gathered around to witness the deeds to Katharan given to Lord Keiriom. They opened it in a private room to be safe.

"They say the smell alone of that box opening killed some of the fairest maidens present. The maids were confused by the vomit they would later clean up. The box was burned and buried.

"By the time the third shipment of hands arrived, Keiriom realised his mistake and went mad himself, abdicating the throne. Katharan was in the middle of an uprising that went down in history, and Liarsbane was sealed away through lock and chain, never to face daylight again."

She smiled a cruel smile as Malik thought of the disaster. He thought of everything that she had said, and soon the pieces started to fall into place.

Give me all of your kingdom's lands.

Take me to him.

Pick me up.

Let me go.

Tell me what mistakes I made.

All his commands had been followed, but also not. He had commanded obedience, but never received what he asked for. Keiriom had asked for lands... he had received hands.

"The ring twists the words to sound different..." he muttered, finally realising the truth. Hands. Shake. Kick. Pet. Yell. The words were changed ever so slightly but it made the effect completely different. The Phantom who lied and commanded his way through life could no longer trust his own words.

Vallie had returned to her lord, whispering in his ear. He nodded and Malik was pinned to the floor, something soft shoved into his mouth. The lord stood.

"Well, Phantom, alas we will have to reconvene to-morrow, once we have taken stock of the treasury you were claiming to protect. Unfortunately, if one coin is missing, we will have to postpone your execution until you let us know where you hid it. Take him away."

———

HONESTLY, for how unused it seemed to be, the prison was relatively clean. Four walls, metal bars, a bed with actual covers. He had been in worse places.

That didn't help ease his mind though. The one thing Malik had learnt about Brythan's ways; he had a darkness to him, and his prisoners learnt that fact very well. They would be unlikely to give the thief much chance to rest, once they chose to find where all of the castle's treasures had been stashed.

It took a full hour to shake away the shock he was feeling at being caught, beaten, mocked, imprisoned, and cursed—this was clearly the Phantom of Scratton's darkest hour. As his mind began to turn again though, he realised that a story with this level of defeat would only sing his praises higher if he escaped.

The world would know of the great Phantom and how he overcame Lords, curses, and the gods themselves in his great escape with riches in tow. They would laud him higher than any thief before or after. Malik would get the recognition he deserved.

There was only one problem. There was no plan.

It had been a very long time since Malik had stolen without a detailed plan. Not since his family cast him aside as a child for not being a prodigy at age five. Back then he had been young, naive, and lucky to survive. He had learnt so much from other thieves, surpassed them all in the process. His first heist proved his parents wrong, as he stole enough to leave them on the same streets they had cast Malik out to. They had not survived as well as he had.

Still, Malik was more prepared than when he was a child. The advantage of playing a guardsman meant he had time to survey the castle, to know its layout. To hear rumours of weak points and secret passages. He had even found his way to the prison before. That was the biggest stroke of luck to him. There was a word that would save him in this moment.

Contingency.

The Phantom of Scratton was perfect, but even perfection did not account for random chance. He always knew he might be imprisoned this night, even if Malik had thought it would be as the guard waiting to be interrogated.

He reached into the hole in the floor designed to hold... well, it was better not to think about it. It had been months since a prisoner had been in the castle, and even longer since the hole was last used, at least from what the guards had told him. While 'inspecting' to make sure someone couldn't crawl up through it, Malik

409

had planted his means of escape. It had been clear no human would be able to fit into such a hole, not that it led anywhere, but a single lockpick would go undetected so long as the toilet remained unused.

So, the world's self-proclaimed greatest thief had a lockpick, a mental map of the castle, and a single exit point designed to be easily accessible. The guards would be on high alert, but Malik had fought worse odds and survived. A memory of escaping the gambling den of Washu flashed in his mind; the only time Malik had actually needed to crawl through a waste hole to escape. He shuddered at the thought. He could still smell it in his nightmares.

Before starting, Malik looked at his hand, at the rosy gem adorning his finger almost mocking him. He would need to be careful once he was out. His usual ways might backfire.

Most locks were like butter to those who knew what they were doing. To Malik, they were like popping a balloon. It took a small tap, a quick kiss, and the magic click happened almost immediately.

Ever sloppy with defences was the palace of the Lord of Albunath; with Malik caught they had likely lowered their guard. A foolish mistake—if anything now that he was in their grasp, they should tighten their defences.

As he made his way to the prison stairs, Malik tested his body piece by piece. Those kicks had done some damage, but thankfully it was nothing major. He was bruised—more so in his pride than his body—but all in all he was mostly capable for what came next.

The door to the prison was shut, a blessing in disguise for the guilty who had escaped their cell. Still, with guards on the other side, it was hardly an ideal barrier before the convicts. There was one way in and out of this place; or, at least that's what they thought.

A paranoid lord was either stupid or genius, Malik had always thought. They became so worried about things going bump in the night that they prepared far too much for it. One of the first lords of Albunath had worried about invading armies of elves, even if the rumour had them on the other side of the continent at the time. They had decided to make secret hiding holes throughout the castle, a stupidly expensive and futile job by today's standards, but with so many 'servants' to do his bidding before they 'retired', it was an easy task back then.

It was a not-so-hidden secret to the workers of the castle that these tunnels existed; most would assume these spaces to be collapsed by now. Most people hadn't spent nights finding them. Other lords had tried to bury them, paranoid as they were, but in time the information was lost.

Malik had found collapsed passages all over the castle, from the kitchens to the Lord's bedroom, which must have seemed like a great idea until an assassin had discovered one. All the entrances had been destroyed of course, but the secrets behind the walls laid for those who were willing to find them. Feeling across the wall towards the back of the jail, he found what he knew was there.

On paper, the tunnel in the prison had collapsed after an escape attempt by a prisoner who just couldn't handle the finer steps to freedom. Sure he had broken out of the jail, had even made it outside, but in failing to consider where to go after escaping much like a novice acrobat, he hadn't stuck the landing.

Unfortunately for the palace, the papers failed to

mention what a terrible job the demolishers had done. Malik couldn't help but wonder if they had taken the 'good enough' approach to the situation. 'Good enough' was part of the reason kingdoms fell to Malik's words.

It hadn't taken much to get the entrance ready, should he require it. Nothing of course to make it too noticeable to the other guards, but with a few simple rocks moved and a shovel for some of the heavier bits, Malik had made a hole into the hidden areas of the castle during his free time.

It was always going to be a tight fit, and without clothes to soften the blow, the Phantom's body started to take the damage that he had faked for the fight with himself, highlighting every pain he had already caused. It took at least an hour before he was through the rubble, an achievement, even if a little problematic, knowing that someone could check his cell for him at any moment.

Once past the jagged rocks the tunnel opened up, enough that he could stand on his own two feet once more. Not bright enough to see his hand in front of his face, or a wall for that matter. Light was a luxury he couldn't exactly afford though.

Malik knew two things. First, he had no idea where these tunnels would come out; he had wanted to explore, but it would have let the other guards know the tunnel wasn't fully collapsed. He would have until daylight to find a new exit.

The second—and more worrying thing—was he could not escape without clothes. There was no chance of freedom if he ran through the city half naked. He'd be caught and dragged back to the cells the second a guard laid eyes on him.

He would aim for the servant's quarters, grab an

outfit, and make his way to the window by the infirmary disguised as a worker. So long as they didn't know he was missing, they wouldn't bat an eye at a random employee roaming the halls. The castle had caught its rat; they would not worry about any mice scurrying about.

In the darkness that engulfed him, Malik took a silent step into the abyss, hoping to find an exit before the abyss stepped into him.

BY THE TIME Malik stumbled upon an exit, time had passed. How much time exactly, he was unsure, but enough to plant the seed of worry in his chest. First light —that was how long he had to get some clothes and reach the exit. Nowhere would be safe once the castle woke up, not even these tunnels.

He had almost missed the hidden door, blended into the wall in the dark. Malik supposed that was the purpose. Feeling around, he found something loose but stuck in place. Hidden levers had a specific feel; if you knew what you were looking for, you could find them by touch alone.

The ancient mechanism rumbled to life. Malik had always wondered how old technology always seemed to work, no matter how much time had passed. It wasn't like that these days where a drawbridge could collapse due to a rock getting stuck in the cogs. They just didn't make technology like they did three hundred years before he was born.

There was something blocking the door, which was probably why it had remained functional; no one knew there was an exit here. Pushing the block, he frowned when he heard little objects falling from it. They weren't loud, making a thudding sound rather than a smashing one. When he made enough space, Malik understood the noise.

The library was a beautiful room, a place the lord took his guests to show off his vast collection of knowledge. Malik despaired; this would have been the perfect room to steal from later. Now he wouldn't be able to. He doubted he would ever return to Albunath now that they knew his face.

Still, the advantage was that this room wasn't far from the servant's quarters. Malik would have to brave a hallway or two, but he was much closer than he had assumed he would be.

Reaching the intimidating wooden door that held all the knowledge the lord had likely never read, the thief slowly opened it to the bland hallway that it was affixed to. He breathed a sigh of relief. It wasn't morning yet. It probably wouldn't be long until it broke, but the castle was still asleep at this moment.

Stepping out the man was—for the first time since he was searched—keenly aware of how little clothes he had on. The wind in the air seemed to grab at him, washing itself up and down his body as a not-so-gentle reminder of the lack of trousers. Malik shivered and, as much as he wanted to run for clothing, made his way quietly through the shadows of the hall.

This was the Phantom in his element, no one was better than him at sneaking through a place undetected. The man was alert, but couldn't help his mind wandering to the early days of being the greatest thief of all time—currently self-proclaimed—but after today, who knew?

It was not long after Malik had been thrown from his house for the simple act of not living up to expectations of the exploitative that he, going by the name Renold so as to not allow his family to find him, had learnt the true power of lying. Renold had enrolled in an acting school... well, 'enrolled' assumed the people knew you were taking the class. Sitting in the rafters of the theatre, it would become a secret joy that those no-bles had no idea he was not meant to be there.

At the start, Renold had needed to learn to look the part. A good disguise was half what you said, and half how people saw you. If he walked into the school wearing rags, he would be thrown out like the rest of the common rabble.

Still, one could always be acquired with the other. Renold had been born in that moment, a rich noble shamed by his peers, put into rags and forced to go to the shops to get new clothes. His words carried him through every statement, and every demand was met with sympathy. They ate the lies off him like he was a three-course meal. He was sure the viscount who got the bill a few days later was both surprised and angry by the mistake.

The thought ignited his finger, as if the pink dia-mond was reacting to the memories of the lies that pushed Malik forward, the things that kept him alive. The blushing beauty that ensnared him was not amused by his persuasiveness.

Easy for you to complain about, he thought looking down at the curse on his finger. *You never had to lie and steal to get by.*

The burning seemed to calm down at the thought, this thing—Liarsbane, apparently—was now attached to someone who had mastered the craft of lying. The fact that Malik not only survived, but thrived, with his words would just anger it further.

Still, as he pried open the door to the servant's quarter, his mind refocused on the task. This was the most likely area of someone being awake, with them getting up early to prepare the castle for the lord's awakening. That was all part of the idea of stealing their clothes as well.

He opened the first cupboard and had to laugh at himself. As funny as it would be to escape in a maid's outfit, Malik felt that it would make him stick out in the streets just a little. It took a couple of drawers before the thief found what he was looking for. The cleaning clothes, those designed to get dirty. He avoided anything high class, as Malik knew that the lower street would recognise a butler running out of the city. He needed his presence as common as it came. It did help that those wearing these plain brown clothes would be mostly invisible to the guards, who would feel sympathy for any wearing them, knowing the dirty jobs they had ahead.

It was the perfect outfit to escape into the night. Not the best fitting, but not the worst. The smell was tolerable, although Malik planned to get a bath in as soon as he was safe.

"And who would you be?" a stern voice uttered, as Malik was halfway through pulling the shirt on. He froze. A guard coming to do rounds? From the voice, she commanded authority. But that was fine, Malik could handle himself.

"Sorry, ma'am, after all the confusion last night, I couldn't sleep. I thought I'd get ready to start my day." He heard a quick *hmph*, and a sigh. Always a good sound to Malik; she was letting her guard down.

"Yes, well, good show. At least they caught that

Phantom. We don't need the rabble down in the slums slinking their way through here."

But as Malik's head popped through the shirt, she gasped. There were only a few reasons a person would gasp in this situation. None of them particularly great for him, except the one where she was gasping at his beauty—which he understood—but better not take the chance on vanity at this time.

His hand was over her mouth before she could scream. Malik knew faces; he always took in the scene of a room, lest he need to recognise someone later. He had seen the throne room and everyone in it— this woman was not there.

Which meant from the fear in her eyes, she was likely one of the head maids, one who knew every servant. The woman had known something was wrong the moment his head had appeared.

Malik put on a threatening smile, the type you make when you are about to let someone choose how long the rest of their life would be. It was all a bluff. The Phantom was many things—a swindler, a rich man, a fear in the heart of an entire class of people—but he was not a murderer. It was the one rule above all others. The only thing that separated the common rabble from gentleman thieves was how they reacted when things went wrong. A thief would silence their victims with their fists; Malik used his words.

"Okay, here's how this is going to work," he said, putting a little more pressure on her neck. Intimidation was his best asset and he was going to use it. "I am going to walk out of here. You, my lovely dear, are going to sit there and be quiet until the sun comes up. Got it?" His grip tightened once more. If not handled correctly, she would lose consciousness soon. That didn't worry Malik; at least if she was asleep, his command would be followed.

He felt her go limp for a second but then she nodded her head . That was a good sign of compliance. He let go running for the door. Malik didn't need to wait to see if she did as he asked, already running for the exit.

Just as his hand reached the door, he heard a crash from behind. The woman was throwing things around the room while trying to sit down. The noise was quiet, starting with clothes. But when she managed to knock a vase over, Malik knew it was really time to run.

He was halfway down the hall when the door smashed open, the woman shouting profanities, still trying to knock over everything. The thief turned to look and was surprised to see her sitting down. Something wasn't right. She was half obeying his—

The ring, Malik realised. It changed something in his order, and she was following the things he had said to the letter. Clearly the word that had changed was something to do with being quiet, but he had no time to contemplate the details. The guards would be here any moment, and the castle would not be too happy to learn of his escape.

The plan was dead. It was time to improvise. A word that Malik hated with a *passion*. There wasn't a good way to explain why he was walking away from the screaming now; he was wearing cleaning clothes, and the guards would know he had just come from the direction of said noise.

The infirmary and the window he had left un-guarded wasn't far, but there were still at least three turns between him and freedom. Around the first was a guard on his way to the noise. Malik nearly panicked, but so close to the scene one lie would work without fail.

"It's the Phantom! He's escaped!" he screamed into the guard's face. Without missing a beat, he sidestepped the now wide-eyed man, who was reaching for something Malik didn't care to examine given the circumstances, and fled with all his might.

A loud noise sounded behind him, and soon others would follow it, an orchestra of problems for the thief. The guards were alerted, and they would be looking for anyone suspicious. A cleaner running with an ominous —currently burning—pink ring would certainly qualify for that.

Indeed, as he turned in the last corridor towards the window, it was as if fate was conspiring against him. Three guards rounded another corner, making the crossing of their paths inevitable

It was the expected "Stop!" Malik heard, but then one looked down at his hand, and very quickly drew his sword. The other two followed suit. The thief stopped; they knew who he was. The man had seen the ring. He had been in the throne room.

Malik wasn't the weakest, but even he knew that it was foolhardy to rush three armed guards, with no weapons, no strategy, and no hope. He was not getting out of that window without a sword piercing him. The only thing he had on him was the clothes he wore, and a ring that seemed to be enjoying the show, lighting up in delight at the troubles that found the thief. It was quickly becoming a bane to his very existence..

The thief had a flash of inspiration. He wasn't much of a gambling man, but when he looked down at his finger, he remembered Vallie's words. It would compel others to do as he said, even if it changed the wording slightly.

It would be a risk, but it wasn't like Malik had a choice. Other guards would be appearing soon. He needed just a moment's distraction, and the one thing he did know about this ring was the trance-like state it put people in.

He charged the three, pointing at them.

"Run away!" he shouted at the three men. Two didn't react, but the middle guard gave the tell-tale signs of the compulsion. It seemed the ring only affected one person at a time.

The other two guards charged at him, knowing, through the most basic of maths, that they had the advantage. The thief barely dodged the first sword swing aimed at his legs. Malik could only assume the order right now was dismember, not kill. They would have gone for his vitals otherwise.

Unfortunately, the other guard was waiting for Malik. He aimed for the leg as well, a certain hit, and the Phantom wouldn't have time to react. With a leg pieced —or worse, removed—he'd never be able to get up to the window. This time he was caught.

"Tag! You're it!" he heard from the third guard, as the man pushed the person trying to kebab Malik. The sword still managed to slice his leg, but not deeply. Adrenaline took him the rest of the way, ignoring any pain as he used the little leverages he had set up a week prior to reach the window.

He jumped, thankful no one had noticed the barrel of hay he had placed there for cushioning. Using what little energy he had left, the Phantom of Scratton made a dash towards the streets. All he needed to do was mix in with the crowds down below. Just a bit further.

His leg buckled.

Commotion sounded from the castle, but try as Malik might, he could not command his leg to move. So close to freedom, yet so far. Just a little more energy and he would have made the greatest escape of all time.

"Are you okay?" The voice came from beside him. He didn't recognise it—he did not know many feminine voices—but it came with genuine concern. It wouldn't be castle staff; they would be screaming to the lord by now. He could only hope she would be an ally to his cause. The lord had little love for the lower quarter, and in turn there was little love for Brythan in the city. There was a chance, however small, that this person might help.

Malik had no choice; he could feel the exhaustion starting to take hold. The beatings, the insults, the escape, all of it had been too much on one man.

The world was blurry, his thinking impaired, but a small part of the thief's pride still made him turn to see his new ally, even if his eyes could not make out any details.

"I'm sorry, I'm about to pass out. Carry me away from here," was all he managed, before the darkness took him to fates unknown.

THE SMELL of lavender was strong, an earthy but pleasant smell of mother nature. It filled whatever room Malik awakened in, and long before he opened his eyes, the thief couldn't help but give a quick sigh of relief; a prison wouldn't smell like this.

"Awake?" a male voice called out, clearly waiting for a sign of life. "Good. Up now." It was like gravel to the ears, almost like it understood the words spoken, but didn't care to use them correctly. There were few races in the world that did not use the common tongue frequently enough to master it.

His eyes confirmed his suspicions, as they fought against the notion of remaining open. The sun had never seemed so brighter, and seemed to shine a pale green off the large figure's head. The gruff voice belonged to an orc. But he was sure that the voice that had been there in his last moment of consciousness had been female—maybe she had asked this man to carry him. With his muscles it wouldn't have been a challenge. Thankfully, the older man had done an alright job of patching up Malik's leg. Nothing fancy, and he would likely still need to see a doctor, but the pain was manageable.

As the Phantom forced himself from the realm of sleep and out of the rough bed, he smiled at the rustic and simple nature of the room. Lower quarter for sure, not quite the slums, but close enough to the wall that there was a good chance at escape now.

"Thank you for saving me," Malik said, remembering his manners. Large, green, and muscular this simpleton might be, but still a saviour right now, and, possibly with a little persuasion, maybe Malik's ticket to leaving the city unnoticed.

The man stood up and walked towards the thief. "Me no save. Daughter save." The giant creature hugged Malik, practically crushing him in the process. "You son soon. Me happy."

Whatever little air hadn't already left Malik's lungs from the hug now vanished. He was speechless as the hug ended, and the Phantom was allowed to breathe once more.

It took a moment to find his voice. "Sorry, when you said son... could you explain? I think I hit my head harder than I realised."

The orc looked annoyed. "Daughter bring you home. Said you want marry. She happy. You marry Rikella." It wasn't a question.

He may have been losing consciousness fast at the time, but he knew his words. Carry he had said, *carry*. He may have slurred the words a little but even so, there should be no mistake. Who would even marry someone they found dying in the street next to the castle?

The answer to his concern began to burn, almost like it was mocking him. He could swear he heard the ring laughing at the misfortune now befalling the Phantom of Scratton. It couldn't have made it worse for the thief if it tried.

Orcs were very protective of who they chose to spend their lives with. They chose a mate for life, and it would be the end of one or both of their lives before that vow was even questioned. If Daddy here was convinced that this love was to happen, Malik would be in for a painful time.

Marriage was a prison to the freethinking thief. He understood why people did it, even hoped in his old age he would find someone to care for him as he spent every penny he ever stole. But Malik was still young; there were too many kingdoms to exploit and treasures to steal for him to be chained down now.

The man looked at the orc and weighed up all the options. He could lie, but that would do nothing, and the ring might make the situation worse. He could command the orc to let him free, but the power of the ring was how he got betrothed in the first place—it was unpredictable.

That left one option, something that left a sickening feeling in Malik's stomach. He had only relied on such a daring move a few times, and vowed to use it only as a last resort.

Malik would tell the truth.

"Look, I'm sure Rikella is lovely, and will make any man happy. But she isn't marrying me out of love." He held his hand up. "This is a cursed ring that twists my words and forces people to obey. I asked her to *carry* me. I'm sorry. The effect will wear off soon enough and we can all go back to our lives. What do you say?"

Rikella's father's eyes burned into Malik, like the ring that had caused the problem in the first place. "You control Rikella? She made to love? Then you made to love too! You want out of promise, there be only one way!"

He was picked up and thrown into the other room, and there he met his blushing bride to be. She wasn't bad looking, but honestly Malik couldn't work out how anyone managed to navigate a kiss involving tusks. Certainly, love knew no limits.

She was far more humanoid than her father, a half-orc to be sure, but the green of the skin was only highlighted by the purple flowers they seemed to be cultivating here. It probably was a nice, if very specific, flower shop—at least until the thief found himself being thrown into it.

The orc stepped out and banged his chest. "Might make right!" It was an old traditional rule of the orcs, back to their chieftain days. A decision could only be made by the strongest. Malik was certainly not that.

"Daddy, please, don't kill my mate!" Rikella stepped between them, giving a moment of peace as the father halted in place. The Phantom of Scratton was so far out of his element. There was no planning for this, no emergency planning for things going wrong. This orc was going to fight him, and there was little chance of escaping. Malik didn't even know where the exit was.

"He turn daughter mind. He make you love. He say no to wedding. Me make him marry you. Might make right."

Rikella turned and faced her soon to be husband, with a mixture of sadness and anger in her eyes, as though her mind was fighting the ring's control .

But unfortunately, her orcish half decided to step out the way, and the barbaric ritual returned with permission this time.

Malik was left in front of a giant humanoid creature who would have loved nothing more than to beat the thief's head in, then march him down a lavender infused aisle. The thief had no weapons, no plans, no clue what to do. The only thing he owned was the clothes he had stolen, and a pink ring that seemed like it was enjoying this situation a bit too much.

An idea popped into Malik's head. It wasn't a good idea. It wasn't a nice idea. It wasn't even a kind idea. Heck, it was barely an idea at all, but if it got him out of here, he'd take it. He took a deep breath and thought of the story of the Mad King. He both hoped and dreaded that this would work.

"Wait. You... I never did get your name. Oh well, I have one thing to say to you. Give me your lands"

Malik hoped this was his way out. The orc would remove his own hands, since the ring would misinterpret the words as they had for the previous Lord of Albunath.

The compulsion washed over the dumb creature. Malik couldn't be entirely sure if the vacancy of the eyes wasn't always there. Taking the moment to stand up, he felt a flush of victory as the beast just stood there, processing the order that would save Malik's life and what was left of his virtue.

Then the father took another step towards Malik.

The thief began to panic. Did it not work on idiots? Did it not compel people if it was intentional? There were rules he didn't know about this thing; he shouldn't have put any faith into it.

Malik took a shaky step back, but the orc was too quick, grabbing him by the scruff of his shirt, then dragging him out of the lavender shop. Whatever he had hoped would happen, didn't. Liarsbane couldn't speak, but he could hear it mocking him nonetheless.

Being dragged out to the street would draw attention, and, with the Lord looking for him, that was the second to last thing he wanted to happen. The bottom of that particular list, of course, was the beating he was preparing himself for.

Thrown like a doll that a little girl had gotten bored of, he landed in something soft and grainy. As he scooped up a small handful, he poured the yellow substance on himself.

Sand...

"Give me your sands."

Malik started laughing hysterically, even as the ring burned his finger more from the backlash of the compulsion. He had tried to use a curse to his advantage and it had backfired on him. He was out of plans, out of chances, out of hope. Liarsbane wanted Malik pummelled, and it was not going to let him use it to get what he desired.

It would never allow him to trick people again, never allow him to convince people with his words.

This cherubic looking devil that had attached itself to him had robbed him of the *one* thing in his life he was good at.

The laughter continued on, echoing through the city. Malik couldn't care, he was done. Beaten. Defeated. Useless.

And yet, there was a small flame, the flame that Vallie had sparked in her mockery of him, that roared to life as he sat there looking at his new father-in-law, as he contemplated the children he and Rikella would have. The flame got stronger as he considered everything he had yet to do, every great heist he would miss due to this damn ring.

The flame pulled him to action. He would *not* let this be the final resting place of Malik, Phantom of Scratton and greatest thief of this kingdom. He wasn't about to give up and live the life of Malik the flower shop owner. The fire showed him what he would lose by giving up. He felt his grip tightening and, as if his brain had finally started ticking after all this time, he knew he had everything he needed to escape handed to him.

Standing once more, the pains he had felt this day waned in his passion, and he smiled at his wife-to-be's father.

"Might make right." He nodded as the orc cracked a smile, acknowledging the challenge. The beast ran at the thief, a carriage charging at a rabbit.

Except this little bunny knew where to kick, at least metaphorically. In reality, just before the orc reached him, he threw the sand he was holding onto and ducked.

The sand hit its target, blinding Rikella's father and allowing Malik to make a run for it. He couldn't help but shout back, "Might makes right, but speed makes freed!"

The roar behind him only made him run that bit faster. Still, it didn't take Malik long to get his bearings... and just like that, the path was clear.

He darted through alleyway after alleyway, injured leg burning but still granting him freedom with every painful step. He avoided the main streets, lest the guards—or worse—the orc, found him. It was a longer path to the carriages but it was also the safest route.

He wished he could stop by his safe house and collect his stolen loot but really, that would be awaiting him when things calmed down. Right now his only goal was survival. Malik slowed down as he rounded the corner, looking at the busy network that was the gates to the city.

It took him a few seconds to see that searches of cargo had increased, clearly due to the guards looking for his escape. But that was fine. There were experts of hiding people coming in and out of the city, and an increase in searches just meant an increase in how much it would cost.

Malik 'accidentally' collided with a couple looking lovingly into each other's eyes as they went to explore the markets, much to the annoyance of the ring he wore. It was probably infuriated at the money pouch he had relieved of funds in the collision, but that only fuelled his flame more. So what if the ring didn't like stealing? It had no power if he didn't stop to say sorry.

Tossing the coins at one of the carriage drivers, the man nodded. It was someone from the underground Ger was affiliated with. There were no words, no questions. Malik hid in the secret compartment and waited until the carriage set off. Trust was nothing in the underground, nor were explanations; the only conversation Ger and this smuggler needed was in the language of coin.

Smuggling was about what you could get away with. Guards were dangerous but once they found something small, they would stop looking for something big. The smuggler knew his game, carrying around a small piece of contraband that the guards would take notice of. Not once would they ever notice the hidden compartment. After all, why investigate something human size, when the man was so useless he was caught with something in a matchbox.

As Malik felt the bump and harshness of the road outside the paved tiles of Albunath, he sighed a deep breath of relief. Trapped in his coffin style accommodation, he thought of the fire within that had pushed him forward.

The feeling was there, the need to prove himself superior to the mocking Vallie. The want to upstage everyone that had caused him issues this day. The honour of besting this curse attached to him, to beat it, and stand above it.

It had been his pride that pushed him to victory, and doubt that had clouded his judgement. He would be better than everyone. He was the Phantom of Scratton, and Malik would not rest until that name was feared once more.

First things first though... he needed to undo this curse.

———

MARY WATCHED as the creature crawled towards her. Part of her knew that she should be concerned but fascination had taken its hold on the girl. She watched on as the mass slowly writhed its body forward.

Long ago, mother had made Mary aware of an important life lesson: "Monsters are not to be feared." But as the limbs came into focus and the outline of a human silhouette formed, the rest of the lesson echoed, "not while the madness of man is more destructive."

Admittedly, she couldn't be certain the thing coming towards her was mad; honestly even the human bit was up for debate. But anyone crawling towards the town well, through a field that the cows used to free themselves from the burden that comes with having multiple stomachs, was either very hurt or at a level even the Mad King wouldn't have fallen to.

Either way, Mary didn't feel any threat from the man. His eyes were focused entirely on his goal—the well. Likely he hadn't noticed the girl who was enjoying the sight. Did her enjoyment of this say something about her? She wondered, as the man's plight continued endlessly onwards.

The smell hit her before she reached an answer. It took away any thought as she began to understand that this man's life had been going downhill long before he had reached the bovine latrine. Mary had never once questioned what despair smelt like, but, in that moment, she knew without a shadow of a doubt.

Mary couldn't decide whether it was kindness or hope that the well remained uncontaminated that led her to raising a bucket ready for him. Through the exhaustion and layers of mess, bruises were evident. This man would have struggled to fetch it himself, the only other choice being to climb into the well. As fun as that might be to watch, she didn't think allowing the town well to be poisoned would be great for survival.

If this man could get substance from wood, Mary was sure he'd have tried to eat the bucket. She used the uneaten container to draw more water, not a word shared between the two. The silence was broken as curiosity took over.

"Tough day?" She mused aloud. It was met with a laugh, not a joyous one, but a desperate one, of adventures and misadventures, of tales too traumatic to tell. It hurt to hear, followed by the rasping words of the traveller.

"Would you be shocked to know that I've had worse?"

For the harshness of his voice, his words pulsed with the sweetness of honey. She couldn't help but feel pity for this stranger. Mary couldn't decide where the feeling came from, but it made her want to help.

"If you want some food, we could use some help at the farm. Wouldn't be much but we can at least get you human again."

There were no lies in her words. Her father was looking for help after an unfortunate collision with a pig had left the man with an unfortunate case of twinge back. He'd be right as rain in a few weeks, but the crops would suffer by then.

"Can I..." The stranger trailed off, the words caught in his throat. There was a story there, but not one he'd be telling today.

The man wobbled to his feet and slowly stuck his hand out, intending to seal the deal with a handshake. Revulsion of touching his hand quickly mixed with curiosity at the pink jewellery that adjoined it. A person who sold something like that would be made for life. This enigma of a human was only becoming more interesting to Mary.

He lowered his head as he realised the shake wouldn't come. Instead, he sniffed. "Would be delighted. Would I be able to have some food before I start? I haven't ea—" His hands clasped over his mouth.

The world blanked as a pink mist enshrouded Mary. She could see the words the man had said, with the mist wrapping around them. There was mischief all around at what it would do, it was pondering, enjoying itself. It grabbed for a word and froze.

Whatever the magic was, it seemed to smile, which was impressive without lips. Mary couldn't be sure but it seemed like the creature was judging the man's words and liking what it saw. She could feel the honesty behind the stranger's intentions in that moment, his sincerity. *He won't run, he will work as promised*, the mist seemed to confirm as it let go of the words.

Then it vanished, as did the memory of the moment for Mary.

"Sure. My mother should be finished cooking, she always makes far too much anyway." Mary chuckled. "Your choice, but I'd wash up first."

The man looked shocked, like the idea that she would agree had never occurred to him. Slowly, he came back to himself and simply nodded, choosing to keep his mouth sealed, lest he undo whatever had surprised him.

Together, they set off for a long day of honest work, and the man looked at the ring upon his finger, no longer burning with intent.

EPILOGUE

One by one, the stories around the table rose and fell into silence, broken by the crackling flames in the hearth. The bartender waited, idle in the shadows, to see what happened when stories, deep trauma, and secrets were spilt forth. Curiosity etched itself onto their face as the participants of this particular experiment sat at the table. Some rested their hand upon their item, others peered into the glass as though wishing for another dose of magical persuasion. None moved.

The bartender turned away, disappointed by the lack of reaction. They heaved a sigh. Maybe the next group would prove more entertaining.

Violet light spilt across the barroom floor as the lantern was uncovered. Sullied ghosts slunk into perception, hovering at the fisherman's side as, one by one, the group looked between each other. Their eyes flicked in unison to the bartender's back.

A warhammer was gripped, a scarf flung over a shoulder, and a golden flower touched for reassurance. One pair of eyes wandered to the waistcoat pocket of the small gnome sitting beside him, but an elbow in the ribs remarked on the futility of trying to rob someone with a warning bell.

The woman held the casket tightly, her eyes on the table, as the lanky human beside her turned a pen in their fingers.

In a single moment, a question was asked into the silence as the bartender worked, oblivious to the shifted attention behind them.

In the next, their answer sounded from the pocket of the gnome.

Ping.

ACKNOWLEDGMENTS

Ashley Bravington - Brewing Storm

I have to begin my acknowledgements thanking my wife Cherie for the encouragement she has given me while writing Brewing Storm and for letting me have Saturday mornings to write. A huge thanks to Renee for organising the Tales of Ale and Chainmail anthology and Von for helping with edits and suggestions, it has been an amazingly fun project to work on with SkyNation and my fellow authors. Last of all I'd love to acknowledge Gravitydefyingturle and the rest of the Discord writers team for the weekly sprint sessions, working alongside other aspiring authors and talented world-builders kept me motivated and listening to their wonderful work helped keep me enthusiastic when I was lugging around the writer's block.

Jonathan Maloney - The Timepiece

For everyone who pushed, pressed, encouraged and in times of need outright bullied with a brandished newspaper to get this story told—thank you, for giving me the confidence I needed. And for everyone else with a quirky little character they might be thinking of—bring them out. Give them life. You never know where their adventures might bring you.

Dave Deickman - This Terrible Paradise

To Renee April, thank you for being the driving force behind this project, for dedication and direction seeing this through and being an awesome friend.

To Dan, Dylan, Brian and Lisa Deickman, Tate Avey and Stephanie Cammack, Kaya and Tyler Cox, Bri Sullivan, Ryan Maroney, Denny and Sarah Nelms, Deston J Munden, thank you for all of your love and support reaching this point and continuing to believe in myself.

To Harberion, thanks for the tattoo art.

Kate Longstone - The Casket

Kate would like to thank Renee for her support, guidance, and enthusiasm for my work, without which this story would never have been completed. Thank you also to all the members of the SkyNation writing group, for their encouragement, friendship, and giving me the confidence to share my work.

Lucina Nyx - Grit and Glimmer

I want to give a massive thank you to Renee April for seeing potential in me and selecting me for this project. Being a published author is something that I always wanted, and this was the perfect opportunity to get over that hurdle. I really can't thank you enough. I also want to thank Artemis.Your constructive criticism, constant support, and reminders to be kind to myself during many moments of self doubt were invaluable. I couldn't have done this without your help. I appreciate you.

Crystal Roles - The Golden Bells

Even the smallest of stories have come from a long line of people fanning a spark. My mum, who read to me before I could, then ever on afterwards. All the librarians grinning widely as I wheeled my mountainous piles past the check out to take home. People who believed I could write (shout out to my grade six class with Mrs Stott who let me change their names and re-create them in weird and whacky ways!) Thank the universe for the strange and wonderful ways stories form in my head - this one came from a strange union of the nursery rhyme Hickory, Dickory, Doc and the random prompt: what if a questing party started in a bathroom?

Thank you SkyNation for writing sprints: being silent together with purpose and giving the words of encouragement to allow myself to write have done more for me than I could ever express. Thank you Ren for thinking of me for this project and for all your support, insight and laughs along the way. Nuuuug nug nug!

Thank you my precious little boy, you have made me more of myself than I have ever been. Finally, thank you to my life partner Jordan, who gave me the space to heal and create worlds only whispered about. Space to write, space to babble enthusiastically, the space to just be. Thank you for seeing, and loving, me.

Thomas D Moore - A Liar's Bane

As a writer of a thief, I feel it is important to steal some acknowledgements for all my family who were very patient with my strange ideas, and let me express myself how I chose to.

Ingram Content Group UK Ltd.
Milton Keynes UK
UKHW041354290623
424255UK00004B/15